BELVEDOR AND THE FOUR CORNERS

THE BELVEDOR SAGA | VOL 1

BELVEDOR AND THE FOUR

CORNERS

ASHLEIGH BELLO

Win or die. Whichever her fate,
freedom is certain.

NORTHWOODS
HOUSE
Publishing

BELVEDOR AND THE FOUR CORNERS
Copyright © 2014 by Ashleigh Bello

First Edition: December 2014
Second Edition: September 2016
Third Edition: October 2020

Cover design by Mirella Santana.
www.mirellasantana.com.br
Cover photography by Jessica Truscott (Faestock).

Map and chapter illustration copyright © 2021 by Jessica Khoury.
All rights reserved.

Other publications by Ashleigh Bello in the Olleb-Yelfra Universe:
Belvedor and the King's Curse
Belvedor and the Desert of Secrets
Belvedor and the Trail of Fire
Belvedor and the Golden Rule
A Myrmaid's Kiss

For more information, visit: www.ashleighbello.com

ISBN-13: 978-0-9987974-4-1
ISBN-10: 0-9987974-4-8

10 9 8 7 6 5 4 3 2 1

For Grandma Farley,
You filled my life with love
and taught me to share it with the world.
Rest in Paradise.

For the World,
You're the inspiration for my imagination,
always reminding me that magic will always exist.

CONTENTS

CITY OF THE FOUR CORNERS
THE JAR OF STONE
UNDOR
Agrarian's District
Healer's District
Vanishing Tunnels
Creator's District
Warrior's District
Tombs
Draminet
NICORA FOREST
BLACK SAND DESERT
BELGRADIA
Fate's Pool
KAMPAULO
MORIAMO
HIGH CITY OF SAINDORA
SEA OF SAINDORA
Empress Isle
NW
N
NE
W
E
SW
S
SE
OLLEB YELFRA
LIZARD INK

BLANCOREN MOUNTAINS
NORTH LUOSE
SOUTH LUOSE
ZAMBIENTH
The Greenhouse
LANZATARÉ
Island of Idris
IMPENETRABLE FOREST
The Treehouse
Starr Caverns
GUANAMARA

PART ONE

JAR OF STONE

ARIANNA BURIED HER FACE in a pillow, trying to block out the world. A bell sounded from the city center, the sharp echoes of the brass piercing the otherwise quiet morning. She groaned as the noise filled her head, heralding the start of yet another dawn she couldn't escape.

"You heard the bell. Get up! Ten minutes to be in line, or it's the Pit!"

Rolling onto her back, eyes pinned to the ceiling, she mused over several ways she could end the life of the regulator harassing her and her bunkmates out of bed. Alas, all of them ended up with her dying too. There was truly only one way out of this place.

Ticking down the days in her head, she forced herself to face the frigid morning.

In just a few months' time, she'd reach her eighteenth year and consequently become a contender in the annual Free Falls

Festivals for the chance to earn her future.

She took a deep breath.

Just a few more months.

Arianna had held tight to this dream of freedom for her entire life. Although she knew that success in the Free Falls would be a bittersweet one—*Free* for the slaves who earned their citizenship and *Falls* for the ones who died—she took comfort in that she wasn't alone. Her hopes, dreams, and this nightmarish reality were shared by all.

If not for the promise of competing in the looming festivals or the elders who brought stories of cities beyond these walls, Arianna might have thought that there was nothing more to this life she'd been handed. She would have known nothing of hope. But, through the mandatory lessons she sat through each day, she quickly came to understand that everyone born to the Olleb suffered the same endless beginning, burdened with the weight of shackles until their eighteenth year. Under the King's law there existed a thriving world outside of this place, the true Olleb-Yelfra, maintained by wise, loyal, able-bodied citizens. And the preservation of this world was only possible because the Free Falls weeded out the weak.

Arianna was determined not to be labeled as such, and she was determined to join that free world, too.

One misstep, one mistake could rip away all she had worked for since she stepped foot in her prison, the City of the Four Corners. There were so many ways to die in this dreadful place, so many ways to fail. Thus, she trained hard, holding tight to her thread of life alongside thousands of other desperate young slaves, waiting for the moment when she could finally join the Olleb as a true citizen.

Slave. She cringed as the word bounced around her mind, the only title she'd ever known and a testimony of her unfortunate status. *Survive.* That was another word she knew well, her single most important goal, for the threats in the Jar were constant. A blade to the throat during a duel, a stray arrow, frostbite—there was never a moment to rest.

"Get moving," snapped the regulator, drawing Arianna away from her jumbled morning thoughts.

She recognized how close to freedom she was—she could almost taste it—so now wasn't the time to slack off or get on the wrong side of the regulators. Obediently, she pushed the covers to her feet.

Floorboards creaked as the thirty other girls rushed to gather their weapons and robes. Her muscles ached with every movement as she climbed down from her bunk to join them, but it was a satisfying pain; it reminded her of yet another win she'd achieved during a recent practice duel with a peer of equal skill. Still, in the end, Arianna knew there was only one fight that truly mattered.

No number of victories could outweigh the outcome of the Free Falls Festivals.

As she placed her feet on the wood floor, the ice-cold panels against her toes made her instantly alert. She dressed quickly, slipped on her boots, and then moved to where cloaks hung on a wall near the door. A deep red colored the fabrics, and silver numbers embroidered the front of each.

Arianna searched for hers—there, number twenty-two.

She reached out to it, unable to stop a frown from wrinkling her face as she stroked the old cloth.

My name is Arianna Belvedor.

Not wishing to stare at the number a second longer, she yanked the robe off the hook and draped it over her shoulders. The heavy fabric was a welcome warmth on her skin, sweeping the floor as it fell down around her body.

She collected her twin swords next; the weight of the thick, bronze blades in her hands reminded her of her purpose. She secured them in their sheath across her back and found her place in line among the others.

"Let's go!" barked the regulator.

She didn't want to, but he pushed open the door, and they marched out into the cold, one by one.

SNOW BIT AT ARIANNA'S SKIN and dotted her dark hair white, the same as every day. Try as she might, there was just no preparing for that kind of cold. She could never stop the shivers from coursing through her body, and the burn of the icy wind made her eyes well with tears no matter what she did. Pulling her hood tight around her head to shield her face from the biting flakes, she gazed toward the sky. Each morning, she found herself searching for the sun, but lately there was a permanent blanket of gray blocking it from view. If she was lucky, it might peek through the clouds to warm her skin for even just a few moments, but most days she wasn't.

As much as she despised those clouds, the view of the ashen-faced mountains that encased the Four Corners was ten times worse, impossible to ignore at almost any moment spent outside. They trapped the city in a wide, jagged cage with perilous peaks that reached toward the skyline like a claw, locking in the gray and barring out the light. It created the perfect prison, and it earned the city a nickname—Jar of Stone.

Thousands of slaves marched in silence alongside Arianna under the darkened sky, under the watch of the mountains. The snow turned brown beneath their boots as they trudged forward in a familiar rhythm. In a crimson flock, they passed the many crumbling buildings that made up the small district until a deep hole spread out before them. They maneuvered around the Pit with ease, their breath hitched in their throats out of respect for those who had perished.

Arianna's eyes were glued to the swelling blackness of the Pit as they passed, straining to see so far down with no help from the sun. Still, she spotted some of the skeletons glinting in the dark. Needle-like rocks and rotting bodies lined the bottom.

"Hey! You wanna join 'em?"

Arianna jumped as the voice pulled her from her thoughts. She hadn't realized she had stopped, holding up the line behind her. The regulator leading her group got down from his horse and stormed over to her side, grabbing ahold of her arm.

"There somebody down there you'd like to see, Twenty-Two?"

She could think of a few names.

Digging his fingernails deep into her skin, the regulator pushed his weight into her so that she had no choice but to lean back, half her body now dangerously hovering over the side of the Pit. From this angle, Arianna could see the bottom with alarming clarity. Her heartbeat quickened as all her hopes for a future seemed to vanish into its depths. If he let go of her arm, she would surely fall to her death. She was unable to tear her gaze from the abyss threatening to swallow her, her curiosity replaced by terror as the sunken faces of the dead stared back.

Just as she was counting the seconds until the end of her life, the regulator moved, allowing her to regain her footing.

"Don't make me ask twice," he said, waiting for an answer as he itched toward his swords.

Flinching away from him, she shook her head.

"No," she said.

Her whisper was sucked down into the darkness of the Pit, and every time her heart throbbed, she thought it might jump right out of her chest to follow.

A gruff laugh escaped his lips.

"Then eyes forward," he replied.

He poked her in the shoulder, on her double-digit iden-
tity, gesturing for her to keep walking. Her knees shook as she
moved on as quickly as possible, and she kept her eyes down
until they arrived at the city center—the Square.

They passed under a low bridge, and a wide, open area
stretched out around them, people pouring in from all sides.
High stone steps encircled the space and created an amphithe-
ater-like structure with pillars at the top.

Arianna eventually found the nerve to lift her gaze from
her boots and peered again to the sky, past the crumbling pillars and past the people below. Wind pounded against a raised
flag that stood tall as a centerpiece of the Square. She studied
the embroidery while waiting for the gathering to commence.
Faded reds, blues, purples, and greens were woven into seg-
ments, a pattern she could retrace by heart if she had to. They
formed a circle which signified the emblem of the Four Corners and the four districts within the city.

As was the daily morning routine, the regulators sat comfortably atop their brawny horses in black, hooded cloaks,
herding the non-citizens into lines facing an elevated platform.
It was a large structure that towered over the crowd as the stage
of the amphitheater. And, on this particular day, Arianna
stood at the front, just below the platform, wishing she could
be anywhere else.

She studied the stage as General Ivo surveyed the red sea
of prisoners from underneath his hood, waiting for everyone
to assemble. His dark, brooding glare matched well to his
known ruthless character. Black robes, lined with red fur and
emblazoned with the golden snake of the King's Crest, swept
the floor at his feet, and a scar slashed across his face like a
worm crawled atop his skin. He also wore a sharp sword at his
belt, one that she'd seen in use plenty.

Behind him, a massive painting created the backdrop on a
black wall. The same golden snake intertwined itself between

two blazing swords, the symbol of Arianna's district. Every time she looked upon it, she thought the symbol quite plain— swords to depict the Warrior's District.

Such a superficial view of what it takes to be a warrior.

A familiar hum buzzed throughout the Square until General Ivo raised his hand. With his gesture, the crowd was promptly silenced. Arianna stood to attention, her arms flat at her sides as he walked forward, hands behind his back, preparing to speak. Though, before his lips parted, something caught his attention, and hers too. A loud whisper was coming from behind her in the crowd.

Arianna bit her lip, unsure of where to look as the hushed voice faded away. *Too late.*

Nothing went unnoticed in the Warrior's District under the general's watch, and right now his eyes were unblinking. He scowled down at the crowd from the stage, and Arianna froze. She felt his gaze burning straight through her center as he searched their faces for the culprit. Then, a stone-faced regulator started to march toward her from his post at the front. Her stomach churned as he neared. This was too much suspense for just one morning, even in the Jar.

To Arianna's relief, the regulator merely pushed past her, instead reaching for a small girl who was standing only one row back. She recognized her as a tenth year.

The girl kicked and screamed as the regulator dragged her to the foot of the stage by the collar of her cloak. He looked to the general for instruction, and Arianna held her breath. After a moment of contemplation, General Ivo gave a single nod— that sinister 'you-know-you're-done-for' nod she'd seen too many times to count.

The regulator acknowledged his unsaid command and locked eyes with the terrified child. "Should have shown some respect," he grumbled in a low voice.

The girl's cries had drowned out his words for the most

part, but Arianna stood close enough to hear the tragic ending they promised. Some days General Ivo gave second chances, but today he seemed to be in as foul a mood as ever.

Arianna could feel the heat from the nervous crowd rising around her, everyone fidgeting uncomfortably as the girl was escorted from the Square, headed in the direction of the Pit. Nobody dared make a sound, not a peep as her cries faded away into nothing.

Arianna closed her eyes, shaking her head at another wasted life. The girl should've known better.

She couldn't resist the small sigh of relief that left her lips when all was quiet again, hoping no one else would notice.

I'm still safe. I'm still here. Just survive.

Her eyes flew open as the general again prepared to speak, as if nothing at all had transpired. His calm demeanor baffled her because inside her own head she was screaming. It was a silent scream that echoed into every corner of her mind until she felt numb and the voice died away. She always took care to silence it, for otherwise she'd have gone mad with grief long ago.

As Arianna tried to focus on anything other than this fresh reminder of death, a sudden quiver rolled across her skin. She knew she was being watched, as though her body could sense the glare of eyes on her back. She glanced slightly to her left and found the culprit. Her friend Liam was standing only a couple people down, and his shaken expression reflected her own worry. They looked out for each other. Life was a little easier that way.

She nodded to him in reassurance, and then put her focus forward.

General Ivo raised his right hand, and the crowd mirrored his movement as he balled his hand into a veiny fist and placed it on his chest above his heart.

"Hail to the King! Hail to Lord Devlindor."

His voice, such a terrible one, made Arianna want to stick her fingers in her ears, but she straightened her back and repeated the daily verse. Her words melted in with the other mindless voices around her, the phrase tasting so wrong on her tongue. She'd be hanged if she voiced it, but she couldn't help but hate King Devlindor. Her loyalty to someone who squeezed so tightly at her life made her dizzy at times.

According to her teachings, this was the way of the world, and promises of citizenship and all the riches that came with it would apparently wipe away the memory of this gruesome chapter of life for all who made it to the next. Freedom supposedly changed people, and Arianna prayed it would change her, too. However, no matter what anyone said, she knew in her heart that she'd have to experience this change for herself to believe it—to believe in the King.

Just survive. A few more months.

"Dismissed," said the general as the echo of voices ceased.

The crowd dispersed to their daily routines, and a dull chatter filled the air as Arianna headed to the Dining Hall. She walked by the Pit on the way, but she didn't dare look down.

MASTER BELL

THE DAY DRAGGED ON after breakfast, and each day was quite the same as the last. For the first few hours, Arianna attended lessons in the Learning Center. And while her eyes remained strictly focused on the elders teaching, her mind daydreamed throughout the history of the King's many accomplishments, of great battles won, and his long-standing reign over the Olleb. Her thoughts wandered so far off at times that she could swear she had walked in the footsteps of a royal or had been knee-deep in the mud, fighting for her people with a shield and sword in hand.

Alas, this was not the case.

After emerging from her vivid imagination, she spent the rest of the day losing duels to her trainer, Master Solomon Bell. Too many to count on her fingers and toes.

"You mustn't falter again, Arianna!" screamed Solomon over the clashing of metal.

Sparks flew as he danced around her in intricate circles. His sword cut through the air with skill and thwarted each attack she attempted.

"I demand your attention. Your enemies demand your attention!" His sword landed hard on hers, and she wavered under the pressure. "Draw your mind to the battle at hand, and leave your thoughts for a more appropriate time."

With one hand behind his back, he never took a hit.

Arianna jabbed her twin swords at his midriff, but he swatted them away with seemingly little effort. She lost her balance and fell to her knees on the stone floor of the sparring room, the impact rattling all the bones in her body. She tried to stand up, though not quickly enough as Solomon lunged forward again, brandishing his weapon.

In the next moment, Arianna felt the familiar sensation of cold steel against her neck. Her sweat dripped onto Solomon's blade, and she wiped it away.

"Yield," she said with a heavy sigh.

Her swords fell to the floor, the sharp sound of metal on stone making her wince. Another battle lost to Master Bell.

He laughed with an energy that boomed off the walls.

"I see nothing funny about another loss," said Arianna, trying to keep her cool as she pushed aside his sword.

"No, of course not. I was merely contemplating the choice to switch from wooden blades to metal," he said. "Dear girl, I feel as if I could give you a sword with a mind of its own and it still wouldn't puncture my skin."

Solomon flashed his pearly teeth and leaned against a wall, folding his arms across his chest.

Arianna considered him now as she caught her breath. He'd dedicated the last several years of his life to preparing her for the ultimate battle. If not for him, she was sure she'd be dead by now. Somedays, his lessons were the only thing that kept her sane and they were really all she had to look forward to on any given day. He constantly urged her to keep faith and remain focused, even if he tried her patience at times.

"Are you giving up so soon?" he asked, a smirk on his lips. "Why, I've barely broken out a sweat."

Arianna's pride got the best of her then. In one swift move, she got back to her feet.

Tightening her grip on the hilts of her blades, she shifted to a wide fighting stance and readied her weapons. The bronze felt too heavy in her hands, and her muscles ached from so much training, but she found the determination to challenge her master from somewhere deep down, even if the effort seemed futile.

"Again!" She ran forward to attack, and Solomon answered with a bow.

Such a gentleman.

She roared in frustration as he swiftly sidestepped her attempt, slapping the flat edge of his steel against her back. It stung, pulsating across her skin. She stumbled forward into the full-length mirror that stood against the wall.

A large crack spread down the middle, making her take pause. She saw the glass now reflected a broken image of the Warrior's Crest, which was displayed on the other side of the room, and a distorted reflection of her.

Turning away from the mirror, she regained her balance and steadied her swords, crossing them at her chest. Solomon beckoned her forward, and the clashing of metal began again. The image of the cracked mirror stayed in Arianna's thoughts all the while, distracting her from the duel. The reflection she'd seen reminded her so much of the broken, lost child she used to be.

I'm not that weak girl anymore. I'm stronger now.

She knew she might never win a battle over Solomon before the Free Falls, this master warrior who had earned his honors in the real world after achieving real victories. But Arianna took pride in his teachings and would keep trying. It may have been nothing more than luck that she had secured an apprenticeship under him in the first place, but she had never once taken it for granted. No matter how hard he pushed her, she knew that, in the end, she would have a better shot at freedom than most of her peers—thanks to Solomon.

Still, at moments like this, when he'd broken her down and worn her out completely, Arianna couldn't help but wonder why he'd ever given her a chance at all.

"BUT... WHY HAVE YOU chosen me as an apprentice, Master Bell?" said Arianna as she knelt before him in the Square, her hands and knees dirtied from the muddy ground.

She had just finished a successful practice duel with a boy from her group, but it had surprised her when Solomon declared his decision in front of the panel. Slaves were hardly ever chosen for private training before their fifteenth year. Besides, Arianna thought it obvious that her dueling partner had let her win. Liam always took it easy on her, and she hadn't put up the grandest of fights compared to others she'd seen.

As soon as the question had spilled from her lips, she regretted it. A hooded regulator hovered over her with his hand raised, ready to strike her for speaking out of turn. Before his palm could reach her face, Arianna's reflexes took over. She dodged his hand, and the regulator tripped sideways, falling forward into the mud.

Her twelfth-year peers watched with horror-struck faces as other regulators closed in to drag her away from the Square for sure punishment.

"No, wait," she begged, struggling against them as they clutched at her arms. "It was an accident!" She had never felt so terrified in all her life.

Solomon raised his hand.

"Let her be," commanded the master swordsman. "She has made only a small offense. It's nothing to get excited over. Besides, I'll enjoy teaching her the hard lesson of respect in training tomorrow."

The regulators gave their distance, and Arianna fell to her knees in relief.

She studied the ground, afraid to meet Solomon's eyes for fear they would match the threat of his voice.

"Please, forgive my behavior. I meant no disrespect, sir," she said, her voice barely audible.

"Look at me when you speak, girl!" he demanded.

She lifted her head.

Strangely, there was no hint of anger on his face as she had anticipated by his tone. In fact, his eyes gave her a sense of reassurance and warmth.

He strode down the stone steps from the evaluators' stand, and, for a moment, Arianna thought him a king. His white velvet and fur cloak sparkled in the daylight, and crimson silk trimmed the edges and lined the inside. On the back, embroidered in the same shining thread, the crest of the district completed his regal appearance.

Solomon brusquely lifted her to her feet by the hook of her elbow and whispered in her ear.

"I chose you because you are worth choosing."

His words were quite unexpected and ones that she would not soon forget. Arianna had never been worth anything to anyone before.

Unbidden tears welled in her eyes, and the surrounding regulators grew smug with satisfaction. They probably as-

*sumed Solomon had reinforced their desires that she be pun-
ished for embarrassing one of their own. She would have assumed it, too. It was unlike master warriors to be kind.*

*"You're now dismissed. Lessons begin at dawn," he said
with finality.*

"ARIANNA, YOU'RE UNFOCUSED TODAY," growled Solomon, regaining her attention. "Where's your head at lately?"

Arianna could sense his growing impatience with her, but
she was exhausted of late. She found that the closer the date of
the Free Falls got, the less she could coax her anxious mind to
sleep at night—let alone concentrate during the day through
vigorous training.

"Master, it pains me that you worry so much. You know
you've taught me well," she replied with a smirk, faking confidence. She sprang forward again. "Am I not match enough
without adding my intellect to the battle?"

Solomon didn't respond, but the frown on his face told
her enough of what he was thinking as they continued to duel.
He clearly wasn't amused by her sarcasm.

Arianna tried to appear brave, but he intimidated her. His
disappointment intimidated her. *Can he tell?*

Although somewhat humbled by the bad knee gained during his time serving the King, Solomon's skill had never failed
him as far as Arianna was concerned. He cleared her by a full,
shaved head, so she had to stand tall to meet his gaze.

He could pass for forty, but his eyes gave him away. No
slave knew the age of any of the elders that ran the district.
Why, even King Devlindor had just celebrated his third cen-
tury, and his portraits still looked youthful. For all she knew,

Solomon could be one hundred and fifty. He claimed twenty-nine, but Arianna knew better. His wisdom far outreached such a small number.

His gaze trained on her as he calculated her next move.

"If you were any match at all, I might actually make an effort," he replied, all traces of amusement gone from his voice. "I would return us to the wooden blade for fear you might cut out my heart." Arianna felt all the blood drain from her face. "Alas, you're neither match nor worthy opponent for an old cripple like me. Not today, anyways."

There was no time to react to the sudden whip of his blade and rapid maneuver of his leg, bad or not, as he spun around her. Moments later, Arianna lay flat on her back once again. She winced as her wavering confidence was instantly replaced with the sinking feeling of shame.

Solomon peered down at her, shaking his head as his sword scratched at the fabric above her heart.

Arianna pursed her lips together, averting her eyes.

"Let me up, you old fool!" she snapped. "Will you never give me credit for my skill? Haven't I accomplished enough to be forgiven one bad day?"

Solomon lifted his weapon, his dark skin gleaming with sweat.

She opened her mouth to speak again, but the words caught in her throat when she saw the look on his face.

"I'll give you credit for your skill once you win a battle over me," he said, calmly, turning on his heels.

He walked to a bench at the far side of the room to sit down and take a sip of water. A barrel of weapons was within reach, so he switched out his sword for an axe.

Arianna scoffed.

"I'm tired of these games," she said, jumping to her feet. "No one has *ever* beaten you, so how could I? What more could you want me to prove? I am a warrior!"

She looked away from him and glimpsed her reflection once more in the broken mirror, the crackling flames burning in a firepit across the room offering an ominous background.

"Arianna Belvedor, a skilled slave of Warrior's District." His words were drawn out, as if speaking to a child. "Perhaps you are the most talented, disciplined fighter of all the children who train within the city. But that is all you are and all you fight—*children*," said Solomon, a fire growing in his eyes.

He cupped her chin in his hand, demanding her attention.

His calloused palm felt rough against her skin, and she noticed dark scars on his hands and arms, the kind that could only be seen up close.

"If you want to live longer than a day as a citizen of the Olleb, then you must learn to think outside of this childhood," he said.

Arianna tried to pull out of his firm grasp, but he wouldn't allow it.

"Master, I'm not a ch—" She faltered as his voice drowned out her words.

"Your eighteenth year is upon you. You must be prepared! Beyond these mountains is a land vaster and more dangerous than you can possibly imagine. And these dangers won't stop the tips of their swords at the nape of your neck. They'll drive them through your skin until your blood stains their hands and your life leaves your eyes. They'll show no mercy to a young woman who hasn't yet had the chance to learn the trickery of the world. That's why I push you so hard."

He let go but held her gaze.

"You're no warrior yet."

Arianna recoiled at the harshness of his words, like a slap to the face. They painted a vivid picture, and one much different than that she'd been fed in the Learning Center. It wasn't the first time she'd heard such a speech, and from the life she'd experienced thus far, she already struggled to believe that the outside world could be much better. But still… she hoped, and she didn't want his words to wash those hopes away—they were all she had to keep her motivated to survive.

"I know all of this," she said, though without much conviction.

Solomon scowled.

"You know nothing! You've won many battles over your matched opponents but never killed more than a beetle under your toes. Heed my warning, Arianna. You may be granted freedom for the skill you show in practice, but can you live long enough to enjoy it?"

She prayed so.

"The land beyond here, which you call freedom, is no kinder place than this children's nightmare you're locked in. It will demand the skill of both your body *and* mind if you're to survive its battles."

He turned away from her.

Arianna couldn't help but feel weak and small in his presence, his words weighing on her until they inevitably sank in.

"I'm sorry," she forced out.

"Don't be sorry, be smart!" he retorted, whipping back around to face her.

She froze, his voice ringing in her ears.

Storing his wisdoms in her heart, she knew Solomon truly wished for her survival. He'd given up years of his life to help her succeed. So, whatever freedom truly meant in the end, she would keep training hard for him, even if she didn't quite understand her destiny yet.

With nothing left to say, she picked up a single sword and steadied it in his direction. Besides, he called for action, not words, and this she could deliver with spirit.

Solomon softened as he looked at her. A warm smile twitched across his lips, and he let out an exasperated sigh.

Arianna knew he was proud of how far she'd come, even

if he never really spoke it aloud and even if *she* tried his patience at times, too. Before him stood the same girl he had first looked upon five years earlier, yet she knew how much she'd grown since then. Her short, dark curls now hung long past her chest. Her thin arms and legs were now lithe and muscular from training. Even her boyish features had curved and smoothed out into a strong, young woman, one who could now hold her own on the battlefield against her peers. Not quite, but almost there. *Almost* a warrior.

"What I want is for you to show me what you've learned from all these years of practice," said Solomon.

Arianna stood taller, her sword hand steady as a rock.

Matching her fighting stance, Solomon raised his axe and signaled for her to attack. "Show me that you're a child no longer, and I'll show you a warrior's respect."

Arianna nodded respectfully to accept his challenge, and he returned a welcoming smile. With that, they sprang forward, the explosion of metal both deafening and sweet to their ears.

UTOPIA

"CAN YOU HEAR ME? Arianna, for bloody sakes, open your eyes!" The voice seemed familiar, but it sounded muffled and distant, like someone spoke to her through glass.

Am I underwater?

Arianna's eyes sprang open to find a vast, cerulean sea of some type of liquid that behaved like water—and yet, clearly, was anything but. It surrounded her from every direction, entangling her already wild hair.

Glancing around, she found no indication that anything else existed outside of this place, no surface and no bottom to this abyss. And while the strange substance felt somehow warm and comforting, as if she could melt right in to be one with the liquid, the silence that accompanied it made her feel exceptionally alone.

Is this freedom… or death, perhaps?

Her gut told her that she had the choice of whether to stay

or go, and her decision came easily. It might be nice to just stay in that depth of nothingness for a while. She enjoyed being warm for once.

Thus, Arianna mindlessly floated around for what seemed like hours, making no attempt to leave, and quite relishing this rare feeling of comfort. After a long time wading through the liquid blue, she noticed the faintest of lights in the distance, so faint that she wasn't sure if it actually existed.

Do I even exist anymore?

The nimble glow grew brighter, and she decided that it must be real enough. Especially as she was the only one around to decide what was and wasn't real.

She couldn't resist the temptation to get a closer look.

Swimming toward the light, Arianna followed a trail of golden glitter. Deeper she swam until the liquid turned a dark sapphire and familiar chills started to creep under her skin and curl around her body, leaving the purity of warmth behind.

Still, she swam on, chasing the light. To her shock, the trail vanished and left her with only pure darkness as a companion.

"Arianna, come back!"

The same voice from before boomed in her ears, its echo rippling the liquid around her skin. Then, her body suddenly went rigid, as if a shock of lightning seared straight through her bones. She began to choke on the watery blackness. It poured into her lungs, burning her throat.

Arianna's screams came only in the form of bubbles as the liquid continued to fill her body. There was no point in struggling; she let go and closed her eyes, leaving the nothingness behind.

"There's my girl. Good as new, aren't you?"

Arianna blinked open her eyes to find Solomon hovering over her with a relieved expression.

She felt miserable, so she looked away from him to try to

hide her shame. Pale lavender walls stung her eyes in the dim light of a small fireplace, and a tall cabinet sat in the corner. A couple of chairs lined the wall to her left, positioned next to the fireplace, and there was a stove on the other side. It was all very familiar.

Arianna had spent countless hours in this well room, staring at those ugly walls. It was connected to Solomon's private sparring chamber. Should any accidents happen during a duel, as they often did, Solomon would take her there to heal.

"What happened?" asked Arianna, finally forcing herself to speak. The disdain in her voice was palpable. She knew what had happened.

Putting her attention back on her master, she found Solomon with his hands resting on his hips and a triumphant grin on his face as he gazed down at her. Again, all very familiar.

"I won," he replied.

"Shocking," she said, flatly.

Solomon shook his head, trying to hide his amusement.

"Oh, cheer up now," he replied. "You put up a damn good fight! I thought today was going to be a wash, but you surprised me there at the end." He gave her a gentle pat on the head in reassurance.

Arianna grimaced at the touch, a sudden throbbing ache in her brain making itself known. She lifted her hand to her face to inspect the cause; to her horror, she felt a large lump growing above her eye. She let out a moan, gazing past Solomon to the ceiling.

"You were out for a while this time," said Solomon, something of concern in his voice. "It's nearly nightfall." Arianna glanced toward the window; no light filtered through from the outside save for the glow of the torches that lined the Dueling Arena walls.

"Yeah, well I suppose after the hundredth concussion, I might stop waking up as fast. You're lucky I even came back this time. I almost decided not to." A flicker of a smile hid the truth of her words.

"Ara, I'm not at all worried about your physical health. Although, maybe I *should* stop going for the head if I want you to remember anything I've ever taught you," he replied, smugly.

Arianna almost chuckled, but it hurt too much to laugh.

"To be quite honest, it's your mental health that concerns me." His tone grew serious, and Arianna knew he was about to lecture her again. "I know you've been having strange dreams. I heard you just now, mumbling in your sleep."

He opened his mouth to say something more, but then seemed to think better of it.

"It was nothing. Just a dream," she replied with a shrug. "Lighten up—"

"Never take a dream lightly!" barked Solomon. Arianna was taken aback. "A mind is a mystery to both man and magic. Therefore, it must be respected. Do you understand me?"

Arianna's eyes widened as the word 'magic' rolled off his tongue. It shocked her silent for a moment.

The King of Olleb-Yelfra forbade anyone, citizen or slave, to even utter opinions on such topics, themes of nearly forgotten fairytales. And severe punishment answered those caught with an imagination outside of the law.

"Master... what do you mean? That word is forb—"

Solomon paid her no mind, continuing his sermon.

"Our minds are what make us unique," he said more calmly now. "They're why we choose the paths that we do. Your mind knows more about you than you do yourself, and it holds the key to your past, present, and future. If you respect that, then you can open up doors you never deemed possible."

Arianna tried to speak up again. "But you said mag—"

Solomon held his finger to her lips. "Just hear me," he implored. "Your mind never sleeps, and that's why you dream. If you start to pay more attention to both worlds, rather than just the physical one, you may be in for a wonderful surprise."

Solomon's words of wisdom always left Arianna dizzy, but to his credit, there usually ended up being some important meaning behind them that she'd come to understand later. As she tried to decipher yet another riddle from her master, she wondered what experiences lay in his past to have equipped him with such wisdom in the first place.

"Master Bell, as usual, your insight is very refreshing," she said, a smirk on her lips.

"I know," he said with a wink.

Solomon relaxed in one of the chairs now, sipping at a cup of tea that had been prepared. He looked so assured that his lessons for today had been received, but Arianna was still determined to ask the question burning on her lips.

She lowered her voice to a whisper. "Now, what's this about mag—"

"Welcome back, dear!" came another voice.

Arianna pouted at the interruption as a woman waddled into the well room, planting a routine kiss on her head.

Solomon glanced up from his tea, catching Arianna's eye. As if reading her mind, he shook his head.

Arianna didn't have to decipher this gesture. It was a clear warning not to speak anything more on the subject, especially with another in earshot. She trusted Solomon with her life, but she was wise enough to know the danger her question posed. Storing her curiosity around the taboo word for later, she put her attention on her caretaker, who was already examining her wounds with gloved hands.

Caretaker Cyn came as one of the perks of having a private trainer like Solomon Bell. She was gowned in long, yellow robes that clung to her plump curves, and a tiny gold snake ensnaring a red heart was stitched to the cloth above her chest.

"This might hurt a little," she said.

Her hair waved in auburn locks to her shoulders, tickling Arianna's cheeks as she began to gently daub medicines onto a gash on her arm.

Arianna winced as the medicine made contact, but she could see the healing begin immediately.

"That really stings," she said, sucking in a hiss through her teeth.

"It's almost over, dear," replied Cyn. "Just a bit more to go."

Arianna nodded for her to continue, biting her lip to try to sway her mind from the uncomfortable sensation. No matter how familiar this sting was after so many years, she just could never quite grow used to fresh pain.

"Solomon Bell, I'll not have you banging this girl around anymore. She'll be dead before the Free Falls if you continue at this rate," said Cyn as she smeared a sticky green ointment over Arianna's lesser bruises.

She spoke to him like a child to be chastised.

Arianna averted her eyes, trying to suppress her grin, but she secretly cheered her on as Cyn gave Solomon a taste of his own medicine.

He frowned, setting aside his cup.

"All right, Cyn, I'll let up a bit. I just want her to be ready for what's coming. It's just around the corner, you know?"

"Well, she won't be ready if she's lying in a bed bleeding out the side of her head, now will she?" retorted Cyn, wagging her finger at him.

Solomon groaned in annoyance, throwing his hands to the air. "She also won't be ready if she can't dodge a sneak attack from less worthy opponents!"

There was something about Cyn that made him unable to keep his usual calm, and there was something about Solomon that made Cyn want to keep egging him on.

They continued bickering back and forth for another hour

until all of Arianna's wounds had healed.

When Arianna peeled away the dried ointments, her bruises had vanished to perfection, the aching gone. The gash on her arm still felt a bit sore, but it would feel good as new by morning.

Arianna stretched out her muscles and stood. At Cyn's insistence, Solomon gave her the rest of the night free, so she had a couple of hours to kill before curfew. She pulled on her cloak, gloves, and boots, and rushed out of the well room, knowing she'd be back there soon enough—Solomon would never ease up on her training just because Cyn had told him to, not so close to the end.

Having unscheduled breaks in her day didn't happen very often, so Arianna planned to take full advantage of it tonight and headed to her favorite spot in the district. When she exited the private sparring room, the wafting smell of snow, blood, and sweat immediately filled her nostrils. She was standing in the Dueling Arena, a vast, open area covered with a dirt floor and surrounded by high, red brick walls. Lanterns were placed evenly around the perimeter, and their flames flickered against the subtle wind, giving the space a soft glow on this cloudy evening.

She walked toward the barred gate on the far side of the arena. Letting the walls guide her, Arianna passed about sixty other doors to private sparring rooms much like her own, and she could hear the echo of battle faintly sound from within.

In the center of the arena, warrior-slaves of all ages were strewn about the grounds, enduring group training sessions, their masters yelling commands at the top of their lungs. There were the wounded, dead, or fighting—nothing in between and nothing out of the ordinary. They conducted drills or dueled one-on-one, wielding a myriad of weapons against one another. Swords, axes, flails, daggers, bows, and anything else that had a sharp point were all fair game in the Dueling Arena.

Leaving the safety of the wall behind, Arianna danced around her peers with caution until she reached the tall steel gate that served as the entrance and exit. It hovered over her like the looming mountains, a cage within a cage. Regulators stood on either side, preventing her from leaving unnoticed.

"Where do you think you're going?" said the woman.

She had a fierce scowl as she pointed her spear at Arianna.

"Master Bell has given me permission for early leave today, ma'am," she replied, unfurling a small parchment from her pockets. It had a note scribbled on it and Solomon's seal. "I'm headed to the Square for the rest of the evening."

The regulator snatched it from her hands to examine.

"Go on, then," she said after a moment, reluctantly lifting her spear.

Arianna gave a slight nod of thanks and then slipped out, the whispers of the regulators' disapproval trailing behind her.

The Warrior's District wound like a giant serpent that coiled into itself, and the path to the right would take her directly to the Square. Arianna turned to the left.

Walking toward the west side of the city, she came upon the Well Center which looked like a warped sphere pressed into the ground. Caretakers, like Cyn, ran in and out of the graying lilac building as they tended to the never-ending onslaught of injured slaves.

Farther up the road, Arianna passed the Dining Hall, a long, rectangular structure made of stone that looked like it might cave in on itself at any given moment. The food served there replicated the same lifeless color as its exterior, and when she moved downwind from the building, she had to hold her breath as the repulsive scent of slop enveloped the air.

More shoddy structures were sprinkled on her path as she neared the edge of the city, each with a purpose that kept the Warrior's District occupants somewhat alive until they inevitably gained freedom through death or citizenship. Leaving them behind, Arianna came to a halt in the face of the mountains, lifting her eyes to their snow-topped peaks. Rumors declared it a dead man's journey to try and trek over Blancoren, so people always went under.

Hundreds of paths beneath the mountains created the maze of the Vanishing Tunnels. And each district within the Four Corners had access to a tunnel entrance that connected one to the other or that could lead a traveler out of the city altogether; that's the path Arianna had her eyes set on.

Just survive.

She knew the story well. With only one way in or out of the endless labyrinth, elders controlled the maps that could let one navigate the Vanishing Tunnels safely. No slave had ever tried to escape before—unless the rumors proved true. But Arianna seriously doubted that anyone would be so stupid as to ever attempt such a death sentence.

She lowered her eyes to the wide hole carved into the mountainside. It looked as if something had bitten a chunk right out of its icy walls. And just like the Dueling Arena gates, there were regulators who guarded this at all times.

Arianna averted her eyes and moved on quickly, appearing as if she were headed to her designated sleeping quarters. Luckily, no one questioned her.

If she continued in a circular path along Blancoren, she would pass the district staple that was the Learning Center and eventually end up right back where she had started. Instead, she kept toward the barracks where she and the other slaves slept. Hundreds of these structures splashed up against the mountain walls. Fixed to rotting wooden stilts high above the ground, they always seemed to sway slightly in the wind.

Arianna circled the quiet street to make sure she was alone. Everyone was still busying about in the center of town, so she felt safe enough from prying eyes. Still, her heart always raced when she snuck away to her favorite place—breaking a law and risking her life in the process.

She ducked under the barracks and out of sight.

Some things are worth the risk.

After a few more minutes of walking, the smell of rotting wood began to sting her nose. Arianna knew she was close to her destination, so she let her fingers trace the frozen rocks of the mountain until they found a particular stone. It was the size of a small child, and it wobbled under her touch.

She pressed her fingers against it and it fell inward, landing with a thud, creating a small hole in the wall of Blancoren. Arianna stared into it, seeing only darkness and remembering clearly the dark moment which had led her there so long ago.

"I'M TRYING. REALLY, I AM," said Arianna.

Her breath came heavy, and her hands shook.

"Not hard enough!" screeched her group trainer. "Pick up your damn sword, you lazy excuse for a girl!"

Another attack was aimed toward her head, but she lifted her heavy wooden weapon in defense. She moved quickly enough to block the strike, but the weight of the blow left her back on the ground and sweating in a panic. Mud covered every inch of her, and her elbows and knees were scratched and bloody.

"Come on. Get up!" said her opponent, a boy in her ninth-year group. Everyone always praised his skill. "Practice makes perfect, and I'm barely getting any today with you."

His sword was pointed at her face, ready for her next feeble attack. He looked like a real warrior standing over her then, wearing his scars proudly, his weapon hand steady as a rock.

"I swear on the High King, if you don't get back on your

feet, I'll have you thrown in the Pit, Twenty-Two," said the trainer.

Nothing scared her more than the Pit. No slave could survive such a punishment. Yet, even with the fear of that fate weighing on her, she knew she couldn't win in this moment.

"I can't fight anymore. I'm not strong enough," she stammered. "I yield." Her sword fell to the ground.

The others in her group laughed. All except one, a flaxen-haired boy who just stared in the other direction—Liam Black.

"You're pathetic. Absolutely not worth a single second more of my time," said the trainer. "In this world, you earn your freedom! You'll be lucky if you ever even see a glimpse."

She wished for that luck with her whole heart.

He turned and walked out of the Dueling Arena with his students at his heels, leaving her alone with the boy who mocked her with his smile and his wooden sword. As beautiful as he was to look at, she only saw him with hate in her eyes.

"Next time at least make it a fight," he said with a toss of his hair. "You'll be dead and buried in the tombs before you reach your next ceremony."

Tossing his sword to the ground, he spat at her feet. Then, he left her there alone, whistling the tune to the 'Song of the Free Bird' as he went.

A few weeks later, he died, his slave number recycled back on the list for some future warrior to be burdened with.

"This is the destiny you choose if you forget your place here," General Ivo said. "Look upon the child that was supposedly destined for greatness, worshiped for his skill by you all. Now, he's nothing more than a rotting corpse for his blatant disrespect to the elders."

The ninth years were all gathered around the general to hear, and Arianna had found herself at the very front. General Ivo looked down into the Pit, and she followed his gaze.

"May freedom find you in death," he added with a sinister

smile as he dropped a single white flower into the Pit.

Arianna had never before seen such a beautiful flower outside of books and scrolls. She couldn't tear her eyes away from the darkness as it swallowed it whole. She wondered at that moment if the general spoke the truth.

Would his soul be set free even though he died a slave?

She hoped not. She hated that boy even in death.

"Mark my words," said the general. The entire crowd was silent. "You're nothing more than a number here, and I'll not hesitate to snuff out the slightest hint of defiance inside of these walls, for there is only room for the most honorable outside of them. Dismissed."

The crowd dispersed back to their duties, and Arianna found the motivation to train harder.

ARIANNA'S NINTH-YEAR GROUP trainer stayed faceless in her memories, but she remembered his remorseless voice well. And she could still see the little boy's wicked face smiling down on her after she'd lost that duel. Left alone in the Dueling Arena with nothing but her shame and humiliation, Arianna had desperately wished for a way to escape and gone to hide under the barracks. Miraculously, something had answered her prayers. When she leaned against a loose rock in the mountainside, it had fallen away, revealing a secret hiding spot like none other. Now, at seventeen, she'd traveled there countless times, forever reflecting on that crucial day in her past and on how far she'd come since.

After crawling inside the hole, Arianna replaced the stone in the wall, becoming blinded in momentary yet familiar darkness. After a few seconds, her eyes adjusted and the ceiling of the hidden cave began to glow like sparkling red and gold lanterns hung just for her special arrival. Millions of firebugs hummed a few feet above her head, guiding the way. The light they surrendered swirled all around her, making her feel reenergized.

As she traveled down the long, narrow passage, the air grew warm and welcoming. Some minutes later, the tunnel ended and a large opening spread out before her, lit even brighter by firebugs than the entrance.

"My paradise," she said as she took in the brilliant backdrop. This utopia had birthed a fighter, given her the motivation for a future such as this.

From the mouth of the cavern, the chamber unwrapped into a huge dome bigger even than the Dueling Arena, and firebugs covered every inch of the walls and ceiling. The top of the cave jutted down like inwardly built crowns, sparkling with dripping water. And massive, glittering, green stones projected from the walls or rested in the hot springs that submerged the center of the floor.

Arianna removed her heavy cloak and clothes, stripping down to her undergarments. It was freeing to shed the material reminders of the Warrior's District and feel the warm air on her exposed skin. Here, she was simply Arianna.

She placed her belongings in the mouth of the tunnel and went to where a high cliff protruded from the side of the cave. She knew foot holdings led up to the top, so she began to climb. From up there, she could see other twisting tunnels on the far side of the cave, much like the one that had led her here. They taunted her to explore, but she had never found the guts to venture farther than this place. She chuckled to herself at even the thought.

There was a stream of water pouring down from an unrevealed source high above her head, so Arianna tore her eyes from the tunnels and fixated on the waterfall instead. It never failed to awe her as it crashed to the pools below in thundering waves. She reached out to let the water flow between her fingers for a moment. Then, she faced the edge of the cliff and sprinted forward.

The ground disappeared, and her body reveled in the rush, in the adrenaline, as she fell through the air. Nothing else mattered until her feet collided with the hot springs below. Waves splashed all around her body, engulfing her in a sweet sensation as she plunged down through the water.

For many years Arianna had practiced moving herself through these hot springs, and it always made her proud to think of how much she'd learned. In the Warrior's District, the regulators rationed water for drinking and bathing purposes only, so she was a self-taught swimmer. Making her way back up for air, she reached the surface with ease and floated around the giant pool on her back for a long while.

The temperature increased in the middle, so her tense muscles started to relax with the heat. And the waterfall rolling down the side of the cliff behind her created soft waves that massaged her skin; Arianna closed her eyes, imagining that the world outside the Four Corners must be this peaceful.

Her mind at ease and dancing with thoughts of battle, Arianna suddenly heard a subtle splash at the opposite end of the hot springs.

With swift reflexes, she let her body submerge.

All but her nose, eyes, and forehead melted into the water as she tried to blend in with the shadows where firebug light didn't reach, her curly locks drifting in a train behind her. More splashing noises sounded in the distance, and she grew terrified at what might have joined her—the only other living things she'd encountered here over the years were firebugs.

Trying to see what had caused the disturbance without getting too close, Arianna stayed stone-still for fear a monster roamed the surface. Even though the law forbade such wild imagination as lurking monsters, stories still orbited the district through whispers and gossip. Every slave had heard their fair share from the older groups at bedtime when they'd exchange exciting tales with the regulators out of earshot.

Now, as Arianna waited for whatever it was to reveal itself, she recalled these nightmarish stories from her youth; tales of scaly creatures that prowled dark waters and ripped apart the bones of careless wanderers burned in her mind.

Her fear grew thicker, thinking of Solomon as these fables clawed their way into her thoughts.

Why does he always have to be right?

Arianna realized she could not truly form a picture of what the real world might be like. Surely not filled with the bloodthirsty creatures of her imagination? Determined to find answers, she held her breath, careful not to make any sound as she waded closer.

Impossible!

Her eyes widened for only a moment at what she saw. Then, she took a deep breath and slipped the rest of her body underwater to hide—there was someone else, another person, in her utopia.

4

GHOST

DEEPER AND DEEPER ARIANNA DRIFTED under the dark waters. She prayed her movement wouldn't stir any attention from the surface, but she needed a closer look to be sure that what she'd seen was no illusion.

Kicking her legs with practiced speed, she headed in the direction of a massive jade rock sunken near the bank on the other side. She only had a minute or so to reach it, or she'd have no other choice but to resurface for air midway and reveal herself. Her thoughts reeled with the unpleasant possibilities of what she might soon encounter. How could she feel unsafe here, in this place that was her own?

Without a sword, she was vulnerable to danger, to a threat that was never supposed to be. Arianna carried only a small dagger strapped to her thigh—a gift from Solomon on the day of their first lesson together and something she made sure she was never without. She knew nothing really of treasure, but this was hers. Patting the dagger's sheath, Arianna made sure it was safely secured and couldn't fall loose in the waters as her mind continued to suit up for battle.

Soon, her lungs started to tighten and her muscles tensed, begging her to breathe. Just when Arianna felt likely to drown, her hands grasped the giant rock, and her body came to rest against the smoothed sides. Without hesitation, she used the stone as leverage to launch herself up toward the surface.

As Arianna broke through the water, she inhaled with a gasp that filled her lungs with delicious life. Then the air left her lips, flowing back out of her body in a long, noisy exhalation that she hoped went unnoticed. All was quiet now as she took in her surroundings, only the drone of the firebugs glued to the walls could be heard. And what she thought she'd seen, only moments before, was gone.

Arianna closed her eyes, relaxing a bit when she saw there was no one there.

Maybe it was just my imagination.

After moving around the jade rock to the shallow part of the waters, she rested her feet on the muddy bottom.

"The dark does play tricks," she said to herself, though her gut was still knotted with doubt.

"Indeed it does," answered a voice.

The words startled Arianna so much that she slipped backward into the water, stirring the mud.

Regaining her footing, she slid her dagger out from its sheath and held it at the ready as she turned in circles to locate the owner of the unknown voice. The weapon felt too light in her hand, but she knew that its sharp blade proved a lethal threat to anyone who found it in their back; it had come in handy a number of times when she'd been jumped in the district by those who had desired to remove her from the competition or make a name for themselves. Alas, the only thing their surprise attacks had accomplished was making a name for Arianna as Solomon Bell's prized apprentice after she'd put them in the Well Center.

Arianna kept a tight grip on the dagger now, but it was hard not to be distracted by its beauty, a treasure indeed. Its blade sparkled like tiny, black diamonds in coal, and a bright blue material—surely inspired by the sea and the sky in a tangled battle—formed the hilt. Traces of deep violets and greens laced the blue as an elaborate outline of a winged beast or god (she couldn't be sure which) made up the guard. Finally, a large, black jewel encasing a sliver of bright yellow, like a captured lightning bolt, completed the pommel.

"Who's there? Show yourself at once," shouted Arianna, pointing the dagger in every direction.

The firebugs in the vicinity took flight in a cloud of golden light that momentarily disarmed her, scared her. For the first time since that humiliating duel with the little boy, she felt truly unprepared for battle. Not only had she been taken off guard but this was *real*, not a practice duel, and she had no idea what to expect from it.

"I'm not hidden," said the voice, with a delicate laugh. It belonged to a girl. "You simply can't see me because you're not looking right."

Arianna took a couple steps farther up the bank, peering around the sunken stones. Still, she saw no one.

Who is this ghost?

"Over here!" The girl's voice was loud, echoing off the cavern walls.

Arianna whipped around and let her dagger fly through the air toward the sound. She'd been so sure of her aim.

The dagger fell to the waters with a splash.

"Tricked you." The ghost girl snickered.

"Face me, you coward," growled Arianna, balling her hands into fists.

"Your startled heart has lost you your knife, and I'm the coward?" the girl replied. "I don't think so."

Arianna struggled to keep a hold on her temper as her fear was quickly overshadowed by her pride. She may have felt frightened at this unexpected encounter, but she'd also spent every day of her life preparing for a real fight. So, weapon or not, she wasn't going to give up without one.

"Enough," she said. "Come out from the shadows, and I'll show you my heart!" She threw her arms out wide in challenge, her patience at an end.

"Very well," the girl replied.

Arianna had pinpointed the sound now and knew her throw had not been far off. This ghost girl had to be on the other side of the large jade stone at her front. She jumped forward, fists raised and ready.

Again, she found nothing.

With a roar of annoyance, Arianna splashed her hands around the area at her feet, searching for her dagger until she felt her fingers slip on the cold metal of the hilt. She wrapped her hand around it, pulling it out from the water.

"Too late," said the honeyed voice that haunted the cavern. "Let the water claim your weapon, or I'll claim your life. I offer no other choices."

Arianna could sense the glare of eyes on her back and the threat of a weapon joining them. She was stunned, waylaid by a voice. This girl… or ghost, whatever she was, had her cornered. Fortunately, Master Bell had taught her well in all areas of battle and conflict, including when to honorably surrender, so she drew a piece of his advice from her mind.

'Never bargain with your life. It's always an unwise gamble if, in fact, the right hand leaves you lucky and the left leaves you dead.'

She could see now the wisdom in what was once just a hypothetical situation. For all she knew, this ghost girl could have a sword an inch from the back of her neck. On the other hand, she could be playing tricks. Arianna wanted the truth of the matter before she gave up her dagger, her dignity—but the wisdom of her master and trusted friend urged her not to.

'If it's your weapon or your life, choose life,' he had once said. *'Maybe then you'll live to fight another day.'*

In a slow gesture of forfeit, the black blade sank back to the floor of the hot springs, and Arianna raised her hands above her head; Solomon had ensured she was quite accustomed to this move.

"Yield!" she spat. Such a sour-tasting word.

"Wise decision," the girl replied. "Look up."

Arianna felt all the blood rush from her face at the command, any fear she had left replaced with pure loathing as she finally laid eyes on the girl behind the voice who claimed victory without a fight. She certainly wasn't a ghost, but a dagger would have done Arianna little good, assuming this girl was quick with a bow and arrow.

The girl was perched atop the tall jade stone which Arianna had been so certain she'd find her behind before. Lean muscles tensed as she tightened her draw on the bow string and arrow, and long arms held the weapon steady at her chest—eyes focused with well-trained form. Arianna didn't know much about handling a bow, but she knew enough to trust her gut; this mystery girl had a sharp aim.

"Clever trick, playing the heights to your advantage," said Arianna. "I'm impressed."

Inside her head she was screaming at herself for not considering that as a hiding place in the first place.

In the Warrior's District, the law required slaves to learn and accomplish the basic skill level for at least three weapons. Arianna had chosen archery as one of her three but never took it past the early stages. She left the bow to practice the mastery of her swords as most of the other warrior-slaves did.

She, like many others, were of the mindset that a true warrior was molded by a weapon with a blade. Thus, people often teased archers during their trainings; some said they would never even need to show up for battle since they could fight from high ground or in the safety of the trees. Arianna was finally seeing the proof of that, but it didn't much matter that she found the tactic cowardly. Somehow, she found herself without bow, without sword, and without dagger… no battle to be fought.

If she made one wrong move, she could end up with an arrow in her belly. And as miserable as district life proved to be, she refused to let hers end in the bowels of the Blancoren Mountains.

"I told you that I yield, *ghost*," said Arianna with as much contempt as she could muster. "Unless you plan to kill me, please lower your weapon." Her body slumped in defeat, and she narrowed her eyes as a last-resort scare tactic.

"Fine." The girl eased her stance. "But if you try for your dagger again, I'll release my arrow."

"And if it missed my heart and fell to the water to lie with my dagger, then where would we be?" Arianna stared up at her in defiance.

The girl glared back with large, pastel blues which stood out bright against her porcelain skin.

"You're pretty bold for someone with an arrow pointed at them," she said. "I never miss a target. Unlike you, it would seem."

Arianna gritted her teeth to keep herself from responding.

Despite her quick mouth, the girl appeared physically delicate, with cherry-colored cheeks and straight, sun-yellow hair that swept just past her shoulders. Arianna knew she could easily take her in a fair fight, weapon or not, if she had the guts to come down off that rock and face her. This girl probably *had* to hide behind her bow in the face of danger; this thought placated Arianna some as she found the calm to focus.

"So, now what?" she asked, fidgeting, her hands still raised.

"Now, we talk." The girl scooted forward on the rock. "Who are you, and how did you find this place?"

"I should ask you the same thing," said Arianna, taking a step forward.

The girl shook her head slightly, pulling back again on the bowstring.

"I'll be asking the questions here," she said. "Don't move again."

"Fine," snapped Arianna. She hated being interrogated by someone—who could not be much older than her—in *her* secret hiding spot. "Mind if I put my hands down, then, at least?"

She gave her a curt nod, her expression still wary.

Arianna rested her tired arms at her side and reluctantly began to answer the questions. "My name is Arianna Belvedor, Warrior's Distri—"

"A slave of the Jar?" The girl's face instantly lit up as Arianna's words caught on her tongue. "I just knew it, but it's unthinkable, really. How did you find these caves?" she asked, eagerly. "How did you get away?"

"I… well, that's somewhat of a long story," said Arianna, taken aback by her sudden change in demeanor.

"Give me the short version, then," said the girl. "I don't have much time. Does anyone else know of this place?"

"I never thought so before," said Arianna, "but, clearly, I was mistaken." She sighed, gesturing to the girl with a wave of her hand. "I found these caves when I was young, by accident. I've been coming here since my ninth year."

"Just here?" said the girl. "Well, it's no wonder that we've never crossed paths, then." She nodded to herself, understanding something Arianna did not.

"What do you mean?" she asked.

"I mean, have you ever traveled through any of the other tunnels that lead away from here?" The girl cocked her head to the side as she examined her from her perch.

"No, just the one that leads me back to where I come from," said Arianna.

"Well, I have, plenty. I even mapped some of them out so that I wouldn't get lost," she explained. "This is my first time stumbling upon this area, so that's why we've never crossed paths before. It's beautiful, isn't it? There's quite a lot hidden down here, but I've never found a way out…"

Arianna perked up at this, all ears now.

"You didn't realize, did you?" she continued, noticing her change in interest. "We're in an unmarked part of the Vanishing Tunnels!"

Arianna lost her footing a bit.

She'd always suspected this but had never proved the theory as curfew always prevented her from exploring for too long. Maybe naivety had poisoned her mind before, but now the magnitude of her betrayal of the law scared her more than ever. She knew that entering the Vanishing Tunnels was a declaration of an escape attempt from the city. If anyone found out, she'd face the death penalty—the Pit. Then again, she'd always known her unauthorized adventures to this utopia already posed a great risk, even if she had never really connected the dots as to why.

Have I found another way out of the Jar?

Suddenly, the ghost girl slid down the jade stone and landed in the shallows with a splash. She hurried out of the water.

"Wait!" said Arianna, wading after her. "Who are you? I have a right to know."

"My name is Lessa… Lessa Thur," she said as she yanked on a long, blue-hooded robe that had been strewn on the ground.

Arianna noticed it had fur lining and a number embroidered at the shoulder in silver. She recognized those robes. She owned the exact same ones in red.

"You're a slave, too, aren't you?" she said, pointing an accusatory finger.

Her mouth hung open at the dangerous confirmation; the number one rule in *The Laws of the City of the Four Corners* stated that slaves were forbidden to interact with those from another district. Of course, no one paid this law much mind. It was unimaginable that anyone could ever break it—no one could ever escape their district.

But now...

"Yes," answered Lessa, slinging her bow across her back and running away. "I am. Nice to meet you, Arianna Belvedor of Warrior's District."

Arianna's mind reeled with questions as she stared after her, still standing in the shallows of the hot springs. She wanted to know everything in an instant. How had she found these caves, and what was her district like? What year did she claim? Was she really trying to escape?

Before Arianna could even form a question on her lips, Lessa had disappeared into the blackness of the tunnels.

"Please, wait. Come back!" Arianna shook her head of the curiosity overwhelming her mind and tried to run after her.

Half a dozen tunnels opened up on this side of the hot springs, and Lessa had vanished into one of them—but which? Arianna had been so taken aback and lost within her own thoughts that she couldn't be sure.

Did that really just happen?

She struggled to comprehend the myriad of emotions playing around in her head. As she leaned her back against the cavern wall to try to catch her breath, her body began to vibrate. The walls felt as if they pulsed with strange life, so she placed her ear to the rock, waiting again for the sensation.

After a minute had passed, the heavy vibrations shook her once more, and Arianna's heart nearly stopped as she realized what it was.

"No, no, no," she said, pushing her body off the wall.

The subtle vibrations had been caused by the sound of the district bell signaling curfew; she only had eight minutes left.

With all that had happened, Arianna had completely let this slip her mind. She needed to be in her quarters by the tenth ring or she was dead.

That was two.

She raced to where her belongings were piled, pulled on her cloak, and tied the belt tight around her waist. Then, she shoved on her boots and dashed to the other side of the hot springs toward the entrance of her district. *Three.*

Dirt and tiny pebbles fell free from the ceiling of the tunnels with the muffled vibrations of her fast-ticking clock as she navigated the familiar passage. *Four.* She pushed her legs faster, trying to fight gravity with her feet, and the firebugs buzzed in uproar at the disruption. *Five.*

Rasped breaths strained her lungs, and the weight of her robes and wet clothes slowed her down. *Six.* She could see the end up ahead now. The faint light of the district spilled through the cracks in the loose rock. She slid the stone to the side and slipped out, unnoticed. *Seven.*

As soon as she was out of the tunnels, the deep vibrations shifted to a piercing sound as the bell sang out through the night. *Three more minutes to go.*

Arianna never stopped running.

Her lungs burned from the frigid air, and her wet hair and clothes had quickly begun to freeze over. If her secret spot within the tunnels wasn't so close to her sleeping quarters, she'd have no chance at all.

Eight, almost there.

She lost her balance as a boy accidentally collided with her.

They both tumbled to the ground in the snow, Arianna's knees and palms scraping on the icy surface. Locking eyes with him for only a moment, she pushed back to her feet. She wondered why he'd also cut curfew so close and if he had a secret hiding spot too. *Nine.*

Arianna ran faster now.

The threatening voice of the bell enveloped her body, but she could see her sleeping quarters up ahead. Her feet thundered down, each step raising a cloud of dust.

Ten. The door to her barrack stood open, and Arianna leaped the stairs in two bounds, landing in a pile on the floor.

The regulator slammed the door shut behind her—she'd made it.

As she lay there panting, Arianna wondered if the boy she'd crashed into had made it back as well. Would he be missing from the daily lineup tomorrow? If so, his body would be at the bottom of the Pit by morning, so she would see on her way to the Square. She tried not to care, but every bone in her body did.

After a long moment, she regained her energy and walked to her bunk where her roommate, Pippa, sat waiting to scold her about curfew. The girl babbled on and on about the regulations as Arianna dried off and readied for bed.

Removing the dagger's empty sheath from her thigh, Arianna felt a pang of sadness, but she wouldn't linger on it now. Too many wonderful things had happened this night to steal her focus. At that moment, her relief at making curfew shocked her into a fit of infectious giggles, if only to drown out Pippa's voice.

And soon the whole room stirred in rare laughter that nobody questioned. When the laughter had died away, silence replacing it, everyone tried to sleep.

Tonight, for once, Arianna was thankful not to be inundated by restless thoughts of battles won and lost, or dying in the mountains, or the festivals inching nearer. Not like usual. Now, there was only one thing that pressed on her mind— Lessa Thur, 'Ghost Girl' of the Four Corners.

ARIANNA TRIED TO SLEEP, but her mind continued to race. She saw hundreds of colored images swimming around the back of her eyelids like a pond of dancing fish—Lessa Thur with a bow and arrow aimed at her back, Solomon with his sword to her neck, the waterfalls in her secret cave. It felt like she had only just fallen asleep when a nightmare snapped her wide awake. She found herself tangled in her blanket as it wrapped around her like a prickly cocoon.

The bitter air had dried her throat, and unbidden tears streaked her face. She clutched at her chest as her heart thrashed against her ribs, her mind clinging to the already fad-ing nightmare of her mangled body and chilling black eyes.

Whose eyes are always watching me when I sleep?

Arianna looked around the silent room to see if her room-mates stirred at her disturbance, her eyes adjusting to the dark. Some gazed at the ceiling, lost in their own thoughts, but most still slept. She sat up in her bunk only to be confronted with a pair of squinty, blue eyes framed in an upside-down, freckled face and a mop of brown hair.

"Bad dream?" asked Pippa.

Arianna gave a weak nod, wiping away the remnants of her tears with the blanket. She felt no shame. All of the slaves ex-perienced nightmares. Although, she wondered if it was nor-mal to have the same one so often, wondered what Solomon might have to say about that.

Pippa offered her a warm smile.

Out of all of the girls she roomed with, she liked her best. They had become good friends after a time.

"Me too," she replied with a yawn. "Try to get some rest."

She rolled back over in her bunk, humming a song that Arianna knew well:

I see you down below,
As I'm flying in the sky,
Up above the mountains
To the other side.
The air here is sweet,
And it's warmer by the sun.
Nobody can catch me,
No one, no one.

Can you see me so far up,
As I'm soaring 'cross the sea?
Higher I go,
No jar can keep me.
My hope keeps me lifted,
My wings help me fly.
I am free,
I'm free in the sky.

Now I only see ahead,
As I'm sailing with the clouds.
Drifting with the wind,
Happiness I've found.
Free and alive,
Goodbye, I've left my past behind.
It is my dream,
Finally, I am free.

As the tune wound to an end, Arianna heard someone snif-
fle from across the wide room. She sighed.

Lying back on her pillow, she tugged the blanket to her
chin and let the song wash away the dark fragments of her
nightmare. The 'Song of the Free Bird' always drove the fear
away, her hopes lifting and soaring with the lyrics as she vowed
to one day be liberated from her cage. Just like the little bird
in the song, she would one day taste her freedom.

With happier thoughts, Arianna drifted back to sleep—a
rare dreamless and quiet one.

SUNDOWN

WAKING TO THE BELL the next morning, Arianna let out a big yawn. She felt hazy, as if still in a dream.

"Did I only just imagine her?" she said, tossing with her confusion and excitement at such an experience from the night before.

"Imagine who?" asked Pippa.

She startled Arianna out of her trance, her eyes reminding her of Lessa's as they peered down at her with such curiosity.

"Don't worry about it!" She didn't mean to snap at Pippa, but the secret scared her just as much as it excited her. No one could ever know about their encounter, about any of it.

"Well, sorry," she said, affronted. "But if you don't want people to ask questions, then maybe you should watch what you say in your sleep. You mumble about the most *interesting* topics."

She rolled her eyes and disappeared back onto her bunk.

Arianna chose to ignore her, sliding out of bed and pulling on her robes as she prepared for the morning march to the Square. *Do I really talk in my sleep?*

"She's right, you know," said a voice that made Arianna's skin crawl almost as much as General Ivo's did.

She turned to find Grinda Risso still in her nightclothes, resting on her pillow with her arms behind her head and her lips twisted into a wicked smile. Her friend sat next to her, doting on her in a way that made Arianna cringe.

"Mind yourself, Risso. I'm in no mood to play games with you today," said Arianna, tensing up at the sight of her.

Grinda laughed, sitting up. Then she swung her legs over the side of the bunk as her minion moved behind her to begin brushing her silky, black hair as per custom each morning.

Arianna glared at her rival with as much disgust as she could so early in the morning, but it annoyed her no end that there *was* something dangerously appealing about her.

Grinda Risso—or, more appropriately nicknamed, Red Risso—was one of the fiercest slaves in the district; she was not to be trifled with. The two girls had always butted heads since they both claimed private masters of an exceptional sort, and Arianna knew she couldn't wait to sink her teeth into her. Grinda had never been too shy about that desire.

"Oh bother," she cooed, flipping her hair back as her friend worked to comb out the tangles. "And I had rather hoped to play today. I do apologize, little Ara. I always seem to forget that you can't make your own decisions regarding *playtime.* One of these days, I'm sure Master Bell will grant you permission to battle with me."

"I can practice with whoever I want, when I want," she replied, clenching her fists.

"Well, it's just been such a long, long time since I've put in my request with your master. Does he still refuse to let us duel? It's too bad you're treated like a slave and a child. It must be terribly boring to be so sheltered," she said in a voice so smooth and so sharp that it pierced straight through Arianna's practiced indifference.

She grasped the edge of the door, trying to see past her emotions. Solomon wouldn't want her to mix with the likes of Grinda Risso so close to the Free Falls Festivals. Sucking in a deep breath, Arianna turned to leave, respecting her master's wishes.

"That's what I thought," said Grinda. The laugh that followed pushed all of Arianna's reason out of sight.

"You want a duel? *Fine*," she snapped. "But be careful what you wish for."

Stop talking, stop talking.

"Meet me in the Square at sundown!"

Too late.

Arianna locked her gaze on dark, gray eyes that smiled back in victory. She couldn't deny the piece of her that yearned for Grinda's head on a platter after all these years dodging her insults. And though normally she was able to tune her out altogether, this morning she was completely unfocused.

The words had just slipped out without her control.

She had invited Red Risso to a Warrior's Challenge with her bunkmates to bear witness—and there was no taking it back now.

The girls in the vicinity began to whisper enthusiastically, and Grinda flashed a toothy grin at Arianna.

"Lovely," she said with a wink. "Sundown it is."

Arianna's heart dropped into her stomach.

What have I done?

She recalled a buried regulation which forbade intentional killing during a training duel, but accidents did occur and the general almost never penalized for it. Who was he to care if a warrior-slave lived or died? They were just numbers to him, to be checked off a list.

Since she was chosen as Solomon's apprentice, Arianna had only ever trained with him or a few trusted friends at his approval. As such, they always took extra precautions not to drastically hurt one another when they dueled. Caretaker Cyn was talented, but even she had her limits.

Grinda knew no such boundaries. And a Warrior's Challenge often ended fatally for one opponent—they were extended for the whole purpose of proving one's skill in front of the district. People didn't tend to hold back, least of all Grinda Risso.

Several of her previous challengers had suffered injuries so catastrophic that the Well Center could do nothing for them, and they eventually died. Of course, Grinda's master always passed the losses off as accidents, so she never received more than a slap on the wrist from the regulators. Besides, they enjoyed the battles with the bloodiest endings the most.

Arianna hated to socialize with her at all, but sharing the same quarters made it very difficult not to cross paths. Solomon would be irate when he found out what she'd done. Alas, not even he could halt a Warrior's Challenge. If she wanted to keep her respect in the district, she'd have to honor the challenge and put up a damn good fight.

The weight of potential consequences followed Arianna like an ominous shadow all the way to the Square and filled her head with nothing but worry as she repeated the daily verse hailing King Devlindor. As soon as General Ivo dismissed them from the lineup, she found herself marching toward the Dining Hall in a daze. When she reached it, she saw her usual breakfast duo already lounging in the scattered sun.

A boy with chubby cheeks and kind eyes, just two years younger than her, swayed back and forth on his feet, trying to catch the sporadic rays. He barely reached her neck in height, and his form lacked skill, so Arianna sometimes practiced with him in her downtime to help give him an advantage with his peer group. He still had a lot to learn and wasn't the quickest to catch on, but she wanted Noah to have the best chance at his freedom ticket when the time came.

He deserved something good after his time here.

"Mornin' there, Miss Belvedor," he said with a mock bow as she came to join them. "Breakfast awaits us. What do you think we'll be eating today?" He chuckled to himself.

Arianna didn't crack a smile. "Not today, Noah."

His brow furrowed. He looked somewhat hurt, and she felt another stab of guilt in her chest.

"We waited for you back at the Square. Rough night?"

Arianna looked around Noah to Liam at his side, also trying to savor this rare, beautiful morning.

He had shed his cloak, wearing only black pants and a white shirt that stretched tight around his muscular body. She blushed as a ray of sun gave him a sudden spotlight. Still, after a lifetime of friendship, she had never quite grown used to how beautiful he was.

"You don't know the half of it," she said with a sigh. He opened his mouth to question her, but she cut him off. "Where are your robes? You'll freeze to death."

"I'll be fine," he said, stretching his arms. "I was just getting some early practice in, so I'm all warmed up."

He feigned wiping sweat from his brow but then slipped back on his cloak.

"Show off," said Noah, tackling him in good fun.

They both fell to the ground, wrestling for only a few seconds before Noah was pinned down.

"Better luck next time, kid," said Liam, hopping to his feet and dragging Noah up with him.

He ruffled his shaggy orange hair, but Noah batted his hand away.

"Please, I was hardly even trying," said Noah, flexing his non-existent muscles. "It's just that I haven't eaten yet. Don't have my strength. You got off lucky."

"Right…" said Liam with a smirk on his face. "Come on, then." He put his arm around Noah's shoulders. "Let's get you fed and energized. We'll try that again after breakfast."

Liam Black was another skilled slave with a private trainer to his name and one of the few approved fighters Arianna could duel with other than Solomon. They were pretty even in their victories over one another, but Arianna was at least assured that he wasn't *letting* her win anymore. She'd quickly become a worthy, if not better, opponent on the battlefield.

"Hungry?" he asked, turning his attention to her.

Arianna averted her eyes, already starting toward the door. She didn't want him to know about the Warrior's Challenge she had so foolishly rushed into.

"Starving," she muttered, sauntering into the Dining Hall. Liam and Noah followed at her heels.

"It's not often we get a day like this," mused Noah as he piled a glop of food on his plate.

Arianna nodded halfheartedly.

Today, bright sunrays had chased away some of the gloom that always hung in the district, so that even the air warmed a little. But it didn't do anything to change how Arianna felt—sick in the pit of her stomach and cold all around.

They grabbed their trays of food and walked to an empty bench in the middle of the room.

"Ara, come out with it?" pried Noah as he tore into his stale bread and devoured his food. "What's wrong with you today? You're acting so strange." The freckles on his face mixed with crumbs, so she couldn't tell one from the other.

She shook her head, locking into his bright green eyes. "Oh, Noah," she sighed.

Too many thoughts raced through her brain.

Her head sloped to the side to relax on one hand as she stirred her cold slop in slow circles. Liam didn't look up from his food, but she knew he was listening.

"I'm just exhausted. That's all," she finally said, unwilling to relay the full details of her morning's events.

"Care to elaborate?" asked Liam.

She considered them both now, so grateful that they all had each other to lean on when they needed a true friend. Liam always tried to protect them both when he could. During a duel, he wouldn't even let the backside of a wooden sword meet Arianna's skin. He cared about her, and she trusted him. Still, she didn't have the courage to admit to him what had happened. She was disappointed enough in herself without adding him to the mix.

His hazel eyes bore into hers, demanding answers. "*Well?*"

"Nothing," she said, shifting in her seat. "It's just Risso… you know how she's always trying to cause trouble with me. It's awful living with her, really. She's completely cruel, and she needs a night in the Pit, if you ask me."

Arianna tossed her spoon aside and folded her arms across her chest. She didn't even bother to make an attempt to stomach the food today.

Liam seemed content enough with her answer as she watched him relax. And Noah went back to scraping at the bottom of his bowl, pretending to listen.

"What did she say this time?" asked Liam. His eyes narrowed in distaste as he braved the food in front of him.

"Just the usual. You'd think I'd be used to it by now. She really gets under my skin," replied Arianna, growing angry all over again.

Trying to avoid too many details, she chewed on her lip, looking anywhere but directly at Liam.

"Well, just let her be," he said. "In a few months, we'll have the Free Falls and then you may never have to see that snake again. Besides, you know she's just envious that Solomon chose you over her. It's about time she let it go."

Arianna gave a weak smile at the honorable mention. "And much to your credit," she whispered.

If Liam hadn't let her win that duel in front of the panel of judges, in front of Solomon, who knows where she'd be now. He was her truest friend.

"By default, you're the best with Master Bell as your teacher," agreed Noah. "Cheer up, Ara! The sun only shines on great days. Don't let her get to you."

Liam stood up to empty their meal trays just as Grinda and her entourage walked into the Dining Hall. Arianna gulped as she saw him relay a few short words that made Grinda grimace. She wondered what he'd said.

Then Grinda led her group to a table within eyesight of Arianna and Noah, mouthing the word 'dead' through bared teeth and pouty lips that looked as if they'd been painted in blood. Arianna refused to let her see any more weakness, so she put on a brave face as they calculated one another.

She deemed Grinda's appearance a perfect match for her menacing character. Jet-black hair curved inward at her shoulders, and her bangs swooped at her eyebrows, standing out richly against her red cloak. She wore a permanent scowl on her chiseled face, and her skin was as pale as the snow on the ground. But, most notably, her body was strong and supple, a warrior-slave clearly capable in a fight.

Arianna had seen Grinda put on a show many times during other Warrior's Challenges, and she almost always walked away unscathed. Her ferocity and fearlessness unnerved her opponents and made them doubt their skill.

Will I doubt my skill?

Arianna shook her head at the thought and looked away from her future opponent. She stood to leave with Liam and Noah but not before Grinda tossed her one last malicious smile. Then everyone at her table began to snicker.

Arianna cringed, knowing rumors of the upcoming mêlée

would spread soon enough. The gossip would surely catch like wildfire throughout the district, so she wanted to tell Solomon before he could learn the news from somebody else.

Red Risso versus Arianna Belvedor at sundown.

She shuddered at the thought of what her near future held in store. People would fill the entire Square tonight for this Warrior's Challenge, and the battle would be a bloodbath; Grinda would make sure of it. She'd have to give it her all.

Arianna liked the notion of being labeled the best, but labels had never worried her as much as winning her actual freedom. Grinda, on the other hand, took pride in her skill and labels above all else.

But I'm just as practiced. I'm just as skilled.

Arianna's confidence started building, her mind boosting itself with encouragement as she pushed her negative thoughts aside.

I can put her in her place… or in the ground.

She smiled, straightening her back.

Like Liam said, I've been trained by Master Solomon Bell.

"See you soon!" said Arianna, waving goodbye to her friends. She headed off to the Dueling Arena with a little jolt of hope.

Not long after, she came upon the gargantuan gates of the arena and stepped through. She darted around the hundreds of people already on the grounds doing drills and pushed open the door to her private sparring room. After hanging up her cloak, she began to warm up before practice.

Beginning with the muscles in her legs, she sat down on the ground and stretched to touch her toes. Something was off. Her eyes traveled up her thigh, and she was immediately reminded that her sheath wasn't there—and her sheath wasn't there because her dagger was missing, lost to the waters in the hot springs of her utopia. She'd held on to that blade for the better part of five years, and now it was just… gone.

"My dagger," she said, burying her head in her hands as her hope quickly receded. "How could I have been so stupid?"

She hadn't even had a moment to really register this loss, but now was not the time she would've chosen. She couldn't remember a more ill-fated day granted to her. To top it all off, the customary clouds had fought away the sun, and they looked ready to burst at any moment. She lifted her head to look out the small window as lightning pierced the sky in thin, sporadic lines. A loud clap of thunder followed, shaking through to her soul, and her nerves intensified as the thought of her oncoming fate settled uncomfortably in her chest.

"What have I done?" she whimpered as she moved to shut the door to the sparring room.

"I don't know," said a deep voice. "What have you done, Arianna?"

She jumped back, startled as Solomon towered over her in the doorway. His expression looked violent.

He knows.

"Master Bell, I'm so sorry. You have to believe me," she implored. "I should've just walked away. Everything is going so wrong."

She sat cross-legged on the floor, head lowered.

"Tell me that what I've heard is false! Did you challenge Grinda Risso?" he asked as he tied up his horse outside. "Do you have any idea of the trouble you've caused for yourself?"

"I know. I—"

"The Free Falls are less than three months away! If she slights you in front of a crowd during a Warrior's Challenge, then you'll lose all of your honor and never be given a decent placement after the festivals. That is *if* you even survive."

Solomon began pacing around the room.

Arianna said nothing, letting his words sink in.

"You showed promise in front of the panel on your twelfth-year ceremony. I chose you as my apprentice because you exhibited a passion for battle like I had only ever seen in myself."

His hands began to shake and his voice grew louder.

"Because I saw this in you," he continued, "because *I* said it was so, you were given a real chance to prove yourself, an opportunity that few others have earned. Those with private trainers during their district days have gone on to be some of the greatest warriors I've ever seen, but by gods, Arianna, that doesn't mean you're unsurpassed! You could be throwing away your one chance at a future. You realize this, don't you?"

He regarded her with what could only be described as disbelief and disappointment.

Arianna felt so lost. She knew it had all been a mistake. "If I could take it back, I would."

Solomon held his hand up for silence, and she would not test him.

"You have willingly signed up for a fantastic failure," he said. "Pray that luck is on your side tonight because if you're bested in front of the thousands in this district by Grinda Risso, you'll never be taken seriously as a warrior of the Olleb. If you manage to earn your freedom, you'll just find another type of slavery waiting for you outside of these walls."

"Master, please. I didn't mean to..."

Arianna's words barely passed her lips, and she couldn't meet his eyes as he glared down at her.

"You're a fool! And you'll either win or die tonight." He slammed the door to the training room as he left.

Arianna felt complete fear wash over her in that moment, as if living one of her nightmares. Trying to remain calm, she decided the sky could shed the tears that welled up inside her chest and pressed against her heart. She didn't have time for such emotions today. The clouds only sprinkled now. But she knew, without a doubt, there'd be a storm to come later.

WHEN SOLOMON RETURNED, his mood had not lifted, and Arianna struggled through the strenuous training. He never once granted her the friend she needed—only the strict master in him showed up to duel. And though she deserved nothing less, she wished she could break through his cold demeanor with a strike of her blade. For once, she actually desired some of his wisdom, but he left her feeling only more discouraged.

The day continued on this way until what little sun was left in the sky began to lower. Arianna would have gone to the Dining Hall for dinner, but she feared her nerves might show. She knew that by now everyone would know about the Warrior's Challenge, so she didn't dare step foot outside of the Dueling Arena until she had to.

After Solomon left her to her thoughts, she rested for a couple of hours in the well room. But it wasn't long before he reappeared with a resigned look on his face.

"It's about time," he said.

"Better get going, then, I guess," she mumbled.

She turned to the mirror in the corner of the room, taking in her reflection. The crack was still apparent from when she had fallen into it. As she considered herself, gathering her courage, she pulled her hair into a high ponytail that fell to the middle of her back.

For the battle, she donned a pair of black, worn leather pants. She saved these for the rougher fights because the leather protected her skin against the cold and the flat side of steel. Her boots, also black, hugged her ankles, with fur lining to keep her toes from freezing. They had a thick heel to keep her steady and three rusted clasps stitched to the side to hold them tight on her feet.

Today of all days, Arianna wished for chainmail across her

chest to add to her ensemble, but armor wasn't a privilege granted to slaves. The King reasoned it would create weakness where strength should live and had banned the use of it in the Four Corners entirely.

Arianna speculated over the many *accidental* butcheries of Grinda's previous opponents, and supposed that they had probably wished for armor too. One of her simple, black linen shirts would have to suffice. Slashed at her sleeves and stomach from old battles with Solomon, the shirt fit loose on her body. And every time she raised her arms, her belly showed. Stamped on the side of the shirt, the large emblem of the district glittered in red and gold.

"Here we go," she said as she slipped on her fingerless leather gloves.

Instinctively, she patted her thigh where her trusty dagger should be, a routine she'd never even realized she had before battle until now. Her spirits sank even lower.

"All ready now, are we?" Solomon asked, coming around the corner. His mood seemed lighter than before.

"As ready as I can be," she replied. "Master, I'm—"

"I know, child. I'm sorry for being so harsh with you," he said, lifting her chin up high so that she could observe herself properly in the mirror.

Her reflection was split from the crack in the glass. She just couldn't see herself clearly anymore. But the crest of the warrior was mirrored behind her reflection, and Arianna stood tall against that backdrop. At least she looked the part of a strong warrior, even if she felt weak on the inside.

I'm a slave. Until I earn my freedom, I am number Twenty-Two.

Solomon placed consoling hands on her shoulders and stared at her through the reflection. He began to issue the words of advice she had been yearning for all day long.

"You're strong and you fight well," he said. "But, Arianna,

you mustn't let your guard down out there. Not for an instant. Do you understand me?"

She nodded, her bravery starting to return.

"Grinda Risso is a fierce opponent to have," he continued. "She has a pure disregard for her own life, and she fights for blood with no fear of consequence. You must never give her a moment of weakness, or she'll prey upon it until you're on your knees."

Solomon handed her the twin bronze swords, her favorites. She sheathed them across her back.

"You're ready for this. I don't condone it, but you are certainly ready. Good luck," he said as he headed toward the door.

Arianna could hear the wind pounding at the wood, demanding to be let in.

"Master, wait," she said. "Will you watch tonight?"

"I'll be around if you need me," he replied as he slipped out of the room. She listened to the sound of his horse's hooves on the ground until it faded away.

Arianna stood all alone now, only thoughts of the bloody battle to come to keep her company. Fortunately for her sake, she felt a bit better after Solomon's words, her self-confidence somewhat restored. With one last look in the mirror, she donned her cloak and set off.

The harsh wind swirled her hair around and knocked some of her bangs free as she trekked toward the Square; she thought she felt as wild on the inside as she probably looked on the out, making her even less eager to have the whole district's attention.

The sun neared invisible now behind the claws of Blancoren, and the crowd became denser as she approached the battlegrounds, her nerves returning in full force. She pulled her hood down over her eyes, trying to stay as warm as possible, and also trying to hide her face.

Just as twilight settled in, Arianna entered the perimeter of the Square, which was filled by what seemed to be every person, both slave and elder, who occupied the district. They crowded onto the old stone stairs of the amphitheater. Even General Ivo had taken his place on the raised platform along with his regulators.

The Square provided space for the morning lineup and commendation to the King, ceremony celebrations, and the annual Free Falls Festivals. However, on occasion, it also hosted the fiery-hearted slaves who initiated a Warrior's Challenge with one another.

The general and other elders quite enjoyed the challenges as entertainment, and did nothing to hide it. In fact, some trainers even encouraged their apprentices to initiate a Warrior's Challenge for the sake of practice. Some trainers, yes—but not Arianna's. The guilt wound around her heart like new. If she lost, it wouldn't just be an embarrassment for her, it would drag Solomon's good name through the mud too.

Everyone huddled closer together as the night grew colder, and Arianna melted in with the crowd. Mist drizzled overhead, but it would turn to snow and ice soon enough. Arianna hoped the worst of it would hold off until the battle was done. Just then, she spotted Grinda, radiating strength, in the center of the Square. She looked somehow hostile and calm at the same time as she leaned her weight against a tall double-bladed axe—always her weapon of choice.

Grinda had selected a very similar outfit to Arianna's, save for her shirt of the same blood red as their cloaks and her boots tied all the way to her knees. She shed her robes impatiently, her hair skimming the collar of her shirt as she cracked her neck back and forth.

Lanterns lit up everywhere within the crowd to light the way of the battle. Banded together with the sporadic strings of lightning across the sky, they made for an eerie effect over the sea of buzzing red figures itching for blood.

A booming voice quieted the crowd.

"Twenty-Two, make your way to the center if you're among us," said the cool voice of General Ivo from the comfort of his throne-like chair.

Arianna choked on her voice as beads of sweat dripped down her face under the warmth of her fur. Her eyes fixed open, unable to blink.

"Twenty-Two, the time is now if you wish to preserve your honor," he continued in a bored voice.

Her feet felt frozen to the ground and her limbs numb from the cold. She couldn't find the strength to move.

"Arianna Belvedor!" General Ivo shot up from his seat, his roar tearing through the dead silence.

The sound jolted Arianna from her stupor, and she lifted the hood from her face. Stepping forward into the center of the Square, she finally found her voice.

"I'm here, General," she said.

She bowed low, and the crowd roared its delight.

THE STORM

"WHY THANK YOU FOR GRACING US with your presence," said General Ivo, returning to his chair. "You may begin at your leisure."

He gave a bored flick of his hand, and Arianna felt the burn of thousands of eyes on her back.

"Ready when you are." Grinda barely blinked as she changed to a fighting stance. She summoned Arianna forward, with her axe, to make the first move.

Arianna turned away from all of the shouting faces, trying to regain some clarity. Mantras of "*Risso*" and "*Belvedor*" echoed throughout the crowd, the voices bleeding together in a haze. It really wasn't clear who they were rooting for to win.

Arianna slowly removed her cloak and let the cloth slip from her fingers. But, before it could touch the ground, a hand reached out and caught it.

"Don't want this gettin' all wet, now do we? I think it

might rain later, you know." She turned to find Noah with a feeble grin on his face.

"I'm sorry I didn't tell you earlier," she said. "I just felt so stupid."

"It's okay. Don't worry about it, Ara. Just take care of yourself out there."

His tone had turned serious, which just made her feel worse—Noah never really acted seriously about anything.

"I'll be fine," she said. "Remember what you told me? If the sun is shining in the Four Corners, then it must be a good day!" She placed a reassuring hand on his shoulder, forcing a smile. "I can take her."

She looked past Noah and found Liam right behind him. He stepped forward, gazing down at her with worried eyes.

Arianna's heart melted as fear spread across his anxious face. She should've confided in him. Liam always knew how to keep her hopes high, and when she found herself in trouble—as she quite often did—he had always protected and looked after her.

Sometimes, like now, she found those three simple words of affection on the tip of her tongue, threatening their friendship. She remembered them from a fairytale and had caught the elders in whispers over such things, but the idea scared her, maybe even more so than this battle.

She wasn't even sure if her feelings for Liam were real or just a reaction to the onset of nerves. Regardless, she knew not to believe in fairytales, so she buried her words in her heart and tried to focus on what was important. Besides, that type of affection was strongly discouraged for slaves and sometimes strongly punished, depending on the regulator. So, it was better to just wait until after, if she could help herself...

"I can win this." She took Liam's hands in hers. His firm, calloused skin felt rough against her own. "Just think of it as a warm-up to the Free Falls. We're almost out of here. I won't mess this up, promise." She tried to seem brave, but she was sure Liam saw straight through the façade.

He shook his hands free and instead cupped them around her face so that she had to step in closer. Then, he tilted her head up toward his so that his sandy eyes met her own, studying her intently. Something about the way he looked at her made her feel so safe, like if she stayed with him there in that moment everything would turn out all right.

Just when Arianna thought Liam might lean in, her lips parted slightly on instinct; he flinched away.

"Be careful," he murmured, letting her go.

The sudden gesture broke Arianna's daze and ripped away her safe feeling—nobody could protect her now but herself.

She stammered an awkward goodbye as Liam dropped his hands to his sides and backed away toward the crowd with a bowed head. Noah followed his lead, giving her a weak wave.

With no one left to stall her, Arianna reluctantly turned and walked back to face Grinda in the middle of the Square.

"Don't you worry," she said. "I'll make sure your friends collect the pieces when I'm finished with you."

Arianna held her tongue but returned a taunting curtsy.

"Let's get started, then, shall we?" She was tired of waiting for this moment to come, tired of being afraid of what the outcome might be. It was here now, and she was ready to fight.

Grinda's lips curled into a sneer, and then the loud hum of the bell sounded as a regulator slammed a mallet down on the metal. She took the invitation with gusto, swinging her axe mere inches away from Arianna's neck as her first move.

Arianna barely had time to draw her swords, but she yanked them from the sheath at her back and crossed them in front of her face, blocking the blow just in time. The clash made for an earsplitting sound, and sparks sprinkled her cheeks as the axe's blade scraped against her swords.

"Well, don't just stand there, honey! I came for a fight."

Grinda pushed off from the contact and circled Arianna like a vulture on prey, trying to anticipate her next move.

"I was just thinking the same thing," said Arianna.

She took a step forward, and Grinda expertly mirrored her footing, clearly amused at the challenge.

Arianna smirked back, recognizing that they actually had something in common. Now that they were getting warmed up, she realized that this was just as much fun for her as it was frightening—after all, she was a warrior by nature with a fire in her heart that yearned for battle, just like Grinda Risso.

Arianna began to pick up the pace, thrusting her swords back and forth to test Grinda's skill, seeing if she could really keep up. Once they had both had their fun, the crowd overjoyed at such a show, Arianna decided to shake things up.

She leaped into the air and came down hard on Grinda with both blades, knocking her to one knee. Grinda used the axe like a shield and shoved back with impressive strength.

Arianna stumbled but regained balance before she could hit the ground, maneuvering out of the fall and landing in a crouch. Already dripping with sweat, she felt energized by the blast of adrenaline now coursing through her body. Nothing could sway her focus from the task at hand.

I can do this.

They were both at eye level now, low to the ground, and Grinda pounced first.

Ready for her, Arianna sprang into the air, forcing her knees into her chest. The sharp blade of the axe sailed just underfoot, barely missing its chance to sever her feet. She landed hard on top of the flat side of the weapon, pinning it to the ground and forcing Grinda to relinquish her grip. She kicked it out of reach.

Weaponless, Grinda charged at Arianna.

Bad move, Risso.

Arianna felt a burst of arrogance wash over her then. She

tightened her grip on her swords, letting her guard down a bit as Grinda neared, unarmed. But Grinda withdrew a small—yet very lethal-looking—flail from a sheath at her hip. She let the spiked ball unravel in her hand like an uncoiled snake, the flail glinting in the flickering light of the torches posted around the grounds.

Arianna staggered, smug feeling gone, when she spotted the remnants of Grinda's last victim on the steel. It looked as if she had dipped half of the flail into a bucket of scarlet dye and had left it to dry in the sun.

"Red Risso, we named you well," called Arianna over the deafening crowd. Their shouts and screams melted in with the thunder, so she couldn't tell one from the other.

Her eyes on that horrific steel ball, Arianna anticipated the flail being launched toward her face as Grinda advanced with the weapon. Instead, Grinda dived to the ground and rolled forward, thrashing the flail at Arianna's legs. It slammed hard into her left knee.

Arianna's leg buckled and she fell flat on her back, crying out as pain seared through to her bones. When she finally looked up, she found Grinda with the axe again in her grasp, swinging it toward her heart like a tree stump to be hacked open.

There was an intake of breath from all around the Square. But Arianna wasn't ready to surrender. She lifted both swords, screaming from the effort it took to block the axe. Then, she trapped Grinda's legs between her own, causing her to lose balance and join her in the cold mud.

Arianna swiftly got to her feet, wobbling where she stood, her leg aching as blood trickled down her torn pants. Grinda was seething with anger, glaring up at her from the ground, but she wiped the mud from her face and stood again. Pausing for only a moment's breath, they each surveyed each other's conditions.

Taking the first steps, Grinda dropped the axe and once again reached for her flail. She twirled it in front of her like a protective armor and closed in on the small space between herself and Arianna.

Arianna backed away, careful to avoid any more encounters with the spiked ball that had already added her blood to its collection. She danced around Grinda with expertise, even on a hurt leg, emulating Solomon's techniques that gave him such allure during battle. Grinda wasn't half the warrior or opponent he was, so it was easy enough to get a few strikes in with her swords. Yet, she hesitated to deliver a fatal blow.

"Enough of this. Fight me!" Grinda screamed, her voice challenging even that of the crowd's.

How to win this without one of us dying?

Grinda had grown unfocused, tired; she'd exerted too much energy too fast. Arianna might be the only one with a limp right now, but she was sure she could take Grinda out right then and there with one deathly swing of her sword. But that's exactly what was stopping her—death.

Unlike Red Risso, Arianna had never killed anyone before.

"Oh, I see. Did the great Solomon Bell forget to teach you how to fight during all of your dance lessons?"

Grinda threw her head back in a cackle that made Arianna lose any reluctance she had about killing her; all of her frustrations from earlier came racing back to the forefront of her mind. She let out a roar of anger, wielding her swords in a motion that entangled the chains of the flail around one of her blades. It gave her a clear shot at Grinda, and she took it.

Her sword met Grinda's arm with the next lunge, leaving a large gash at her shoulder.

Grinda shrieked, covering the wound with one hand.

"You're lucky," said Arianna. "I missed what I was aiming for." A smile twitched on her lips.

"You'll pay for that," growled Grinda.

She yanked the flail back, and Arianna's sword flew out of her hand. It took her a moment to realize what had even happened.

Grinda now held her sword.

A light patter of rain started to fall from the sky, another clap of thunder shaking the ground under their feet; it shook Arianna back into action, and she found the determination to fight harder as she watched Grinda parade around the Square with her weapon.

I want my sword back.

Arianna maneuvered well enough with just one sword, but she felt at odds without her double team. She ran forward, bringing her lone sword down hard on its twin in Grinda's hand.

Grinda staggered a bit at first, but then she returned the attack. An axe may have been her weapon of choice, but, like any true warrior, she was capable with a blade.

They continued on like this, sword-on-sword, for what seemed like ages, matching each other in perfect unison until Arianna decided to end it. She spun around, throwing her leg out so that Grinda's stomach met her boot with a strong kick. Grinda lurched backward, coughing up blood as she landed hard on her back.

Arianna didn't stop to rest. She leaped into the air, her sword held high above her head, ready to come down with a final blow.

But Grinda was ready too. She relinquished Arianna's sword and reached for her blood-covered flail.

Before Arianna could lay her sword into Grinda, the spikes of the flail burrowed deep into her skin, the chains coiling tight around her arm. She lost her grip on her weapon and on her focus. Her knees hit the ground, and she buckled over, trying to free her arm.

"Is that all you've got?" said Grinda.

Arianna felt a boot collide with her side, her ribs cracking beneath her skin like ice underfoot. She rolled onto her back, crying out from the pain.

"Come on. Get up!" Grinda shouted, her victorious laugh somehow worse than anything Arianna had ever endured thus far in the districts.

The bystanders grew calm now, silently waiting.

Arianna curled on her side, wrapping one arm around her stomach as she struggled to breathe. From this angle, she could see the blood flowing like a river down her arm. The skin had been torn apart at her wrist from where the spikes had ripped into her flesh, and her hand was shaking.

Somehow, she found the strength to get back to her feet, and Grinda gave her the room to stand.

"Solomon should be so proud," she said, slowly clapping.

Arianna lifted her head to the sky and let the rainwater wash over her for a moment, trying to tune Grinda out. There were so many people watching, waiting for her to fail, but she still had some fight left in her yet. Grinda may have control of all the weapons on the field, but Arianna wasn't going to give up so easily.

With a painful warrior cry, she launched herself toward the forgotten flail in the mud and grasped for its long, wooden handle. Arianna swung the flail as hard as she could, not caring about the excruciating pain it caused, and released her grip. The weapon flew through the air, slicing the rain in its path toward Grinda's head.

The attempt took Grinda by such surprise, since she was too focused on gloating, that she couldn't act fast enough to escape its path. The spiked end of the flail caught her in the cheek, tearing the soft flesh as her head pitched sideways.

Grinda's scream made Arianna instantly regret the decision. She was ready for this battle to end. She really didn't want to kill or hurt anyone if she didn't have to... not even

Red Risso. They had both proven themselves worthy of a fight against one another, each bloodied, bruised, and still standing. Did one of them really have to die for this Warrior's Challenge to be over?

The rain fell harder now, softening the ground and cleansing their wounds, as if restarting the battle.

When will it end?

Grinda clutched at her face, blood covering her fingertips. Eyes bulging, she raced toward Arianna, weaponless once more. Fists raised, Arianna readied herself, trying to set aside her own exhaustion.

Forgetting their weapons, the girls instead used their fists and feet to finish the battle, colliding in a tangle of rage.

Moments later, Arianna took a punch to the side with her broken ribs. The next thing she knew, Grinda's foot had smashed into her head. She felt dizzy and disconcerted as she floated to the ground.

When Grinda stood over her to revel in her triumph, Arianna kicked her shin with great force; she fell down beside her, howling out.

The pair couldn't be more evenly matched, and Arianna wished one of the elders would call it as such.

A sword lay just out of reach for them both, and the girls stopped wrestling, spotting it at the same time. Side by side, they both lunged for it, scraping through the mud and ignoring their injuries—Grinda got there first, but only because she had been closer.

"I guess luck is on my side today," she said with a sneer as she limped to her feet and pointed Arianna's sword at her chest.

"Luck doesn't make you the better warrior," spat Arianna, rolling over on her back and pushing herself up on her elbows.

Grinda stepped forward, pressing the blade lightly against Arianna's body and dragging it down to her stomach, a wicked gleam in her eye.

Arianna sucked in a breath through her teeth as if the gesture might offer some kind of protection. She had never been on this end of her own sword before, and she didn't much care for it.

"Say it," demanded Grinda through clenched teeth.

Arianna felt all the blood drain from her face, embarrassment and anger her only emotions now, and the only emotions she thought she'd ever feel again.

"I said, say it!" Grinda's sword hand shook, demanding that Arianna hand over the victory.

"Fine… you win, Grinda," she said after a moment. "I yield."

The words tasted like acid on her tongue, and they were beginning to seem like the most common thing in her vocabulary.

"I'm sorry, what was that?" asked Grinda, cocking her head to the side as she observed her.

Her mouth twisted up in a smile, and Arianna thought it might be the first genuine one she'd ever seen on her face.

"I said—" But before Arianna could mutter the degrading words once more, she felt the cool metal slice through her flesh of her stomach.

"Speak up next time," said Grinda, withdrawing the bronze blade from Arianna's belly.

Then, she tossed it aside, into the bloodstained snow.

ARIANNA'S HEAD SPUN. The pain she felt was so overwhelming that she wasn't even sure if it was pain anymore. She heard someone screaming in the distance but then recognized it as her own voice. Curling to the side to try to find some relief, she felt a river of warm blood pour from her body.

Faces whirled about her, but she couldn't recognize any. And, faintly, she heard people cheering in the background as General Ivo dismissed the crowd. The red of their cloaks swirled together, making her nauseous as everyone left the Square.

Suddenly, she felt as if the earth had flung her into the sky in a painful heave. Then, everything went black.

"Arianna! Can you hear me? Hold on. Just hold on." The voice seemed far away, but she knew it called for her safety. It seemed familiar somehow as the blackness blurred back into color.

"Liam?" She could barely form the word.

"Yes, I'm here. Don't worry, okay? I'm going to make this right. I promise." He wrapped her cloak around her, holding her in the safety of his strong arms.

"I'm not worried," she replied in a slur.

Arianna felt the rain pounding against her face. And the throbbing at her side kept causing her to go in and out of a dark consciousness. She struggled to breathe through the pain. As her head lolled over his arm, no strength to hold it up, she spotted her blood in a long trail behind them.

Everything went black again.

"Bring her here! Hold on, dear!" shouted another muffled voice as a warm light filtered through her eyelids.

Faces blurred about her vision and cold hands ran over her skin. Soft, muted voices buzzed in her ears, bouncing around her jumbled head.

Cyn? She tried to form the name on her lips, but her voice never came.

"Set her down here, carefully now. Gently, please," she heard Cyn command.

"Can you hear me?" asked the deep voice of a man.

"Solomon?" Arianna reached out with her one uninjured arm.

"I'm right here," he said, sweeping her hair from her face. "Cyn, get over here! I'm losing her. Liam, get Noah out of here. We can handle this. We don't need bystanders crowding the room."

The voices whirled and blurred in Arianna's clouded mind, and she desperately struggled to hold on to some clarity. But she just couldn't find the strength.

"Solomon?" she said again.

"Yes, I'm right here." She felt his hand grasp hers.

"You were right. You're always right…" Arianna's voice trailed off, back into the blackness of her mind.

7

THE BATTLE

"I'M TELLING THE TRUTH, TALIS! You must come quickly. There isn't much time," pleaded Solomon.

"Master Bell, this is neither the time nor place for such talk," whispered a small man, scanning for onlookers from the entrance of his home. "Please, it's best you go now."

Talis closed the door in his face.

Solomon pounded his fist on the wood, demanding to be let in, but the man behind the door would not oblige. He began to pace back and forth, clutching at his face under the rain turned snow. With every passing moment, anger began to build up inside of him.

He paused in front of the door, contemplating his options for only an instant, and then a flicker of fire passed through his heart. In one swift action, he lifted his foot and slammed it onto the wood panel of the door.

The door crashed open in a cloud of splintered wood, tearing a gash where the lock used to latch.

Talis jumped up from his chair. "Have you lost your damn mind, Bell?"

Solomon burst into the house and stood in a large common area. A few chairs were seated around a fire, and Solomon saw more doors at the far wall.

"Talis Churry, what has become of you, my friend?"

Solomon lost his fury in one glance at the man's terrified face. He pulled the door shut, set the lantern he'd been carrying aside, and lowered himself into a plush chair across from him, trying to ease his anxiety. The room felt comforting with the fire for light, the walls a soft golden brown and the subtle scent of jasmine lingering in the air.

Talis only stared, unmoving. Then, he seated himself near the fireplace where flames licked at the wood of soon-to-be ashes. He was a short, silver-haired man, and he kept his eyes trained on the fire as if he were searching for something. The flames illuminated his sunken face and the shadows under his eyes. His pink skin wrinkled, but his eyes glinted with untold wisdoms, the same cerulean blue as the lining of his white robes. The long velvet dragged on the floor; the fabric had turned brown at the bottom.

"That was long ago, Solomon," he said after a while, stroking his thick, graying mustache. "That past is behind us now. How did you even come to find me?"

"Fate has led me to your doorstep tonight, old friend. I wasn't searching for you when I ran to the Healer's District, yet here I am. Your door happened to be the first of the master healers I came upon. I'm in as much disbelief as you! Why wouldn't you have told me that you returned to the districts?"

Talis shook his head. "Please, spare me—"

"I will not." Solomon leaned forward in his chair. "How can you deny the renewed path we've been set on tonight?"

Talis pushed himself to his feet, still facing the fire with his hands pulled behind his back.

"Fate has not been kind to me, so I've no faith in her." He spoke in a whisper, pausing to warm his small hands near the flames; they appeared blackened and scarred.

"And to I," Solomon said, lowering his head, "she has shown little mercy, but now I see the light. Talis, please—"

"No," he said with finality.

"You have to listen to me! I need your help," urged Solomon. "There is no one else."

Talis waved his hand for silence, and Solomon quieted, though his patience was waning.

"This girl you speak of… your apprentice. Do you honestly believe she's worth all the trouble?" he asked, narrowing his eyes as he studied him, clearly searching for a hint of folly in Solomon's expression.

"I do," said Solomon. His lips set into a firm line.

"And that is to say that the rumors speak a truth. This we don't know for certain," continued Talis.

He relaxed back in his chair and took a sip from a steaming cup of tea.

"It's no rumor, and we're living proof of that! There are people organizing, people like us who are just waiting for the right time. You know this." Solomon's voice turned cold as he rose from his seat with fists clenched at his sides.

Talis looked up from his tea and set it aside.

"And how can you be so sure there'll ever be a right time?" he said, not intimidated in the least. "We thought last time was the right time, and look where that got us!"

"That history is much too long for a time like this. We can argue about it later," replied Solomon.

He bent down to kneel at Talis' feet, demanding his full attention.

"Brother, please," he urged. "Show me your courage. We

need all the help we can get, and she's special. I can feel it in my heart. You must trust me on this. She could be one of us."

Talis twisted a finger around his long beard as he thought.

"There's still hope out there," continued Solomon. "She's reminded me of that."

"And yet, you tell me she lies on her deathbed? Humph." Talis pursed his lips.

"There's still good in this world, and I made a vow to protect what little is left. As did you! You must remember what we fight for," said Solomon.

His eyes softened a little as he seemed to linger on a distant memory, but it quickly vanished.

"Fight for?" Talis said, his voice pitching. "I fight for nothing now! That past is behind me. I can't help you."

He tore his eyes away only to get lost again in the dying fire, the flames reflecting in his glassy stare.

"Then you're a coward," replied Solomon as he stood again. He felt like a giant hovering over a child as Talis remained in his chair. "I know your soul is calling for retribution, just like mine. Turning your face away from the battle can win no war!"

"I'm running from nothing. This is my life now. I'm retired, Solomon. *You're* retired, and there is no war. There's no one left to even lift a sword. We shouldn't trifle with these things anymore," he said.

"I'm left, and you're still standing here, alive and well. Look at yourself," said Solomon. "You can't tell me that this is how you want to spend the rest of your days, doing nothing of good. Not when there's still hope."

"And what of the others?" asked Talis, bitterly. "What of them and their hope? Their blood is still fresh on my hands."

"Then don't waste it!" retorted Solomon. "Your past is your present, and your present is your past. We'll always be slaves in a world where children are taken from their mothers and caged at birth. Don't you remember the tortures you faced when you were considered a number within these mountains?"

His voice started to steadily rise. "You may have earned your rights and your citizenship to the Olleb, but for what?" he added. "Nothing's changed. Those horrors are just being relived for us by others now. Is this the life you imagined then? Is this the life you fought and bled for?"

Talis met Solomon's eyes.

"This life is void of anything worth fighting for now. I know we tried our hand at uncovering some good, but we wasted a lot of honorable souls doing it. We aren't young anymore. The final hand we've been dealt is a luxurious one compared to what others have suffered. It's time you accept the inevitable and stop chasing fairytales," he said with a wave of his hand.

Contempt took over any compassion for Talis in that moment, and all of the muscles in Solomon's body tensed.

"No, Talis, it's time *you* accepted the inevitable. Olleb-Yelfra struggles, and we can't turn our backs on her. Not when she has entrusted us with so much power. You're still strong! Please, look to your soul. Do what is asked of you. Our land has suffered enough," said Solomon.

He grabbed Talis by the shoulders and shook him violently as if to will the sense into him.

"Our fate is now!"

"I'm so sorry, but I can't. I won't," he choked out. "I wish for no trouble."

He pushed away Solomon's hands with weak effort.

Solomon straightened his back. "Well, trouble has found you, brother."

"Is that a threat?" Talis asked, standing. His fingers twitched by his sides.

Solomon met his stance. And though he stood much taller than the old man before him, something fierce shone in Talis' eyes, evening them out.

"I mean, *Talis*, you owe me this favor," he replied, his voice heavy with an unsaid accusation.

In an instant, he drew one of his twin swords from the sheath at his back. The silver, sleek blade curved slightly, *dangerously*, and an inscription on the metal glimmered in the light of the fire. He brought the blade a pinch away from Talis' neck, grasping the jeweled hilt with two steady hands, unyielding. "What say you now?" he said.

"I say you're a fool to come here this night, and you've forced my hand," answered Talis, his eyes flashing with a hint of silver.

He never even flinched.

In one rapid move, Talis wrapped his fingers tight around Solomon's wrists. The skin-on-skin contact somehow sent a powerful surge of pain through to his muscles, Solomon's body going rigid at the contact. His limbs writhed, and his sword crashed to the ground. He fell to the floor alongside it.

Talis stood over him now, glaring down at him as he slid his fingers across his skin once more. Solomon convulsed again, howling in agony from just his mere touch.

"I knew you were still in there," he said through gritted teeth as his body continued to contort with uncontrollable spasms.

After a moment, Talis let go, and the shooting pain ceased.

"I won't deny that I owe you my life," he finally said, pacing about the room as Solomon pulled himself up to a seated position. "If this is the favor you ask of me, then I'll help you *only* to repay my debt. But this is the last I want to hear of it."

Talis' expression seemed grave and defeated.

"Do we have an agreement?" he asked, offering his hand.

"Fair is fair," replied Solomon with a feeble smile as he let Talis help him to his feet.

Solomon sheathed his sword and made to leave as Talis

grabbed the lantern near the doorway. With just the snap of his fingers, a bright flame sparked and started to lick at the oil.

"Let's not waste any more time, then," said Talis, gruffly.

"Yes, we must hurry. It's a bit of a trek through the tunnels back to the Warrior's District," said Solomon, clinging to this last bit of hope. "If we're too late..." He threw open the door with Talis reluctantly following behind.

"By gods!" gasped Talis when they stepped out into the blizzard. "You came by foot in this weather?" He lifted his hood, tight over his head, to shield his face.

Solomon smirked, shaking his head.

"You should know there are quicker ways to travel when in dire need," he said, lifting the lantern up so that the sparkling flame illuminated their faces. "You're the one who taught them to me."

"*You* should know better than to take such risks," he snapped. "You could've died... or worse, been caught!"

"Trust me, Talis, this is worth the risk," he replied, shrugging him off. "But I certainly don't have the energy right now to get us both back without something going wrong. So, what do you suggest?"

"We can take my horse as far as the tunnels," said Talis. He disappeared behind the house for a moment and came back leading a large stallion. "Can't ride them through, so he'd just slow us down if we take him farther than that. I'll leave him in the stables on the other side of the district and then we go on foot. When we get to the Warrior's District, we'll just have to figure something out. But try to keep a low profile, would you? I know how you can get."

"Of course! It'll be just like the good ole days," sang Solomon, slapping him on the back. "Thank you, my friend."

"I can tell this is going to be a long night," muttered Talis.

As they both situated themselves on the horse, Talis in the lead, something made Solomon turn around, sensing that someone was watching them. Sure enough, when he looked back over his shoulder, he found a young girl peering out of a circular window from Talis' home. Her sapphire eyes lingered on them, an expression of worry and confusion on her face.

Solomon opened his mouth to question Talis; the girl was clearly the age of a healer-slave and should be in her own quarters at such a late hour. But then, he thought better of it—he didn't have another second to spare thinking of anyone other than Arianna and how to save her.

With the wave of his hand, he guided the midnight snowfall to swirl about himself and Talis in a vortex of dazzling white so that it looked as if they were one with the blizzard. Then, finally, they set off toward the Vanishing Tunnels.

THEIR HEAVY FOOTSTEPS ECHOED loudly in the quietness of the tunnels as they left the Healer's District behind. It took them a fair amount of time to journey the paths that led toward the Warrior's District, but they had possession of a map and eventually made it there with no detours.

Solomon came to an abrupt halt at the mouth of the entrance, throwing his arm out for Talis to stop. They could hear the chattering of two guards only a few feet away.

"Of course she's done for," said one of the regulators in a tired voice. "How can anyone survive that kind of blow?"

"I suppose we'll be finding out tomorrow. That sure was some battle, though. I wish more of these kids would hack away at each other," replied his companion.

The regulator chuckled. "Sure wasn't a boring show."

"I'll give you a show," growled Solomon as he unsheathed a sword.

Using only the pommel, he delivered one heavy strike to the back of each of their heads. With two muffled thuds, the guards fell facedown in the snow, unconscious.

"I see you're still practicing old habits too," said Talis, shaking his head.

"They'll be fine," he replied, not sorry in the least. "Come on. We can take their horses, and I'll return them later before anyone notices."

Borrowing the regulators' horses, they started down the twisting paths of the district. A few flames flickered in windows they passed and sporadic lanterns lined the street, but for the most part, darkness shrouded them all the way to the Dueling Arena. Solomon pushed on the gates and they creaked open, the blizzard drowning out the noise.

They made their way to his private sparring room.

After they'd dismounted from the horses, Solomon took a long, brass key from his pocket and inserted it into a lock. The door swung open with a click, and he and Talis stepped inside. Without a pause in his step, Solomon took Talis by the arm and led him to the well room toward the back, where the smell of sickness immediately stung their noses and stifled the air.

The lanterns glowed too brightly in the small space here, not hiding anything from sight—Solomon found Cyn seated in the corner, her yellow robes covered in dried blood and bags swelling under her eyes. And, in the center of the room, was a large blood-spattered bed where a blood-spattered girl lay naked and dying.

Barely able to look upon Arianna as fear gripped his heart, Solomon glanced back to Cyn. She offered nothing of reassurance, just shaking her head in evident defeat.

Solomon took a deep breath, balling his hands into fists, and forced himself to really see his apprentice for what she was—dying, or maybe even already dead.

Arianna didn't appear like herself, normally so full of life.

There were dark bruises all over her body, and her skin had a sickly pale shade to it. He went to kneel next to her bedside and took her cold hand in his, nuzzling it at his cheek as warm tears melted onto her skin.

"It was too much." Cyn placed her head in her hands and began to weep. "I tried, but there wasn't enough time. She's too weak now, and we don't have strong enough healing remedies here in the districts. Her body isn't cooperating with anything I do."

She choked out the sad statement which sentenced the young, budding warrior to death.

"Move aside," said Talis. Cyn barely seemed to notice him in her frazzled state. He grabbed Arianna's hand away from Solomon and pressed two fingers against her wrist. "She still has a pulse but just barely." His expression stayed vague and unreadable.

"Can you bring her back?" asked Solomon.

"I can try," he replied in a less-than-optimistic tone. He moved awkwardly around Cyn, appearing quite uncomfortable at her presence. "Miss, you're the caretaker here, I suspect?"

Cyn nodded, looking to Solomon in clear bewilderment.

"It's all right," he assured her. "Talis is a friend. He's here to help."

"How long has she been unconscious?" asked Talis.

"Almost three hours," said Cyn. "She lost so much blood before we got her here. She needs stronger healing remedies and surgery, but we don't have the tools—"

She could barely push out her words.

"I did everything I could, but there isn't a way to heal her in this state." Her head dropped to her hands again as she began to bawl uncontrollably. "She had so much promise."

Solomon placed a consoling hand on her shoulder as Talis examined Arianna's limp body.

"Don't worry," he whispered in Cyn's ear. "He's the best

healer I know. He'll make this right again."

"It's a miracle she even lasted five minutes," said Talis. "From the looks of her, I'd say she put up quite the fight."

"That she did," said Solomon with nothing but pride.

"Please, leave us now. I need concentration if I'm to have any hope of reviving this child. Go," demanded Talis.

"Bring her back to us," said Solomon, catching his eye. "There's a reason we were reunited again tonight, and that reason is her survival. We *need* her to live, Talis. Trust me on this."

With that, he took Cyn and left the room, leaving Talis to perform the daunting task at hand.

TALIS SAW CYN HAD TRIED to stitch up the deep wound on Arianna's stomach. It still gushed with fresh blood, and the ointments worked at a sluggish pace. Cyn had cleaned and cared for all her injuries with skill, but Talis agreed that there was nothing more she could've done to try to fix such extensive damage in time. Not with the mediocre selection of healing remedies they rationed to the districts.

Arianna's chest rose up and down, too slow not to be concerning and only just noticeable. Scrutinizing the details, Talis scrunched up his face. Any more tampering with her already mangled body would surely result in a swift death.

He knelt down so that his face aligned with hers.

"I don't know if you're worth all this trouble or what you're capable of, but my friend has a great confidence in you. For that, I'll try and grant you one more chance at this miserable life." His whisper evaporated into the hovering silence of the well room.

He got to his feet, head drooped in concentration.

His hair fell down around his face, and his lips moved quickly as a slur of smooth-feeling words rolled off his tongue—words he hadn't used in decades. He waved his hands over Arianna's heart in a ritualistic fashion until, suddenly, her body reacted with a lurch.

"Only those deemed worthy can be restored," he said with shaking hands. "Are you worthy, Arianna?"

Talis felt out of practice, such power completely draining his energy as the foreign language spilled from his mouth, his voice growing louder; Arianna's body writhed only more, convulsing violently.

Just then, a soft white light began to trickle from his palms, spreading about Arianna's body like a glimmering cocoon. As Talis ceaselessly sang his spell, the light grew animated and buzzed across her skin, seeking to awaken all of the nerves in her body.

Arianna continued to tremble in response; yet still, she would not wake.

"*Onasyuda!*" cried Talis with the last of his strength.

The light fell away from her body like glittering rain, melting into the air before it hit the floor. But, when Talis opened his eyes, everything was just as before—Arianna was completely unchanged, her wounds remaining unhealed.

"Seems Solomon put his faith in the wrong child." He let out a long sigh, wiping the sweat from his brow. "King Devlindor has guided yet another wasted life into Death's arms," he uttered to himself, bowing his head out of respect.

Talis gently placed a white sheet over Arianna's lifeless body, so that the only thing of her he could see was her limp hand hanging off the bed. He hurried to exit the room, leaving the last of his hope behind.

PART TWO

# DEAD

"NO, YOU LIE!" SCREAMED SOLOMON as he slammed Talis into the wall. Cyn sank to the floor beside them.

"Solomon, the girl is dead. I did all that I could, but her body rejected the—"

He glanced uncertainly at Cyn, but she paid them no mind.

"—the treatment. I'm truly sorry," he said in a soft voice. "She just wasn't strong enough." He placed a gentle hand on Solomon's shoulder, pushing him to arm's length.

Solomon shoved Talis' arm aside and stormed into the well room, wanting to see her with his own eyes.

"Arianna?" he mumbled as a tear escaped his control.

He quickly wiped it away and went to stand beside the bed, too afraid to lift the sheet that covered her.

Talis watched from the doorway along with Cyn, who couldn't seem to bring herself to enter.

"No, this wasn't supposed to be," said Solomon, shaking his head. "I don't understand why your magic didn't work. You must've made some mistake!" He slammed his fist into the wall in front of him. "Maybe you didn't even try. You've lost all your confidence. Tell me, Talis! Did you try?"

His voice cracked as he looked back to confront him.

Talis stepped inside the room then, pulling the door closed as he did.

"I was dragged here tonight to revive a girl who was already cold to the touch!" he snapped back. "It's a terrible risk and often a waste to use magic to try and bring back the dead. You never know what the magic could do to a person. Who they'll be, after. That is, if they even wake, which is an extremely rare occurrence with the *Onasyuda* enchantment. Mind you, I still gave it my best effort to will her back to life."

Solomon ignored him, fixing his eyes on the bed.

He heard Talis walk slowly toward him from the doorway. "Solomon, friend—" he said, forcing the last word between his lips.

"No, don't," said Solomon, squeezing his eyes shut as he grasped Arianna's cold hand.

He still couldn't bear to lift the sheet. He couldn't bear to look.

"The spells we mastered and practiced for so many years… well, I don't have to explain to you the kind of power we possess," continued Talis. "I know you were never fond of practicing healers' magic, but it doesn't work the same way your defensive spells do."

Talis paused for a moment, seeming to search for the right words, but Solomon couldn't focus on him anyway.

"No matter the level or expertise of any sorcerer, healing magic, like all magic at its core, can only be summoned. It can't be wielded to obey every command as you command your sword. It can be conjured for a purpose but never controlled once it's been called. Not unless the magic submits itself in its own right," he said.

"Are you saying your magic *chose* not to help her?" hissed Solomon, barely able to subdue his anger. "I thought you were supposed to be a master healer. You're supposed to be the best!"

"I'm saying that I beckoned the strongest curative magic that my old knowledge could evoke. Her body wouldn't accept it. Or, maybe, the magic wouldn't accept her." Talis glanced toward the bed. "One can never be certain."

"If there's nothing more you can do, then just go," barked Solomon. "I don't need any further lessons in magic. I'm a master, too, and I won't hear any more of your excuses. You have failed me."

Talis let out a heavy sigh. "She's passed on, Solomon. You must accept that." He started toward the door. "I really am sorry for your loss."

Just as Talis was about to leave the well room, Solomon shrieked. His eyes were pinned on the bed and his mouth hung open in pure disbelief.

"What's happening?" asked Solomon. "What is this?"

"I don't believe it." Talis walked up to the bed and stripped away the sheet that covered Arianna's body.

Arianna remained still as ever, but a warm light radiated underneath her skin, making her glow from the inside out. Seconds later, the light concentrated into a luminous orb at her stomach, glowing dim within her body like a clouded sun. Gradually, it began to rise until it pressed out of her skin, a ball of burning white fire. It stretched and coiled all around her body with a mind of its own.

"Astounding," whispered Solomon. "I've never seen anything like this."

"Neither have I," said Talis, shaking his head. "*Onasyuda*

magic materializes differently almost every time. You know that, but I was certain it hadn't worked. I've never known it to take so long." His eyes stayed fixed to Arianna. "If she wakes, there's no telling who, or *what*, she'll be."

"She will be just fine," said Solomon, willing it to be true with all of his heart.

"Prepare yourself," said Talis. "Good or bad, magic is famed for its consequences."

As the fiery orb danced around Arianna's body, Solomon and Talis could only watch, sharing in the wonder. Right before their eyes, her wounds melted away and her bruised flesh was painted with life again.

"Is she… alive?" breathed Solomon, grabbing for Talis' hand and squeezing it tight.

The orb passed over Arianna's heart, stalling there before absorbing back below her skin. Then it exploded into sparks of colorful magic that seemed to seep throughout her veins, lighting up every inch of her for a brief moment until the magic disappeared.

Before Solomon could even bring himself to blink, Arianna's eyes flew open, flashing with a silver glow. He ran to her aid, cupping her face in his hands. Her skin was warmed and softened from her corpse-like state, and he relished this unexpected gift of life.

"Solomon? What's going on?" she asked, clearly disoriented as she looked around the well room.

A wide grin stretched across his face at the familiar question; it seemed as if Arianna had just awakened from another strenuous training session with him.

It was just like any other day—except everything had changed. "A miracle," he said, glowing with happiness. "A miracle has happened for us all this day."

AFTER SOLOMON RELINQUISHED his hold on Arianna, Cyn came bursting through the door. Immediately spotting Arianna, she blundered through the room and pulled her into a warm embrace.

"Mercy, I don't believe it!" she said as she looked Arianna up and down. All of her wounds had vanished. "But how…"

Arianna shook her head, just as dumbfounded, and Cyn squeezed her tighter.

"You're suffocating me," said Arianna, her voice muffled by her robes.

"I might be able to offer a bit of an explanation," said Talis.

Arianna pulled away from Cyn and glanced his way, again lost for words. *Who is this elder in my well room?*

"How do you feel, Arianna?" he asked in a gentle voice, coming up to the bed as Solomon and Cyn gave them space.

Arianna shrank back from him, suddenly aware of her nakedness. She swung her stiff legs over the edge of the bed and wrapped herself in the tattered, bloodstained robes that had lain at her feet. The fabric felt warm and welcome against her skin.

"I feel extremely muddled," she said, pulling her fingers through her matted hair as she tried to make sense of things.

"Yes, of course." Talis waved a hand as if her confusion didn't concern him in the slightest. "But, physically, how do you feel?" he asked with an excited gleam in his eye.

"As good as new, I suppose," she said, examining her arms and legs. "I feel… perfect, actually. But I'm very confused."

She pressed her fingers to her forehead, trying to assemble all of her thoughts, but they just kept blending into a giant lump. She needed some clarity.

"Who are you? What happened?" she asked.

She let the questions pour from her lips, desperately wanting the solution to her tangled mind.

"I remember the battle and the taste of blood in my mouth. I remember the pain and *Grinda*." She could barely force the name from her lips. "Then…"

"Then what, Ara?" said Solomon. "What did you see?"

She looked up at him, feeling more lost and scared than maybe ever before.

"Then there was only darkness, and I couldn't swim out of it this time," she said. "I tried, but I couldn't…" Her voice trailed off as she tried to grasp onto her memories.

"It's okay, dear," said Cyn. "Take your time. What happened after that?"

"Well… then I did." She ran her fingers through her hair as she thought. "I swam out and woke up here," she mumbled.

It all sounded ludicrous to her, so she started to panic, her heart thrumming at an uncomfortable pace inside her chest.

"Please, rest your mind. Breathe," said Talis. "I'll explain as much as I'm able. My name is Master Talis Churry, and your master guided me here tonight from the Healer's District in order to help you. You see, I possess some special qualities that he believed could help save your life."

He sat down on the long mattress beside her.

Arianna looked down at her now unscathed hands, turning them over and massaging her fingers.

"What kind of special qualities?" she asked, studying his unreadable face.

Can I trust this stranger?

His azure eyes reminded her of someone she knew, but she couldn't quite place it. Everything was a blur, and she needed answers. Waiting for him to speak, her patience waning, she noticed Talis' attention flick uneasily to Cyn; she was seated on a chair now by the back wall, fanning her face.

Solomon suddenly rose to his feet.

"Cyn, please allow me to escort you back to your quarters now that we know Arianna will be okay," he said in a soft voice, walking to her side. "You must be exhausted."

"Yes, I am rather tired," Cyn replied with a yawn.

She straightened out the wrinkles on her robes and attempted to collect herself. Then she scuttled over to Arianna and planted a kiss on her head.

"Welcome back, dear," she said before walking out of the well room.

Solomon spoke to Arianna before leaving.

"Listen to him," he said. "I've always told you that this world hides many secrets. Well, this will be one of them."

"But—"

He shook his head, and Arianna swallowed her words.

"Don't hinder your mind with thoughts of true and false, Ara. Let it be vulnerable to explore all the possibilities… as it does when you dream. Do you understand me?" He tapped his temple, his expression serious, anxious even.

Arianna's thoughts drifted to one of Solomon's most recent lectures.

'Your mind never sleeps, and that's why you dream. If you start to pay more attention to both worlds, rather than just the physical one, you may be in for a wonderful surprise.'

Arianna nodded her agreement but said nothing. She wished very much that Solomon and Cyn would stay. Alas, they left, and she sat alone with the stranger who called himself Talis Churry. When the door swung shut, he picked up the conversation right where he'd left off.

"I'm a sorcerer, Arianna," he said with a smile on his lips.

She was staggered by his words, and a wave of anger washed over her.

Is he joking? An elder making light of such illicit subjects, and at a time like this?

"I don't understand what you mean…" she said after a moment. "Are you trying to get me in trouble? We shouldn't be talking of such things."

"Enlighten me," he said, cocking his head to the side as he considered her.

"Sorcerers are the stars of prohibited fairytales that have trickled to my ears, sir. I don't partake in them. It's against the law," she said, firmly. "Is this a test or something? Tell me who you really are."

Talis matched her stony stare, saying nothing as they looked upon each other in silence for what seemed like a long time. His words bounced around in her head as his eyes bore deeper. *'I'm a sorcerer.'*

Arianna's head started to spin, and her thoughts drifted to Solomon and his counsel. She needed him there. The false declaration haunted her, but she couldn't grasp why.

Could he be serious?

She shook the idea from her head, but she couldn't shake Solomon's face from her mind. He had seemed so keen for Talis to speak with her alone and for her to listen.

Arianna shuddered, feeling vulnerable and lost as Talis' eyes seemed to see straight into her soul. *'I'm a sorcerer.'*

His voice rang in her ears as she started to second-guess this reality, the darkness threatening to claim her once more. Silent tears rolled down her cheeks, and she looked away, embarrassed by his scrutiny. The staring contest was over.

And still, Talis Churry said nothing.

Grasping a thought amidst the chaos in her mind, Arianna reached at least one clear conclusion with ease; even if nothing else was certain, she knew that she was lucky to be alive—and also that she shouldn't be.

Something brought me back from the dead.

A SORCERER

"SAY SOMETHING," SAID ARIANNA, letting her mouth explode with the words scratching at her teeth. "Have you really just introduced yourself as a sorcerer? Are you sticking with that? If so, I guess I'm actually dead."

She chuckled to herself, thinking that maybe she was.

"Please, just tell me who you are and what happened. That's why you're here, isn't it?"

"Well, Miss Belvedor, you did have *quite* the epic battle. Or, so I hear anyways," said Talis, breaking his wordless streak.

Arianna opened her mouth to retort, but he cut her off.

"To answer your questions, yes, I am a sorcerer," he said. "And, no, miraculously, you're not dead." He winked.

"Sorcerer, huh?" Arianna scoffed, thinking this old man had reached far past his expiration date to be of any value for this world per the King's criteria of worthy Olleb citizens. He was clearly insane.

"Actually, it surprises me that you're even familiar with the term," he replied. "I thought such talk had all but died out in the districts."

"Laws were meant to be broken," she said under her breath.

Of course she knew the word. King Devlindor forbade imaginative subjects such as these, but gossip spread and children talked. Some got caught and paid the price, but others lived to tell the bedtime stories. It was unavoidable not to *think* about these things, sometimes, but Arianna would never voice them.

She valued her life and her future—now more than ever.

"Shall I continue?" he asked after a long pause, running his fingers along his thick mustache.

"You're an elder and may do as you wish," said Arianna, gesturing a polite wave and hoping she came across as relaxed.

However outlandish his claim might be and despite the fear fluttering in her heart at the topic, she couldn't deny that she was a little curious to hear more.

"Let's see, where to begin?" he mused, tapping his fingers on his knee.

Talis' eyes examined the ceiling as Arianna examined him.

He looked an odd sight sitting in her well room, with his long, silver hair and fancy robes. She'd seen elders from other districts before—they were permitted to travel back and forth through the tunnels as they pleased—but not this up close. There was something about him that put her on edge. She didn't trust a word he said.

'I'm a sorcerer.'

"How about the last thing you remember," said Talis. "I think that will do. You told me you were consumed by a darkness that trapped you? Something like that, yes?"

Excitement was thick in his voice as he pried.

"Yes, I was stuck in an… unending blackness. There was nothing to be done," answered Arianna, her voice low as she recalled her strange struggle after the end of the Warrior's Challenge. "I suppose it was only a nightmare." Strange, though, that it felt like anything but.

Talis leaned in, his chin resting on his hands. "Tell me more. How did you find your way out of the dark?"

Arianna searched her cluttered brain for answers and seized a faint memory from before she had awakened. The image was fuzzy, like a fading dream she was desperate to savor. But, in her soul, she knew that it had somehow, inexplicably, been a real experience.

"I... I followed a light. It led me back here," she stuttered as she tried to turn the memory into fathomable words.

Talis clapped his hands together, making her jump.

"You truly saw the light?" he asked.

A hint of a smile began to shine in his eyes.

"Yes! Is that somehow amusing to you?" she retorted, utterly exhausted by this conversation. Then she remembered herself and that she was speaking to an elder. "I know it sounds absurd, sir, but that's my last recollection before I woke up here in this bed." She folded her arms across her chest, looking at her hands.

"I'm sorry if you've taken offense," said Talis with a satisfied sigh. "It's just... you really are a miracle. Solomon was right to put his faith in you."

He was nodding his head, reassured of something she didn't understand.

"What do you mean?" asked Arianna, annoyed by the cryptic statement as more questions flooded her mind.

"What I mean is that you lay dead on this very mattress. Not near-dead. *Dead.*" Arianna tried to let that sink in, but she really couldn't. "Yet here you are because you chose to follow a light that came to you in the shadows. You chose this path, Arianna. It led you here."

He gestured to the room around him, but it was clear to

Arianna that he spoke of a second chance at life.

"I can't be sure that I made any conscious choices, Master Churry. It's all just a blur," she admitted, bowing her head.

She felt as if tears might overwhelm her at any moment.

"Well, it would appear that you did. In my experience with life and death, it's much simpler to be consumed by the unrelenting darkness. It's always easier to just let go. The real struggle is holding on to what little light has been left to us."

He feigned grasping the air and opened his fist to reveal nothing.

"Those of us who never let it out of our view are sometimes gifted second chances at the world." He winked a blue eye at her as she tried to process his riddle.

Arianna decided to dig deeper for answers.

"Master Churry, do I then have you to thank for my life?"

"Well, that I can't answer." He smiled. "I suppose I am the sorcerer that beckoned the light which guided you here. I did not, however, direct its path by any means. Nor did I choose the path for you to follow."

His words only left her more and more baffled. Arianna wanted to trust this man as Solomon had said, but he made it so very difficult.

"Forgive me, but how can you summon a light into my subconscious?" she asked, almost in giggles at her illogical questions. "Because, if I was, in fact, dead, then my memory must've taken place inside my head... like a dream." But not.

The thrill of such forbidden talk started to lighten her mood as she continued to play along, her cares slipping away.

"Now that will take much time to explain. Why don't I start a pot of tea, hmm?"

"Please, let me," said Arianna.

She pushed herself off the bed, wobbling at first as she stood. She walked toward the small stove near the back of the room and rekindled the coal's dying flames to heat the kettle.

She sat herself at the foot of the bed like a child waiting for a story to be told.

"I'll start somewhere near the beginning," began Talis. "As I've already confided to you, I *am* a sorcerer. Mostly gifted in the art of healing. Though, I have a range of other talents."

Arianna clung to his words.

"My duty is much like that of Master Bell's. I have a young apprentice in the Healer's District, quite as spirited as you, and I'm a notable figure in my area of expertise," he continued. "Do you follow?"

Arianna nodded.

"Good. So, what do you know of magic, girl?" he asked.

Arianna's wandering mind snapped back to reality.

Magic?

It had been one thing when Solomon alluded to the dangerous topic—she knew him, trusted him. But he wasn't here now. Her reflexes told her to run away from the conversation. And yet, her instincts told her to stay.

After a moment, she felt compelled to answer the question.

"Well, in the Learning Center, the educators only taught us that the notion of magic came from an old fable thought up by those who let their imaginations run astray. These were people not fit for our world," she said, recalling the lessons of long ago when she had first been brought, as a small child, to the Warrior's District. "Those who told lies and stories that alluded to a strange existence before King Devlindor have been, and will continue to be, eradicated from the Olleb. That's why the subject is so forbidden." She placed her fist to her chest. "Hail to the King."

She gazed at the ceiling as she tried to process her own depiction of magic, never having much thought over it before.

"Yet, I guess… I'm still unsure of what magic is supposed to mean, even if it is just part of someone's wrongful fantasy. I've heard different tales here and there of such talk, of magic making the impossible happen, but they're just old stories made up to defy the law by those who take pleasure in the risk. They're not real." She peered into her childhood for the scarce information. "No one knows what came before King Devlindor," she added in a whisper. "It's treasonous to even consider a 'before,' but, if this so-called magic did ever exist, it doesn't anymore."

Arianna knew it was all just an elaborate lie. Stories of magic were just that—stories. But what was this man getting at by bringing it up now? Talis clearly had done so purposefully. There was a reason they were discussing this, something that had to do with her, and she wanted to know what it was.

"Well, take a guess. What do you think it would mean, if it were real?" asked Talis, considering her intently.

Arianna let out a small, nervous laugh, thinking again of her last lesson with Solomon.

'*A mind is a mystery to both man and magic,*' he had said.

"I suppose, if I had to make a theory, I would guess that magic was something intangible to the touch since it's linked to the mind."

She chewed on her lip as she thought.

"And probably uncontrollable if the King felt the need to make the topic punishable by death to even speak of," she continued. "Even though the idea of magic was *only* a figment of someone's imagination." Her brow furrowed at that stark realization. "He controls everything, even life."

Even now, after just earning it back by some phenomenon, Arianna's life sat in his hands.

Talis nodded in agreement, his expression solemn.

"A wise conclusion. You're very bright for your age and predicament. It's good you stick with your instincts," he said, leaving her more to speculate about.

He crossed his legs and then leaned his face in closer to hers, as if to whisper a secret.

"You're absolutely right, you know? Magic is intangible and irrepressible. But you're wrong about just one thing."

Arianna arched an eyebrow at him.

"Magic is real and has survived the destruction of the Olleb. It burrows through the trees and the mountainsides. It runs deep through the waters and in the sky. Magic energizes this world and can never be fully destroyed or oppressed because… well, to put it simply, it connects us all. It brings balance to the world, and I can see it's had plenty to do with your creation."

Arianna's mouth dropped open at his description.

Magic doesn't exist. Sorcerers do not exist. And I want nothing to do with any of it.

As Talis rambled on, a part of Arianna tried to block out these crazy notions. Yet, the other part listened quite intently.

"Although King Devlindor would have you believe there was never a trace of enchantment in this world, he couldn't deceive us all," explained Talis. "He knows himself this is an impossible endeavor, but he has tried to hide it from the citizens of the Olleb, with great effort, by ruling with an iron fist. Without magic, the world would cease to exist, and there are still people alive today who know this truth."

He sighed, letting his eyes close for a moment.

"Regrettably, though, he has wiped out a large portion of the magical entities that used to reside in this land and has hidden these atrocities under centuries of lies. There was certainly a 'before' to King Devlindor's reign," he said, sternly. "Because of his corruption, the balance of the world is no longer equal. That's why we suffer so. As his tyrannical grip tightens, the magical properties of the Olleb weaken, possibly forever if he continues to take us down such a dark path."

Seeming to grow angered by his own story, Talis momentarily retreated into his thoughts, looking down to his lap.

His words formed a picture that Arianna could not even

begin to fully comprehend. She had never known a better world, let alone an enchanted one, and thus had no indication of what 'better' would really mean or why he would allude that her suffering, and everyone's suffering, wasn't somehow normal.

Yes, Arianna hated the King, but she accepted that hatred. The regulators in her district had all once been slaves just the same. And Talis and Solomon had been raised in the Four Corners. This was the world they lived in, and she had never had a reason to believe before—not from history, or her teachings, or experience—that it should or could be any different.

This is life.

For centuries, Olleb-Yelfra had survived under the rule of King Devlindor. And Arianna considered that if there *was* ever anything before this time, it seemed irrelevant now.

Suddenly, the kettle screamed from the corner and Talis left Arianna on the floor to contemplate her thoughts. He returned with two steaming cups of tea.

Arianna let hers cool before attempting to taste the flowered water. It refreshed her dry tongue, and her body welcomed the nourishment after such a catastrophic day. After a couple minutes of silence, the conversation picked up again.

"This magic you speak of. You think it's why I'm here now, don't you?" asked Arianna.

She had to assume that was why he was trying to explain it to her—to explain away her mysterious memory.

Half of her stubborn-self thought it best to just stick to the dull reality she'd always known, one where the word 'enchantment' had no place. But the other half wished with all her soul that his words spoke a truth about a world once filled with color. About a world where Kyrone Devlindor was not a king.

"Yes and no," replied Talis, lifting his cup to his lips. "You're here because I sent the magic to you, but *you* had to make the choice to accept it. Do you understand?"

"I guess so," she lied. She sipped her tea.

"Magic is everywhere," said Talis. "Some, like me, can summon it more naturally than others. Just as some are affected by it more easily. I sense that you're strongly connected to this enchanted side of nature."

"Why?" she asked, taken aback by his assumption. "What's any of this have to do with me?"

Everything in her mind and body rejected the idea that something, regardless of what it was, could be connected to her without her knowing. Yet, she still wanted to believe in something more. Her mind reeled, tugging to both sides.

"When Solomon brought me to your bedside, I looked upon a corpse, Arianna. You were as good as dead. The spell that I conjured to heal you, the *Onasyuda* enchantment, failed in front of my eyes. You were gone," he said. "And frankly, I didn't expect anything otherwise."

She held her breath during his recollection of what had happened to her after the battle. Finally, he was going to provide some of the answers she desperately searched for.

"Then, minutes later, you were glowing like a star," he continued. "It was as if the spell I had called for sank into your soul and waited there for you to grasp it. And so you did! The light blessed your body and healed you inside and out."

His infectious excitement made Arianna smile, but the story was just so incomprehensible.

How could that be true? That I actually grasped onto some magic light?

Arianna let her fingers graze her stomach where she remembered Grinda stabbing her with her very own sword. Although it was faint, she could feel the rigid lines of a scar there.

"You must be flowing with the magical blood of your ancestors," said Talis. "I would guess you're a descendant of a very powerful line for this magic to have connected to you in such an extraordinary way. Like I said before, Solomon was right to put his faith in you." He took another drink.

Arianna's curiosity was piqued further at this last statement, so she tried to pry just a little deeper.

"And what faith might that be?" she asked.

Talis looked up from his tea and stared at her for a moment. Arianna wondered what he saw in his mind's eye as a wounded expression flickered across his face.

"Another day, perhaps," he said in a masked tone. "You've had enough wonderment for one night, I take it."

The sad expression wiped from his face.

Before Arianna could form her next question, the door to the well room swung open. Her stomach twisted in knots at the sudden intrusion. It took an interruption for her to remember that this discussion violated so many rules.

Arianna relaxed when she saw that it was only Solomon. He had just returned from escorting Cyn back to her home.

"Please, sit," said Talis, gesturing to a chair as Solomon strode across the room.

Solomon removed his cloak and sat down.

"So, what've we learned?" he asked, turning to Arianna.

A wary expression settled on his face as he crossed his legs, visibly tense.

"Too much," she said, shaking her head. "Solomon, how can any of this be true? It's all very overwhelming. Have you heard his explanation? Do *you* believe this talk about…?"

Placing her head in her hands, Arianna tried to massage away a growing headache.

Solomon stayed silent, and Arianna glanced up, waiting for an answer. She wished that someone would tell her exactly what to believe. In the end, she knew she'd have to make the decision on her own, but she needed Solomon's insight first.

"Yes, I know," he said, his voice solemn. "I'm sorry. You must be shocked at all of the information, but don't bid it unwelcome. Just give it time to settle."

Solomon turned to Talis, who finished his last drops of tea and stood up from the bed.

"We need to get you back to your district before anyone misses you," he said. "I can never thank you enough for your help tonight, but I don't want anyone raising questions over her recovery."

"Consider my debts paid," said Talis with a low bow.

Solomon drew him into a hug that Talis reluctantly returned, making Arianna wonder what kind of relationship these two had once shared. It was obvious that they knew each other well.

"Take care of her, Solomon. She may have swayed my stance on rekindling my old ways." Talis chuckled and his belly shook beneath his cloak.

"It only takes a little faith," he replied, flashing a grin at Arianna.

"Be safe and mind that storm," said Solomon.

Arianna glanced toward the small window on the far wall. Wind pounded large snowflakes against the glass, demanding entrance. She shivered, looking away.

"Farewell, Arianna of Warrior's District." Talis spoke as if there were some underlying joke to his words. "I enjoyed breaking the law with you this night. Until we meet again."

"Goodbye," she said as he made to leave. "Oh, and Master Churry, I've decided that I *do* have you to thank for my life. So... thank you." She felt certain at least with that decision.

He smiled.

"Please, call me Talis," he said with a nod before pulling the door closed behind him.

After he'd left her and Solomon alone, Arianna begun to feel a slight fear creep up all around her again; all the information he'd given her had only led to a thousand more questions. *Sorcerers? Magic? Healing lights? An Olleb history predating the High King?*

None of it had any place in her world.

Before more worry and confusion could consume her mind, she felt a welcome hand on her shoulder—Solomon there by her side.

"You put up a good fight today," he said.

She scoffed at his lame attempt at consoling her about losing to Grinda.

"I meant in here." Solomon pointed at her head, and they both couldn't help but smile a little.

"Thanks," she mumbled. With that, she felt her body and mind shatter like glass. Throwing her arms around him, she sobbed into his shoulder.

"I should've never challenged her. I'm so confused. And what's all this talk about magic? And King Devlindor? Please, I need some clarity." Unbidden tears warmed her cheeks.

"In time, Arianna," he said, patting her back. "For now, you need your rest. We must figure out what to do about introducing you back to the district. I'm sure everyone assumes you're dead. We couldn't possibly present you now. You haven't a scratch!" He gazed at her with pride.

"Oh," was all she could manage.

She really couldn't even consider that problem with all the other things rolling around in her head.

"Don't worry. I'll take care of it all. I already have an idea," he said. "But you understand that you can never mention Talis or, obviously, all you've learned and experienced here today to anyone, right?"

"Not even to Liam—"

"Not to anyone," he said, firmly. "Understood? This is of the utmost importance, Arianna."

Arianna shrugged with no strength left to argue. Her head felt heavy as she began to feel the weight of all the stress this long day had delivered.

"This really is a matter of life or death. Tell me you under-stand. It doesn't matter if you choose to believe him or not, but no one is to ever hear of these occurrences," he said in a voice only strict Master Bell used, not Solomon the friend.

"Yes, I understand, Master," she whispered.

"Good. I'll leave you now, then. I have to prepare your... re-entrance to life, shall we say?" He caressed his goatee, lost in thought.

"So, what should I do then?"

"Just sleep. You've been through a traumatic experience. Relax your mind and your body, and I'll be back in the morning with food and more information. I promise."

Arianna gave a weak nod.

"And, Ara... I'm glad you decided to come back." Solomon gave a warm smile, and she returned it the best she could.

After he had left, Arianna felt more alone than ever. Only her thoughts kept her company, and they stabbed at her brain in a sensation just as unwelcome as when Grinda Risso had stabbed at her flesh.

She relaxed her head on the fresh sheets and pillow Solomon had brought upon his return; her eyelids drooped and reality became fogged.

THE WALLS OF THE BLANCOREN MOUNTAINS stand firmly in place around the Jar, around me. Wind stirs the gray snow in swirls about my head, leaving my hair damp and loose in ringlets over my shoulders. The white garment on my skin is thin, and my shoes are absent.

I wish I had my swords.

A frosted mirror faces me, affixed to the mountainside. I

study myself and pale chestnut eyes regard me with harsh satisfaction. Yes, these are my eyes, but something isn't right; they begin to shine a radiant silver.

The reflection in the mirror doesn't seem like me. She's so beautiful—a beauty I don't think I could ever achieve. I move back, and the figure copies my footsteps.

My heart begins to drum inside my chest as I study her, throbbing to the beat of her heart.

Could that really be me?

I feel drawn to her, to my reflection.

I want to run, but I can't. Instead, I step forward in the snow, and I raise my hand to touch the frosted glass as she does the same. It's ice cold against my palm.

Then, suddenly, I begin to panic. My hand is frozen to the mirror, and I'm unable to pull it away.

The girl who is me throws her head back in laughter, her voice a honeyed sound that sends warning signals to the pit of my stomach. I scream as the girl shifts—she's no longer my reflection.

As she changes, new, dark eyes bore into mine. But nothing else is visible as black smoke envelops the mirror. Then something changes, and I'm no longer stuck.

No… this is much, much worse.

I feel myself being pulled forward, my body sucked into the glass, into the walls of Blancoren. I cry out for help, but my voice is lost to the howling wind as the murky eyes keep close watch.

Now I lie motionless in the soft snow, blood staining the clean cloth on my skin. It spills from many wounds, coloring the virgin snow a deep red. I feel no pain besides the absence of my sword. And my voice is suddenly missing.

I can only lie there, still as stone.

The only thing I see is Blancoren, the thing I least wish to look upon before I die. I try to shut my eyes to no avail.

They're frozen in place like the rest of me. Then something moves in the distance, and I realize I'm not alone.

A figure in long black robes steps forth from the shadows. Ruthless black eyes drink up my pain, taunting me. They're the same eyes as from the mirror.

My sword!

The jeweled hilt sparkles in one mangled hand, my blood-stained dagger in the other. The intruder on my death lets the dagger drop down beside me, the snow wiping the fresh blood clean off the metal. With the tip of my sword, the monster pushes the damp hair from my face and then drives the steel through my chest with exquisite force.

I can feel now.

I stare into the sinister face of my murderer before I'm ripped from my body. I hear his cackling laughter drifting farther away, and the light dims as if only from faint candles in the sapphire sky. Now I'm gazing into my own lifeless eyes as their strange, glowing light darkens. My body is tattered and gored, still as a statue in the snow. My gleaming sword protrudes from pallid flesh, lathered with fresh blood.

I smell a sweet scent and look toward the sky. Large snowflakes drift down toward my body. And as they drift nearer, I realize this isn't snow at all.

Such a sweet smell—the smell of flowers.

White flower petals fall through me from the dark abyss above, layering on my body below. A plain stone cross hovers in the night as if hung by some invisible string attached to a star. 'May freedom find you in death' is carved into the stone.

The stranger melts away into the darkness then, leaving my body alone in this open grave. His monstrous laughter still echoes off the walls of the mountains, off the walls in my head.

"At least you're one with your sword," I note, in my ghost-like state. Then I'm gone.

LESSA THUR

"WHAT ARE YOU DOING AWAKE at this hour?" asked Talis as he kicked the snow off his boots. He let his cloak billow to the floor.

"It's nearly dawn," replied Lessa as she retrieved the fallen robes. She hung them on a hook between the door and a circular window. "Where did you go last night? Were you with that man again?" She couldn't help but pry.

"I allow you to live here on one condition," he said with a yawn. "That you mind your own business. Do you recall this conversation?"

His tiredness made his would-be-stern voice sound lazy and unguarded.

"I do," she replied. "But I'm also inclined to mention that I rise with the sun. I don't care about your late-night activities. In fact, *Master*, I wouldn't even be receiving a chastising from you if you'd gotten a decent night's sleep for once."

She wagged her finger at him, a smile on her lips.

"Oh, no, no, no. I'm too tired for this," he said, dismissing her with the wave of his hand. "I'm off to bed. If you don't wake me, you'll live to see another day." He disappeared through the door of his bedroom.

"Just a few more to go until the Free Falls!" she said.

"I'm counting the days," she heard him grumble.

She laughed to herself, knowing he enjoyed her company more than most.

"Actually, Lessa," called Talis from his room, "since you're up at the crack of dawn, you might as well do something productive with your extra time. Practice yesterday's lesson, and it's about time you refill our prillyberry stock. We'll resume regular training after the morning commendation to the King. I'm going to try to get a couple hours of rest until then."

His door slammed, vibrating the floor beneath Lessa's feet.

"Yes, Master Churry," she said with less than enthusiasm.

After donning clean blue robes and orange-tinted boots, she left the house.

Lessa blinked her eyes several times, adjusting to the new light. The snow glittered brilliantly at this time of day—early morning before the district stirred and had a chance to muck everything up. Nevertheless, she wished it to disappear. She yearned for the warmth of the sun on her skin and for the kiss of heated wind on her face. She knew it existed outside of these walls somewhere far, far away; she'd read enough about the different terrains of Olleb-Yelfra in the Learning Center to know that the Blancoren Mountains weren't all there was to life. This icy existence numbed her nerves, but Lessa was more than ready to feel… feel anything at all.

She yanked up the hood of her cloak, pinching it together at her neck in a failed attempt to keep out the cold.

Trekking through the snow, she speculated about her master's latest adventures. He often disappeared after lessons nowadays. The dark man had appeared nearly a month ago now, calling at their doorstep in the middle of the night. Since then, Talis had been sneaking off on a regular basis, and she knew that the strange visitor must have everything to do with his secret escapades.

Though Lessa prodded Talis with endless questions, trying to get him to reveal anything about his evening disappearances, he never budged. But she wasn't one to give up on a goal and was certain she'd get him to talk soon enough. Especially given that she was his permanent house guest now. As Lessa walked along, mulling over her bittersweet predicament, she recalled the day of her fifteenth-year celebrations when Master Talis Churry had selected her as his apprentice.

"SLAVE NUMBER TWENTY," said a bored woman as she read the roster at the front of the panel.

Lessa made her way forward, kicking pebbles as she went. Lifting her eyes to the elders, her attention strayed to the wall behind them, settling on a vast painting of hands cupping water and a golden snake—the Healer's Crest.

A fragile-looking man she knew by the name of Talis Churry surveyed her, but she wouldn't let their eyes meet as she looked anywhere else.

"The healing concoction you made was quite powerful," he said after a moment, twisting his beard around his finger. "Much more effective than that of your peers. Impressive for one so young. With proper training, you could have endless opportunities as a healer of the Olleb." He leaned forward from his seat, as if to demand that she look at him. "Would

you like to be my apprentice?"

Lessa couldn't help the lump of anger growing in her throat as his question rolled around in her mind, not really understanding why it irked her so much.

"Do I have a choice?" she muttered, reluctantly finding his water-colored gaze.

As soon as their eyes met, Lessa felt her skin flush. She didn't like this attention one bit. She knew she had a knack for healing, but all she wanted was to keep her head down, survive the Free Falls, and get out. The last thing she desired was to become the center of attention as some renowned elder's project to parade about the district.

"You always have a choice," Talis replied.

Lessa couldn't help but scoff at this absurd statement, crossing her arms at her chest. She couldn't find any words to speak, the lump of anger only growing larger as she tried desperately to swallow it for fear it might cause her to say something she'd certainly regret.

"Why, aren't you the cautious one?" he said with a chuckle, a curious twinkle in his eye as he regarded her.

Lessa opened her mouth to retort but caught a regulator's threatening gaze. She let her mouth close as she registered the warning, dropping her eyes to the floor.

"It seems you may need some convincing in whether or not to accept," said Talis with an expression that sat somewhere between shock and amusement. "I offer you mastery in the art of healing and survival. I offer you the best chance at earning your freedom. I offer you advice and knowledge of the unknown. And, ultimately, I can offer you the world should you succeed." Talis leaned back, patiently waiting. "So, Lessa Thur, I'll ask you again. Do you want to be my apprentice?"

Lifting her gaze from the floor at the mention of her name, Lessa saw herself mirrored in his eyes. An impenetrable silence hung in the air as she tasted the words he fed her—she really didn't have a choice. No healer-slave had any choices in the face of their elders, let alone a master healer. Though, if she had, she would've definitely said yes.

Talis Churry was quite convincing. So much so that she almost believed she had actually made up her mind herself.

"I accept," she said in a quiet voice, humbled by his promises and the regulator at her back.

"Good," he replied. "We begin your lessons tomorrow."

A WOLF HOWLED IN THE DISTANCE, breaking Lessa's pensive state. She picked up the pace, walking toward a tall building—the Dining Hall. Her stomach grumbled, so she pushed open the doors, the musty smell of grime filling her nose as she searched for anything edible.

It was eerily quiet in the hall, everyone still at their barracks, but when she peeked through to the kitchen, she found a team of men and women busying about. They wore light orange uniforms and hats spotted with cooking stains as they furiously prepared for breakfast.

A man looked up, eyeing her.

"Hey, you there! What business do you have in here? Two more hours 'til the kitchen's open. You better get moving if you know what's good for ya!" He waved a wooden spoon in her face.

Lessa scurried out, not trying to get into any more trouble with the elders than she already had. She'd burdened Talis enough as it was.

"Sorry," she muttered. The door swung closed behind her.

As she headed back through the Dining Hall, Lessa suddenly felt the burn of eyes on her back and turned around.

The same man who'd just yelled at her in front of the kitchen crew had tiptoed up behind her. He was on the shorter side for an elder, barely clearing her in height, and he had a pudgy face that wrinkled when he smiled.

"Here you go, Lessa," he said with a wink. He plopped a juicy red apple into her hand. "Now quit poking your face around here before you get us both in trouble."

Her mouth watered at the sight of such a delicious treat.

"You had me fooled, Nico! Thank you so much. I really owe you one," she said.

"Anytime, kid! And there's more where that came from if you survive the Free Falls. Keep your head on straight." He waved her off as he ran back through the kitchen doors.

Lessa slipped back outside, sinking her teeth into the sweet skin of the apple and savoring every bite. Eager to reach the Field, she jogged up the hilly street with a new energy. There she could clear her head a bit before the bell inevitably sounded and launched her into another hectic district day. She sulked at the thought of any more training.

Picking prillyberries didn't rattle her mind as much as trying to get Talis' concoctions just right. He had put a lot of pressure on her shoulders after taking her under his wing, and sometimes she thought all she was good for was disappointing him.

For the past two and a half years, he'd worked tirelessly to prepare her for the Healer's District Free Falls Festivals (which occurred during the first week of the month-long festivities). Talis seemed very pleased with her progress up to this point and had no doubt she would pass the ultimate test, but the problem came with her other talent—a gift for catching the regulators' attention.

There was something about Lessa that just made her stick out from a crowd. She had recognized this about herself from a young age and thought it possibly due to a combination of her pale skin and fair hair; it was as if she had been born from the snow. Talis also often said she was too smart for her own good, and she supposed that could be true as well. Her smart mouth had sounded in the wrong place at the wrong time, usually in speaking up for someone else, on various occasions. And, because she was so good at being noticed—despite desperately wanting to blend in—on those various occasions, the regulators had found reason to punish her.

In her district, the King had instated a penalty for disobedience called the Poison Cure with the idea that he could 'cure' the insolent slaves of their dishonorable behavior for the promise of a better future. That is, if they survived the poison.

If they didn't...

'*Then obviously they weren't worthy of freedom,*' her district general had declared. '*Hail to the King!*

Twice Lessa had been given the Poison Cure for speaking out of turn, yet somehow she'd overcome its toxic effects. Her two-time, miraculous survival shocked and awed the elders, including Talis—though she'd always wondered, in the back of her mind, if he hadn't had something to do with her curious recovery, for he was always there by her side when she opened her eyes. After the second time she survived the Poison Cure, at the turn of her seventeenth year, Talis had taken full responsibility for her for fear the regulators might put her to death just out of spite.

Lessa remembered the conversation like it was yesterday. Lying half-awake on the bed in her private well room where she and Talis frequently trained, she'd listened as the district general and Talis had discussed her future in the Healer's District in strained whispers. Talis pleaded for her life, claiming he valued it because he'd put so much time into her training and that her skill proved superior to her peers; it would have been a wasted investment if she were to die.

And, after much debate, the general ultimately granted

Talis' abnormal request because of his valued contributions to the Olleb's healing sector.

Lessa was very grateful that her master had essentially rescued her from a sealed fate at the hands of the regulators, but she still felt so ashamed that he'd had to risk his reputation on her. Memories of the excruciating pain caused by the Poison Cure still lingered as bitter reminders of her place in life, but she knew she held a place in his old heart, too. She couldn't bear to disappoint him further after all he'd done for her.

As she passed the perfectly stacked barracks of all the other slaves on the way to her destination, she counted herself so lucky. She lived a very luxurious and quiet life now compared to probably any other healer-slave who'd ever stepped foot in her district. Having been permitted to reside in Talis' quarters instead of the barracks so that he could keep a strict eye on her, Lessa never had to mingle much with her peers or the regulators anymore. Aside from attending the mandatory commendation to the King each morning and keeping up with her daily lessons at the Learning Center, it was just her and Talis.

Smiling to herself at the kindness he'd shown her and at the fact that she'd ultimately gotten her wish to not be the center of attention, Lessa hurried on to complete his chores. Eventually, the steep, paved path she climbed turned to rocky land as the Field loomed ahead—the only place in the Healer's District with some life to it.

She came upon a long, wooden fence and gated entrance encircling a vast, hilly area. After swinging the gate open, Lessa clambered up the rocky length of land until she stood on flat ground. A non-spectacular view of the district spread out before her. Large buildings dotted the barren land with little to linger on, and grumpy regulators began to trickle out into the streets As they prepared for the start of another day.

The view didn't stretch very far beyond that before the walls of Blancoren blocked her line of sight, only making her itch to see more. Tearing her eyes away from the mountains, she started forward, passing through an area with shoddy structures that housed a variety of items that she and her peers could use in their healing mixtures.

As she trekked deeper into the Field, the ground became hidden under a thick blanket of snow. And tall black trees with thin branches shot up high into the sky, making intrusions on the clean, white ground. She always thought it looked as if some sort of monstrous creature clawed its way out of the earth.

A large boulder caught her eye as she zigzagged between the trees, following a familiar path to where she knew the best prillyberries grew. At Talis' behest, she had concealed a long-bow and arrows in a hole under it—the law prohibited weapons within her district, other than those owned by the regulators.

It had been a wonderous surprise when Talis had taken her to the Field one early morning to introduce her to the weapon. Though they'd both be in a heap of trouble if she were caught, the fact that Talis had sanctioned it made her feel a little less scared about breaking this rule. It was as if his word were some type of shield against danger at times. Nevertheless, only in seclusion did Talis permit her to practice her aim, the trees giving the perfect cover for arrows astray. And, each time she let an arrow fly, she found it just as thrilling and satisfying as the first—to break one of the King's laws.

Lessa gave the boulder a longing stare but continued past it. She didn't have time for that this morning.

Tilting her head back to survey the treetops, she spotted layers of fluorescent-green prillyberries, hung like prizes for the taking, on the black, snow-cluttered branches. Most of her peers didn't bother picking these since it was such a hassle. However, as they were the prime ingredient for Talis' restorative recipes, she would need to gather a lot.

At her feet, a couple of ladders and baskets lay buried in the rising snow for exactly this purpose, but Lessa preferred climbing the traditional way. Talis not there with disapproving eyes, she slung a basket around her arm and grabbed ahold of the lowest limb. Placing her foot steady at the base of the tallest tree in the middle of the thicket, she began the long climb. Up, higher and higher, she went, the wind stinging her face and whipping her hair into her eyes.

"There we go!" she huffed with one last lunge into the air.

She straddled a branch that looked like it could hold her weight. From up here, the view became a little more appealing, and the air was crisp but refreshing, instantly readying her to the challenge of a new day.

Lessa took a moment to look around, the Healer's District appearing so small now. It made her yearn to climb up even higher in the sky, and she savored the quiet the treetops gifted her. Here, she felt the most alive, like she could momentarily fly. Alas, reality forever squeezed at her fantasy.

No matter how high she climbed, Lessa knew she could never clear the talons of Blancoren. This depressing thought shook her out of her tempting imagination.

She began to pluck at the prillyberries, dropping them into the basket on her arm. The berries felt ripe to the touch, plump with the delectable red juices which made for good medicines. Once the basket was quite full, she prepared to climb back down. Something rustled in the sparse leaves above her head, snow sprinkling her hair.

She looked up but found nothing there.

Her skin prickled, feeling her presence joined with another in this wayward sky. Listening to her instincts, Lessa decided to get back to the ground as fast as possible. But, before she could start the climb down, the sound of a small branch snapping rippled through the silence.

"Who's there?" she called to the wind in a shaky voice.

The howling breeze stole her words as a light snow shifted from the canopy, trickling into a swirl around her body.

There, again at her back, she heard the crunching of leaves and saw a couple of prillyberries fall at the disturbance. Glancing up, she noticed the snow had been brushed clean off a limb. An unsettling feeling in her gut warned her to be cautious; there was definitely something sharing her tree, though she knew that birds flew far clear of the Field.

Steadying the basket in a tiny nook against the tree trunk, Lessa reached for a thin branch overhead. It strained at her tug but held its own as she pulled herself up to a standing position. Carefully using the branch as leverage, she leaned around the huge trunk of the tree, as far as she could manage without falling, to try to get a better angle to see.

A pair of bright orange eyes appeared from out of nowhere, gleaming only inches from her face.

Lessa felt a scream catch in her throat as she lurched backward. She tried to cling to the icy branch with her feet as she felt her body sway, struggling to balance, but she lost her footing in the next moment.

Her weight pulled too much on the tiny branch she clung to, and it cracked. She felt the rush of air at her back as she fell toward the ground, the basket of prillyberries cascading down with her. Her limbs flailed as she attempted to grip anything at all, and the scream which was stuck in her throat before was now released at full force, shredding the quiet morning to pieces.

As the treetops moved farther and farther away, she spotted the same pair of large, peachy eyes glaring down after her from their cover. And, as their eyes met, what followed was a searing pain unlike anything Lessa had ever experienced before, a hundred times worse than the Poison Cure.

She wasn't even sure now if she was still falling or if she'd already crashed into the earth.

Had it been seconds, minutes, hours?

The pain never lessened. But, through the pain, Lessa felt a single tear warm her cheek, a warmth she clung to amidst the overwhelming and sudden cold until, finally, the pain ceased and she felt nothing.

SUNDAY

"BUT IT'S BEEN WEEKS!" SAID ARIANNA, pacing around the sparring room with her swords in hand and wishing she could be anywhere else. "I'm losing my mind. Please, just let me out for a little bit. I promise I'll be careful."

"You know we can't take that risk," said Solomon. "I've confided to General Ivo that you've only barely survived the Warrior's Challenge. He thinks you're still bedridden, but I assured him that Cyn and I could have you well enough to perform by the time the Free Falls Festivals begin. You can still have a fair shot at earning your citizenship."

Arianna feigned listening, tired of this speech and desperate for a change of scenery.

"With the exception of me, Cyn, and the general, the entire district believes you to be dead," he continued, clasping his hands behind his back as he lectured on. "If you were to be seen, we'd all be beheaded for disloyalty. General Ivo wants no mention of you until the festivals. He can't have it known that he's permitting the existence of someone weak enough to be on the brink of death. It's against the morale that feeds the city, and he won't have that tarnished. If I hadn't vouched for your full recovery, he would've already tossed you to the Pit."

"Of course I'm so thankful to you, but isn't there—"

Solomon crossed his arms at his chest. "No buts! You'll just have to stick it out a few more weeks," he said, rejecting Arianna's thousandth plea to go outside. "You should consider yourself lucky after all you've been through. You'll be out of this place soon enough."

He patted her on the head.

"Easy for you to say," she grumbled, swatting away his hand. "You're not hiding away in the shadows."

"What do you mean? I'm always in the shadows! *See?*" He pinched at his skin, throwing his head back in laughter.

"Very funny." Arianna couldn't help but feel her lips tweak up in an unwelcome smile at her master's infectious optimism, but it quickly vanished.

"And what of my friends?" asked Arianna. "Liam and Noah should know I'm not rotting at the bottom of the Pit right now. They'll be devastated to know we lied."

"Absolutely not. It's just too risky. I'm sorry," he replied. "Your friends may grieve for you now, but you can mend those relationships later. We've been over this, Ara. This is for your own good. If you want out of the Four Corners alive, you'll listen to me."

Solomon was nothing if not sincere, but it didn't soothe Arianna's frustrations in the slightest. She craved conversation with her friends or to breathe fresh air, and there was nothing he could say to push those yearnings away as they continued to fester in her mind.

"Your bed is comfortable, your food is fresh, you have access to your training facilities at every hour, and you're away from the prying eyes of your rivals. You're dead to them! Imagine the uproar you'll cause when you step out at the Free Falls Festivals with vengeance on your plate."

Solomon studied her, his look thoughtful.

"Just hang in there. Your lessons are done for the day. You're free to do as you please *inside* of these chambers," he said, his voice daring her to defy him.

She groaned, resigned to his commands.

"If you're so bored, study the material Talis has generously left for you," added Solomon with a knowing expression. "You've barely glanced at any of the parchments."

Arianna felt her heartbeat quicken at just the mention and she looked away.

"Where has he been lately?" she asked, trying to seem uninterested. "Is he coming back?"

"I'm not really sure," he replied, shrugging his shoulders. "It's getting awfully close to the Free Falls in the Healer's District, so maybe his own apprentice is demanding his full attention, quite like mine." He winked. "I'm sure we'll see him again soon enough."

Arianna assessed the stack of yellow-tinted scrolls in the corner of the room near the firepit. Talis had brought them from his personal library, and she couldn't help but ponder at how such parchments came to be in his possession in the first place. He'd offered them to her in an attempt to sway her beliefs and deepen her understanding of magic, but she still shied away from the theme on instinct.

So much had changed so suddenly for her after the Warrior's Challenge that she yearned for things to just return to normal. Scrolls supposedly about magic and sorcerers, like Talis claimed to be, were not part of the ordinary she was trying to get back to. From her brief skimming, they told more stories of an enchanted world before King Devlindor's crowning, tales that stretched her sanity too far.

Her small, meek world had spread a little wider with such descriptions of ancient magic, these bizarre children's stories. But even if, by the *slimmest* chance, any of it proved to be true, Arianna didn't see how colorful stories of the past could mean anything to her future.

Besides, if she'd gleaned anything from her lessons in the Learning Center it was that she was not keen on studying. The scrolls were the last of her priorities. Right now, all she wanted was some fresh air to sort her mind.

Her gaze followed Solomon as he threw his cloak around his shoulders, the red and white contrasting strikingly against his dark skin. Then he padded to the door.

"Just read," he said as he slipped out. "I'll be by tomorrow to check in."

"See you," she said, barely able to push the words from her lips as they pressed into a thin line.

Arianna wanted to scream as she was left alone again, the Jar tightening its grip even more on her freedom.

ARIANNA WOKE LATER, buried in a pile of molding scrolls. She hadn't really retained anything she'd read and felt groggy as she longed for the outdoors.

After picking herself up off the floor, she walked to stand in front of the cracked mirror near the weaponry. She pushed the tangles out of her eyes to observe her reflection and thought she had grown a bit, curved out more. Her muscles felt ripe and ready as she moved her hands up and down her body. Though, she also noticed that a new pale shade claimed her normally tan skin color.

She frowned as a strange sensation tugged at her heart, a

longing for the freedom to wander around inside the mountains she hated so much. She clenched her fists at the ridiculous thought; never before had she imagined any type of freedom within the mountain walls.

"That's it!" Arianna said as a dangerous idea entered her mind. "The mountains…"

She went to the window. Night had already fallen, but there were still people around. Curfew hadn't yet passed.

A long snowstorm had recently subsided, so she wouldn't have that to cover her. The idea was risky, but excitement coursed through her veins and washed away her reason. She pulled on her comfy leather boots, wrapped her cloak around her body, and tightened her hood about her face. Then, she slipped out of the door and left the sparring room behind.

The cool outside air immediately invigorated her, clearing her mind of the fogginess that had crept over it during these last monotonous weeks. It smelled like blood, mud, and sweat, and she welcomed the familiar scent. Basking in the glorious chill of wind on her skin, Arianna felt renewed in body and soul. A deep respect for the outside world, of nature, settled with her then—she wouldn't take it for granted again.

Taking in the Dueling Arena, she saw that most of her peers had already left for the day, though there were a scattered few who still practiced. Their wooden swords splintered and cracked with repeated blows against one another, so they paid no mind to Arianna. She moved around them with stealth, quickening her footsteps.

When she reached the tall gate, she saw the regulators normally posted there had also gone.

It must be getting late.

Arianna gathered her courage and stepped into the street, hoping she could reach the mountains without anyone noticing her. With her hood pulled low over her face, she kept her head down and eyes averted.

When she came to the crossing that would lead her either to the Square or toward the barracks, her curiosity got the best of her and she went right. She wanted to lay eyes on the place where Grinda Risso had beaten her. When she did, memories of her lost battle flashed in her mind, lighting a fire in her heart that called for revenge.

I surrendered.

If there's one thing Solomon had taught her about the honor of being a warrior in Olleb-Yelfra, it was that the word 'yield' during a duel should always be respected.

All of a sudden, a familiar voice trickled to Arianna's ears. She tore her eyes away from the grounds of the Square and surveyed the stands. There she found Pippa seated on the stone stairs with a group of their seventeenth-year peers.

"Any idea who might be your biggest competition now, Risso?" she asked in a small voice.

Arianna grimaced at the mention of her adversary's name.

What is she doing with Grinda?

Only morbid answers came to mind.

Arianna snuck closer to spy, wishing to pull her friend to safety from the snake pit that she had clearly gotten trapped in. She guessed that Pippa saw her own lack of talent as detrimental to her future, with the festivals so close, and was trying to connect with others who exerted strength for support—now that Arianna was, to Pippa's knowledge, dead. After all, that was why she had clung to Arianna in the beginning. And Grinda probably allowed it if only as a happy reminder to herself that she'd killed Arianna Belvedor.

But Pippa was so kindhearted, and the last thing Arianna wanted was her failed Warrior's Challenge to result in her friend getting mixed up in the wrong crowd right before the Free Falls because she was scared or lonely. Even as different as they were, after sharing a bunk for so many years, their friendship and alliance had grown naturally. She wanted Pippa to survive this place, and hanging out with Grinda Risso was not the way to do it.

What are you doing? You should know better.

Grinda bared her teeth at Pippa, and then a large, curly-haired boy in their group spoke on her behalf.

"Red Risso has no competitors!" he spat.

Her friends emphatically agreed, and Pippa turned red.

"Quite right you are," said Grinda, rubbing at a nasty scar on her face.

Arianna smiled to herself, thrilled that she'd left her with at least something of payback for such a dishonorable ending to a Warrior's Challenge.

"I buried Arianna in the dust, or have you forgotten?" she said, turning a burning gaze on Pippa. "Now, unless you know of someone else that needs to be eliminated… say a squeaky, fragile girl such as yourself, please do shut up so that we can all enjoy what little time we have to ourselves before curfew."

Pippa shrank down where she sat but said nothing.

Fighting every urge to reveal herself, Arianna gritted her teeth at the mistreatment of her friend. The last time she followed her hasty ego, she died, so, unless she planned on taking out Grinda and all of her friends by herself, she had to walk away. Turning back in the direction of the barracks, she left the Square and poor Pippa behind.

ARIANNA FOUND HERSELF CROUCHED below a familiar space underneath the barracks. She placed her hand on the loose stone of the mountainside, and, just like always, it fell inward. She slid into the hole and replaced the stone. Moving down the dark tunnel, which forever burned golden and copper by way of the firebugs, it wasn't long before Arianna was sucking in the warm and welcoming air created by the hot springs. The happiness from being back in her underground utopia enveloped her inside and out, making her feel more alive than ever.

She took in the area as if for the first time. Gazing up, she saw the mouth of the large tunnel expanding over her in an astonishing arch, offering her entrance to what must be a magical place by Talis' standards. She savored this momentary freedom, spinning around in circles with her arms out wide. This place was sacred in her mind.

Suddenly, a new thought occurred to her and she stopped spinning—her revered hot springs weren't hers alone to cherish as she used to believe. In fact, she stood in a *shared* secret utopia. A blurred memory of a young woman in blue robes pointing an arrow at her chest made her heartbeat quicken.

Where is Lessa Thur?

Arianna had no more answers about the ghost girl of the tunnels than she had on the night they'd met. But, now that her mind was clear and she had time to spare outside of Solomon's watch, she was finally ready to solve the mystery put on hold, to find out who this person was who had stumbled upon her sanctuary.

Arianna shrugged out of her robes and kicked her shoes to the side of the swirling pools, pondering the origin of the girl. The water looked enticing as it cascaded down in front of her in thick strings of blue and white, its warm spray showering her like a welcome rain. Before long, she dived in, letting the waters engulf her in a liquid paradise. Kicking her feet, she surged back up toward the surface and broke through in one fierce thrust.

For a while, she just floated around in a blissful state of mind, trying to picture what Lessa's district life might be like compared to hers. She knew some details about the other three corners in the city, but not enough to form a tangible picture.

As her thoughts drifted alongside her in the waters, the recollection of her lost dagger suddenly popped into her mind. She waded toward the giant jade rock in the shallows.

When Arianna reached it, the firebugs took golden flight at her intrusive touch and entwined her in a soft, radiant light. It transported her back to the moment of her first exchange with the girl who played in the shadows.

'Let the water claim your weapon, or I'll claim your life,' Lessa had warned.

Arianna shook her head at the memory, shocked once again at being accosted in her own secret sanctuary by another warrior of sorts. Now, after all that had happened since, she felt almost pleased at the confrontation that had lost her the dagger; it made her consider that the outside world must not be as dull as she'd always assumed if such surprises could occur in the Four Corners. Lessa had proven to her that life held a lot of mystery still to unravel—just as Talis and Solomon were constantly trying to force her imagination even wider.

For what seemed like an hour, Arianna searched near the spot where her dagger had fallen. Her eyes combed the still, glass-like waters until she was certain it was gone. Saddened by the sure loss of her precious weapon, she made her way to the edge of the hot springs and got out.

After squeezing some of the water from her tangled hair, Arianna glanced longingly toward the mysterious tunnels that bordered the other side of the vast chamber. Lessa Thur had disappeared down one of them, and part of Arianna hoped for her to return—longbow, arrows, and all. She resolved to offer her hand in peace should they ever meet again. After all, if Lessa had found her way to this cave of wonders from her district, then she must've been hiding from something too.

She's a slave just like me. How different can we be?

Curious to explore, Arianna slipped on her boots to protect her feet and then wandered toward the other tunnels, regarding the magnificent structures. Tilting her head up, she gaped at the crowning mouths of the various passages.

Where do you lead?

There were six tunnels looming before her, so she scoped out the entrance of each one until she got to the one in the middle. The mouth of this tunnel was a bit smaller in comparison to the others but still large enough to walk straight through without having to duck.

She advanced a few paces in and accidentally kicked something hard. Looking down, she froze in disbelief. Just below the hovering stalactites in the entryway, there, in plain sight, lay her beloved dagger. It dazzled in the light of the firebugs, as if they lit the way back to her secret treasure.

Arianna knelt down to pick it up and turned it over in her fingers, basking in its unfathomable beauty before tucking it carefully away in one of her boots. Her skin still dripped with water, and she wore only coverings on her chest and hips besides her shoes. But the added weight of the dagger on her body again made her feel as if she were fully dressed and ready for battle. She let out a heavy and happy sigh, feeling that this discovery had granted her a twinge of release at the giant lump of stress building up in her chest over the last several weeks.

Her gaze lingered on the place where she'd found the dagger, and she noticed that a piece of folded parchment had been placed under it. Arianna didn't hesitate to pick it up, the paper feeling damp and worn against her fingertips. In her eagerness to unfold it, she tore a small rip in the soft sheet. Though the rip scratched right through Arianna's name, she knew it to be addressed to her. Scanning the flawlessly-inked letters, she only took a moment to admire the elegant calligraphy before she began to read:

I owe you an apology for how things transpired when we met, but one can never be too careful when breaking the law. There just wasn't time for niceties, as I'm sure you're well aware. I can't imagine that the rules differ much in your district. Precaution was certainly needed in the circumstance. Though, after much thought, I now realize I'm too intrigued to care about the consequences of our meeting, and I'd like to possibly see you again… if you're still alive and ever read this, of course.

I understand that this is a huge risk for us both, but it seems we're already used to taking it. So, if you're up for the challenge, I'm curious enough to try. After all, you're the first slave I've ever met outside of my district!

Meet me here again if you can. I'll return every Sunday around the same time as before since I've no way of knowing when or if you might see this letter. Also, please accept the return of your dagger as a peace offering. It seems a precious possession, and I'm sure you must be fond of it. Besides, we're not allowed weapons in my district, and I've already broken that rule plenty without this added to my plate.

In hopes that we meet again,
Lessa Thur of Healer's District

At the bottom corner of the parchment, Arianna saw that Lessa had drawn an exquisite replication of her dagger.

Lessa Thur of… Healer's District. Is this really happening?

As the words from the letter began to sink in, the thrill of it all began to overflow Arianna's mind. She knew she must see this girl again; they seemed as if they shared a single mind. And, as unthinkable as it might be, the worn parchment in her hands was the only proof she needed to be certain she wasn't dreaming.

"Damn!" said Arianna, slapping her hand to her forehead. The water on her skin made the contact sting.

How many Sundays have already passed?

She started counting in her head but became muddled. Time seemed so foggy since she'd been locked up in her dungeon of a room. Just then, a thought struck her.

"There was hardly anyone on the streets when I left," she exclaimed out loud. "People were lounging in the Square. Today must be Sunday!"

Her voice echoed off the walls of the cavern.

But still, how many Sundays have passed since that night?

She frowned, uncertain, but guessed somewhere around five or six. Glancing back at the letter, she reread it three more times as her mind whirled in anticipation.

Today is Sunday.

After a taste of something new and forbidden, Arianna couldn't wait to find out more. This could be her chance to find out a real, solid piece of information about the rest of the world and take a break from pondering the bizarre riddles the mystic Talis Churry had left to her.

She ran back for her robes which were sprawled across the cavern floor near her familiar tunnel. Arianna pulled them on in haste, stashed the letter in a pocket stitched into the lining, tied up her hair, and sat at the mouth of Lessa's passage to wait for her to come.

She waited and waited and waited until she heard the unsettling vibrations of the bell signaling curfew. The firebugs hummed in tune to the sound. She knew from Lessa's letter that it would be curfew in the Healer's District as well.

It's too late for her to come now.

Arianna paced nervously, her thoughts rolling around her head in a jumble as she tried to guess why she hadn't shown.

Maybe she was too tired from training. Maybe it wasn't safe to come tonight. Or maybe she gave up waiting on me.

It had been more than a month after all.

As Arianna continued to speculate over the possibilities of Lessa's absence, her mind kept stopping at one conclusion—Lessa had lost faith that she'd ever return after their encounter.

If this were so, and Arianna truly believed that it was, she would have to find Lessa herself. She felt braver on her second chance at life, like maybe she held more purpose than just marching to the beat of the Warrior's District bell like everyone else. Arianna already was *not* like everyone else—she had died and come back to life, had two renowned elders whispering outlandish notions of magic in her ears, and had formed an acquaintance with a slave from another district.

An insatiable curiosity had formed within her the very moment she'd read that letter, a yearning for adventure that burned at her skin and clawed at her mind now that she'd had a little taste. And with it, an idea formed, urging her body forward and willing Arianna down a dangerous path. Her legs moved, and she followed their lead without thinking, as if her feet had a mind of their own. The firebug glow on the ceiling of this jagged tunnel allowed her to see, and though the nerves in her body rattled her bones, her mind pushed her forward relentlessly. Arianna wanted answers and would go and get them herself.

She was going to find Lessa Thur.

12

INTRUDER

FARTHER AND FARTHER ARIANNA WANDERED into the twining tunnel. With every step, her courage became more defined. *I will find Lessa Thur.* This passageway didn't differ much from the one leading back to the Warrior's District like she had expected. Firebugs lit the way like gleaming lanterns attached to the walls—just the same.

She came upon a small open area covered with gray, translucent stones that reflected the light of the firebugs. The lustrous, ashen gems caped most of the floor and jutted out in all directions from the walls. Arianna couldn't help but gawk as she stepped into the vortex of dancing lights. Her soul blazed in happiness at such a sight, much like the first time she'd laid eyes on her hot springs.

There was nothing more raw or more beautiful in the Jar than what she'd found buried beneath the mountains; a spark of defiance whizzed through her brain and heart as she looked on. All her best experiences came when defying the rules and expectations set for her.

And she rather enjoyed doing things differently.

As Arianna soaked in the sight of the jeweled cavern, her eyes began to adjust to the splendor, and she detected more. Four small passageways were carved out from the far side of the cavern. Her spirits sank—she didn't have a clue as to where to go next.

Just then, she remembered Lessa speaking of her makeshift map and threw her hands up in frustration. It only occurred to her now that this was why she'd needed it.

Arianna had never ventured beyond the safety of the hot springs before. She was only familiar with the one long tunnel which led her directly to and from her own district, so she had never needed any help with navigation. Her surge of bravery began to founder, and she took a seat on a wide, flat facet of one of the gems. Resting her chin in her hands and contemplating turning back, she racked her brain for guidance.

Her eyes dropped to the muddy floor as she thought, studying her footprints in the muck. Then, as if a lightning bolt had run through the stone, she jumped up from her seat with an idea. Eyes still glued to the ground, Arianna placed a heavyset boot against one of the footprints she'd spotted. In comparison to her own, the footprint was much narrower and shorter by at least two inches.

"It doesn't match!"

Her voice bounced off the glassy rocks and ricocheted all around the chamber like a mocking chorus.

This has to be hers.

She turned in circles, careful of her footing, until positive as to which direction the footprints led in. Then she headed with as much gusto as before toward the tunnel off to the right.

Never losing sight of what she hoped to be Lessa's tracks, she started to hum a familiar tune, its sound echoing all around her like a companion and making her feel even more confident in her decision. Though the beautiful vision of the jeweled chamber eventually shrank back behind her, nothing could stop her from trekking onward.

Arianna continued to follow the footprints deep into the twisting tunnels, but she noticed after a while that the light had begun to fade as the firebugs grew sparser. Before long, complete darkness swallowed her. She was a warrior, though, and kept the brave face of one as she carried on, careful of her footsteps while using her hands to guide her. Warriors didn't give up, and Arianna wouldn't either—nonetheless, her heart thrashed against her chest in defiance of her courage.

After some time feeling around the cave, Arianna felt something cold and brittle against her fingers, not like stone. She pushed on it and a dim light sprinkled her face. Vines crumpled and splintered at her force, and she fell forward into a soft pile of snow with a sigh of relief. The sudden cold shocked her at first, but she welcomed the outside air.

Wary that she might very well be in the Healer's District, she crouched down low and scanned her surroundings. The hole she'd fallen through was expertly concealed under a cover of nature, barely visible to the unknowing eye. The frozen roots of a large tree enclosed the small opening to the tunnel, and a thick blanket of snow kept the space well hidden.

As her eyes adjusted from the pure darkness of the tunnel to what was now a glaring white with the strike of moonlight atop the snow, Arianna realized that she was standing in some sort of scant forest. The area was littered with blackened trees, their limbs stretching tall toward an equally black sky. And with the mountains as their backdrop, Arianna wondered if they too were dying to escape the Four Corners.

Somewhere in the distance, a wolf howled at the moon. The sound woke her to the task at hand.

How to find Lessa Thur?

Not wanting to linger for fear she might get caught or that she'd talk herself into going back, Arianna slipped on her gloves and lifted up her hood. The warmth of the hot springs had long since dissipated, so the familiar cold of the Jar was starting to creep back into her bones, along with her nerves.

This... is the Healer's District?

So far, it didn't look like anything much at all, but Arianna was feeling more than uneasy to be sneaking around the unknown, an intruder on the night. And yet, this was also the most thrilling moment of her life thus far. She started through the forest, carefully climbing downhill—as was her only option from here. Wobbling a bit on the uneven ground in the dark, she hopped from tree to tree for cover.

Arianna paused for a moment at the tree that marked the end of the forest. She pressed her body against its trunk to hide; the earthy smell of bark sunk into her nostrils, just as welcome as the scent of freshly baked bread (something she'd only had the pleasure of smelling, never tasting). She smiled at the sensation. In the Warrior's District, all the trees had been hacked away and repurposed for weaponry, firewood, or any number of things that their parts proved good for. She'd never seen so many unwounded and alive in one place before, but she rather enjoyed this added element of nature.

Looking around the trunk of the tree, she noticed a long fence bordered the forest, and a gate swung back and forth, creaking in the wind. A battered sign clung to it that read 'The Field.' As she examined what lay beyond the fence from her hilly perch, she finally saw the true Healer's District. It sprawled out below from this place, still under the watch of the moon and washed in a dim lighting from the several lanterns placed up and down the streets.

Arianna couldn't look away, her eyes seemingly frozen open as she stared down at a replica of her own home. Her lips curled at the sight. She even saw the same barracks gathered in bland rows against the mountainside in the distance as well as other familiar-looking buildings scattered about. As far as she could tell, the Field and the pattern that this district was laid in were the only discernible differences.

The roads of the Warrior's District she walked each day coiled into themselves, all connected in some way. Here, it seemed that the paths zigzagged and twisted in abstract designs that she didn't understand. She supposed there was probably some order to them she'd see if she lived here. Nevertheless, the Blancoren Mountains formed a wide barrier around this district and all the paths within, creating an almost identical prison to her own. She knew in that moment that she never need bother to lay eyes on the Creator's or Agrarian's Districts—each of the Four Corners was the same nightmare.

Suddenly, Arianna didn't feel so out of place anymore. She scanned the road leading down from the Field, searching for any sign of regulators. The path was clear.

They probably already finished the headcount hours ago.

Arianna resolved to head through town to the slave barracks in search of Lessa. She would try to find a way to leave her a note or some clue that she was still alive and willing to meet. She started down the single pathway that led from the Field to the rest of the district. There was no turning back at this point.

Her crimson robes stood out dangerously against the new fallen snow, making her a walking display of treason. But she focused on anything other than that, keeping her eyes peeled. Curfew had surely passed by now, so she hoped there wouldn't be any questioning eyes to dodge. Drawing her cloak tight around her body like a cocoon, she swathed every inch of skin, trying to hide beneath the cloth as if it granted her invisibility. There was no cover whatsoever as she walked the space between the Field and the looming buildings, so she hurried through the open streets.

After what seemed like ages, a tall, bland building that she immediately recognized came into view—the Dining Hall.

Arianna ducked into the shadows of its walls. At least it offered her a small shelter to safely calculate her next move; she mapped the streets with her eyes, committing them to memory, as well as the way back home.

Before she could decide which way to go next, the rumble of voices rose from down the street. Every muscle in her body clenched at the sound. Arianna had no choice but to stand perfectly still, watching in horror as the light of a lantern bounced toward the Dining Hall, threatening to chase away the shadows that hid her as the voices grew more distinct.

"I'm telling you, Rod, I saw something just there. Look for tracks," someone said in a low voice.

She heard a loud thump as faces came into view.

"Those are *our* tracks, idiot!" someone shouted back. "Did they really have to put me on duty with you tonight?"

They were so close now that Arianna could see their faces clearly—regulators, of course. Another staple ingredient of a district in the Four Corners that Arianna would have been more than happy not to find here. Their horses pawed the ground impatiently as they surveyed the area.

"Sorry, Rod. It's just... the general warned us to be even more vigilant with our patrol," he said, scratching at the growing lump on his head. "You saw Gavin, right? His body was completely shredded by the mouth of the Vanishing Tunnels." He lowered his voice. "I'm a bit on edge is all."

"I understand," said Rod with a knowing sigh. "I still can't believe the wolves got to him. You'd think with all these damn healers around that he would've survived."

Arianna listened intently, trying not to make a sound as she glued herself to the wall at her back.

"He was a good man," replied the other.

"Don't worry. We'll catch the wolf that did it," growled

Rod. Their voices grew fainter. "It's been several weeks now, but I'm sure he'll be back for more blood."

Once the regulators had gone from earshot, Arianna let her breath escape in a long exhale. She didn't realize how still she'd been standing until all her muscles relaxed, causing her to buckle forward from the sudden freedom. She remained in the shadows a moment longer, watching as their sleek, black robes disappeared into the night.

That was too close.

Spying on regulators in the Healer's District suddenly made the stakes all the more real, and she decided to turn back if she didn't reach her destination soon.

Arianna chose to explore a path in the exact opposite direction as the regulators had gone.

There was definitely no movement in this part of town, so she felt a little safer, but she'd lost sight of the barracks where she was sure Lessa would be.

After a while, a line of very polished buildings came into view. Flickering candles shone through polished glass windows and neatly stacked stone and brick created splendid structures, all of different shapes and sizes. The buildings were grand indeed—clearly not meant for quartering slaves.

Arianna looked around and spotted a sign that read 'Supreme Way' in gold lettering.

This must be where the elders live.

In her district, the roads created a pattern so that a warrior-slave never need pass near the elders' homes. Unless escorted by an elder, someone caught snooping around there would suffer severe punishment; it had happened once or twice in her time that one of her peers had been too curious, too careless, got caught and paid the price. Arianna laughed to herself now thinking that what she was doing was ten times worse—the most careless and curious a slave had probably ever been.

And still, she wandered farther down the street, imagining

what luxuries probably lay behind each door and wishing they were hers.

Solomon had invited Arianna into his home once during her younger years, and she remembered the splendor well. It was unlike anything she'd ever witnessed before in her district. Just that little glimpse of a finer life had inflamed her desire to get out of the Four Corners and see what she could make of the world—but she'd always wondered if that hadn't been why he'd brought her there in the first place.

Now, in this surreal moment, that motivation was being renewed. Though, with no one around to tell her what to do or how to feel or why to fight, it felt different than before.

As Arianna tried to make sense of her feelings, she noted that the elder homes here made a much softer impression than the ones in the Warrior's District, the roofs clinging to pastel walls like the rounded tip of a mushroom. Lavished with soft-colored stones and bricks, and gentle designs here and there—she thought there was something warm and welcoming about them. The untouched snow at the doorsteps and the steam billowing from the chimneys gave a homey sensation that Arianna had felt little in her life.

She listened for voices as she tiptoed along, trying to minimize the crunch of compacted snow under her boots. With no instated curfew, elders—masters, regulators, caretakers, trainers, cooks, and the like—could leave their houses whenever they pleased. Someone could walk out into the street at any moment and spot her. So, she moved carefully on, stopping only in the shadows as she traveled the path.

Whispering silent prayers as she walked, Arianna noticed silver-plated names hung on each door. She studied the first.

Yuna Riggs, Caretaker.

No lights shone through the windows in this house as she crept by, but a shudder through her body sent warning signals to her brain not to linger. Reading more names as she hurried past other homes, Arianna searched for a different path to take toward the barracks.

Nikola Crane, Regulator.
Lavaden Lark, Trainer.
Talis Churry, Master Healer and Trainer.
Atellis Otten, Regulator.
Lorundin Land, Caretaker.

Arianna had walked by two other houses before she realized what she'd read.

Talis Churry?

She'd been so absorbed with locating Lessa that she hadn't even considered that she might also find Talis here. She doubled back.

He was an elder, of course, and she still didn't quite trust him, so she wouldn't be knocking on his door for a friendly hello. But, now that Arianna stood at his doorstep, her interest stirred. Talis had visited her and Solomon from the Healer's District on several occasions since the night of her death—mostly to whisper things with her master behind closed doors. Recently, though, he'd stopped visiting.

Arianna let her curiosity for Lessa slip away momentarily as she tiptoed closer to Talis' home, wanting to learn a little more about the *sorcerer* of Supreme Way in the Healer's District. A lantern flickered in the circle window she crouched beneath, and smoke poured from a chimney, mixing with the fast-moving clouds in the sky. She lifted up on her toes and peered through the window.

The house looked even bigger on the inside, and Arianna's eyes grew wide as she spotted Talis. He sat in a large, leather chair with his legs perched up as he warmed by a fire. Arianna relaxed a little at just the sight of a familiar face in these unknown parts. Observing him there, so still, she realized he slept soundly, the faintest of snores reaching her ears through the glass.

She also saw a cup of steaming tea had been placed on the table.

So like Talis.

Her mouth twitched up into a smile as she spied; she wanted more.

Slinking off toward the back of his quarters, Arianna was glad to find more large windows at her disposal. She placed her fingers on the ledge of one and looked into a different part of his home. This dark room contained only a desk littered with parchments and books, and a shelf that reached from the ceiling to the floor held more of the same.

She moved to the next accessible window; this one was ajar. Her eyes followed the soft, trembling light of another lantern set atop its sill. With the aid of the flame, she could clearly see what was inside.

Arianna's mouth fell open, and she regarded the reflection of her own shocked face in the glass of the window, her chestnut eyes fixed open. "Lessa?"

Could it be?

She squeezed her eyes shut for a moment and shook her head, trying to get rid of what was clearly a trick of the mind. Hesitantly, she peeped open an eye, but the image didn't sway.

There lay Lessa Thur, Ghost Girl of the Healer's District.

Arianna smiled with caution.

Now I see what has Master Churry so tied up.

Her snooping had surely paid off. Though, what Lessa could possibly be doing in Talis' home was an entirely different riddle to solve.

As she considered Lessa in this sleeping state, Arianna noted her slow breathing. *Too slow...*

Something about her seemed off; her head rested on a white pillow, and a thick fur quilt was pulled up to her chin.

Almost as if someone possessed her body to do so, Arianna pulled the window open and slid inside to have a better look.

And, just as she'd learned from countless lessons from her cunning master, she was careful not to make any sound as she snuck around.

The light of the lantern flickered from the onset of the wind, creating a frantic light that bounced across the walls in the dark. The space looked simple except for the duvet and some paintings, but it was much more comfortable than any room Arianna herself had ever slept in.

She moved farther in, and her muddy boots stained the lavender rug on the floor.

Gaping at the portraits decorating the room, she realized that a couple even resembled the secret beauty of her utopia—*their* utopia. A myriad of emerald and gold paint strokes could be seen in those displaying the hot springs, while others depicted monochrome abstracts of what looked to be various landmarks in the Healer's District.

Arianna's lips pursed in a hard line as her eyes settled on the outline of the Blancoren Mountains; the black and white image reflected exactly how she normally felt when she looked upon them in real life.

Still, she couldn't deny this portrayal of the mountains was beautiful—even if in a depressing way.

As she circled the room, Arianna discovered even more pictures and sketches piled in a neat stack on a desk. A large oval mirror hung just above it. Arianna studied the frame of woven silver. She stole a look at her reflection, her expression turned solemn, and she wiped the dirt from her face.

I don't belong here.

But, oh, how she wanted to—the flame of desire to get out of this place and move on to a life more worthwhile burned even brighter inside of her, now more than ever.

Turning away from the mirror, Arianna began quietly thumbing through the paintings on the desk. She stopped on her fifth finding and stifled a little chuckle; it was an image of her dagger. The painting held just as much fascination as the tangible blade now snug in her boot, and she noticed a signature in the corner with the same curly writing as the one on her letter from Lessa.

An artist and an archer. Who would've thought?

Arianna replaced the painting back among the others.

Her curiosity satiated, she turned around to observe the sleeping girl who had launched her into this unthinkable adventure.

"What's happened to you?" she murmured.

Lessa slept, motionless, but her eyelids moved slightly as if she was witnessing something vivid and alive within her dreams. A light sweat covered her forehead, and her fingers twitched every so often.

She didn't *look* like she could be woken, but Arianna tried her luck anyway.

"Lessa, can you hear me?" she whispered near her ear.

Placing a hand on her arm, she shook her with gentle urgency. Lessa's skin felt cold beneath her hand, and she didn't seem to notice her touch at all.

In the next heartbeat, Arianna heard a noise sound from somewhere else in the house. She glanced to the door and held her breath. Thinking it Talis, she decided to take leave immediately before her luck ran out.

In haste, she searched for some plain parchment, ink, and a pen. She found what she needed on the desk and wrote a quick, sloppy letter:

To Miss Thur of Healer's District,

I hope this finds you well. I've received your invitation and would like to accept. In fact, I was so eager to meet you that I followed your footsteps from the tunnels. Thank you for leading the way.

I see that at the moment you're quite unwell. When you return from your subconscious, I'll be waiting there on Sunday, in our secret paradise.

In hopes that you wake soon...
Arianna Belvedor, Warrior's District

A rush of excitement overwhelmed Arianna as she folded the letter and placed it underneath Lessa's pillow. She decided her time had been well spent and quickly clambered back out through the window. Before jumping down to the ground, she turned around for one last look at the ghost girl, wondering if they'd ever meet again or if this secret would die with them, hopefully outside of the Jar.

Alas, a pair of fiery eyes, certainly *not* belonging to Lessa (or any human for that matter), met hers instead.

Arianna screamed, panic overcoming her senses; there was an intruder inside the young healer's bedroom.

Her hands flailed, and she fell backward into the plush snow, knocking the lantern down with her. The glass shattered and the flame blew out, leaving her surrounded by darkness. She heard the pounding of footsteps as Talis burst through the door of Lessa's room.

Nerves rattling her body, Arianna crawled toward the side of the house just as Talis stuck his head out of the window.

"Must've been those damn wolves again," she heard him say, pulling the window shut.

Arianna didn't dare look back as she got to her feet and ran as fast as she could toward the Field.

Those eyes.

It was all she could do to keep her mind from spinning with concern; she worried for Lessa, who lay helpless in bed with some strange monster lurking about her room, and hoped Talis could care for her. Though, she doubted the old man would be able to fight off such an unknown invader.

Arianna reached the secluded entrance to the Vanishing Tunnels, ducking in through the vines. And although she'd left the Healer's District behind, she still didn't quite feel safe with those horrible, blazing eyes lingering in her mind.

13

THE AWAKENING

LESSA'S EYES FLEW OPEN as something soft tickled her face. She groaned and reached for her pounding head.

"You're finally awake!" said Talis, glancing toward her from near her window.

He was at her bedside in an instant, examining her.

"What's going on?" she asked in a slurred voice that sounded dry and unfamiliar.

"You fell from a rather tall tree in the Field," he replied.

A hint of anger laced his words, but he kept it at a simmer. "You've been in a deep sleep for nearly two weeks now while your body healed," he added. "I wasn't sure you would even wake after such a fall."

Lessa turned her gaze on him, and his expression softened. He placed a hand on her forehead for a moment.

"You're burning up," he said, clearly worried. "I've been

giving you medicines while you slept to help the healing process along, but that fall did a number on you. How do you feel?" His eyes searched hers for any hint of pain.

"I feel like I just fell from a tree," she said, massaging her temples. She forced a smile on her lips but it didn't fool Talis.

"You really ought to take more care of yourself. I know you like climbing, but I always knew something like this would happen." He fluffed up the pillow behind her head. "It was lucky that the snow helped break your fall. I managed to fix your broken bones with the last of the prillyberry brew, but it took you much longer to wake than I would've expected."

"Was it really that bad?" she asked.

Talis nodded, and a frown wrinkled his face. "Never do that again, you hear?"

"Trust me, I won't," she said, feeling as if she were experiencing the aftereffects of a Poison Cure.

"When you didn't show up for the morning commendation to the King, I went searching for you. It's a good thing I found you when I did," said Talis. "Look, you're as good as new. My remedies worked like magic!"

Lessa's eyes widened as the banned word rolled with ease off his tongue, but she didn't call attention to it. She could barely think straight as it was without questioning him over such a matter.

"I'd say," she replied, carefully stretching out her arms and legs. "The last I remember, my body was in a tangled heap before I blacked out. You're wonderfully gifted, Master. I'm not really sure how you do it. I don't think I could ever heal such an extensive injury."

Lessa shook her head at the idea, and Talis gave her a thoughtful look.

"I'm sure one day you will," he replied. "Otherwise, I'm not as good of a teacher as I thought!"

Lessa tried to laugh, but the gesture pulled out aches from

all across her body that she hadn't before noticed.

"I'm still in a bit of pain though, I think," she said with a grimace.

Talis tugged on his beard as he surveyed her condition.

"I can fix that," he said, hurrying out of the room.

Lessa heard a clatter start in the kitchen.

With Talis out of the room, she pushed herself up to a seated position, testing her strength. Then, she reached for something to tie up her sweat-drenched hair; it made her cringe the way it clung to her skin. Pulling her locks into a ponytail, she ran her hand across the back of her neck, trying to get the thin, stray pieces to behave. Unexpectedly, a stinging sensation surged throughout her body at the touch.

Flinching at the unpleasant tingle, Lessa pressed at the sensitive spot on her neck again, finding it jagged and raised.

What in the world?

She grabbed for a small hand-mirror on her bedside table and tried to angle it to see. But no luck. She just didn't bend that way.

Planting her feet on the floor, she was happy to find that her legs still worked, even if they were a little wobbly. She stumbled across the room to her desk where there was another, larger mirror. Angling the small one in her hand so that the back of her neck was reflected in the bigger one, she glimpsed what was causing her such irritation.

Lessa gasped at what she saw and felt the mirror slip from her hand; it fell to the floor, shattering to pieces.

Tiny shards of glass scattered in a threatening maze about her feet, but she didn't much care as she bent down and scooped up the largest piece, tilting it so that she could once again see the abnormal spot on her skin—an iridescent-silver and spiral scar had formed on the back of her neck.

The luminescent mark stood out like a coiled, metallic serpent painted on her skin. In a way, she found it stunning in contrast to her paleness, but it also made her extremely wary. This scar was definitely new, and a *peculiar* one at that. She supposed it had been earned from her fall, but she'd never seen anything like it before—not on herself or anyone else.

Talis blundered back into the room with a tray of steaming tea and what looked like one of his famous restorative concoctions.

"What are you doing out of bed?" he snapped, narrowing his eyes at the mess.

Lessa quickly yanked her hair tie out so that her blond locks cascaded back down over her shoulders, hiding the strange scar from view. If he'd already noticed it on her, he didn't say so.

"I just wanted to stretch my legs," she said, tiptoeing around the glass and crawling back into bed. Even such little movement had exhausted her.

"Well, you must feel very weak after such a long time unconscious. Rest a bit and drink these," he said, setting the tray at the foot of her bed. "Tomorrow we'll get your body working properly again."

Lessa reached for the cup of tea. The porcelain felt wonderfully warm against her palms, and the brew smelled of sweet jasmine, perfect to quench the insatiable thirst she had felt upon waking.

"Thank you, Master Churry," she said, before drinking it too fast and burning her tongue.

"We've already lost two weeks of preparation, Lessa. We can't waste any more time getting you up to speed," he replied with a stern expression. "The festivals will be here before you know it." Taking the tea from her hands, he replaced it with another cup.

Lessa frowned, his reminder of the Free Falls just as sour as the smell of the new brew tingling her nose. But she obediently lifted the cup to her lips and forced the cold liquid down in one gulp. Her eyelids almost instantly drooped as Talis took the empty cup from her hands.

"What day is it?" she asked with a yawn as the red liquid from the concoction dripped down her chin, staining the white pillow behind her head.

I'll have to clean that later.

Her thoughts blurred, and her body went numb as a pleasant sensation spread across her limbs.

"It's Sunday," replied Talis before he left the room.

Sunday?

Lessa sensed the importance of the word, but her thought was swiftly whisked away into a vast, clouded pool of memories. She felt it slip from her grasp as her mind melted into an enrapturing dream of jeweled labyrinths and brilliant waterfalls. Then, her dream shattered into something darker, and she fell through a snow-cluttered sky, a pair of orange eyes glowering after her.

I4

THIS IS HOME

THE FIREBUGS BLAZED IN A SPIRALING GUST around Arianna as she raced through the tunnels under the Jar. Their golden light blended in with the red of her billowing robes, making it seem as if she ran through a vortex of roaring fire. She slammed her body against the rock of the entrance to her district. Falling through, she landed on her hands and knees with a crash. After putting the stone in its rightful place, she jogged toward the safety of the Dueling Arena, sweat dripping down her forehead and cheeks.

Looking back behind her, Arianna noted the hundreds of identical sleeping barracks that housed her peers. It was odd to be running away from them, since she no longer slept there, but she also didn't mind it at all.

Deep shadows swallowed them in the night, making it appear as if giant wooden cages had been fixed to the side of the mountain.

Stopping for a moment to catch her breath, she tilted her eyes up toward the moon.

Strange… to feel more trapped with a wide view of this sky than when I'm hiding below the mountains.

She laughed at the bizarre thought and guessed the time to be around midnight or later. Deep, indigo shadows blanketed the sky, and the moon was a rich orange as it peeked out of gray, ribbon-like clouds—but only just. Distant, starry globes also sprinkled the dark where the clouds parted.

It was a beautiful night, even for the Jar.

Arianna continued down the familiar path at a slower pace. Eyes still glued to the sky as the full moon rose into glorious view, she was reminded of…

Those horrible eyes.

"Hey, you there!" a husky voice called from up ahead.

Horror replaced anything she was feeling before as the sound of a galloping horse slowing to a trot reached her ears.

With so much excitement overwhelming her mind and the false sense of safety from being back in familiar territory, she'd forgotten to lie low. *Stupid. Stupid. Stupid!*

Only now, as reality sank in, did Arianna realize that the *glorious* moon had washed her in a hazy spotlight. She stood out in full view atop the snowy ground, not even a single shadow to hide her face.

She stayed frozen as the horse came to a stop a few feet in front of her. A tall man in glossy, black robes and the golden snake of the King's Crest embellished across his chest jumped down to face her.

Arianna stiffened, unable to blink as she studied him.

His face looked jagged, and his eyes matched the black of his uniform. His arms rippled with large muscles that overshadowed a rather round belly, and a thick, calloused hand clenched the clean, silver handle of a sword at his hip.

Arianna turned on her heels, attempting to escape in the

opposite direction—she was confident she could outrun this regulator on foot, and he'd lose precious time to catch her in clambering back up on his horse. But, as soon as she spun around, she collided headfirst into another regulator who had snuck up from behind.

He grabbed her by the arms and shoved her to the ground. With a groan, Arianna rolled over from her back to her hands and feet, her hair falling down over her face as she glared up at the two men; they had her cornered.

"Gotcha," he said. His horse had been tied up several paces back, so he must've crept over on foot to help his partner make sure she couldn't get away.

Arianna locked in on his dark green eyes as he crouched down in front of her, so close that she could see the white around his jade irises. He had stringy blond hair that brushed the top of thick eyebrows and his robes fluttered out behind him like a cape in the wind.

The name 'Das' was embroidered on his chest in the same golden thread as the snake on his cloak.

Before Arianna could even gather her thoughts, the other man had yanked her up to her knees by her hair. Once again, she looked upon the starry sky as the regulator forced her head backward so he could look down at her face.

"So, who do we have here?" he asked, his grip sure.

"Quite the surprise tonight," Das replied as his piercing eyes devoured every inch of her. He stood back up, hands on his hips. "What's your number, slave?"

Arianna said nothing. If she revealed herself, they would know Solomon had lied about her death and it could cause him a whole mess of trouble. She couldn't risk endangering her master or Cyn, not after all they'd risked to help her.

The husky regulator at her back clutched a handful of her curls and tugged hard. Arianna winced, a headache already forming.

"My friend here asked you a question," he hissed, lips curling over yellow teeth.

Then she saw the distinct glint of steel moving back and forth as Das withdrew his sword and waved it about.

Arianna's eyes clamped shut, comprehending her fate.

Home sweet home.

Das used the tip of his weapon to caress her exposed neck. She would have flinched away but the other regulator kept her firmly in place, still gripping her hair.

"Would you prefer to identify yourself now?" he asked.

To tell or not to tell? Arianna considered the options as the point of his sword kissed her skin; with each one, she could only see herself as dead or *dead.*

There was really only one choice that she could make which might buy her some time—silence.

She pressed her lips into a tight line.

"Kill her if you must," said the other, "but the general may want to make a show of it. We haven't had someone break curfew in a while. Just give me a little warning this time if you do plan on getting rid of her now. I don't want blood splattering my cloak again." His voice sounded much too casual to be mulling over her death.

Das didn't relax his stance in the least, and Arianna readied herself for his slender blade to push straight through her neck and out the other side. She didn't move a muscle, didn't even breathe. She wouldn't give them the satisfaction of a struggle.

"Of course, Akias," he said after a moment, tapping a finger to his chiseled chin. "How shall we punish you, then? The Pit, perhaps?"

Hearing the Pit laid out in front of her as a possible fate made Arianna go numb, her bravery in the face of sure death fleeing away.

Let me go!

The wordless voice of her mind exploded with a scream of

anger and fear unknown to her as her future vanished before her eyes. But still, she wouldn't let them see. Trying to remain calm on the outside, Arianna racked her brain for an escape.

Then, an idea struck as if a rescue rope had been dropped from the heavens—she reached for it.

My dagger.

She'd almost forgotten their reunion after its long absence from her side. If she made any wrong move, though, Das would make a hole in her throat for certain; she couldn't reach for it now in this position. But, if she survived long enough to get off her knees and get her hands on a blade, she just might have a chance to get out of this alive. After all, she was Solomon's apprentice for a reason.

I just need a weapon.

"Let's search her robes," said Das to Akias with a nod. "I'd like to know why she's out past curfew, and so very late, before her blood gets on my sword."

Flicking his thin blade at her shoulder, he pushed aside her curls to reveal the number 'twenty-two' stitched to her robes.

"Twenty-Two," hummed Akias as he too leaned over to see. "Why are you out here, then?"

The hint of a smile grew on Arianna's lips as she realized they had no clue who she was—that Slave Twenty-Two of Warrior's District, the renowned Master Bell's apprentice, had been defeated and, supposedly, *killed* during a Warrior's Challenge. If they tossed her in the Pit tonight, Solomon and Cyn would be saved the effort of trying to reintroduce her to the district with some farfetched recovery story ahead of the Free Falls. So, at the very least, something good could come from her death.

Akias' hands began fingering within her robes in an uncomfortable search for a clue as to her previous whereabouts. Above her, Das wore a huge grin; he pressed his sword in a tiny bit more, daring her to move, and she felt a warm trickle of blood run down her neck.

"How is she?" he asked, licking his cracked lips.

Arianna sucked in a breath through her teeth at the discomfort, focusing her thoughts on her dagger and trying to keep quiet.

Just survive.

"Maybe we'll save you for a snack," said Das with a foul smirk on his face. His eyes followed the unwelcome hand beneath her cloaks.

"I think you might have a little more bite than you can chew here, *Das,*" spat Arianna, his name like tar on her tongue. She just couldn't help herself that time.

"Oh, feisty, are we? That's an unusual way for a slave to speak to an elder with a blade to their throat. You must not have been taught any manners during training." With the flick of his wrist, his blade twisted ever so slightly. More blood. "That's okay. I like a little bite with my food," he said with a gleam in his hungry eyes.

Arianna felt the threat of oncoming tears and didn't say anything further, fearing they'd surely fall if she did.

"Found something!" said Akias, finally ending his search.

Arianna felt his fingers clasp around Lessa's letter and was utterly relieved that she hadn't hidden it too well for the sake of her dagger—and her temper. But its contents really wouldn't help her much in this situation. Her fate was sealed.

Win or die.

"Now, what do we have here?" asked Das.

"Have at it," said Akias, handing him the crumpled parchment. He stood, throwing Arianna on her back on the icy ground.

This could be my only chance.

Das and Akias were momentarily occupied with their findings, so she rolled over to her side, curling her legs into her chest as if she were wounded. Then, she quickly shifted the dagger from her boot, hiding it within the cloth of her robes so that they wouldn't notice. Das stepped over to her in the next moment, fixing the point of his sword back at her neck as she lay in the snow. He began to read the letter out loud, stumbling over the first part due to the tear she'd accidentally made in the parchment.

They might know her number, but they didn't know her name. And she wouldn't be giving that up easily.

I am Arianna Belvedor.

Das held his sword hand steady as he recited the letter, one which had been meant only for her eyes. With each treasonous, inconceivable word that left his lips, his voice began to shake and eventually trailed off completely at Lessa's signature. Mouth agape, he let the letter float to the ground.

Arianna clutched her dagger, ready to fight.

"Akias, she's... she's... been to the *Healer's* District!" he shrieked after a moment, finding his words.

Akias fetched the fallen letter with shaking hands to read for himself. "Impossible," he breathed, a tremor in his voice.

The regulators both stared down at her with expressions of pure disbelief. Arianna just glared back, patiently waiting for her moment to strike.

"What is this? Is this true?" roared Akias, spit flying from his mouth. Was that fear she saw in his eyes?

She said nothing—if her adventure, that letter, marked the end of her life now, Arianna decided it had all been worth it if only to see this perplexed, powerless look on a regulator's face.

"Don't worry yourself so much," Das said to Akias. "If she doesn't wish to speak, General Ivo will see enjoyment torturing the answers out of her." He turned his gaze on her, and it seemed as if he were amused. "But, I must say, this is a first."

He kicked at Arianna's feet as if she were some ragdoll to be toyed with, and she was sure her face had turned the color of bright red rage in response. Without hesitation, she moved up to her elbows, challenging the tip of his sword and forgetting her fears to make room for her dignity. She was so *tired* of being threatened. Her entire life was one threat after another—she just wanted to live, really *live*, or be done.

"Come on, Das," barked Akias, clearly troubled by what he'd read. "Quit playing around. Help me tie her to my horse. We need to get her to the general at once."

Das laughed haughtily, lifting his sword as Akias knelt down in front of her, reaching out to pull her to her feet.

It's now or never.

Arianna cleared her mind. She held the dagger so surely that she felt the grooves of its intricate pommel imprint on her palm. She angled it at her side beneath her robes, positioning it just right. If she moved quickly enough, she could bury the weapon in Akias' ribs before either of them could comprehend the assault. She'd fight back to the death—just as they'd taught her to do over all these years.

Arianna noticed a flicker of movement from the corner of her eye. The sword Das had threatened her with only moments before had dropped to the snow at his feet.

In utter confusion, she and Akias looked up.

Das was standing where he'd been before, but his hands hung loose at his hips and his eyes bulged wide with horror. A sword protruded from his neck and then was swiftly sucked back into the darkness of the night. Blood rained to the snow as he fell to his knees, a whimper escaping his lips; Arianna was both shocked and pleased to watch the life in his bright green eyes, like poisoned stars, be snuffed right out.

As Das fell to join his sword, Akias jumped up in a whirl of black robes, reaching for his weapon with impressive speed for a man of his build. Arianna, on the other hand, remained low to the ground, having the good sense to crawl away.

In the next blink, she heard Akias screech; a severed leather-gloved hand landed at her feet moments later. Then, with a crash, his body hit the ground like a stone. His cloak was drenched in blood, and the golden snake at his chest dripped red as she stared into Akias' deadened eyes.

Mud, blood, and snow.

These things Arianna knew well. But dead regulators at her feet? That was something quite different. Gathering the remnants of her courage, she lifted her gaze to their executioner as he stepped forth from the shadows.

"Solomon?" she whispered with a sigh of relief as the formidable master of swords looked down upon her. She released her grip on her dagger.

Though, as Arianna registered the rigid lines of fury on his face, her relief quickly reverted back to fear—she thought then that she'd rather face General Ivo.

15

WOLF OF THE EAST

SOLOMON LOOMED OVER HER like a tower swathed in black, and Arianna shriveled in his powerful presence. Glossy beads of sweat glimmered on his forehead, and piercing, dark eyes narrowed sharply in her direction. His lips formed a hard line where she was used to seeing smiles, and his right hand gripped a jeweled sword with an arched blade that she'd watched him wield in lessons too many times to count. Though, never in this way. Never with the intent to kill. Dripping fresh blood onto the ground and warming the snow, it lingered at his side as if hungry for more.

Arianna was unable to move nor speak as she locked eyes with the regulator slayer, and Solomon didn't blink when he stared down at her, his gaze burning a hole in her heart; it felt like he were seeing straight through her body. The veins in his hand bulged as he clenched his weapon, and he seemed to grow angrier with every excruciating second that passed. Arianna was humbled by the immense power that radiated off him—her maker, her *master.*

For the first time, she truly feared Solomon Bell.

Averting her eyes to the ground, she said, "Master Bell—"

"Look at me when you speak!" His voice stung like a cold slap to her face.

The memory of their first encounter flickered through her mind as Arianna obediently lifted her eyes to his. Except, this time, there was no warmth in his expression and his voice matched the callous look on his face. "I'm—"

Solomon sheathed his sword in the scabbard at his hip and marched away before she could push out another word. His white cloak lay across a low stone wall a few feet back—he preferred to fight without it. He picked it up and placed it around his shoulders. Then, he walked back to Arianna and lifted her to her feet by the hook of her elbow.

She didn't risk speaking another word after that. He turned his back to her and began to head up the path. Struggling to follow his long strides, she had to jog to keep up.

As they ran together through the district in the dead of night, it began to snow. Arianna looked toward the sky, finding only black and gray swirls of color as the icy flakes melted on her face. It reminded her of one of the monochrome abstracts she'd seen in Lessa's room.

Lessa Thur. Talis Churry. The Healer's District. Those horrible eyes. Dead regulators.

What was I thinking?

Tearing her focus away from the sky, she studied the embroidery of the Warrior's Crest at Solomon's back. His robes glittered as they rolled behind him, making him one with the dancing snow. He lifted his hood up to shield his hairless head, the red silk lining sliding effortlessly across his skin.

He glanced back at Arianna over his shoulder. Not a

glance, a *glare.* "Put your hood up!"

She did as he commanded without question.

They passed the Dining Hall. Its front doors swung open, creaking back and forth on the wind. The Well Center loomed just ahead, the dark transforming it into some kind of unnerving lump on the land rather than a place for healing. Instinctively, Arianna started to veer in the direction of the Dueling Arena—Solomon turned to the right.

"This way," he growled. Arianna quickly changed course, wondering where he was leading her.

To my death, perhaps.

Not moments later, Solomon whipped around to face her, a fire blazing in his eyes. Arianna gasped, holding her hands up to shield her face as he suddenly lunged for her, pulling her around a corner and slamming her into a wall of an unknown building. He strapped his strong arm across her chest like a belt so she couldn't move.

Arianna pulled a breath in through her teeth at the abrupt force and squeezed her eyes shut, readying herself for pain. The whine of horses trickled to her ears from the other side of the wall, so she knew they'd crossed into elder territory where the Warrior's District Stables were kept.

Master Bell wouldn't kill me.

Still, she couldn't help but think the worst.

Finding the courage to open her eyes, she saw that Solomon had also flattened himself against the wall at her side. Stern eyes bore into hers and he lifted a finger to his lips, daring her to speak or move; Arianna had never been so unable to do either in her life.

Paralyzed by fear of her master's wrath at her betrayal, she hadn't even noticed the clacking of hooves from up ahead until quite some time had passed. Voices grew audible, and Arianna's panic swelled in another direction as a regulator stopped her horse right near their hiding place.

While the roof of the Stables sheltered her and Solomon in the shadows, nothing tangible separated them from the regulator. Arianna prayed that the darkness was enough, but she trusted it little. Her heart beat frantically inside her chest as she watched and waited, hoping Solomon couldn't hear.

"R.J., where have you been?" called the deep voice of a man. Another horse trotted up the lantern-lit path to meet the woman. "Where in the King's name are Akias and Das? Why aren't they with you? There's been a slave out of bed. The general is handling this one!"

"They… they're dead," stuttered the woman, her face as white as the snow on the ground. Arianna slightly turned her head to see Solomon's reaction, but his expression hadn't changed. "They went ahead of me to do rounds, and when I rode to catch up, I… just found them…"

'Dead?' mouthed the other regulator, clutching the reins of his horse.

R.J. nodded. "I came back this way to find help."

Arianna had trouble telling some of the regulators apart in the district since there were so many of them, but she'd definitely seen this woman terrorizing her and her friends before. With interesting tattoos peeking out of her robes, spiked hair, and parts of her head shaven in fascinating patterns, she had a sharp style, not easily forgotten. Though, right now, Arianna thought her disheveled expression made her seem extremely mismatched.

A regulator… frightened? Mismatched, indeed.

It was a very odd thing to even consider, let alone actually witness, and Arianna couldn't look away.

"What do you mean *dead?*" the man replied, his words trembling. He was tall and lean with rich brown skin, and dark hair tied up in a tight knot at the top of his head that made the skin pull across his face in an unnatural way.

He slid down from his horse, as if the ground beneath his

feet might wake him from a nightmare.

"I mean *dead*, Mundar. It was a bloodbath," she replied. "Who could've done this?"

The chatter of more voices flitted up the street from a different direction as a gaggle of laughing regulators joined Mundar and R.J. The thick scent of whiskey wafted in on the wind that followed them, making Arianna's nose wrinkle. The elders were frequently drinking some form of ale or malt to dull their senses and get through the cold days, so she was familiar with the smell. But it was yet another perk of citizenship she hadn't yet tasted.

"What are you two moping about?" said a belligerent man.

He slapped Mundar across the back, and he buckled forward from the force.

Snapping out of his stupor, Mundar came back with a fierce uppercut to the man's jaw. He fell like an axed tree to the ground with a groan.

"Calm yourself!" said R.J., hopping down from her horse to pull Mundar away.

A man with ruddy hair and freckles stepped forth from the group, a smirk stretched across a face that was very easy on the eyes. He reminded Arianna of Noah.

"Was that really necessary now?" He held out a hand to help his friend to his feet. "We're just having a bit of fun," he said with a snicker, hands on his hips as he turned to face Mundar. "Maybe you should join us next time."

Mundar growled in frustration, stomping over to him. He grabbed him by the fur collar of his robes, whispering something in his ear. Arianna couldn't hear, but she could guess the topic. The already pale regulator blanched at Mundar's words, stumbling out of his grasp. Collecting himself, he addressed the rest of the group.

"All right everyone, there's been a situation. Das and Akias have been found *murdered* near the slave barracks," he announced, his casual demeanor shifting to one of authority. There were shocked murmurs all around, and Arianna could only imagine the thoughts swirling in their minds at such news. Regulators didn't get murdered in Olleb-Yelfra—that was *their* profession. "Listen up! You're now all on duty."

She watched this man with interest and noticed elaborate designs woven into the black of his uniform in red and gold, shimmering faintly as he moved. And bright red fabric lined the interior of his robes, similar to Solomon's. This regulator stood out from the rest, and she recognized him after a moment as the general's right-hand man, Sir Dean Westing.

He looks too young to be a leader.

Yet, with his command, the lively, drunken group immediately shifted into what looked to be a practiced and capable unit of warriors. Even the drunk man who before seemed on the brink of losing his stomach had lost the wobble in his step.

Westing paced before them with his arms behind his back.

"Ida and Orlene—" he started. Two women stepped to attention, hands on the handles of their swords. "—I want you both to go with Mundar to check out the scene of the crime and wait for me there. Snoop around a bit. If you find anything interesting, hold on to it." He stopped pacing, olive eyes gleaming with excitement, like he'd waited his whole life for such a thing to happen under his watch… for such a challenge. "And don't move the bodies. I want to see this for myself. I'm certain the general will, too."

Moving as one, Ida and Orlene gave a slight bow of acknowledgment. Something about them seemed resourceful. Dark brown hair fell in waves around their faces, and their golden-brown skin matched their eyes. Arianna found it impossible to tell one apart from the other. She would've thought them twins, but there was no way to be certain—in Olleb-Yelfra, siblings were always forced apart.

The women entered the front door of the Stables.

"And bring me a damn horse!" called Westing.

Pressing her ear against the wall at her back, Arianna could hear them moving around inside. Not long after, they came out mounted atop two slender horses and leading another larger one behind them by the reins; Westing took hold of the horse's harness and told them to be off.

Mundar gave Westing a curt nod and hopped back on his horse. In the next blink of an eye, he was racing down the street, Ida and Orlene following closely behind, their horses kicking up a cloud of snow as they went.

When the three regulators had rounded a corner and were out of sight, Westing took a deep breath, putting his attention back on those remaining.

"All right… the rest of you, wake up the crew and gather in the Square to wait for instructions," he commanded. "If someone is out here killing regulators, every one of us needs to remain vigilant. R.J., you'll be coming with me. I want you to inform General Ivo of everything you saw tonight so we can hunt down the culprit."

"At your service, sir," she said, settling back on her horse.

Westing mounted his horse now as well. "Let's make sure that whoever did this wishes they'd never been born!"

"Hoorah!" shouted the regulators, lifting their weapons to the air.

They scattered in different directions, leaving only Sir Dean Westing and R.J. in Solomon and Arianna's view. With everyone gone, Westing grew visibly more alert, scanning the area with a warrior's instinct now that all was quiet. And, for a moment, his gaze paused in their direction.

Arianna felt her chest tighten, and every second that he didn't blink felt as if years stretched by. She held her breath like there was a dagger to her throat.

If I can see him, can he see me?

She prayed for better luck than that.

"Ready?" said R.J., giving Westing a strange look.

"Yes… let's get going," he responded after a moment, peeling his eyes away from the shadows of the Stables.

Just as soon as Arianna's imagination had conjured up the worst possible conclusion to her adventure gone wrong, Westing and R.J. rode off into the night.

Solomon released his hold on Arianna, and she staggered forward. It felt as if she'd never once breathed in her life, the air flowing back to her lungs in one big gulp. She stole a glance at her master after she'd caught her breath, but his mood had only seemed to worsen; he just stood there, so still for a moment, staring off into the night like he was searching for something. Arianna desperately wanted to know what he was thinking. Then he took her again by the elbow, leading her away.

They continued down the same path as before, the same path R.J. and Sir Dean Westing had also just taken. Parts of the ground here were covered in a thin layer of ice that cracked loudly in the silence of the hovering night. And the muddy paths she was used to had turned to sleek slabs of black stone, made even more beautiful under the sheen of glittering snow.

Eventually, they came across a coiling street of neatly lined dwellings, each quite eye-catching in their own unique ways— as if the makers had been trying to compete with the neighboring homes to see which would turn out most impressive. Arianna knew immediately where she was and where they were headed; she'd visited Supreme Way of the Warrior's District before with Solomon. But she'd been quite young then, and everything had looked so much… better.

Now, after nearly being executed by Das and Akias, regulators who maintained permanent residences here like all the rest of the elders, it made her sick to see how comfortable her captors were kept. The Jar she lived in and the Jar that Solomon, Talis, and Cyn lived in were not one and the same.

She gaped at the homes as they walked, grandiose things that shone silver-washed in the moonlight, like the shimmering metal of a blade. Unlike Supreme Way in the Healer's District, each dwelling was built of the same hoary stone, making the street seem cold and unkind in the night. However, in the day, Arianna knew they looked much different—splendid and striking structures which stood out against the backdrop of the mountains; at least, that was how she remembered Supreme Way from long ago.

"This way," whispered Solomon. "Hurry!"

He gestured for her to stay close and started to weave between the homes. She crouched down low, careful not to make a sound as she crept along in Solomon's footsteps. Taking care to duck beneath tall windows with candles flickering on the sills, Arianna could've thought that time had hiccupped and accidentally launched her back to the Healer's District to spy on Talis and Lessa.

After a few minutes, voices coming from different directions filtered to her ears on the wind. She knew that the regulators were swarming Supreme Way now, following Sir Dean Westing's orders to rouse everyone they could in an effort to hunt down the assailant—to hunt down Solomon.

As she stayed close to her master, dancing around the spots of lantern lights and keeping to the shadows, Arianna felt her stomach churn at the dire consequences of her choices—not only had she betrayed Solomon's trust but she'd gotten him in a whole mess of trouble.

"We're here," he said after a while, leading her to the back of one of the homes. Arianna didn't recognize it from the outside in the dark, but she knew it was his.

Wooden steps led to a small balcony that hovered just over the ground with a back-door entrance to the house at the top. Motioning for her to wait, Solomon produced a silver key from his robes and climbed the stairs.

The sound of footsteps quickening around the corner reached her ears—snow crunching underfoot. Arianna moved to hide herself under the small space between the stairs and the ground, without a moment's hesitation.

"Bell, there you are!"

Solomon cursed under his breath.

Arianna peered through the cracks and saw Sir Dean Westing at the foot of the stairs; he glanced down, as if he'd felt the burn of eyes on him from below.

Arianna froze, trying to make herself as small as possible, wishing she could just vanish into thin air.

Could this night get any worse?

"Sir Dean, to what do I owe the pleasure?" said Solomon.

"I've been searching everywhere for you," he replied, sharply, looking away from the floor and instead at Solomon. "Where have you been? My men were at your door only minutes ago."

"Oh, I do apologize. I'm a heavy sleeper, but I was roused by all the commotion," he answered in such a casual tone that Arianna almost believed his lie. "What's happened? Is everything okay?"

His response seemed to satisfy Westing, but frustration still laced thickly in his voice.

"I see…" he said. "Well, you must come with me now that you're awake. General Ivo requires your assistance. "Two of our men have been murdered." He cleared his throat. "Das and Akias."

"You don't say?" said Solomon in a high-pitched voice quite unlike himself. He straightened his back, trying to act surprised in a way that made Arianna want to burst out in laughter despite the horrifying situation.

"How can I be of service?" he added when Westing raised an eyebrow at him. "Who could've done such a thing?"

"Mundar caught a young slave near the Dining Hall

shortly before we found them dead. She's being interrogated as we speak."

Much like Arianna, Solomon gaped at this new information but recovered his composure in record time.

"You mean to tell me you think a *child* murdered Das and Akias? That's absurd! Das was one of the most skilled regulators in the district. And Akias... he was a beast of a man. To be bested by a child—"

"Not a *child*, a warrior-slave," snapped Westing. "And if you have any other suspicions, Bell, best tell me now. We need all hands on deck." His voice was all but condemning.

Arianna balked. She would've lost a limb if she'd ever spoken to her master like that.

In one quick move, Solomon leaped down the stairs, the key dropping from his hand with a small clang on the wood. He stood nose to nose with Westing now, his expression just as threatening as when Arianna had first laid eyes on him this night. He was in as foul a mood as she'd ever seen him and wouldn't have been surprised if he pulled out his sword right then and there to feed another regulator's life to it.

"*Sir Dean*, if you improperly address me again, I'll see to it that you're buried alongside your fallen friends. You may be the right hand of the general, but the general is the right hand of me," said Solomon, towering over him with a warrior's confidence only earned from many victories.

Westing shrank before him like a child, and Arianna pitied him slightly. She knew the feeling well; it seemed Solomon Bell hadn't a fear in the world, and she wondered if she'd ever be as strong as him one day—she hoped.

"I've slayed many men for less," Solomon continued, "and I'll not be belittled by the likes of you. My title has been granted to me by the High King of Olleb-Yelfra. I'm here by *choice*, unlike the general or even you for that matter. If you forget your place again, I'll set your soul free in the Tombs of

Blancoren. Do I make myself clear?"

Even Arianna shivered at his statement. It was considered a horrible fate to be buried there, in the tombs under the mountains. No slave—not anyone—wanted to be stuck in Blancoren forever, not even in death. There would be no freedom in that ending.

Westing stood his ground for only a moment before he found his humility. Then he bent to one knee.

"Please forgive my offense, Master Bell, Wolf of the East and Great Warrior of Olleb-Yelfra. I humbly ask your mercy."

His eyes didn't leave the ground.

Arianna had never seen Solomon enforce his true power over anyone before, aside from Das and Akias, that is. Moreover, she'd never heard him be called by so many titles in one sentence. She realized only now that he ranked *higher* than General Ivo. How could she betray someone so influential? Someone who probably held the power alone to grant her freedom if she proved herself worthy? She prayed this was all just a dream, a nightmare she might soon wake from.

Though, at the same time, she reveled in the fact that this 'Wolf of the East' had chosen her to receive his guidance and friendship. The best of the best had shown her the ways of the sword and of the world. Now, he even doubled as her rescuer. He'd committed an act of treason on her behalf—a *slave*.

My name is Arianna Belvedor.

Solomon turned on his heels and walked away in the direction they'd just come from. Westing was still bent at his knee, his fists clenched at his side.

When he stood, Arianna saw that his hand rested on the hilt of his sword, his face boiling red. If he attacked Solomon from behind, he could very well win.

Coward, she thought. *I won't let that happen.*

She readied herself, hand on the pommel of her dagger. Maybe she would have to use it tonight after all.

As she watched him intently from the cover of the stairs, Westing finally let go of his sword and, reluctantly, followed Solomon's lead. Moments later, she heard the pounding of hooves on the ground as they rode off.

Alone now, Arianna scampered up the steps and retrieved the key that had been covered in a thin layer of snow. She wiped it off with the sleeve of her cloak and undid the lock. A click sounded from the door as it creaked open. She slipped inside and re-locked the latch.

Once safely inside, a surge of emotion overwhelmed Arianna, as if she could finally feel *all* her feelings now that she was no longer in danger. She clasped her hands over her mouth and leaned against the door for support, struggling to control the waterfall of tears threatening to cascade at any moment.

A flickering fireplace crackling in the center of a wide room instantly chased away the cold from the outside, beckoning her closer. On the floor before it lay a huge, white, fur pelt; Arianna studied the head of the animal, teeth and all, and recalled reading of it in the Learning Center. She was drawn farther into the room; her fingers skimmed the top of a long, ornate couch, soft gold ringlets stitched into crème-colored cushions. Placed directly in front of it stood a low, wooden table with elaborate designs carved into every panel. And tall candles, gold and bronze trinkets, and thick, dust-covered books decorated two tall shelves on either side of the fireplace—this place had definitely evolved since the first time she'd been here. Simple Solomon seemed to like a little splendor after all.

Thoughts of the recent events stirred unpleasantly in Arianna's mind as she settled on the rug before the fireplace. On the wall above it hung a grand oil painting full of color that she'd certainly never seen before. Animals that could never survive in such a brutal terrain as the Jar filled the canvas with life, and a painted river sparkled like sapphires under a sky brushed with soft clouds and a beaming sun.

Arianna couldn't help but smile at such a peaceful picture and wanted only to be lost in it. She curled into a ball on the floor and wrapped herself in the comfort of her robes, contemplating the story of the colorful world depicted in the portrait and wishing it were hers.

This was all just a big mistake.

She wished for Liam, for someone to confide in and to help her plan a way forward. Because, right now, she didn't see how she could ever earn her freedom after what she'd done. Wiping the tears from her eyes before they could fall, she drifted into a deep sleep—into dreams and into the painting.

It came alive all around her, transporting Arianna from her scarred reality and into the serenity which hung on Solomon's wall. The warm water lapped at her ankles and animals darted through long, swaying grasses as the suntanned her face.

Was there ever a life such as this?

HER EYES FLEW OPEN to find Solomon sitting on the couch, watching her, the dwindling embers from the fireplace reflecting in his stare. He still wore his muddied boots and looked as if he'd only just arrived.

Still hazy with sleep, Arianna sat up, sitting cross-legged on the rug. She waited for him to speak first.

"We need to talk," he said after what seemed like ages. His voice was quiet, his expression unreadable.

Solomon pulled something from his robes and laid the object on the table between them. Arianna's eyes grew wide as she looked upon the letter from Lessa.

She groaned as her stomach knotted, wishing she'd discarded it earlier or set it on fire. Anything other than carrying it around in her pocket—this letter had caused her nothing but trouble tonight.

"Regulator Orlene found this during the scan of the area," said Solomon. Arianna chewed on her lip, waiting for him to deliver worse news.

"Lucky for you, the incriminating part of the letter has been damaged. They don't know *who* this was addressed to. However," Solomon continued, "a Lessa Thur of the Healer's District is quite clear as the sender."

Arianna rubbed her temples, trying to relax her frenzied mind. She'd been so worried about herself during all this that she hadn't even considered the damage this could do to her newfound, unlawful acquaintance.

"Arianna, this letter was meant for you, or am I mistaken?" asked Solomon, pointing to the uncanny drawing of the dagger he'd gifted her. He held his breath, probably praying that he was wrong.

"You're not mistaken," she whispered, barely able to withstand his reproachful gaze and knowing it impossible for him to look more saddened or betrayed. "How did you get it away from the regulators?" The words trembled from her lips.

"I have my ways, but it doesn't much matter at this point. All of the district regulators are hunting for whoever this 'Lessa' is right this very minute… and I'm leading the charge. They've already apprehended another girl who they are certain was the recipient." Arianna gulped, wondering who had taken the fall for her mistake.

Solomon leaned forward. "I'm going to need answers. *Now*. And don't leave anything out." She certainly wouldn't.

Arianna gave a single nod of her head, and the fire crackled behind her, licking at the tension between them.

Solomon sat back and crossed his arms. "Good," he said.

"So, tell me, then. Where have you been hiding?"

Taking a deep breath, Arianna started from the very beginning. She explained about the boy who'd broken her pride during her ninth year and the cave of wonders which had rejuvenated it. She told of the Ghost Girl of Healer's District who'd cornered her with an arrow in some secret section of the Vanishing Tunnels and of her encounter with the moon-eyed monster in Talis' home.

Every secret she held spilled from her like rain from a broken sky. Only in her honesty did she even realize she'd kept so much hidden. When she finally finished, her mouth hung dry with nothing left to say.

Solomon stayed silent as he gazed past her, to the painting.

16

CELLMATE

ONE WEEK HAD PASSED since Arianna's confession to Solomon. It was another Sunday night. Arianna paced back and forth in her secret cavern, waiting.

What's taking them so long?

The waterfall thundered down behind her, filling the silence that seemed to echo into every corner of her mind.

"Arianna?" came a shy voice all of a sudden.

This is it.

She whipped around to find Lessa Thur standing just a few feet away from her at the mouth of the tunnel which led to the Healer's District. Arianna gave a small wave of her hand.

"Hi." That was the only thing she could think of to say as nerves overcame her vocabulary.

It had been nearly two months since their first meeting. Two months since the day her world had begun to spiral out of control. In just that short amount of time, Arianna's life had been turned upside down. Or was it right-side up? She still didn't have the answer, but change it had.

And in two months, she saw Lessa had changed as well. Her hair appeared much longer than she recalled, waving down past her shoulders in golden streaks, and she wore a cloak of pure white lined with sapphire blues and lush fur trimmed down the sides. It seemed too big on her. Or maybe she looked thinner than before?

In any case, something about Lessa was strong and healthy now—not like when Arianna had spied her in the Healer's District, bedridden. It seemed as though she glowed with the same excitement on the outside as Arianna felt on the inside.

As they contemplated each other, Arianna spotted the most curious addition of all to Lessa Thur. What she had at first thought to be the hood of her cloak turned out to be a small, furry, white animal with big, orange eyes perched on her shoulder. The creature was mesmerizing.

Arianna could only gawk. "Is that…?"

"A monkey," answered Lessa, patting it gently on the head.

It was something Arianna had only ever seen in books in the Learning Center and once in Solomon's colorful portrait. How strange to find it in this setting, morphed from ink and paint into *real*, breathing life; it clearly belonged to a different world… one Arianna hoped she could also belong to one day.

It curled its long tail around Lessa's neck as it scanned the hot springs. Then, its eyes, like bright burning coals, found Arianna's—she remembered those eyes. She stepped back in caution, but Lessa inched closer, letting its tail curl playfully around her neck.

"Don't be frightened," she said with a thoughtful smile. "This is Sano. He found me in the trees."

Arianna opened her mouth to speak, to scream, to question. Really anything at all, but nothing came out. This creature was unfathomable. Lessa being here, in this underground, was unfathomable. All of it…

Unfathomable.

Before she could find the words to say or the emotions to feel, another surprise came stalking out from the same tunnel.

"Talis!" Forgetting everything else, Arianna ran to him. "I'm *so* sorry, Talis—"

He put a finger to her lips.

"It's good to see you, Arianna, but don't apologize," he said. "It's not necessary. Fate is fate, and I daresay your little adventure was just the beginning of what she has in store for you. You can't argue with destiny now." He strode over to Solomon. "I believe you taught me that. Right, Bell?"

"Don't let her off the hook that easy," said Solomon, slinking out of the shadows and walking over to them. Arianna fidgeted under his scrutiny, moving back to give them space.

"What an enchanting place they've found here," said Talis, the twinkle of firebugs reflecting in his awed gaze.

"Indeed," said Solomon. They shared a look, like some untold secret lingered between them. Then he and Talis walked away, toward the edge of the water.

Arianna watched the two with intrigue, trying to wrap her head around this new situation. How bizarre it was to see Solomon and Talis fitted into the backdrop of her utopia, her safe place to hide—and yet, fit they did. The jade stones twinkled in acceptance and the firebugs swirled in tornados of light high above their heads, welcoming them just the same as they had Arianna, and, she supposed, Lessa too.

Suddenly, a shared secret didn't seem so bad anymore.

Talis ran his fingers along the wall of the cavern, caressing the jutting jade stones. A second later, she heard him suck a breath in through his teeth and abruptly pull his hand back.

"Sharp little beauties," he said.

The two masters stood only feet from the girls, so Arianna could detect the blood trickling down Talis' pale hand.

"Are you okay?" said Solomon.

"Oh, I'll be fine," he replied. "Just a small cut. Nothing to fuss over."

"So I see," said Solomon with a smirk.

Arianna's eyes grew wide in disbelief as she saw the tiniest hint of a sparkling light emanate from Talis' palm. Then, just as soon as the light had come, it disappeared along with the blood and the cut.

Where's the wound?

She stood on her tiptoes to try to get a better look but saw nothing now. There was no hint of blood anywhere. That is, *except* on the stone that had pierced him.

"What are you looking for?" said Lessa, turning her head in the same direction.

Her voice made Arianna jump. "It's nothing. I just... I swear my mind is always playing tricks on me in these caves."

She shook her head of the riddle and took a deep breath before facing Lessa again; she looked just as bewildered and nervous as Arianna felt at this reunion, aided by their masters.

Arianna prepared her next words carefully as Lessa fidgeted with her robes. She had wanted to say them for so long, and nothing—not the strange animal on her shoulders or her vivid imagination—could put them off any longer.

"I'm sorry I wasn't more... cautious. You're in this situation because of me," she said, bowing her head.

The caves quieted, as if they respectfully waited for Lessa's reaction. Even the firebugs seemed to stop humming.

"When Talis told me the regulators were coming after me because of the letter I had written, because of you, I *was* angry at first," she said. "But Talis is right. Fate is fate, and this is ours." Lessa pulled a parchment from her own robes, and Arianna recognized the letter she'd left under her pillow in the Healer's District. "Frankly, if you hadn't come looking for me first, I probably would've made a similar choice. Neither of us are very good at following the rules, are we?"

Arianna felt her mind instantly relax with Lessa's kind words. She'd been ready to face the worst for getting her and Talis into such a mess with her recklessness, but they didn't seem to harbor any anger toward her. The guilt she'd been carrying all this time began to dissipate, little by little.

"I am sorry, though," said Arianna with a solemn smile. "I hope I can make it up to you... to you both."

"Thank you," said Lessa. "But I was getting bored stiff anyways. This next chapter will probably be a lot more exciting, if you ask me!" She flashed a warm smile. "This old man had me training day and night after the accident until Solomon showed up to warn him of what'd happened. I try to look on the bright side. At least I've wriggled my way out of the Free Falls." She feigned wiping sweat from her brow.

Talis scowled. "But you haven't wriggled your way out of the Four Corners. Have some humility. You're not out of this yet," he said, looking at Lessa sidelong as he came to stand next to her. "Only if the gods are on our side do we have a prayer of actually getting you some resemblance of citizenship now."

The sharp pang of guilt stabbed at Arianna's chest again.

"We won't leave Lessa behind," said Solomon. "I'll figure out a way to get her out safely once Arianna wins her freedom. And at least nobody is looking for her in the Warrior's District anymore. In those robes, I think she could really pass as an elder from the Healer's District if I train her right. It's risky, but with my influence, she has a good shot at fooling the system all the way out of here.

"I hope so," said Talis, wearily. "We haven't got any other choice."

Solomon laid a hand on Talis' shoulder. "If anything goes wrong, I will protect her. I promise you that."

Talis gave him a firm nod. "I know you will," he said.

"Slave to elder in a mere night?" cooed Lessa, tugging at

her fancy robes as she tried to sway the darkening mood hovering about the small group. "I'm sure I could get used to this life. Maybe I should be *thanking* you, Arianna!"

Talis grumbled something that sounded like swearing, causing Lessa to erupt in a fit of giggles that cracked right through this scowl. Her laughter, so genuinely bright, lit up the cavern, forcing a smile on Arianna's face. Solomon joined in with his own booming laughter that always made Arianna's heart leap, and the four got to know each other a little better; she was glad Solomon's temper had softened now after such a dreadful week, and she hoped it stayed this course.

"Lessa, it's time you properly meet Solomon Bell," said Talis after the laughter had subsided. "He's an old friend of mine and Arianna's master trainer. The universe has played an interesting card by introducing both of our apprentices. He'll take good care of you until we figure out how to handle this… situation. Preferably in a way so that we can all leave with our heads intact."

"How do you do?" said Solomon, taking Lessa's dainty hand in his. He bowed low, flashing pearly teeth, and Lessa flushed a bright pink.

"Pleased to meet you, Master Bell."

He gave her a wink and then shifted his attention to Sano, still sitting comfortably atop Lessa's shoulders. "Ara, I believe you've found your fiery-eyed monster," he said with a chuckle. "You might want to watch your back at night. Sure you'll be okay?"

Arianna turned red, pursing her lips. "I will survive," she said, folding her arms across her chest.

Lessa looked from Sano to Arianna in confusion as Solomon tickled the monkey under its chin.

"Tell you later," said Arianna, rolling her eyes.

"So…" said Solomon, turning to Talis, "is that what I *think* it is?" He nodded to Sano, a strange twinkle in his eye.

"I believe so," said Talis. His mouth twisted into a smile.

"Well I'll be damned!" said Solomon with the clap of his hands. The sound resonated throughout the cavern as he and Talis shared another glance.

"It's just a monkey," said Arianna, frustrated at the secrecy. "Why are you both acting so strange?"

"Just admiring two promising young girls," said Talis. "There's more hope than you know in your futures."

Lessa raised an eyebrow at her master. "Do you always have to be so cryptic?" He only shrugged, and Lessa pouted.

Arianna chuckled to herself, thinking that she at least didn't have to deal with their mysteries on her own any longer.

"So, how did you come to find Sano?" asked Arianna, changing the subject.

Lessa's face lit up as Sano finally became the topic of choice. "I had a terrible fall from a tree when I was gathering fruits for some healing mixtures. I don't really remember much from before the fall, but when I woke up, Sano was there." She patted his head and Sano cooed. "Master Churry said he'd found him by my side in the Field. Can you believe it?"

"He was very stubborn," added Talis, hands on his hips. "I tried to send him away, but he kept following me. I had no choice but to take him home too."

"I've never seen a monkey before today," said Arianna. "He's quite extraordinary. May I?" Her voice came out small and hesitant; she still needed proof that it was indeed no monster. She'd hardly even ventured this close to a horse in her district, always fearing the regulators on top, so animals in general were not something she was accustomed to.

"Sure, he's very friendly."

Arianna stepped closer, removing her gloves. His fur felt soft beneath her fingers, like newly woven fabric, as she gently stroked him. And she noticed his tiny paws were a shining silver on the padding—strange. She couldn't recall that feature from her studies on different creatures of the Olleb, but she found it the most striking feature of all, aside from his eyes.

Sano crooned at her touch, pushing his small head into the palm of her hand.

"Good, he likes you," said Lessa, her nose crinkling as she smiled.

Arianna grinned. Sano truly *was* extraordinary.

"Perfect!" Solomon's voice sounded loud over the drumming of the waterfall, startling Sano so much that his hair stood on edge. "Glad we're all acquainted. Now this will be tricky business, but I believe it's our best plan of action. Do you have everything you need, Lessa?" he asked, morphing into serious Master Bell.

Lessa had a large pack slung across her back along with her longbow. "Ready as I'll ever be," she said, sucking in a big breath through her nose.

"Good. We better be off, then. Help Lessa with her things, will you?" he said to Arianna. "We'll need the cover of a crowd to smuggle you in. It's too risky now to be sneaking around after curfew with so many more regulators on duty after dark."

Arianna took the heavy rucksack from Lessa so that she only had to worry about her bow and arrows, and Sano.

"Master Churry," said Lessa, hugging him tightly around the waist. "I'll really miss you."

He blushed, returning the embrace.

"I'll miss you, too," he said so quietly that Arianna almost didn't hear. Then he turned serious, pushing her to arm's length. "Take care of yourself and stay out of trouble, you hear?" Talis glanced between Arianna and Lessa, concern or worry in his expression. "The both of you. I *mean* it. I'll be down for the Warrior's District Free Falls soon enough to cheer you on, Arianna. The Healer's District will begin the festivals in just a few days, so it won't be too long now before I can join you all again."

The annual Free Falls Festivals traditionally lasted for one week per district, consecutive to each, and Arianna's came last—less than five weeks away now.

"How could we get into trouble with such little time?" said Lessa, grinning from ear to ear. Arianna liked her already.

Talis huffed, looking to Solomon for reassurance. "Are you sure this will work? Lessa can be quite the bad luck charm at times. Don't let her smile fool you."

"Don't worry. I have experience in dealing with similar… misfortune. Remember when we were their age? So young! So clueless." His eyes shifted to Arianna, but her scowl only made him smile more. "Besides, they'll never think to look for Lessa in the Warrior's District after the search party I led. Sir Dean Westing's already informed your general that she needs to take over from here. Everyone's trying to keep this very quiet. Two slaves from different districts meeting can't get back to the King without someone losing their head. Her only chance now is to hide where they've already looked."

Talis sighed. "You're right. The regulators in the Healer's District have been watching me like a hawk since your general called for an investigation into Lessa. It was all I could do to keep her hidden before we could arrange this plan." He brushed his hair back. "It's been quite exhausting, really.

"Well, you can relax now." Solomon placed a hand protectively on the girls' shoulders. "The regulators in our district have already executed a slave who was out past curfew the same night this all started. They've held her responsible for the murders of Regulators Das and Akias. With her unfortunate death, the commotion has died down a lot on our side… save for the increase of patrol and punishment in general." Arianna looked to her feet, remembering all the other reasons she had to still feel racked with guilt, probably forever. "In fact, it's you who should be careful since they know of Lessa's treason. Will *you* be all right?" Solomon looked truly concerned.

"Oh, I'll be fine," said Talis, wriggling his fingers.

Solomon returned an understanding nod, and Arianna started to wonder again…

Where is his wound? How did it heal?

"They're speculating I've done off with her myself," he added. "Lessa was always misbehaving, so rumors have started up that I had quite enough and poisoned her with one of the very concoctions I trained her to brew for the Free Falls."

Lessa's mouth dropped open. "That's mortifying!"

"For you, maybe," said Talis with a shrug that made her fume. "For me, it's the perfect reputation-builder in the Jar. Will probably keep them from snooping around long."

"If not, I'm sure your magic fingers will keep them at bay," said Solomon with a laugh.

Arianna stiffened as the illicit word of her nightmares resurfaced. Stealing a glance at Lessa, she saw she fidgeted uncomfortably as well.

"Now if that's all, we should really be going," said Solomon. "I don't want to risk the bell sounding before we're safely settled."

"Farewell and see you soon, then," said Talis, shaking his hand before stalking off toward the passageway to the Healer's District. "And take care of that monkey, Lessa!" His voice faded as the mouth of the tunnel swallowed him.

"Come on," said Solomon, gesturing for the girls to follow his lead. "Let's not waste any more time."

He led the way back past the steaming hot springs toward the Warrior's District, having to duck his head to clear the low ceiling of the tunnel. When they reached the small entrance to the district, he rolled the loose stone to the side, crawled out, and scanned the area. It was nearly curfew; waves of red-robed warriors scurried back to the safety of their quarters—barracks which they were now crouched beneath.

After the scene from yesterday, nobody would dare be out by even the first ring of the bell. No slave had ever been tortured for as long as a week before. But, unfortunately, there was a first time for everything in the Jar.

Solomon and Lessa slid out first from underneath the barracks. They blended into the crowd as elders, slaves cowering away from them as they walked with confident strides; Solomon had been right to suggest Talis give Lessa one of his cloaks. Draped in the same white fabrics and furs as Solomon, she looked like any other elder—the Healer's Crest shimmering at her back in azure threads.

Arianna kept her eyes pinned on them as they traveled farther down the path, feeling less nervous with each step they took. Solomon stayed close by Lessa's side, Lessa keeping her hood tight about her face for extra protection from prying eyes. But elders from all districts traveled anywhere they pleased without restriction. Even citizens could visit from outside of the Four Corners to watch the Free Falls Festivals take place, so it was normal this time of year for many new faces to wander about—nobody noticed her.

Once they'd disappeared down the windy road, Arianna slipped out to quickly follow in their footsteps. She tried to dodge the people flying through the streets but found it an impossible task; they didn't try to avoid her as they had done Solomon and Lessa, because she was *one* of them. Everyone was clearly on edge more than normal tonight, scurrying this way and that in a panic. The next thing she knew, she was tumbling to the ground after a collision with someone who'd seemingly appeared from out of nowhere—he'd been standing still, as if a pillar of stone, in the middle of the street as the crowd rushed around him.

"Eyes open!" growled what was surely a regulator in an unforgiving mood.

Arianna looked up, finding none other than Sir Dean Westing glaring down at her with a broadsword in hand. His robes hung around him with an impressiveness most couldn't achieve, and his blade caught the firelight of a nearby lantern, making her squint as the gleam shone directly into her eyes.

"To your feet," he spat. Saying a profuse apology out loud and an even stronger prayer in her mind, Arianna slowly rose.

He pulled her closer by her collar, searching her face.

Please don't recognize me.

Akias and Das hadn't, so she could only hope.

Arianna was so close to Westing now that she could smell the thick scent of ale on his breath. She grew hot under his scrutiny, beads of sweat gathering on her skin. Her gaze dropped to his polished boots as she waited for judgment.

"You look oddly familiar," he said after a moment.

Arianna said nothing, but her mind screamed in panic.

He knows!

Westing tilted his head, scratching at the stubble on his chin as he tried to place her. "I'd wager you've been in trouble before with the regulators. Second chances are quite rare in the Jar, and we *certainly* don't give out thirds. What's your identification number, slave?"

Arianna froze. "I… my…" Her hair covered the dooming silver twenty-two on her robes.

"Out with it! What's your numb—"

"Sir Dean, give the orders now," came a sharp voice from behind. "It's time for curfew. The assembly will take place in the Learning Center. Tell the others, and don't make me wait."

Peeking over Westing's shoulder, she noted black boots and a thick, fur-lined cape draping over the back of a brawny horse.

"And save a seat for Solomon by my side," he added. "He's been quite the asset as of late."

Westing turned and bowed his head low, forcing Arianna's down with him. "Of course, General," he said, hardly able to hide the jealousy lacing his words.

Arianna's mind flip-flopped as she laid eyes on General Ivo; she'd, thankfully, never been this close to him before, and she fought the urge to run. For a fleeting moment, she actually felt glad that Westing held her upright. Her knees shook uncontrollably, her fate hanging in the balance between one ruthless regulator and *the most* ruthless regulator.

"Today is your lucky day," hissed Westing, turning his attention back to her as the general rode away. "I don't have time for this now. Get out of my sight!" He threw Arianna to the snow-covered ground and stepped over her body, the bystanders giving him clear passage through the crowd.

Arianna couldn't have run faster if she tried, the ring of the bell buzzing in her ears. She didn't stop until she'd reached the gates of the Dueling Arena.

Everyone had already emptied from this part of the district, so she moved freely across the vast grounds toward her sparring room—toward safety. Lessa and Solomon greeted her at the door, a mixture of worry and relief plain on their faces.

"I'm glad you made it," said Solomon with a sigh, resting his hand on her shoulder. "I'm sorry, but I must be off now. I'm expected at an assembly. Cyn will bring food later once the meeting commences as regulator patrol will be much less then. In the meantime, please show Lessa around her new home." He scooted Arianna inside. "And fill her in on the recent events, please. Best we're all in the know going forward."

With a smile of reassurance, he left—this time locking the door behind him.

The girls stood together in silence, Arianna taking a moment to let the warmth radiating from the firepit thaw the cold that had settled in her heart from the awful encounter with General Ivo and Sir Dean Westing. Lessa scanned the large training room, and Arianna wondered what she thought of it. Arianna knew it would certainly be a change from her previous housing arrangement. It smelled like sweat and smoke, and dirt clung to every surface, but it would have to do.

"Nice place," said Lessa after a moment.

They both laughed, breaking the awkward silence.

"It's not much, but its home for now," said Arianna, shrugging her shoulders as she moved farther into the room. "And it's a lot less crowded than my former sleeping quarters."

Lessa walked farther in, setting her longbow down and inspecting the area. "Your Master Bell seems wonderful."

"Talis too. We're lucky to have them as our trainers." Arianna snickered. "Although, I think Solomon may trade me in for you if he gets the chance. You're much more polite."

"I think he might regret it if he did," said Lessa. "I'm not sure I could hold my own with a sword." She was drawn to the barrel of weapons in the corner as Sano jumped down from her shoulders to explore the room alongside her.

"We can fix that," said Arianna, her cautious excitement beginning to grow now that the first part of their plan had been a success. She still had a lot to learn about Lessa, but at least she wasn't alone in this anymore.

As the girls warmed to each other, settling in to this new normal, they sat by the fire and began to examine their chaotic worlds, each divulging stories of their not-so-different experiences, life-altering choices, and daring dreams. And, as the minutes passed by, Arianna's guard fell away quickly until there was nothing of it left. She decided to take the leap and trust Lessa fully as Talis and Solomon did, relying on their better judgment. Though Liam was her closest friend, she couldn't pull him into this mess. She made peace with this new chapter in life, which wouldn't include him for a while.

17

FALLING STAR

PEERING TOWARD THE DOOR, Arianna heard the soft click of the lock, anxious to see who came to visit. Feeling a little on edge from so much change overnight, she clutched the handle of her dagger; it was secured snugly back in the small sheath strapped at her thigh. The door burst open, and a delicious scent filled the room followed by Arianna's rosy-cheeked caretaker—she'd arrived with supper.

When Cyn set eyes on Arianna, she gushed and flew across the room, almost dropping the tray of food she carried. Lessa caught it just in time as Cyn flung her arms around Arianna's neck, knocking her backward.

"*Oh!*" she sobbed. "Oh, dear, it's been so long since Solomon has let me see you! He's got no right. Let me look at you." She pushed her to arm's length, examining every inch of her with a furrowed brow.

"Relax," laughed Arianna, wriggling out of her clutches.

"It's just been a week. But I'm very glad to see you too."

"Oh dear, has it really only been seven days?" she said, clapping her hands with a sudden burst of realization. "It feels so much longer." She turned her sights on Lessa. "And who might this lovely young lady be?"

Lessa, who observed from a corner, stepped forward to introduce herself. She extended her hand and a warm smile.

"My name is Lessa, ma'am. Lessa Thur," she said in her sweetest voice as Cyn took her hand.

"Well, aren't you a beauty. But shouldn't you be in your sleeping quarters by now?" Cyn glanced to the old clock that hung on the far wall and began biting one of her nails. "Oh, my… *Yes*, it's well past curfew," she said, almost to herself. "The regulators will do more than slaughter you if they find you out now. After what happened to that young girl who murdered those regulators—" Cyn repressed a shudder.

"What has Solomon told you?" asked Arianna, prying a little so as not to divulge too much information to her caretaker. She didn't want to rope her into anything more than she had to, and clearly she wasn't expecting to find Lessa here.

"He just told me to bring you dinner and that you were hungry enough for two. Good thing I brought extras!" She smiled and looked around. "Where did I put all that food?" She began wandering about the room, scratching her head.

"I set it here, ma'am," said Lessa as she waved her hand toward the large tray on a table up against a wall.

"Do call me Cyn, dear. How old do I look?" Her eyes grew wide as she smoothed out her hair. Lessa chuckled, Cyn offering her a wink. "Now, tell me, what's going on here, *really?*" She placed her hands on her hips as she narrowed her eyes at the both of them.

Arianna glanced at Lessa for help, but her lips were sealed tight. She had hoped Cyn would forget her questions; it surely wouldn't be the first time.

But, unfortunately, tonight she was very persistent.

Feeling quite unsure of how to handle this situation, Arianna let the silence drag on. She knew Cyn to be an honest friend, one of the few elders who hadn't let the Jar turn her heart cold—she truly wanted Arianna's survival. Though, she also knew her to be an unruly gossip. Her brain filtered nothing out, and her mouth simply said whatever thoughts flitted through her mind. It would be quite risky to confide such a large secret to Cyn. Especially when Arianna knew she still struggled in keeping the last one; it was a miracle the entire district didn't already know of Arianna's inexplicable recovery, but Solomon kept her on a short string with that one. He'd have her head if she talked.

Cyn glanced back and forth between Lessa and Arianna, but neither of the girls said a peep.

"You know, that Solomon has about run his course," she said, tapping her foot impatiently. "I'm going to have a serious talk with him soon." She tried to stare Arianna down, but she wouldn't go for it, smiling sheepishly in response. Cyn whipped around to wag her finger at Lessa instead. "I don't know who you are, child, but I'm *certain* you aren't from around here now that I get a good look at you."

Lessa opened her mouth to speak, but Cyn held up her hands and scrunched her eyes closed.

"No, I don't even want to know! I'm stressed enough with the festivals just weeks away. People are dying left and right. Oh, Solomon will hear from me all right." She was all but muttering to herself now.

Lessa and Arianna tried to hold their laughter behind their teeth, but it proved difficult as Cyn continued to ramble and fume, her face taking on an abnormal cherry-colored flush.

"Bye, dears," she said with one final huff. "I'll be back tomorrow to deliver your meals. Just let that Solomon try and stop me. Oh, and I snuck you a little something special, Ara."

She nodded toward the food. "I thought you could use a treat being cooped up in here for so long. Make sure to share now." She pinched their cheeks and flew out the door.

This time Arianna heard no click; the key lay forgotten on the tray of food.

Dinner looked superb, Arianna's mouth instantly watering. Solomon's weeklong punishment had consisted of making her stomach the worst of the worst from the Dining Hall, so this meal looked like a juicy feast in comparison. She assumed it the leftovers from the elders' selection tonight and was more than happy to take their scraps. The two girls pulled up a couple of chairs, split the food and began to eat.

Arianna dug her teeth into the large chicken breast as Lessa fed tidbits of fruit to Sano. He licked at her fingers and nibbled at crumbs before crawling away to a corner to chase spiders. As they made their way quickly through the main course, Arianna turned her attention to the mysterious lidded plate.

"I bet this is the surprise Cyn was talking about," she said through a mouthful, setting the lid aside. A small silver platter had been piled with different shapes of pastel-painted pastries and slivers of something sweet-smelling sprinkled on top.

Lessa's mouth fell open, and Sano scurried back to investigate but she shooed him away. They each took one, plopping the small pastries in their mouth with one bite.

"By gods," gasped Lessa, closing her eyes as she savored the delectable treat. "This is the sweetest thing I've ever tasted!"

"*Mmm…* It's like biting into a cloud," squealed Arianna in delight as she licked her fingers of the crumbs. Both girls fell into a fit of sugar-induced giggles, reaching for more.

"Can you please pass the water?" said Arianna, nodding to the silver carafe Cyn had left for them. "I'll grab us some glasses." She ran into the well room and pulled two copper goblets from the cabinet, then she set them on the table.

As Lessa tilted the carafe, a dark red liquid scented like

honey and bark dripped into the first goblet.

"*Oh?*" she said, just as surprised as Arianna to see that whatever was in the carafe was, in fact, *not* water. "I think this will be the real surprise." She grabbed for the other goblet and filled it to the brim before pushing it over to Arianna.

Arianna sniffed at the drink, wrinkling her nose in suspicion. "What... is it?" She recognized the smell but couldn't quite place it.

Lessa looked at her with a dumbfounded expression. "Why, it's wine!" she exclaimed. "I've seen Talis drink it plenty to know, but I've never been allowed a taste. He said I was already 'pampered' enough as it was and denied it to me." She rolled her big blue eyes.

"Well, he wasn't wrong," chided Arianna, recalling the charming room where she'd slept.

She stared into the deep red of the drink, thinking it looked quite a lot like blood. She'd tasted enough of that already and didn't like the idea of drinking it out of a goblet. She shuddered at such a thought.

Maybe this is more to Grinda Risso's taste.

And then, Arianna remembered that wine, like whiskey, ale, malt and a number of other brews, was only meant for the tongues of elders, only meant for citizens of the Olleb. The thought of tasting such a thing *before* passing the Free Falls was strangely empowering. "I've never tried it before, either," she said, mulling over this realization. "But... I suppose there's a first time for everything." She held her cup to the air as she'd seen the elders do before, feeling inspired.

Lessa clinked her goblet to Arianna's. "Cheers," she said with a big smile, repeating a word that was typically announced before the first drink. Then, they both took their very first swig of wine.

Arianna couldn't help but notice that neither of them had

felt inclined to say the phrase she'd heard the elders customarily shout after—Cheers… *to the King!*

Arianna pushed the thought from her mind as it swirled with dangerous desires and touched the cup again to her lips, sipping at it cautiously to start. The wine went down smoothly, quenching a different kind of thirst. She lifted the glass and drank more, the liquid making her tingle from the inside out.

"Now I see why all the fuss," said Arianna with a satisfied smirk. Lessa nodded emphatically, and they both reached for more, letting the wine wash away their worries.

"So, tell me," said Lessa after a short while, "who *did* the regulators blame for the deaths of those two that Solomon killed?" Her eyebrows lifted as she crossed her legs, visibly anxious to get some information.

Arianna blanched, almost choking on the food she was chewing. She grabbed for her wine and threw the rest of it back in one gulp, trying to wash away the foul memory. For a week, she'd been trying to process the events that had transpired the night she had snuck away to the Healer's District. The memories still sat clear and fresh in her mind, trapping her in that horrific scene. It was all she could do to distract herself from them—she could feel the shiver that had run down her spine when Akias searched for the letter. And Das' unsettling voice still rang in her ears as he threatened her life with his sword. Even the blood—it still stung her nose as they fell before her eyes, dead by Solomon's hand.

Alas, Lessa's question discomforted Arianna even more so than that of her vivid recollections.

Who did they blame? Who had suffered on her behalf? Who had they killed instead of Solomon?

Lessa poured Arianna some more wine from the carafe—Cyn had seemingly left them a never-ending supply to pair with their sweets. "I'm sorry. I shouldn't have brought it up," she said, picking at her food.

"No… it's all right. You should know. Solomon wanted me to tell you," said Arianna, tracing the brim of her goblet with her finger. The wine really *did* look like blood. "It's just that I knew the girl. We were roommates, actually." She tried to swallow the lump in her throat, but it wouldn't budge. "Her name was Pippa."

As Arianna relayed the terrible events from the week prior, starting from when Akias and Das had caught her red-handed, Lessa cringed at the detail, clinging to every word.

"… Then, when Solomon returned back to his house that night, he explained what would happen next," continued Arianna, her voice falling to a whisper. "He told me that the general had already declared the murderer by the time he'd arrived at the gathering at the Square and that she would be severely punished." She studied her hands. "You see, just moments before Das and Akias were discovered dead, another regulator, Regulator Mundar, had made a find of his own and had already alerted General Ivo."

"What did he find?" asked Lessa, leaning in and almost spilling the contents of her wine.

"Not what… *who*," said Arianna. "Another girl, Pippa, had also snuck out after curfew that night. She was apprehended in the Dining Hall, a building very close to where I was with Das and Akias." She remembered how odd she thought it was that the doors to the Dining Hall had been ajar that night. "Apparently, Pippa tried to run and might've gotten away, but by that time, the whole force was out hunting for a slave out of bed. They were looking for *me*, and so they caught her easily." Arianna laid her head and arms across the table. "Solomon said she swore that it wasn't her who'd killed those men and that she didn't have anything to do with the letter or Healer's District, and of course *we* know she didn't, but the evidence against her was unquestionable. They even found blood on her hands and cloak!"

"Really? But she clearly didn't kill those regulators, so… whose blood was it?" asked Lessa, scratching her head.

Arianna just shrugged her shoulders. "My thoughts exactly," she said, "but it's irrelevant now. All the evidence was there. Of course, Solomon tried to make General Ivo see reason. The possibility that an inexperienced girl like Pippa could've bested two strong regulators is ridiculous."

"He just wouldn't rationalize, then?" said Lessa, trying to understand.

"No, he wouldn't," said Arianna, her remorse threatening to break her. "And it wasn't just about the murders, it was about Pippa somehow arranging a meeting with a healer-slave, which is maybe seen as an even worse crime. In any case, General Ivo isn't a very *rational* person. He rules by making examples of people with any excuse, so he deemed Pippa at fault for the murders and had her tortured for days before he threw her to the Pit, just to prove a point."

Arianna stifled a sob, and Lessa stared off toward the fire.

"Talis said the regulators are all still dumbfounded about our letter," said Lessa. "Sounds like if they don't find me, they'll try to forget anything even happened."

"But something did happen. Pippa died." Arianna balled her hands into fists. "It's all my fault!" she shouted. She banged her fists on the table, and their drinks sloshed onto the wood. "She was my… my *friend.*"

Arianna couldn't control the painful emotions threatening to overcome her now while Pippa zigzagged through her thoughts. She squeezed her eyes shut and covered her ears as her friend's faint, tortured screams reverberated through her head. For almost a week she'd had to endure this heart-wrenching sound coming from the Square—it was a sound that she would never forget. Feeling as if the wine had messed with her mind and tapped into a corner of it that she'd desperately tried to block out, at that moment, Arianna began to weep uncontrollably for the pain poor Pippa must've felt.

"Solomon said the regulators made a show out of her torture in vengeance for their fallen officials," she said through clipped breaths. "I was glad to be holed up in these chambers then. I didn't have to watch. Still, though, I heard the screaming." Nobody in the district could've blocked out that sound.

Arianna's chest constricted with agony as her heart pounded through the pain. And she tasted salt, so much salt, as tears ran down her cheeks and wet her lips. It was as if she'd never cried before. Lessa laid a consoling hand on hers, allowing her to shed her grief.

"On the way to the caverns today to meet you, I passed by her final resting place," she said, finding a sudden calm. "I could barely stand to look." An image of the ravaged girl at the bottom of the Pit consumed Arianna—every part of Pippa's body had been visible, in excruciating detail. Her pale, blue eyes bulged from her head, and her hair was matted with blood.

It's all my fault.

Never again would she hear Pippa's sweet lullaby coaxing her nightmares away.

She died because of me.

Never again would she have to withstand the droning lectures of her caring friend when she cut curfew too close. But, oh, how she wished she would.

She didn't deserve this.

"During our last encounter I even… I *yelled* at her," said Arianna, shaking her head, disgusted with herself. A deep chasm of regret formed like a stone in her gut.

The two girls sat in silence for a long time thereafter, sipping wine and picking at their food. All the while, Arianna tried to replace the image of the girl in the Pit with a Pippa she remembered—as a beautiful, kind soul soaring over some great sea, forever free like that lucky bird in the song she held so dear.

"This isn't your fault," said Lessa, softly. "It was just… a *horrible* coincidence. Even if no regulators had been found dead, she would've still been caught and punished. You know that. She was out past curfew with blood on her hands. She would've been sentenced to death regardless of your actions." Lessa glanced again to the fire, seeming to disappear in its flames. "It's the King's law that killed your friend. This is *his* world, and she broke his rules and got caught. The only thing you're at fault for is maybe too much luck on your side." She looked her in the eyes then. "Arianna, we're so *lucky*. But don't blame yourself for this. It's much too big a burden."

Arianna averted her eyes to the table, staring at the key Cyn had accidentally left with their tray of food.

"I suppose," she said in barely a whisper. "I just wonder why Pippa was even out past curfew in the first place. It wasn't like her. She was always so punctual and obedient."

A dark thought crossed her mind, a clue that dangled in her memories. For now, she chose to ignore it; she had enough on her plate without adding to the pile, but she knew it'd be there when she was ready.

Taking a deep breath, Arianna wiped away the evidence of her tears. "Come on," she said to Lessa. "I want to show you the rest of your new home." She drummed her fingers on the table near the food tray before shifting the key into her pocket.

"I like how you think!" said Lessa, beaming up at Arianna.

"And grab your bow," she added, trying to put on a happy face. "It should be safe enough now to show you the grounds. There aren't sleeping quarters near here, and the regulators will be patrolling elsewhere."

Lessa stood, quick to follow Arianna as she collected her twin swords. "Sano, don't cause any trouble!" she called.

They walked to the unlocked door of the sparring room and threw it wide open.

AFTER ENSURING NOBODY WAS IN EARSHOT, Arianna walked along the grounds with Lessa at her heels, explaining the routines of a warrior-slave. As she talked, she permitted the fresh air to wash away her troubles, to momentarily let her mind be free of thoughts of Pippa. The breeze bounced back and forth between the high walls of the Dueling Arena, whistling around the architecture which seemed to be inspired by Blancoren itself.

"It's a jar within the Jar," Lessa noted before looking toward the sky. "It's quite something, huh? Definitely nice to see at least one familiar face."

Arianna tilted her head back, following Lessa's gaze. She saw the moon, a full, bright globe of orange light, and had never witnessed so many stars dotting the night before—never seen the sky so clearly. "Yeah…" she whispered. "It is."

As they looked on, the sky suddenly rewarded them with something even more spectacular.

"Look there!" said Lessa, pointing up.

Arianna gaped as a blazing trail ran across the sky, a giant star seeming to soar through the night, tiring of its sedentary life and searching for adventure. "It's as if the gods have lit it on fire," she said, holding her breath while it passed.

As it slashed the darkness open, like a sword made of light, Arianna wished desperately for such a power. She'd never before seen something so mysterious nor beautiful in all her life.

"Do you think so?" asked Lessa, a strange expression crossing her face. "Maybe it's running from something. Or maybe it was made of fire to begin with and just learned how to fly."

Arianna smiled. "Whatever the case, I hope it will survive." They watched until the fiery star fell out of sight behind the walls of the Blancoren Mountains, darkness shrouding them once more.

After setting her swords on the ground, Arianna tossed a quiver of arrows to Lessa. "I want a rematch," she said.

Nocking an arrow on her bow without a second thought, Lessa let it fly through the air, too close to Arianna's head.

"Are you mad!" she whispered, frantically, ducking out of the way. "I've had enough near-death experiences, if you don't mind." She whirled around to see where the arrow had landed, and it vibrated dead center of a target a few feet away.

"I'm sorry," said Lessa. "You seem to be a bit disgruntled. Would you like another demonstration?"

Arianna pivoted, expecting to see Lessa, but instead found another arrow breezing past overhead. It split the first one clean down the middle, the wood curled and splintered.

"What the—" Her mouth dropped open.

"Over here," said Lessa, tapping her on the shoulder from behind. Arianna jumped, sending Lessa into a fit of laughter.

"Gloat much?" she scoffed, hands on her hips.

Lessa couldn't breathe through her laughter, just nodding in confirmation.

"Well, I admit, you are *pretty* good with your weapon," replied Arianna, conceding to the fun.

"Many thanks," replied Lessa with a low, mocking bow.

Arianna unsheathed her dagger. With a flick of her wrist, she sent it flying in Lessa's direction, missing her only slightly—*and* intentionally. It sliced through the air and landed on the same nearby target with a thud.

"Call it a tie?" said Arianna, unable to hide her smirk.

"I suppose I haven't got a choice!" They shook hands, amused at the competition. "So, are these just for show?" asked

Lessa as she gestured to the swords at their feet.

"Not at all," said Arianna. She bent down, resting her hands on the hilts of her weapons. And, in the blink of an eye, she spun around in a whirl of red robes, locking Lessa's neck between the two blades, careful not to graze her skin.

Lessa froze, wide-eyed and gaping.

"I have my tricks as well," said Arianna. "I've been practicing for the Free Falls with these ever since I can remember. I hope they don't fail me when the time comes." A dark, brooding cloud of worry suddenly hovered over the fun as she let the swords swing down at her sides.

"Don't worry," said Lessa, quite serious. "I'll be there cheering you on. You'll be competing for both of us now."

"So, have *you* ever handled a sword?" asked Arianna, trying to steer her thoughts in a different direction.

Lessa shook her head.

"That changes tonight. You can't be in the Warrior's District having never held a blade." Arianna dropped the swords to her feet and gathered up two wooden ones which had been left discarded on the grounds. She tossed one to Lessa, who didn't hesitate to catch it.

"Shall I call you master, then?" she said, smiling as she tied her golden locks into a ponytail at the top of her head, before setting aside her bow and removing her cloak.

"If it pleases you!" Arianna laughed. She removed her cloak as well and began to circle Lessa, sword raised.

"Now, bend your knees and steady your sword, like *this*," she commanded. "You must be firmly grounded so you can have complete control. I'm going to test your stance." Arianna slammed her sword down on Lessa's without much warning.

Lessa wobbled at the weight but then found her balance, copying Arianna's instruction.

"Good," said Arianna, nodding. "Again?"

"Again!" said Lessa, flying forward.

Splinters of wood whizzed in all directions when their swords collided, and sweat drenched their skin as they trained through the night.

For exactly what, though, they were uncertain.

18

TRUTH BE TOLD

THE GIRLS UNDRESSED AND WASHED for bed in the wee hours of the morning, worn out from the night's activities.

"What's that there?" asked Arianna.

"What's what where?" Lessa said, turning her head from side to side, looking for something amiss.

"That, there on your neck." Arianna pointed at her back.

"Oh, it's just a scar from when I fell from the tree."

"I've never seen a silver scar before. How could a wound heal like that?" Arianna leaned closer to get a better look. The mark on Lessa coiled in a spiral of silver, as if the trim of an elder's cloak had been stitched to her skin.

"Your guess is as good as mine," she replied with a shrug.

Sano appeared on her shoulder. He curled his tail around her neckline, covering the scar from view. As Sano's bright orange eyes flicked between them, Arianna became once again transfixed by the creature. She still couldn't believe something so small and gentle had given her such a fright before.

What kind of warrior is afraid of a monkey, of all things? She would never ask that thought aloud.

Lessa dropped her voice to a whisper, stealing a nervous glance over to a table in the far corner of the room, one covered in parchments and scrolls. "I notice Talis gave you some reading material as well," she said. "What did you… think of all that?"

"I honestly don't know," replied Arianna, tersely, scurrying away to pretend to be occupied with cleaning up the food.

What did she have to do to let this topic leave her be?

Taking the hint, Lessa didn't press her for more information, thankfully, but Arianna was certain Talis had told her the same bizarre stories.

Magical, unfathomable stories.

"Solomon will surely have our heads for staying up all night," said Arianna with a yawn, a headache from too many sweets and greedy portions of wine already forming. "Let's get some rest and talk more of it tomorrow."

She knew she couldn't ignore her forever.

"Sure thing," said Lessa. "Oh, and don't forget to lock the door. Otherwise they'll be suspicious of us."

"Good thinking," said Arianna, fishing the key out of the pocket of her robes which now hung on a hook at the wall. She walked over to the door and locked it from the inside.

Then, she led Lessa into the well room where they were to share the single bed normally meant for healing. It was toasty warm in the room when they entered, the small fireplace in the corner doing wonders to heat the space. Arianna silently thanked Solomon for getting it ready for them before he'd left.

"It will be just like sleeping in the barracks again!" said Lessa, clearly amused as she hopped under the covers.

"Lovely." Arianna grimaced. "I just missed sharing my sleeping quarters *so* much." She slid in next to her, glad at least that the bed was plenty big enough for the both of them to lie comfortably. She slipped the key under one of the pillows. "For safekeeping," she added.

Lessa smiled. "In all honesty, though," she said, eyes drooping, "it really is nice to have a friend."

Sano curled cozily at the foot of the bed.

"Yeah," mumbled Arianna, "it really is."

"RISE AND SHINE, LADIES!" Solomon bellowed at the top of his lungs as he swung open the door to the well room and pulled back the curtain from the window. Daylight flooded into the chamber, piercing the pleasant darkness.

Arianna groaned, pulling the covers up over her eyes.

"Good morning!" she heard Lessa sing.

"*Arghh…*" Had she been informed that Lessa was a morning person, she might've fought against this sleeping arrangement. Arianna peeked out from the blankets, feeling like she had only just drifted to sleep. She rubbed at her eyes, as they adjusted to the bright light, and sat up. Through the doorway of the well room, she could see Solomon, Cyn, and Lessa all hovered over a hearty breakfast of eggs, bacon, and bread.

She sniffed the delicious air. "Okay, I'm up!" she said, throwing the covers aside and dragging her feet into the other room to join them. It wasn't every day that fresh food like this was given to her.

"Morning, dear. Here, have some breakfast," said Cyn with a warm smile as she offered her a chair. "Hurry, before Solomon eats it all." Arianna looked from Cyn to Lessa and back, unsure of how to act.

Does she know? What has Solomon told her to explain

Lessa after last night?

"Relax, Ara!" said Solomon in a more jovial mood than usual. "I've told Cyn everything she *needs* to know." So, not everything. Arianna rolled her eyes. "Sit down and eat. We've a long day ahead of us."

With a plop, she dropped into the chair meant for her and reached for a cup of water before chugging it down; water had *never* tasted so good than on this morning. She groaned again, squinting her eyes as her head gave a sharp throb. Then, she started in on the bread, relishing every warm, soft bite.

I could certainly get used to this.

"Could you be more of a slob?" gasped Cyn, wagging her fork at Solomon as he shoveled his mouth full of food. Scraps fell to her lap and Sano leaped after them, making her squeal in amusement.

Before Solomon could retort, Arianna chimed in to save herself from an even worse headache. "What have you planned for us today, Master Bell?" she asked.

"Well, you and I still have to pack in a lot of training before the festivals," he said. He turned his attention to Lessa. "And I believe Talis has left you some lessons as well? This will be no time to slack." He raised his eyebrow at her while he shoved another forkful into his mouth.

"Yes, of course he did," replied Lessa, less than enthused.

She'd learn quickly that Solomon was probably just as much a stickler as Talis had been when it came to training—it wouldn't matter to him that Lessa was a stowaway from the Healer's District. He wasn't one to permit slacking under his watch.

"If you're all going to start poking swords at each other again, I think I'll be off now," said Cyn, getting to her feet. "I have business to attend to in the Well Center later, so I've left you some other provisions to carry throughout the day."

"Thank you!" said Arianna, her mouth full.

"It's my pleasure, dear," she said with a grin that made the skin around her eyes wrinkle.

They all waved goodbye to Cyn, cleared their plates, and set to work. Arianna started off with a warm-up stretch to work out the dull ache that had set in her muscles after practicing last night with Lessa and to wake herself up.

"With barely a month 'til the festivals, you'll have to train doubly hard," said Solomon, doing the same.

Arianna nearly fell out of her form. "Where did the time go?" She ran her hands through her hair, and they tangled in the messy morning curls.

"Don't worry. You're already ready. I just need to tweak you a bit," said Solomon with a nod, hands on his hips as he looked her up and down. "Shall we begin?"

He invited her into the sparring space.

With a heavy sigh, Arianna glanced at Lessa—she was dutifully unpacking her rucksack. Leaving Sano to his own devices as he bounced about the room, she placed a number of strange mixtures on a table near the back wall. There were a few jars holding some kind of red liquid and a sticky, white paste that she began to carefully measure out in doses. Lessa tossed them all in an empty bowl, added water and then prodded them with a wooden mixing tool; the contents smoked in her face, making her cough loudly.

Arianna balked as a rancid smell immediately filled the air.

"Everything all right over there?" called Solomon, pinching his nostrils shut. "That doesn't smell like healing to me."

"Yeah," she grumbled, narrowing her eyes at the pot. "I just used the wrong measurements, is all."

Lessa didn't even look his way, clearly engrossed in what she was doing; she unfurled a parchment from her bag, scanned the words, and attempted the experiment again, humming something as she went—words Arianna couldn't place.

"Let's go, Ara!" barked Solomon from across the room,

seizing her attention. "I hope you're prepared. I'm feeling very alert today." He twisted her swords at his side much too energetically for her liking.

She slumped, not sure how she was going to make it through the morning, head throbbing as it was, and she internally cursed the elders for inventing such a deceitfully poisonous drink in the first place—But, oh, it had been *delicious.*

"Aren't I always? I just need a minute," she said, trying to mentally equip herself for what was sure to be an excruciatingly long day.

Swords in hand, she sauntered over to Solomon on the sparring floor. Behind him, the painting of the Warrior's Crest glimmered on the wall as an annoying reminder that the Free Falls Festivals were coming—whether she was ready or not. And, this morning especially, Arianna felt the opposite of prepared.

I'm no warrior yet.

Solomon seemed not to notice how out of sorts she was today. Or, maybe, he just didn't care. He rolled out a large mat and beckoned her forward with the point of one of his magnificent swords.

They started slow, just loosening up now with an established routine.

Thrust, parry, step back, step forward. Thrust again.

Swordplay was a practiced dance, a duet between the participants. And this daily warm-up—not worrying about defending against attacks, not trying to draw blood, no winner and *no* yielding—was easily Arianna's favorite part of training with Solomon; it allowed her to really enjoy the art of dueling and to truly appreciate the weapons as an extension of herself. The swords kissed and she heard music. Her arms ached and she felt alive. Outside of her utopia, these moments were indeed her happiest… on a normal day at least.

"You're slow today, Ara," said Solomon, his voice reproving as he lunged again. She stepped back, trying to hide the wobble in her leg as his next move took her by surprise.

The goal during this exercise was to free her mind of what she *thought* he might do and instead feel with her weapon and see with her eyes what he *would* do. Solomon had spent years coaching Arianna to really listen with her whole self during a duel. The tiniest movement of the body—a flick of the wrist, the turn of a hip, the angle of a foot, the height of an elbow, the tilt of a blade, even an expression—could reveal an opponent's next move. And catching a critical detail could be the difference between life and death on a real battlefield.

"I'm just a little tired this morning," she said, matching his footsteps and turning her blade to meet his, over and over. She mimicked his movements as best she could, but right now her best was not even near to passable for Solomon's standards.

After a while, he lowered his weapons with an exasperated sigh. "Well, then, let's get on with it," he said, a bite to his tone. "There's no use with this part of training if you're not focused."

"Sorry," she mumbled, tucking her hair behind her ears.

"Take your position," he ordered. "And remember to use the meditation phrases you've learned. They'll help you concentrate your attacks and make your mind stronger. And clearly you need some help with that this morning."

Arianna nodded, trying not to let him see her skepticism as she readied herself for a real swordfight. In her opinion, the *meditation* words he spoke of did quite the opposite of what he envisioned; they made her lose focus when she let them slip into her mind instead of concentrate on her form. She tended to avoid them altogether when she practiced on her own or with her friends, but Solomon would never let her get away with that during duels with him.

"What's the objective today?" she asked.

"Why don't we keep it simple," he said after a moment of deliberation. "One sword each." He set one of his own aside. "And just try to stay alive. First one with a blade to the throat or heart loses." Arianna pouted, placing one of her swords back in the barrel.

She never, *ever* won against Solomon during this 'simple' type of exercise and more often than not ended up with Cyn having to fix her up at the end. She wished she'd just suggested something herself. Arianna best enjoyed the training sessions where the aim was to knock the opponent out of a designated area or to see who could hold on to their sword for the longest without losing grip; she at least stood a chance against Solomon in those types of spars and could gain some points.

This is really not my day.

The clang of metal on metal rang loud throughout the room as their weapons smashed together, relentlessly. Solomon whirled around the mat like a thundering wind trapped in a bottle, bringing his sword down with all the strength he had, each and every time. It was like he knew she was weathering the effects of no sleep and too much wine and wanted to make her pay for it. At one point, she thought her arm might snap off from the effort it took to block him when he struck.

"Better," said Solomon. "Try that again, but don't dawdle after you land a strike. That's the time to attack harder."

She found herself on the floor again; Arianna got back to her feet, gritting her teeth.

Solomon laughed. "Look who's awake now!"

He ran at her again, sword raised, but this time she didn't play into his hand and instead evaded his attack, returning him a swift kick to the stomach. He buckled backward, but he took her down with him when he fell, trapping her foot with his free hand.

Arianna was staring up at the ceiling again.

Rolling to the side, she had to release the grip on her sword to get enough leverage to free herself from his hold. She scrambled to her feet with a grunt, and raised her fists.

Solomon copied her, also leaving his sword on the floor.

"All right, then," he said. "Come and get me!" They began to circle each other, weaponless now.

Arianna's fists came down hard on his chest, his arms, his stomach—but he blocked, and blocked, and blocked. Sometimes she was dizzied by how fast he was. Even without a sword to aid him. Even for his age.

Master Solomon Bell, Wolf of the East.

He lived up to his name.

Arianna ducked just as he swung another iron fist at her. She was fast too, though, and could hold her ground during hand-to-hand combat with Solomon, could actually land some hits. But they were never disabling. He, on the other hand, with all those muscles, could knock her out cold with just one punch in the right spot.

Jumping in the air, Arianna tried a spinning kick to catch him off guard, but, of course, he deflected it. Again, she landed on her back with an embarrassing thud. She caught Lessa's expression from the corner of her eye, wincing at the sound… or was it at her disastrous showcase of a training session? She just closed her eyes for a moment, pretending not to care.

"We're not done yet, Ara. Stand up and pick up your sword," he commanded, as he went to scoop up his own sword.

Arianna did as he said and then they were at it again, every collision of their blades making her want to crawl back to bed.

"*Luzcora!*" shouted Solomon, midair, just before another strike of his blade. The blow knocked Arianna clean off her feet, sparks sizzling off his sword. "Use the *words*," he said, now fully channeling his master warrior mindset.

She staggered to her feet, bracing herself for another attack before she'd barely found her balance. Sweat dripped into her eyes, her throat burned for more water, and her head felt on the brink of combustion—each strike of his sword like someone taking a hot needle to her brain.

"*Luzcora…*" She spat his words back at him, but they felt silly coming out of her mouth and did nothing for her position. Evading another thrust of his sword, she lunged for his middle. He guarded well, spinning so that his elbow caught her in the ribs.

Arianna hunched over from the sudden pain, unable to hide her irritation anymore. "*Luzcora,*" she growled again after regaining composure. She lunged forward with everything she had, but even she knew the move had been sloppy.

Solomon danced around her with ease, his bad knee doing nothing to ail him; catching Arianna's strike, he sent it back tenfold. Their swords hissed as they crashed together, again and again, and she'd had just about enough as she kept taking on most of the shock.

"Why must I use these words if you barely do?" she said, throwing her sword to the ground and resting her hands on her knees to catch her breath.

Solomon was clearly taken aback from her abrupt forfeit of the duel. Arianna could tell she'd struck a nerve with him now, but she stubbornly held her ground.

"They're all in here," he said, tapping his forehead. "It takes time to master that, though. Don't worry, your power will grow."

"But why should I say these words at all? They don't make me feel stronger," said Arianna. She shook her head, vexed. "They don't make any sense. They don't *mean* anything."

"Because you have no faith!" roared Solomon.

The weight of his words took Arianna by such surprise that she jumped back. Flicking her eyes to Lessa, she saw Solomon had caught her attention as well.

The room stilled, quiet save for the firepit that was forever crackling and the echo of his voice between the walls.

Yet, even in the face of such anger from her master, Arianna's tongue seemed to have a mind of its own. "How can I have faith in a word?" Her voice trembled, no louder than a whisper.

A guttural sound escaped from Solomon then, and he threw down his sword in a rage. Arianna wanted to take back her question, fearing that he might cut her tongue out and toss it to the fire, but reality wouldn't permit that. It seemed everything she did lately let Solomon down.

"I *mean*, you have no faith in anything!" he said, throwing his hands up. "I'm tired of waiting for you to come around. The meditation words are *spells*, Arianna. All this time I've been training you, teaching you, I've been lacing your mind with knowledge of magic, and it's about time you accepted these things for what they truly are." He began to pace in front of her, looking at the floor as if he were struggling with whether or not to continue.

All the air felt as if it had been pounded from her body, and Arianna stood frozen. This subject just wouldn't leave her in peace. It stalked her now and forever, no matter how much she tried to avoid it.

"I wield my weapons alongside knowledge of magic, and so shall you!" added Solomon as if the declaration had been tearing at his skull for years.

Had it?

Arianna stayed silent, but her mind spun with questions.

The meditation words are… spells?

She tried even wrapping her head around the word 'spells.' All this time, years of training, she thought them merely expressions to help her concentration as Solomon had described.

He lied?

Arianna trusted him with everything.

I don't trust him with this.

She felt betrayed, lost as her world swayed.

Solomon turned away from her, unable to meet her eyes anymore. He took a deep, long breath, clasping his hands behind his back as he stared at the painting of the golden snake and swords, studying the serpent that entangled the shining, scorching blades.

"Every exercise I've ever taught you in order to enhance your strength, both physical and mental—they all have double meanings," he said. "You're my apprentice in body and soul, sword *and* magic. Why can't you see this?" His words came sharp, his voice soft. "I've tried to let you discover this gradually, on your own, but time is not on our side, Ara. You must open your eyes to the truth, for what a waste if you don't."

Arianna didn't realize at first that her mouth had gone dry and that she hadn't blinked for quite some time. Then, the shriek of shattering glass snapped her awake. She turned and found Lessa with shaking hands, staring at them from across the room.

"And you," Solomon said, spinning around to face the young healer with an accusatory finger. "Why, your master is also a sorcerer. And a fine one at that! Or don't you already know?" Lessa lowered her gaze to the table as Sano curled protectively in her lap. "Those medicines you brew are full of magical qualities, and the words I hear you whisper while you stir are equally charmed. Olleb-Yelfra *is* enchanted, ladies, in ways you can't even begin to imagine. King Devlindor, try as he might, can never bleed her heart dry."

His words ripped through their world, but Arianna still couldn't fully comprehend them as she searched for anything to grasp onto and make sense of. His statements kept sliding through her mind, one after the other, incomprehensible.

Afraid Solomon might lunge at her in his fury, she walked away from the sparring area and near to Lessa. Never before had she witnessed her master so impassioned, so *impatient,* about her ability to understand something—or lack thereof. And with talk of such a subject, to accept such treasonous, imaginative notions as reality… she didn't think his reaction fair.

Since Talis had entered her life, bringing with him these outlandish assertions about magic and whatnot, Solomon had been willing to accept that she just still didn't know how to believe. How could he expect her to truly consider such stories as truth after the life she'd lived? How had he?

Solomon had only encouraged her to study the material Talis had left and learn for herself—but every word she'd read thus far was foreign. None of it fit in with the tangible world she'd always known, and she wanted to forget it completely.

"Magic is of this world," said Solomon, finding his calm as he looked them both in the eyes. "Open your minds. Can't you recall a time or place when something inexplicable has happened to you? If you can't, then I'll never mention this subject again." His voice came softer now, pleading. "But I *know* you can."

Arianna tried to look away, but she couldn't. Her mind surged, rolling through her memories, unbidden images and indescribable feelings whipping across her mind—the inexplicable force drawing her to the hot springs in the jade tunnels long ago, and the day Solomon chose her as his apprentice, handing her the priceless dagger; her mind spun even more, and she followed a shimmering light back to life after Grinda Risso had bested her. Lessa was there, too, a healer-slave standing by her side in the Warrior's District, watching a star blaze a path through a dark sky.

Her eyes focused back to reality, locking in on the ghost girl she'd found beneath the tunnels. Arianna noticed she rubbed at the mysterious, silver mark on the back of her neck, a testimony to her strange luck after surviving such a fall. But Sano—Lessa gazed at him—he was certainly one of the best and biggest mysteries of them all.

Solomon observed them closely as they dug into their pasts, not hiding his desperation that they understand. "These remarkable gifts are all pieces of the world I speak of," he said, drawing their attention back to him. "Can't you see that?"

"Why do you and Master Churry leave us with only a sliver of information and then expect us to believe?" asked Lessa, her voice cracking. "All we want is to… survive, and it seems like you're making a joke of it. Be straight. What is it *exactly* that you want us to consider?"

Solomon opened his mouth to speak but Arianna interrupted, finding courage to face her master now that Lessa had spoken up.

"Master Churry tells me he's a sorcerer, and now you say you're training us in *spells*," she said. Her hands gestured everywhere in a jumble, mirroring her thoughts. "Do you really mean to say that all these strange things that have happened to us are due to magic? And that somehow the King has tried to hide its existence from us?" She closed her eyes, pressing her hands to her head. "You realize how absurd this all sounds, don't you? What does magic even truly mean? Explain that, *plainly*, and then maybe we'll listen!" She folded her arms across her chest, feeling all the heat rise to her face.

"Magic has no… true definition," said Solomon with a furrowed brow. "One who wields magic defines it for him- or herself."

He began to fidget uncomfortably as the situation spiraled, Lessa and Arianna both now making demands of their own.

"Okay, well, why us, then? Why tell us this now?" asked Arianna, not accepting another vague answer. The questions flew from her lips without her approval, but she was tired of being in the dark about so many things.

"Please, just tell us what's going on. What are you both keeping from us?" added Lessa. "Talk of magic is punishable by death. And I know Master Churry wouldn't risk his life, risk *mine*, for no good reason."

"Do you now? Then I suppose the reason must be quite good," answered Solomon, cocking his head to the side as he studied her. Lessa's lips clamped tight.

"There must be something more you aren't telling us," said Arianna. "Why did you choose me? What exactly are you training me for?"

"You know why I chose you. Don't you remember?" She peered back to the day they first met.

'I chose you because you are worth choosing.'

Her head throbbed even more. "But… for what?" Tears of frustration clouded her vision, but she wouldn't let them fall. "Why have you risked so much for me? Master, *please*, just—"

As if a realization had suddenly dawned on him, Solomon shrank back from the bombardment of questions, waving his hands in the air. "No," he said, firmly. "I won't say anything further now. I'm so sorry, girls. This wasn't the right moment. I… I just lost my patience." He ran his hand across his head, clearly conflicted with something. "One day, soon, I promise you'll come to understand everything fully. Just know that you can trust me, Ara." He glanced to Lessa. "And you can trust Talis." He donned his robes and moved toward the door faster than a whistling wind. "Keep practicing… *all* that we've taught you."

Solomon slipped out of the sparring room before another question could be asked. Arianna and Lessa gaped at each other when he was gone, each with no more answers than the other. Thus, they went about their lessons, separately, deep in thought.

"LUNCH?" SAID ARIANNA, having not a single ounce of energy left to keep terrorizing the sword pell in the corner.

Lessa mumbled her agreement, and they went to prepare the meals Cyn had left.

"What were you taught of magic in your district?" asked Arianna, confronting the matter on her mind.

"I was taught that magic is just a fabrication thought up by people who became overwhelmed by their imaginations, people who never made good citizens of the Olleb," said Lessa, reciting the words as if reading a script. "The only reason that we're privileged to know the word at all is simply to challenge any gossip or tales that still linger. Not that it seems to be working. *Hail* King Devlindor." She rolled her eyes. "You?"

"Quite similar." A laugh escaped her lips, but then she turned serious. "I think Talis healed me somehow, you know. I was beyond repair, yet here I am. No medicine or master healer should've been able to save me," said Arianna. "Nothing could have. I know enough to know that for certain. By gods, I had a sword in my stomach!" She placed her hand over where Grinda's life-ending strike had landed.

"Yes, he told me so," said Lessa, expressionless as she stared off into her own thoughts. "He said he used magic… that he was a *sorcerer*."

"He told me the same thing." Arianna didn't know what to feel.

"It just doesn't seem possible," said Lessa, studying the ceiling, a low chandelier of withered candles hanging above their heads. "But… what if it is?" She looked back at Arianna, scratching Sano behind the ears as he lay across her neck. "What reason would they have to lie, to put their lives on the line like this?"

Arianna shrugged. "And if it was real, and this magic *somehow* played a part in giving me back my life, then is it even so bad? What else is it capable of? Where is its place in this world?" Her musings took her into a different headspace, one that had no place anywhere in Olleb-Yelfra under King Devlindor's rule. "I wish I knew more about the past." She sighed. "Talis said many things that night about it… about what the King had done—" No, she couldn't think like this.

It felt odd, terrifying, to yearn for so many answers when not so long ago Arianna never even had questions. Her world had become so complicated in such a short amount of time. She thought of the educators spoon-feeding them the knowledge they would need to survive in the real world, if they made it that far. Until now, it had never occurred to her that there could be more than their wisdom—more to… *this.*

"The night I came here, Talis sat me down in his study beforehand and told me of his belief in magic," said Lessa with a far-off gaze. "He told me that with it he'd healed you and that this choice, destiny he called it, had intertwined us forever—you, me, Solomon, himself." She trailed off, trying to articulate her thoughts. "I had always hoped there was more to life, but I truly wasn't expecting this much excitement." She smiled, and an expression like wonder played on her face.

Arianna said nothing, taken by surprise at her friend's assessment of all this bizarre information.

"He wouldn't lie to me. Solomon's right. I *do* trust Talis, even if I'm not quite sure with what yet," added Lessa. "But there's obviously a lot more to what they've told us than we realize, and I wish they'd just come out and say it."

Arianna stared at her, dumbfounded.

"Excitement?" she said, tasting the word. Suddenly, she felt her heart pump with the same enthusiasm as it had when she'd set off on her first real adventure to the Healer's District. "I guess this is quite exciting, isn't it? I mean, whether magic's real or not, life just got a whole lot more interesting. Especially with meeting you by such chance."

"Like I said before," said Lessa with a smirk, "we're lucky."

Something sparked within Arianna then. Maybe Solomon's words finally sank in or Lessa's trust in her master gave her the courage she needed to fully trust her own. Maybe the weight of it all was just too much to deny in the end. She didn't know, and it didn't matter—at that moment, she let her mind open wide, changing her beliefs forever.

Just like that, all the wisdom Solomon and Talis had been trying to impart morphed into a reality that Arianna had been trying to shut out. So many possibilities cascaded into her mind, and now she wished she'd paid them more attention before. The girls found themselves enraptured in talks of these magical secrets, contemplating old memories in a different light. In an instant, their glum worlds exploded with life. They believed in *magic*.

Or, at the very least, they would try to validate their masters' theories about magic, giving Talis and Solomon the benefit of the doubt they deserved.

"All of those scrolls Talis left here, have you looked through them?" asked Lessa.

"Not especially," said Arianna, curling a strand of hair around her finger. "I've been occupied with the festivals so near. I tried to skim some, but everything just bleeds together. It all just seemed like nonsense before. But now—"

"Now we read!" said Lessa, clapping her hands together. "My absolute favorite thing to do."

Arianna shook her head in wondrous confusion. She never thought she'd find herself studying for a subject such as this.

They sat down cross-legged on the training mat and got to reading. They pored over the scrolls for hours, trying to sort out all the details they could in one sitting. To say the least, it was all very puzzling and at times even disturbing. And though the feeling of excitement was harder to suppress the more they read on, Arianna couldn't help but still notice the cloud hovering over her head.

Why have you chosen me?

She was desperate to know.

"I think I've found something!" said Lessa, unfurling a long, yellowed scroll that smelled of mold.

It was titled *Olleb-Yelfra the Fallen* and was dated almost three centuries earlier—no true signature claimed the writing.

"Do you think it'll explain more about the Olleb's past? All of these other scrolls and books only talk about charms and creatures that I don't understand." Arianna scratched at her head. "Right now, the only thing I care about is how any of this connects to us," she added, scanning the parchment, doubtful. "Maybe then something will make sense."

"I hope so," said Lessa. "But I tell you, even if I'm trying to believe in all this, I still don't know if I want anything to do with magic after some of the things we've read tonight." She shuddered. "Can you... imagine?"

"I sure am trying to," muttered Arianna, so tired that her eyes burned. "Let's just find out a bit more before we write off a new world of possibility," she said. "It's too late to turn back now anyways." She began to read:

> *Since the dawn of time, Olleb-Yelfra saw many a king and queen. For thousands of years, each kingdom flourished under sovereign rule. It seemed as if the Olleb would relish in a boundless Golden Age. The land was an enchanted place while magic kissed the streams and skies freely. Extraordinary people studied the art of wizardry, and mystic creatures roamed the land. Even common citizens shared the privilege of a magical life while everyone lived in peace. Then, the balance shifted. Where there is light, darkness can always be found. This, I now know for certain...*

Arianna's voice trailed off. She hadn't even realized her hands had begun to shake until she stopped reading. Lessa clung to every word, urging her on, but now that Arianna held the information in her hands, she felt unsure.

Do I really want to know?

She sensed a hard history lesson lay at the end of the script. And something about the words seemed so… true. All her life she thought the world had always been depressing and dark; it had never once occurred to her that something more may have survived before these times. Yet here it was—inked in ancient calligraphy. Just in reading the first paragraph, she felt cheated.

There had been a Golden Age?

Lessa squirmed with impatience, so Arianna stifled her nerves and spiraling thoughts and continued to read. As she did, her mind painted a vivid image of the words on the scroll. She felt connected to them somehow, as if she could see straight into the past through the script. Her imagination spun, and she became lost in the ink, lost in an Olleb-Yelfra before her time. The nameless author guided her through this 'boundless Golden Age,' and her spirits soared with them, throughout a spectacular and enchanted past.

19

THE FALLEN

THE SUN SHONE BRIGHT, and the familiar roar of the ocean played its symphony nearby. A young lord of the palace, Kyrone Devlindor, placed his arm around his cousin, Prince Neas, as they watched the water lapping at the shores of a silver-sanded beach from the terrace connected to his room. From there, Kyrone had to squint to try to see what might've caused the splashing in the distance.

Probably just another mermaid searching for love.

He smiled at the thought as he leaned over the white, marble rail to get a better look. It was doubtful she'd ever find it.

The city swept down below them in stacks around the castle. He could see everything from there—all the land, he was sure. The sun warmed his skin as it kissed the earth and sea, and the air tasted of sweet salt. The low buzz from the city stole his attention as it reached his ears, sounding of life and love as children laughed and young men and women sang through their chores. Kyrone added his own laughter to the mix as a song he knew well rose from the masses:

I asked for some bread, and he gave me a pig,
And that's why I call him my king.
I asked for a wife, a pretty young slice,
And somehow I wound up with three.
Several years later, I'm on my death table,
With one more request for my king.
I said when I'm dead, if my children should beg,
Please only do grant what they need!
He said, 'Yes my good lad, one wife for one man.'
Three is a death penalty!
Then he gave me a kiss, my last granted wish,
And that's why I call him my king.

The song drifted away on the wind along with the laughter, so he turned his attention elsewhere. Leaning over the rail, he glimpsed a budding witch trying to build a sandcastle on the beach, the sand churning in a sparkling gust about the air as her hands flowed back and forth in abstract patterns. After a few novice magic mishaps, and a little help from Prince Neas, the dancing grains settled into a replica of the Kingdom of Saindora, the sprawling seaside metropolis in which they lived. The young lord and prince clapped their approval and support, and the little witch waved back, wearing a proud smile. It was just another normal day. A *perfect* day.

"That was a great duel. You fought well today, cousin," said Prince Neas as he took their swords and laid them against the smooth stone wall at their backs so that their blades caught the sun, glistening white.

They were both bare-chested and extremely sweaty, though Kyrone could *never* understand why his cousin was so much more muscular than him... they trained the same amount. He also found it absolutely absurd how handsome Prince Neas still managed to appear after a duel in this kind of heat; he didn't need a mirror to know that he looked like a drowned rat from the trench.

"Thank you. You weren't so bad yourself," said Kyrone with a smirk. He ran a hand through his hair, trying to tame it, but his thick, black locks never wanted to stay in place.

"Ah, my two favorite boys!" said a tall, plump man with rich brown skin. Everything about him, from his attire to his smile, was vibrant. "The servants said I might find you here." They both jumped at the interruption as King Damas pushed the sheer curtains aside and stepped out onto the balcony to join them.

"Father, you're home early!" said Prince Neas, standing up straight. "What has your journey offered you this time? All is well, I trust?" He embraced the king in a long hug. "Did you run into any trouble while you were away?"

"My young prince, always in a rush for the details," he said with a chuckle. "Come. Let us walk the grounds before supper. I have quite the tale for you."

Kyrone slumped as they headed inside, leaving him alone to admire the view. Unable to stop it, the heat rose to his face, so he turned his back to them, hoping they wouldn't see—with such pale skin, it was painfully obvious when he was embarrassed, or angry, or… jealous; he always tried to remain in control and *hated* feeling anything but, especially when it came to his emotions. Alas, he couldn't seem to shake the sick twinge in his heart that grew bigger every passing sun as he was forced to stand in the shadows and bear witness to a father, a king, who loved his son so dearly; he'd never really had a chance to know his own, and his mother loved him little.

A double-winged dragonfly landed on the floor at his feet, its body a glimmering turquoise and the wings a deep, translucent black.

Such a beautiful creature.

Kyrone crushed it under his bare foot, feeling a stitch of relief in his chest.

Such a beautiful death.

He wriggled his toes in the warm mess of the insect as he studied it. He didn't know why he'd done it and felt a little guilty after the fact, but it was only a bug. And channeling his anger into something else gave him back some control and made him feel better, if only for a second. Nevertheless, a need haunted him still, somewhere deep down, that he ached to fill.

"What are you waiting for?" Kyrone looked up, surprised to see King Damas poking his head out from the curtains. "We're waiting on you," he said.

Forgetting his pain, Kyrone flashed a big smile and followed him inside. The remnants of the dragonfly clung to the bottom of his foot as he went, and a dark gold stain remained on the terrace floor as proof of the creature's demise.

"It's wonderful to see you again, Your Majesty," said Kyrone. He bowed low.

"I won't ask you again, little lord," said the king. "Call me Uncle Damas." He gave his nephew a hug around the shoulders, laughing as Kyrone squirmed under his grip. "I trust you've been taking good care of my boy here?"

"I never let him out of my sight, Uncle," he said, nudging Prince Neas in the ribs.

Together, they left Kyrone's bedroom and walked along one of the many halls that created the enchanting labyrinth that was this palace, eventually winding down a tall, velvet staircase that led to a grand foyer.

A glass-paned window covered the expanse of one wall, light blue swirls decorating the glass in intricate designs that made the chamber glitter like water as the sun beamed through. And an array of jeweled chandeliers clung to the ceiling, sprinkling a rainbow of color across a pink-splattered marble floor that shone like it had been freshly scrubbed.

The Palace of Saindora was airy and bright, mesmerizing and complex, so much wonder woven into its walls that Kyrone thought the architecture to be inspired by magic itself. From this main foyer, marble, granite, and gold branched out to all angles of the palace like veins pumping life into the mortar; they created tall archways and paved halls that led to a vast number of charming chambers and galleries—libraries, kitchens, sparring rooms, gardens, sitting rooms, and more. Kyrone had yet to fully explore whole wings of the castle, though he'd forever continue to try. No door was locked to him as a lord with residence here, each chamber so inviting.

As he continued following in the king's and prince's footsteps, he could not ignore the portraits hung in every corridor, try as he might. Sprinkled with enchantments so that the contents of the canvases moved slightly, the painter's magic had captured every real moment of the past with each stroke of their brush. Thus, the people of the paintings forever smiled down at those who walked the halls of the palace, trapped in a moment in time as they fixed the crowns and tiaras atop their heads or smoothed out their robes while the artists tried to preserve their essence through paint.

Kyrone studied each and every one, finding the faces of renowned witches and wizards, or royal family allies, both human and not. He caught himself frowning as he stopped to consider a huge portrait, marking the end of the hall, framed in crystal—Saindora's royal family.

"Quit gawking at me and keep up!" laughed the prince from up ahead, waving him forward. Kyrone sighed, tearing his eyes away. "We're headed out to the main gardens."

Hurrying to catch up, Kyrone couldn't help but notice that things seemed busier than usual this afternoon. Stealing a glance inside the kitchens, he saw servants preparing for what looked to be a grand feast. Frosting churned in the air as a woman charmed the icing onto a huge cake, a young man diligently following her around the table to precisely place cherries along the iced brim.

That's odd… I don't recall an event planned for tonight.

He assumed the palace attendants were just going above and beyond to celebrate the king's homecoming; the people loved him so much.

Kyrone stalled again to peek inside the throne room, finding no one inside but the guards who always silently stood watch, blending in with the strange statues along the walls as they secured the chamber. Looking up, he saw himself surrounded by the black granite that tiled the whole expanse of the floor, his reflection showing in the mirrored ceiling which created a dome of glass above the windowless chamber. The only real light in this room, save for the sun as it filtered in through the open doors, came from a dazzling diamond chandelier lit with candles.

Still gazing at his reflection, Kyrone felt that twinge in his heart grow a bit bigger again, anger filling the hole all the way up. He tore his eyes away from the lonely boy trapped forever behind a barrier of ornate glass and slipped back out into the hall.

Prince Neas and King Damas had likely already made it to the gardens by now—they weren't anywhere to be seen when he rounded the corner.

Probably wanted quality time together… without me.

He shoved his hands in the pockets of his pants and kept walking, slowly, eyes glued to his feet.

"Ky Ky, is that you over there?" A child's voice reached his ears from a nearby sitting room he hadn't yet passed.

Knowing the voice from anywhere, Kyrone smiled and went to the doorway, forgetting his worries a moment.

His sister, Lady Elisa Devlindor, sat upon a long, cream-colored settee in a room draped with lavender curtains along the walls; it had always been a favorite hiding place of hers. She claimed the pastel colors made her feel cheerful, so he wasn't surprised to find her holed up in there this afternoon. Her diary was on the table, too, always in sight, and he supposed she'd come to jot down her thoughts in private.

"Yes, sister. How did you know?" He shot her a sly smirk, arms crossed at his chest, as he leaned against the door frame.

"I just had an inkling," she said with a giggle.

"You're very in tune for one so young," said Kyrone, knowing that her *inklings* had something to do with magic. She was a strong sorceress and growing at that. Though, not stronger than him. "But aren't you supposed to be taking lessons at this hour? Where are your attendants?"

She pouted. "They're just… busy, you know? Oh, I don't know! *I'm* busy. Now go away. Leave me be."

Kyrone laughed. "As you command, my lady," he said with a mock bow. "One would think you were queen with that attitude, though." King Damas' wife had died several years earlier; it was too bad his sister wasn't yet of marrying age.

Elisa narrowed her eyes at him. "Go away," she said again.

"Yes, yes. I'm leaving," he said. "In fact, I'm going to meet the king and prince in the gardens now if you'd like to join me. I could use an escort. I keep letting my mind wander so far off that they probably think I've gotten myself lost."

Elisa shook her head, and her platinum hair fell into her eyes as she concentrated hard on something.

"What are you staring at—" Kyrone stopped himself just as she failed at charming a pile of feathers, from a mutilated pillow, into the air.

"I see," he said after a moment, noting her frustration.

Then he closed his eyes, a deep breath flowing from his lips. Elisa squealed in delight as the feathers rose all around her in a pink and white twister.

Kyrone laughed, shaking his head at how easy it was to placate his sister. "Keep practicing, Elisa," he said. "You'll get it someday soon."

He left her alone, stepping back into the hallway. As he pulled the door shut, he accidentally bumped into someone.

"Watch yourself!" shouted a dwarf, eyes streaking with silver as he glared up at him. "I've got priceless metal here." The short yet robust creature would appear as just a man—if not for the unnaturally ripped muscles across his body, his long, braided beard and hair, and smug disposition. The glowing jewel embedded into his forearm made Kyrone assume him from the City of Undor. And he carried a bundle of fine swords, probably headed to the royal armory; King Damas had a treaty with several of the dwarf clans around the Olleb, so they often came to trade in weapons and priceless gemstones for a variety of Saindora treasures.

Kyrone mumbled a slight apology, and the dwarf gave him a curt nod, readjusting his pile before continuing on.

Such annoying creatures. No manners at all.

He rolled his eyes when the dwarf was out of sight.

Soon, Kyrone reached a double door made of polished redwood at the end of the corridor. Two servants on either side pulled its large rungs and bowed as the door swung open. "King Damas said they'd be toward the fountains, my lord," one said.

"Very good," he said.

A rush of warm air spilled into the hallway, and Kyrone stepped out into the sun.

This side of the castle opened up toward a breathtaking garden filled with the best of Saindora's nature. Kyrone sniffed at the air, and the sweet scent of flowers filled his nose. Then he followed a pebbled path that slithered through the grass, winding toward a forest that created a fence around the area.

He stared toward the dense woodland—drawn to it—entranced by the fairy dust weaving in and out through the trees.

Kyrone shook his head, closing his eyes.

Never stare too long after fairies!

He knew better than that.

Snapping out of his trance, he finally caught up to King Damas and Prince Neas. They were seated at the edge of a fountain in an area decorated with statues of lovers, friends, and the gods and goddesses who ruled the skies and earth. As the water in the fountain bed danced unnaturally and their eyes flashed with silver streaks, Kyrone saw they were using their magic to splash one another in good fun.

"There you are," said King Damas with a grin, squeezing some of the water from his cloak. "We've been waiting for you."

"Take a nap, did you?" chided the prince. "I think I wore you out after our duel. I'll go easy on you next time."

He, too, was covered in water.

"I just got a bit… sidetracked," mumbled Kyrone, trying not to show his annoyance. He didn't care much for sarcasm, but Prince Neas never seemed to notice.

"Well now that you're here, let's keep walking," said the king. "I need to stretch my legs after being cooped in the carriage for weeks. It's quite a journey from here to the North."

Together, the three nobles walked side by side throughout the gardens, stopping only for a moment to observe the king's horses galloping back and forth in a large, penned meadow. It overflowed with tall grasses, and fragrant wildflowers opened up toward the sun.

"Your Grace, this has just arrived for you from the Nicora Realm." A smartly-dressed servant handed the king a rolled parchment with a fine seal.

King Damas smiled in thanks, and the servant bowed low before scurrying off. Taking a moment to read the letter, he scratched at the graying hair under his glittering crown of solid gold, jewels covering it like a strip of colorful stars as they caught the sunlight. Then he stuffed the parchment in the pocket of his robes and clapped his hands. An array of butterflies took instant flight at the disturbance, leaving the previously painted bushes only green.

"Ah, very good! Very good indeed," he said. "Everything is unfolding just as I'd hoped. A celebration is due, my sons!"

He slapped Kyrone on the back and laid his heavy arms across their shoulders. The embrace felt too warm as his silky cape draped over him. To match the king's splendor, the gold fabric of his robes was woven with rich shades of color on the inside, making the boys' linen slacks appear like rags. It clashed against Kyrone's pallor—although, he rather enjoyed how the cloth felt against his skin.

"Father, what are we to celebrate?" asked Prince Neas, eyes alit with curiosity.

Kyrone considered his cousin… considered that they were nothing alike. His smile was magnetic, and it was rare if he were without it, and his eyes were exact replicas of his father's—as if they'd each been granted two topaz gems flecked with bits of gold to see through because of their royal status.

Whose eyes do I have?

He could barely remember his father's features, and he shared hardly anything of looks in common with his mother and sister.

"Well, you asked how I fared on my journey," said King Damas, his expression ecstatic. "I would say quite well! In fact, I have a surprise for you both." He squeezed them even tighter, forcing them into his chest.

Kyrone and the prince exchanged a confused glance, finding it difficult to contain their excitement now as well.

"*Well?*" asked Kyrone with an eager smile. "Out with it. What is it, then, Uncle?"

King Damas sang in reply, "If I told you, then it wouldn't be a surprise, now would it?"

Just as the sun began to fall behind the clouds, a shadow growing over the gardens, a servant came to declare the feast nearly ready.

"That's our cue," said the king with a wink. "Time to go get cleaned up. I've already had your attendants lay out your outfits for tonight."

Barely able to contain their anticipation, Kyrone and Prince Neas raced ahead of the king back inside the palace to ready for whatever surprise he had in store for them. A short while later, they were escorted into an enormous gallery where a hundred decorated tables had been laid out, the delicious scent of baked bread, pies, and roast meats in the air.

The room was already filled to capacity, people both standing and sitting, and all dressed in their finest gowns, vests, and cloaks. Kyrone even saw his mother, though she seemed more on edge than usual, standing watch over Elisa who giggled in the corner as some boy whispered in her ear from behind. He assumed she was irritated to have to attend another formal function alone—she'd never found another suitor after father had left them and she hated to endure the scrutiny of the noblewomen at affairs such as these.

Aside from his forever-displeased mother, everyone else seemed fully contented, making acquaintance with one another and sharing gossip. They talked of their children's successes at magic school or in coveted apprenticeships around the Olleb. And whispers were rampant about another sailor lost at sea, many taking guesses at the cause—mermaids, pirates, a sudden storm? They also bragged about their recent adventures to other regions and discussed the exciting new births and unions among nobles in neighboring kingdoms. Overall, Kyrone thought it to be a rather large crowd tonight, the conversations blending together in a buzz.

Every noble in the city had shown up, it seemed.

But why?

It was rather unusual that the king would sanction such a gathering on only his first night back.

Suddenly, the room quieted, everyone rising to their feet and staring toward him and the prince. Kyrone didn't have to look behind him to know that King Damas was there.

Never taking these moments for granted, Kyrone beamed as all eyes steadied on him and his family. Then he felt the king's hand at his back, ushering him and Prince Neas down a makeshift aisle toward a table at the front that was elevated above the rest. Other noblemen and women were already seated there, waiting, but three empty places for them remained in the center.

After they climbed the small steps to the table, King Damas turned to face the crowd. His people bowed low and long as he gestured for the boys to stand close by his side.

Everyone applauded his homecoming and he returned a gracious smile.

"Citizens of Saindora," said the king, lifting his hand for silence. "Thank you for joining me this night. I'm truly humbled to see all of your welcome faces after such a long journey." The crowd politely praised him again. "As you probably know by now, we hold this feast in honor of my sons."

Kyrone blushed at this mention, cursing his fair skin again, especially now with so many people to witness his reddening cheeks. He truly did love King Damas; the king had been the only father-figure he'd ever known. And what better family could he hope for than that of *the* royal one of Saindora—one of the greatest kingdoms in all of Olleb-Yelfra?

"They've both recently celebrated their fifteenth birthdays," he added, "so I've fetched them a little surprise." Kyrone and Prince Neas fidgeted where they stood, whispering their predictions behind the king's back. "May I present Master Lethander, Great Lord of the Nicora Elven Clan!" The king held his arm out wide and motioned down the aisle.

The boys gawked in disbelief as a tall elf paced forward. Kyrone knew elves to be quite uncommon in these parts, so this was *truly* a grand surprise, indeed. It was a moment to be marked by history! Known for their knowledge of old magic, elves felt more comfortable in seclusion with their own kind. Still, the collective wisdom of the elf tribes and their many advanced accomplishments had earned the creatures much respect across Olleb-Yelfra.

Kyrone couldn't take his eyes off Master Lethander, gaping all the while.

The elegant creature looked pale—but not sickly as he thought of himself—and his bluish-silver hair grew long yet neatly past his shoulders, slightly pointed ears sticking out. He was bare-chested, wearing only leggings and light green swaths of fabric that swept the floor, making Kyrone think he must've just arrived. And long chains of silver and gold were draped around his neck.

The elf also held tight to a remarkable staff crafted of white wood that had been polished and subtly spun with patterns that probably meant something important to his kind. He gripped to it tightly so that a thin, silver tattoo on the back of his hand became noticeable. It swirled up his skin and looped around his wrist like a band; Kyrone recalled this magical marking. All elves from the Nicora Realm supposedly received them on both hands as part of their coming of age ceremonies.

Bowing to King Damas and the boys, who respectfully returned the gesture, Master Lethander then turned to follow an attendant in waiting.

"Master Lethander has gone to freshen up from his journey. He'll return to dine with us soon," the king explained to the curious crowd.

"Will he stay for long, Father?" asked Prince Neas, hope thick in his voice.

King Damas nodded, pulling the boys in close. "My young lads, I'm proud to say that he shall be your new master!"

His voice echoed off the walls of the feast hall, and Kyrone's knees went weak as the gathering gasped in excitement, everyone thrilled to finally welcome an elf to Saindora for the long term.

"This is a great honor for our family," said King Damas, speaking only to them now. "My journey to their realm resulted in great fortune for us. A peace like none other is spreading across the land, so you must be on your very best behavior from here on out to ensure it remains that way. Elves truly respect the nature of magic, and soon so shall you."

King Damas signaled for everyone to be seated, and a cheerful symphony started in a balcony above the room. Kyrone looked up to see a flute played by hand while other musicians enchanted their instruments into song, the melody mixing in with the jovial voices of the crowd.

Hundreds of servants appeared promptly with silver trays laden with food galore. Children excitedly ran between the tables, whispering secrets and showing off their new spells, and couples began to drift onto the dance floor in a whirl of passion. Endless amounts of wine and ale were also served in goblets of gold, and everyone enjoyed a slice of cake with the charmed icing and cherries on the top. Kyrone couldn't remember a more lively celebration than tonight.

As the evening settled in, the moon pushing the sun away fully, the glass-topped chamber was suddenly lit by floating lanterns, attendants using their magic to set them aflame and keep them in place—he looked up toward the sky, hopeful for the future. Just then, he spotted a dragon pierce through the clouds and fly overhead; it disappeared in a burst of golden flames as quickly as it had emerged.

"Come on, Kyrone. Let's have a drink to celebrate!" said Prince Neas, stealing his attention away as he placed a goblet of wine in his hand. "To new beginnings."

Kyrone smiled. "To a new world," he said.

They clinked their cups and then downed their drinks.

ARIANNA STOPPED READING, overcome with shock and awe and wonder at the evidence she held in her hands—a secret history of Olleb-Yelfra was unraveling before her eyes.

This is so forbidden.

She itched for more.

Lessa grabbed the scroll from her, impatient to know the ending. She recited the script from where Arianna had left off:

> *Master Lethander extended a rare honor to the young lord and prince on this momentous occasion. He was fond of King Damas and his politics, so he had agreed to the apprenticeship as a gesture meant to strengthen their alliance, one that would one day, hopefully, be replicated across other kingdoms and realms. Only witches and wizards with true power and perseverance could become masters in magic. And since Prince Neas and young Kyrone came from notable magical bloodlines, Master Lethander saw raw potential in them; he spent years molding their talents and their minds with the ancient wisdoms of the elves, and they grew powerful.*

While Master Lethander pushed both young men to train hard, most of his praise was, unjustly, afforded to Prince Neas—he quickly excelled in many areas of magic. Through no fault of his own, Kyrone was made to grow envious of his cousin with each turning sun, the renowned elf using his influence to poison the susceptible young man against his own family. Although Prince Neas had so far surpassed Kyrone in the art of magic, he proved inferior in swordsmanship, having let those skills go in favor of mastering new spells. Thus, out of a jealous rage, incited purely by the elf's wickedness, Kyrone killed his cousin during what should have been a friendly duel of swords.

With his cousin's blood on his hands, Kyrone immediately realized he had been manipulated into committing a horrendous act of treason. Not willing to face the sure consequence of death, he tried to dispose of the prince's body in the woodland behind the palace. As he came toward the concealment of the trees, Master Lethander appeared—as if he had known where to find them all along. The elf, in an attempt to seem noble, made to try to heal Prince Neas with his dark magic. Of course, it was all a farce. The prince was dead.

However, Kyrone was wise for his young age and would not let Master Lethander dishonor Prince Neas any more than he already had. Heroically, he plunged his sword into the elf's back as he was bent over the prince, effectively taking the life of the so-called 'great' elf lord of the Nicora Clan. Kyrone then left the bodies at the edge of the forest and plucked up the courage to relay the true events to the king. Not wanting to put his uncle in an even more difficult position by implicating himself in the wrongdoings of Master Lethander, Kyrone claimed the elf had murdered Prince Neas during instruction, indeed to effectively remove the king's heir to the throne and weaken their monarchy—it was, after all, mostly true and the only way to spare the king more anguish.

The people had always loved King Damas, but he was never a fit ruler… a strong ruler. At the first real sign of distress, he went mad with grief and could barely keep the crown atop his head for how much he tried to drink away his sorrows. Kyrone did him a favor when he served him that last goblet of wine; he helped put the poor man out of his misery. Though, King Damas hadn't been wholly useless the years before his death. In fact, he issued the royal decree that would pave the way for the future; it ordered that the Nicora Elven Clan pay, in its entirety, for the heinous crime of their leader. Anyone could see that Master Lethander's agenda had been a well-thought-out strategy to destabilize the kingdom. Accordingly, within weeks of the prince's death, the king's vast armies and sorcerers had slaughtered them all.

There was a lull in such affairs after that. But, following the weeklong mourning for King

Damas, the Saindora City Council crowned the honorable and deserving Kyrone Devlindor as King of Saindora—at the age of just eighteen—as per the last will and testament of the late king. Thus began Olleb-Yelfra's fall into the Dark Ages, some might say. Though, some might also say that what becomes shrouded by darkness slowly begins to see with new and sharper eyes.

In order to help his people see, the young King Devlindor had no other choice but to become a persuasive tyrant—although he didn't care for this label. With his unmatched intelligence, he helped the people of Saindora understand that the deaths of their beloved king and prince were due to the uncontrollable magic residing within the Olleb. After all, none of this would have happened if not for Master Lethander's malicious undertakings. So, to carry on King's Damas' last legacy, King Devlindor swayed the people to his side and sent crusades to contain all traces of magic in the region within the boundaries of the Saindora palace for sanctioned usage. He also insisted on and enforced the immediate cease of use of magic for anyone able; the people fed on the new king's promises and ideals because they were sound. And those who did not, died—for the betterment of the Olleb and everyone's ultimate safety.

With access to so much power and knowledge, King Devlindor was able to stretch his progressive 'magic ban' movement far outside the *boundaries of his kingdom. Only a few years passed before he proclaimed himself High King of all of Olleb-Yelfra, a feat no ruler had ever achieved before. With his reach, he eventually extended the prohibition on magic to every corner of the land.*

Alas, the Olleb burned under King Devlindor's early reign, to no fault of his own. He was forced to use his own magic, and the aid of a very few trusted, honorable sorceresses and sorcerers who understood his hunger for a better world, to dissipate uprisings in problematic areas. With their support, he was able to pass his laws to the fullest extent, banning knowledge and stories of what had been known as the Golden Age. Just to speak of the time proved a punishable act, if only to save the next generations the trouble of reliving such a distressing and chaotic era.

The history of dwarves, giants, elves, fairies, mermaids, and magic all vanished from memory. Dragons and avatars fell to myth. King Devlindor amassed essential literature having to do with spells or the like and burned all other traces of magic schools, libraries, and books to the ground. Even tales of his former fellow kings and queens, and of noblemen and women, quickly ceased, for their achievements had obviously not been noteworthy enough to remember in comparison to his own. And, ultimately, in the effort to cleanse the land of evil and keep the people safe, he exterminated all known magical bloodlines—animal, creature, and human alike. Henceforth, after a time, histories of a Golden Age faded into fiction and the Olleb finally saw peace.

But, of all of King Devlindor's most extraordinary triumphs during his early reign, his most recognized accomplishment was the creation of the City of the Four Corners, a place that ensures nobody can be born royal, or noble, or better than. A place where all men and women are created equal, and face equal opportunity to earn their rights to the astounding new world and order of Olleb-Yelfra.

The idea of the city and its purpose was born after King Devlindor received counsel from a seer (whom he graciously spared during the magic ban crusades) who resided in the palace. She foresaw a future that could—although very unlikely—result in the High King's death, and consequently the end of peace in Olleb-Yelfra, if her advice were not taken into consideration. Thus, for the world's continued wellbeing, the prophecy was written with the seer's binding blood and locked away in the darkest labyrinths of the palace to be seen only by the eyes of those it avowed.

Inscribed by way of:
A Once Noble Man
Born of Noble Blood
To a Once Enchanted Land
And Noble Kingdom

Lessa's voice trembled as she finished, and Arianna felt her emotions in turmoil as she tried to process the abrupt ending to what had started off as such a beautiful world.

"I wonder who wrote that," said Arianna as she scanned the scroll over Lessa's shoulder.

"I don't know," said Lessa as she turned the scroll over in her fingers, stroking the leathery parchment. "But I would bet this cryptic signature was to keep his name safe from the King. Obviously, this was never meant to be seen by anyone in this day and age."

"Does it say anything else about this *prophecy*?" asked Arianna, folding her arms across her chest. According to the text, this prophecy was the reason the Four Corners existed—therefore she loathed it.

Lessa shook her head, stretching her legs across the mat.

"I wonder how Talis even got his hands on a parchment with this kind of information," she said. "Can you believe it?"

Arianna stood up to refresh the dying fire as the room began to grow dark. "The story gives me chills," she said, her mind feeling like it had melted into one of the charred coals she was staring at in the firepit. "How can one person stretch their power so far? It seems as if the path to power was just laid out for him." She came back to sit down, bringing with her the remaining wine from the night before. Her headache had only been made worse after such a story, so what would it hurt at this point? "It was like luck was on his side with every choice." She took a swig from the carafe.

"Maybe it was," replied Lessa, reaching for the wine. "A little luck and a lot of fear from what I can read between the lines." She drank.

"What do you mean?" said Arianna.

"Well, he destroyed all of those people, all of those creatures… for what? To make himself feel more confident, powerful? He was scared at who he wasn't, so he took and took and *took* to try and even things out for himself. He's responsible for so much death." She shook her head, rereading the scroll.

Sano jumped on her shoulder, his eyes scanning the parchment alongside hers.

"Worst of all," said Arianna, "he's responsible for all of this!" She sprung to her feet, her hands waving around as she gestured to everything.

Both Lessa and Sano jumped at the sudden outburst.

Arianna began pacing about the room. "We've been enslaved for centuries because of a king who was frightened of a prophecy? Is that the summary? *Really?*" she said. Her face burned and her hands shook. "There used to be love in this world, and he stole it out of… fear. Yet, we're made to be afraid every day of our lives just to prove that we belong to the world he created to make himself feel… more than?"

Arianna dropped back down, taking another swig of the wine. Sano went to curl up in her lap, and she stroked him, the gesture helping to calm the fire licking at her insides. Lessa was still fixated on the parchment, but she saw a storm swirled behind her eyes just the same.

"Being a slave," said Lessa, "I just thought this was how things were supposed to be and had been forever. To think that people used to belong to their mothers and fathers seems so impossible now. Yet, this script here says it was so." She looked to Arianna. "If what this 'once noble man' wrote is true, then the prophecy might be as well."

She put down the scroll, reaching for more wine.

"What do you mean to say?" asked Arianna, still stroking Sano. "You think there's hope of—" She couldn't even fathom the thought in her mind, that she might hope for the High King's downfall. Even the slightest possibility of such an idea was inconceivable.

She took another sip of the wine and stood to return the

carafe to the table before they got carried away again.

"Maybe you ought to just leave that here," said Lessa. "We have a lot more reading to do."

THE GIRLS CONTINUED TO PORE over the scrolls and books, pouring the wine as they went. They looked for any hint as to what the prophecy might be, anything at all to prove their theories, but the only reference was inked in *Olleb-Yelfra the Fallen*. Most of the other parchments and texts only described different magical creatures, spells, or scattered history that didn't piece together with any of their questions.

One book referenced a story of a man who had been fated to the carnage of a scorned mermaid at sea. Another told the story of a sorry wizard who offered his own children to a dragon in sacrifice for his protection against a curse—the dragon took his life instead. There was an old scroll that described a handsome king who lured suitors to his bed, until his queen found out and had his head. And they read of an enchanted isle where magic flourished in all crevices of the land, a safe-haven for creatures of all kinds; travelers there found themselves very lucky *or* very dead.

The girls skimmed over talk of orbs and spellbooks with strange incantations. They read of distant lands with peculiar names and schools of magic that had once been part of normal education. But none of it mattered. Everything just seemed to blur together in a nonsensical fashion—as expected from a nonsensical world.

Lessa scratched at her head as she picked up another scroll. "It's hard to fathom that this land has seen so much war and survived," she said. "From what it sounds like, King Devlindor almost ripped this land apart."

"It's hard to believe that there once was a time filled with magic after living seventeen years in this wretched place," said Arianna.

"Well, we still have a few more stories on dwarves to get through," said Lessa, unable to stop a smile from stretching across her face. "And let's not forget the fairies and avatars! Whatever that means…"

Arianna shook with laughter, waking Sano from his snooze in her lap. He lazily crawled back to his rightful place on Lessa's shoulder.

"Actually, I could use some fresh air right about now," said Arianna, feigning exhaustion. "All of this wine and magic is going to my head. Want to duel?"

Lessa agreed and got to her feet.

After piling all of the scrolls and books back on the table, they both donned their robes and grabbed the key from under the pillow. In a blur of white and red, they flew out the door.

They were flushed from the wine—Lessa a little pink and Arianna a little red—but the air cooled their blood, clearing their foggy heads. Tonight seemed much cloudier than the last, and the snow gave signs of turning into a blizzard. Still, they took a turn about the arena to stretch their legs, trying to talk of more trivial things than the history of Olleb-Yelfra before King Devlindor.

"Any idea what the Free Falls will be like in your district?" asked Lessa, pulling her hood up. The white fabric of Talis' elder robes blended well with the heavy snow.

All of the blood drained from Arianna's face.

"Not a clue," she said, feeling the onset of nerves. "Last year they were absolutely horrific, though. Seems to only worsen each time, but it's always the same idea. Kill or be killed."

"I'm grateful you got me out of mine," said Lessa with a

sigh. "I *never* thought that would come out of my mouth since I've been training my whole life for that day… but I'm so glad. It's not like we ever had a choice before."

Arianna looked toward Blancoren, wishing she could trade places with Lessa in that moment.

"My district is always the first to go, so they'll be starting shortly," she added. "Last festival they partnered all of the participants up and lathered one of each with a cream made from Night Wasps that literally made their skin melt off."

Arianna shuddered as her imagination painted an all-too-vivid picture of that. "The other had to drink a concoction that caused internal bleeding. The cream and drink were both ineffective for about two hours, but if they couldn't remedy each other before the time was up, then…" She shook her head. "It was just a bloody mess, and that was only the first day."

Arianna tried to shake the image forming in her mind.

"Ours may be even more gruesome with all the hacking away at each other that's involved," she said. "I may be a good warrior, but I've never actually *killed* anyone before." She chewed on her lip. "Being in battle is thrilling. I love it, but I'm not sure if I'm ready to take someone's life. It just seems so—" Her voice faded, and she kicked at an ice patch forming on the ground.

An awkward silence spread between them. Moments later, Lessa tilted her head back, catching the snow on her tongue. Then she started spinning in a circle, taking Arianna's hand in her own and forcing her to spin too. Faster and faster they went, the snow whirling in gusts around them as if they were one with the wind, an orbiting globe of white melting into crimson as their cloaks fluttered behind them. Eventually losing control, the girls fell to the ground in giggles. They lolled there for a few moments, slowing their dizzied heads.

"What do you think will happen to us if I win my freedom?" asked Arianna, gazing up toward the spinning sky and letting snowflakes melt on her face.

"I suppose you'll go on to be a great warrior somewhere," said Lessa. "And I'll sneak away behind you as your caretaker." Something of doubt or shock crossed into her expression. "When the festivals end, no one in the Healer's District will doubt that I'm dead by the hand of my master. I'll be free to do as I please… as long as nobody asks for my identification, I suppose."

"I'll make sure Solomon gets you documented. He apparently has his ways." Arianna smirked at a memory. "I wonder what'll become of our masters once we're free, though."

"Who knows! They'll probably run off to bewilder two new young slaves. I've no idea what to even make of all this information." Lessa moved her hands and feet up and down in the snow for a moment. "Help me up, will you?"

Arianna wobbled a bit as she stood.

She lent Lessa a hand and she jumped up with grace. Staring down at the impressions their bodies had left in the snow, Arianna balked as she looked upon a giant blob rather than the figure of a person with wings like Lessa's.

"Hmm, that really looks like you!" said Lessa, trying to keep the laughter behind her teeth.

At that, Arianna chucked a ball of snow through the air. With perfect precision, a warrior's aim, it landed on Lessa's head, turning her blond head a pearly white.

"Outwitted!" said Arianna with a snicker, hands resting on her hips in triumph.

Moments later, a war of sparkling snow and laughter broke out between them. And though the sky continued to fall all around and the night only grew colder, nothing could stop Arianna and Lessa from enjoying this small taste of freedom.

PART THREE

20

THE FREE FALLS

SOLOMON WAS PACING AGAIN, back and forth outside the well room. Every heavy footstep echoed loudly against the stone floor. "She'll be fine," Arianna heard Talis say. "She's ready. Come sit down."

"I know. I know," said Solomon. She heard the shuffling of steps stop outside the door and then an impatient knock. "Time to go!"

"In the King's name, give her a minute," huffed Cyn.

Just as Arianna reached for the handle, the door flew open and she was gazing up at Solomon.

Cyn fumed, pushing him out of the way to give her some room. "Solomon Bell, if you make her any more nervous than she already is, so help me, I'll whip a sword on you myself," she growled. She stood on her tiptoes to look him square in the eyes. Her face flashed a dangerous red, and Solomon staggered backward away from the door.

"Yeesh! Okay," said Solomon, throwing up his hands and shrinking back. "Relax. I'm just trying to move things along."

Arianna couldn't help but laugh; only Cyn would stand up to the Wolf of the East and live to tell the tale.

Lessa was there, too, sitting at a table beside Talis. "Oh, she's ready all right," she said with a whistle. "Just look at her! No need to fuss everyone. The warrior has arrived."

Arianna took a deep breath and lifted her head high. Chin up, shoulders back, chest out, feet grounded—a warrior's stance, indeed.

Cyn had labored over her all day to ensure she was feeling her best *and* would turn heads at the Free Falls tonight. Freshly bathed and clothed in a new outfit Cyn had made for her, Arianna certainly felt like a new person; she just hoped that after this week was over she'd actually be one.

Her curls were pulled into a ponytail that fell long across her shoulder, loose bangs dangling in her face and framing her eyes. She donned pants made of leather that hugged her skin to let her move freely and comfortably, and she wore a bright red shirt, the Warrior's Crest stitched in gold thread on the back. The same black boots as she always wore were laced up tight, and she had on her favored fingerless gloves to make sure she'd never lose grip on her swords. Her attire was perfect for battle, though not to be complete without weapons—her dagger was snug in its rightful place at her thigh, and her favorite twin swords crisscrossed in a sheath strapped across her back.

Yes, she knew she *looked* the part of a warrior. On the inside, though, she might as well have been a child in group training for the way her emotions were twisting about between nausea and nerves.

Calm down. Deep breath. You're ready for this.

Solomon beamed as he laid eyes upon her, his apprentice.

"You look strong," he said, gripping her shoulders. "Your opponents will definitely fear you. Especially if you keep that scowl on your face the entire time."

She sniggered.

"How do you feel?"

Arianna offered a wavering smile, but he saw straight through it.

"Whatever happens out there, just know I'm so proud of you. Remember that."

She blushed at his declaration as he laid her cloak around her shoulders. She fastened it at the neck, feeling her ensemble complete.

"So, how do we do this?" she asked. Solomon had so far still neglected to tell her of his plan. "Am I expected at the Free Falls… or am I still supposed to be dead?"

Solomon pulled at his goatee. "I've thought this over plenty, and I've decided that your best shot at survival is to use the art of surprise," he said. "I think General Ivo has well forgotten that you even exist with all the commotion of the festival preparations to worry over. He hasn't mentioned you once in weeks, so you'll just simply show up." He chuckled as he sidestepped Cyn's kick. "I thought this the better option rather than reminding him of the 'weakness' you showed in the Warrior's Challenge. If you earn your freedom during the festivals, like everyone else and in front of the entire district, with me backing you up, he can hardly object."

Cyn started to protest. "You're just going to have her show—"

"I like this plan," said Arianna, before Cyn could start another tussle with Solomon. Her thoughts soared to the horrified expression sure to come over Grinda's face when she made her entrance back from the dead—just that look alone would be something to celebrate. "Any idea what I can expect for the challenges?"

"Expect a war," said Solomon. "That's all there ever is."

"You'll do just fine, dear," said Cyn. She gave Arianna a

loving hug, glaring sidelong at Solomon all the while.

"Thanks, Cyn… for everything," she replied. "I couldn't have made it to the Free Falls without you keeping me alive these last few years."

"Oh, all right, then," said Cyn, pulling away. "I must be off now. I'm to help the Well Center prepare for anyone who the general deems worth healing when all of the swords are put away tonight after the first round." She shivered. "Take care… survive. I won't be able to watch." Without another word, she scuttled out the door. Though not before Arianna saw her wipe a tear from the corner of her eye.

"We should be on our way too," said Talis, glancing to Solomon. "I want to get a good spot in the elders' section."

Lessa started to don her cloak as well.

Talis stopped cold, observing his apprentice with wry amusement. "Don't be silly, girl! You aren't going anywhere. It'll be too risky to show your face with so many elders from the Healer's District around today," he said.

Lessa's mouth dropped open as she looked between Arianna, Talis, and Solomon. "But… I promised I'd be there, Master."

She stared at him with big, pleading eyes, and Arianna did too. After a month in such close quarters together, learning about magic together, the two had grown inseparable.

"Master Churry, won't you reconsider—" started Arianna.

"My words are final," he said. Solomon silently nodded his agreement. "Save your charm for another day, Miss Thur. You *will* stay here. We haven't come this far to make mistakes now. It's not worth the gamble."

Lessa opened her mouth to protest, but one look at Talis changed her mind.

"Don't worry," said Arianna, trying to sound brave. "I'll be fine. Thank you, though… your support has meant wonders this last month."

"Well, good luck, then." Lessa gave her a short hug, her sour mood palpable. "I'll see you soon."

Arianna nodded, expressionless as all the blood rushed from her face.

Would she?

Without any other words, the two masters and Arianna left the sparring room, leaving Lessa behind. Solomon locked the door, sealing her in, and then they were off.

Arianna lifted her hood over her head as thousands made their way to the Square from all directions in the district. As they came upon the center of town, she melted in with the sea of people clawing their way up toward the seating to watch.

She looked around, desperate to find a familiar face that wasn't Lessa's, Solomon's, or Talis', but everyone just blurred together as one. Three quarters of the amphitheater was already filled with a herd of blood-red cloaks. The only section not colored crimson stood reserved for the elders and General Ivo, where Talis and Solomon would sit; not many outsiders traveled to the Four Corners for the festivals, but every elder residing in the slave city made at least one trek to a different district for fun.

All the commotion reminded Arianna of her last battle in the Square, but the turnout for this was on a much grander scale. Thus, it made the possibility of failure that much worse. As she pushed through the crowd, trying to keep Solomon and Talis in sight, a chant began to rise from some of the already seated slaves:

> *Can you keep your head?*
> *No true warrior winds up dead!*

Arianna felt a lump growing in her throat. No matter how many times she'd sat through a Free Falls Festival, she'd never grown desensitized to all the death that came with them.

Never once had she participated in those cheers that many of her peers enjoyed on this day every year. Where was the fun in killing and dying? Where was their empathy?

Regardless of how hard she tried to smother her emotions for the sake of her sanity, day in and day out, Arianna had always felt a pang of sadness for the lives lost in the confines of the Jar. And now that she stood as a contestant, she hoped her friends and acquaintances sitting in the crowd knew better than to chant too—they would all be standing in her place soon, with their lives on the line.

"This way." Solomon waved for Arianna and Talis to follow him as he carved a path through the crowd. "This is where we leave you," he said, stopping in front of the section reserved for elders. "Go make your way around to the bottom with the other contenders. I'll slip your number into the pot, so you'll get your chance to fight. Just wait for instructions. The general will be relaying them soon."

"But what if I—"

Solomon rested his hand on her shoulder, stalling her growing panic. "Don't worry, Ara. I *know* you can do this. I have every faith. You were meant to live, and so you shall. It's time to earn your freedom now. Then we can go from there." He leaned in to whisper so no one else would hear. "There's still so much magic for you to discover."

Arianna took a deep breath and put a brave face on for her master. She just had to make it through this week. Then she'd be able to think of the future, to figure out this new enchanted world and what it meant for her. For now, she had to focus on the things in her control.

Just survive.

Talis offered her a reassuring nod, and then they waved goodbye, finding seats among the other trainers who hoped their apprentices lasted the night.

It took a while, but Arianna eventually pushed her way

through the throng of people toward the large group of seventeenth-year contenders. They were huddled about on the floor of the cleared Square, waiting for their destinies. She joined them stealthily, blending in with the other nerve-racked warrior-slaves.

Looking up toward the sky, one streaked with the embers of a faraway and falling sun, Arianna saw the flag of the Four Corners hanging limp in the still air—so many times her gaze had rested upon that flag. So many days had she counted to see the hour when she might look up to it waving over the Square on the day of her judgment.

Arianna let her eyes close for a moment.

Now that day was here, and she hoped to never need look upon it again.

Suddenly, the unmistakable grating voice of Grinda Risso caught her attention. Arianna spotted her just ahead, and it took all the willpower she had not to make herself known. As much as she wanted to cut out her adversary's tongue, she would wait patiently for her number to be called as Solomon had advised. She gritted her teeth, pulling in a deep breath.

Patience.

She just needed patience.

Trying to ignore Grinda, she studied the rest of her peers. Some fidgeted, mulling over their fears in silence, while others, like Grinda, tried to act unperturbed. Arianna wondered what she looked like to the rest as she endeavored to remain outwardly composed, but so far nobody had even noticed her standing in the back.

"I'll be fine. Now go on," came a familiar voice from behind. "Get out of here, and cheer me on like you're supposed to." Arianna's heart began to flutter, and she turned to find Liam with Noah close by his side.

"Okay, okay," said Noah. "I'm going. I'll find you after. Keep your head on out there!"

Liam grinned and rustled up Noah's already shaggy hair. "No true warrior winds up dead," he replied.

Arianna fought the urge to shout out their names.

Between meeting Lessa and pursuing knowledge of a veiled magical history, she'd let thoughts of Liam and Noah quickly fade into the background; they thought her dead, and now that she saw them there, so close, she felt guilty for leaving them in the dark. They'd probably be devastated to know they'd been deceived.

Patience.

"Will this year's contenders please make your way to the front." Arianna felt all the nerves in her body spring to alert as General Ivo's voice rang out across the excited amphitheater.

Heads hung low, the seventeenth years all walked as a group into the center of the Square. General Ivo was there to greet them, perched on the elevated platform at their front.

Arianna, still standing toward the back of the group, raised her eyes to his, waiting for further instruction. Someone grasped her elbow from behind, yanking her so hard that she almost lost her balance.

"What the—" She turned to find Sir Dean Westing glaring down at her.

"I know your secret… Arianna Belvedor," he hissed in a whisper so that only she could hear. The stench of whiskey clung to his breath. "Good luck out there. Hope there won't be any nasty surprises." He laughed and then let go of her arm.

Westing walked across the grounds and up the stairs to the podium. He took his place by the general. His gaze lingered on Arianna for a moment and she thought no one had ever worn such a sinister smile. Then his expression softened; he looked rather at ease at his master's side.

Arianna wished for hers.

What did he mean?

Her mind spun over Westing's words. She kept so many

secrets these days and was sure that any one of them meant a spot in the Tombs of Blancoren.

But he can't possibly know about Lessa or the magic.

If he did, she would certainly not be breathing.

Then it clicked—Solomon had been wrong.

General Ivo had obviously confided in his right hand about her survival. He hadn't forgotten about her at all. On the contrary, it seemed he and Westing had been expecting Arianna to show up today. And from the sound of it, they weren't going to make it easy for her to win her freedom. In fact, they probably would try to ensure that she didn't, just to get back at Solomon for asserting his power over them—Arianna could only hope that the lesson wouldn't cost her life.

The general raised his hand, and the Square fell silent. It seemed as if even the wind ceased howling in order to usher in the start of the weeklong festivities.

Arianna pushed Westing out of her mind.

She couldn't process more than one threat to her life at a time, so she decided to focus on the matter at hand—the Free Falls Festivals. As Solomon had drilled into her head many times, she only had to pass *one* test to be given a clean slate for her epically failed Warrior's Challenge. If they called her number today, she could be on her way out of the Jar in less than a fortnight.

Just survive!

General Ivo opened his mouth to speak, and everyone in the Square leaned in to listen.

"I'm delighted to commence the 287th annual Free Falls Festivals of the Warrior's District!" he said, his voice echoing throughout the amphitheater and reaching the ears of all. "In the good name of the King, let us not waste any time. If you recall, last year's festivities were quite successful. It turned out one of the highest new citizen rates we've seen in the last decade." He turned his attention on Arianna's group, wetting his cracked lips. "I do hope you've all trained as hard as your predecessors, for we have something quite challenging in store for you this week."

Arianna shifted on her feet, trying to keep calm. But even in the bitter cold, she felt her cheeks burning. With one glance around, she saw her peers shared her panic as they swallowed back their tears or fought the urge to run. At the very least, she knew she wasn't alone.

A pair of roaming hazel eyes caught hers a moment later; Liam had spotted her, mouth agape as if trying to decide if she were real or a figment of his imagination.

Arianna's lips twisted up in an apologetic smile. She mouthed 'Hi.'

Shaking off his shock, Liam shoved through the group, coming to stand beside her. Saying nothing, he took her hand in his and squeezed tight. Then they both put their attention back on General Ivo.

"Before we get started," said the general, "let me introduce the panel of judges for this evening. Now remember, you must score a six or higher on average in order to qualify for your citizenship. If you're critically wounded, you will obviously be disqualified." He chuckled along with many others seated in the elders' section.

Arianna chewed on her lip. Everyone knew 'disqualified' was just a fancy word for *dead*.

The general went on to list the names and credentials of the judges, citing their astounding wins during their respective Free Falls years prior, but Arianna could hardly concentrate. She searched the crowd for Solomon and Talis, wanting another dose of their encouragement.

Eventually, she did find a face, but it didn't belong to either of the masters. "Lessa?" gasped Arianna, straining to see so far away.

Sure enough, the runaway healer was seated in the elders'

section directly behind General Ivo's stage at the highest part of the amphitheater, a good distance from Talis or Solomon. Arianna had recognized her sky-colored eyes before anything else; they stood out bright blue against her pale skin. And a pair of fiery ones peeked out from the cover of her hood.

Noticing she had Arianna's attention, Lessa smirked and pulled something out of her robes; it was the bronze key to the sparring room. 'Outwitted,' she mouthed with a discreet wave.

Arianna clasped her free hand over her lips in order to trap in the laughter that threatened to betray her panic. She couldn't believe Lessa's brazenness! It actually rivaled her own.

"Pay attention," urged Liam, tugging at Arianna's cloak.

General Ivo had finished introducing the panel and began to relay the most important part of the festivals—the rules.

"Each slave will have a weapon of choice, per usual," he said. "Whatever means of survival you deem necessary will suffice. The judges will call you out in sets of two by random drawings. When your number is selected, you'll have one hour to fight to the death." He lifted a finger. "One hour to duel."

Arianna looked at Liam sideways as his grip on her hand tightened. His face was white. She looked straight ahead, lips pressed into a tight line.

"Only one of you may survive," the general continued. "The fewer wounds you suffer and the quicker you kill your opponent, the better your score. Should the duel go on too long, you may be in for a surprise to help determine the verdict. While unlikely, if by the end of the hour no one has died, you'll both be executed on the spot."

The smile on his face made Arianna's stomach twist in knots.

"Best you finish the job quickly," he added. "Ultimately, if you're worthy enough to be granted citizenship on this day, you may watch the remainder of the festivals this week in the elders' section." He gestured behind him. "Once this year's

Free Falls are over, the winners shall be guided out of the Four Corners through the Vanishing Tunnels and directed toward your new lives."

Arianna closed her eyes, picturing that life, savoring that beautiful image.

My name is Arianna Belvedor… and I am a slave.

She opened her eyes, ready to face the day which could rid her of that forsaken title forever.

"Now," called General Ivo, again staring toward Arianna's group, "as there are so many of you due to participate in the celebrations this year, we won't have time for everyone this evening. But don't fret, there are plenty of events to be held during the course of the week. You'll have your time to shine in the coming days." He surveyed the crowd, clearly pleased with the turnout. "Tonight we celebrate the strong and eliminate the weak from our world. Hail to the King!"

"Hail to Lord Devlindor!" the crowd screamed back.

"Wonderful," said the general with a smile. "And with that, let the Free Falls Festivals begin!" He finished to a standing ovation and the sharp ring of the bell sounded throughout the Square.

The regulators then ushered Arianna, Liam, and the rest of the seventeenth years to seating behind a large stone wall separating the battle grounds of the Square from their audience. The regulators were also guarding every exit in case a contender got too nervous and tried to run—no one ever got away, but each year someone always tried.

As the contenders awaited their turn, everyone began to grow unnervingly anxious. Arianna watched with hitched breath as a wrinkled woman on the panel, swathed in plush pink robes and rings piled on every plump finger, pulled two numbers from a large, decorated basin.

"Slaves Ninety-Seven and Twenty-Six, please take your place," she called down. Her face sagged in all the wrong places, and her hair hung loose on her scalp.

A tall, lanky boy stood up and dragged his feet to the middle of the Square. A small, timid-looking girl followed. Arianna recognized the boy as Herald—someone she had occasionally trained with in her eleventh year. The girl she could not place.

Herald dropped dead within minutes as the girl buried her axe in his throat. She scored an even eight, and the crowd roared as the first of few earned her freedom.

"I saw you die," whispered Liam now that nobody was paying them attention. "You took a sword to the stomach." He still clung to Arianna's hand, but he focused on the next battle, never looking at her.

"And yet, here I am," she said, her voice soft. She turned her body toward Liam, willing him to meet her eyes.

Still, he refused.

"Arianna," he said, staring toward the battlegrounds. His voice cracked. "I thought... I thought I'd lost you." She could feel his hand tremble within her own. "Do you have any idea what was going through my mind when they announced you dead? I—"

"I'm *sorry*," said Arianna, shaking her head. "I wanted to tell you, but Solomon wouldn't let me. He didn't think it was safe for me to show my face until now."

"What do you mean he wouldn't let you?" he hissed.

"It's so complicated, Liam," she said with a shrug. "I am sorry, but I'm here now. Let's just focus on now. Please, just look at me."

Finally, Liam met her gaze, and Arianna shrank back as his eyes burned into hers. Anger or relief, she couldn't tell.

"You don't understand!" The cheers and chants of the crowd drowned out his voice. "I—"

He shook his head, clearly frustrated at something that clawed at his mind.

"What is it?" pleaded Arianna. "You can tell me."

Liam lowered his head.

"I could've stepped in, and I didn't," he said. "I thought you had her at first." He looked away. "I should've been there for you."

For some reason, Arianna felt he meant to say something more, but she didn't press him on it.

"What happened to me wasn't your fault. You can't protect me all the time," said Arianna, gently. "Not in this world. Let's just get through today, all right? After all is said and done, I'll fill you in on everything. I promise."

He gave her a curt nod.

"If your number gets called, don't let your guard down," he said with a somber expression. "But if you do, I won't hesitate to save you this time."

Arianna flushed. "I never need saving," she joked, trying to lift the mood.

That drew a faint smile from Liam, but she could tell his thoughts were elsewhere, still tormenting him; it made her feel that much more guilty about not finding a way to let him know that she had survived. She trusted him with everything, so as soon as she had an opening tonight, she would tell him the truth. She owed him that much.

They turned their attention back to the battles, but thoughts of Liam and their friendship consumed Arianna's mind. No matter what happened in her future, her bond with Liam could never be broken after sharing so many defining experiences in the Jar. Now, here they sat, hand in hand, blood flying in every direction, at their own Free Falls Festivals.

"Slave numbers Forty-Five and Three Hundred," called a husky man who sat to the right of the woman on the panel.

Not even an hour had fully passed yet and already Arianna had seen three people die and three people live.

The bell sounded again for the next candidates to begin

dueling, and two of her peers began to swing their swords back and forth in a myriad of fancy tricks, each quite skilled. Arianna immediately recognized the girls as long-time bunkmates from her former sleeping quarters and close friends. Their hesitation was plain in their horror-struck faces, their hands shaking as they halfheartedly battled—neither had the heart to kill the other.

Thirty minutes of close calls ticked by as they battled, and then the crowd's attention was drawn elsewhere; two gates on either side of the Square creaked open. Suddenly, the subtle sound of hissing filled the air.

As the ominous noise grew louder, the contenders all peered over the low wall at the snow-covered ground to see where it was coming from. Liam grabbed Arianna's robes and pulled her back just as a long, purple and black snake flew into the air where her face had been only seconds before. "Saved you," he said, finally loosening up a bit.

One of their peers at the far end of the wall proved much less fortunate as a snake caught her in the neck with its fangs. Green venom oozed from her skin, and she writhed in agony for a while before she died.

Arianna watched with revulsion as the regulators dragged her body away. "*Snakes?*" she said with a shiver. "That's the general's surprise?"

She gulped, hoping that Westing's 'surprise' meant specifically for her would be far less... alive.

Arianna cringed away from the wall as she recognized more and more long, scaly bodies slithering toward the only movement in the Square, like someone dragged thick ropes through the snow. Some of the snakes even had two heads.

"That's sickening," said Liam, nodding toward the two girls caught in the middle of their hunt.

Arianna turned her attention to her former roommates and couldn't look away. In no time at all, about twenty snakes had encircled them. The snakes raised their heads, tongues licking the air in menacing taunts as they cornered their prey.

The girls pointed their swords away from each other and toward their new enemies. They stood trapped, back to back and surrounded from every angle. They fought bravely, trying to put down as many of the serpents as possible, but the snake was the King's favored symbol for a reason—cunning and swift, feared and respected, a deadly bite if provoked.

The crowd cheered on the warriors, but to no avail. Their final judgment was obvious to all watching.

The snakes were too quick and too hungry.

No matter how many the girls killed, they each suffered bites to their legs and arms in the process. Green liquid gushed from many wounds, and they became slow, their faces twisted in torment as their screams echoed across the Square, the venom taking its course quickly. The girls fell to their knees, trying to fight off more attacks, trying to fight for each other, but the snakes sank their fangs into their skin again and again.

What was only a few minutes passed by like an eternity. Arianna wished it to stop. Then the bell sounded, declaring the battle over as the friends eventually collapsed in the snow, arms linked, to meet their end together.

The remaining serpents continued to slither about in victory, wrapping their bodies around their kill, but their reign was short-lived too. A flurry of arrows rained down on them from skilled archers hidden throughout the unsuspecting crowd. The spectators swung around in search of those with longbows, cheering them on as their arrows struck the last remaining serpents dead and layered over the girls until they were unrecognizable.

"Next up, slaves One Seventeen and Two Thirty-Four," said the lady with the rings, in a bored voice. "Might choose a different spot on the battlefield… the last pair left it a bit messy."

Two boys hopped the stone wall and sauntered forward. One looked rather confident, carrying a large, two-headed flail. The other brandished a mallet with something less than enthusiasm on his face.

"The one with the flail is Kinas Bleridon. Do you remember him from training?" asked Liam.

"Yes," growled Arianna. "He's one of Risso's lot, isn't he?"

"That's right," he replied. "He's her right-hand man. That little guy doesn't stand a chance. I don't even recognize him."

"He reminds me of Pippa a bit," she stuttered, studying the boy intently. Short brown hair brushed his shoulders, and his eyes were surrounded by a bed of freckles. He could've been her twin.

Liam paled at the mention of Pippa's name as he leaned against the wall. "I don't know why she had to go running around with Red Risso's crowd," he said, shaking his head. "She was smarter than that. She should be here with us right now. I'm sorry... I know you two were close."

Arianna whipped around to look at him.

"I knew it!" she said, all her nerves washed away in a wave of anger over Pippa's unjust death. "Tell me what happened that night. I mean, I heard how she died, but *why* was she out past curfew to begin with? You know, don't you? What was Grinda's hand in it?" She'd had her suspicions about this since the night it had happened, but Liam had just confirmed it.

"Slave numbers Fifty-Three and Six, make your way to the center," called someone from the panel as the regulators dragged the boy's body into a growing pile with the others.

Kinas' flail dripped with fresh blood as he strode back toward his friends, triumphant. Grinda and the rest of their gang showered him with praise. He scored a nine for such an expeditious kill, receiving his freedom card with gusto.

Liam looked at Arianna, his expression somber. "The same thing that always happens when someone joins that lot," he answered. "It was initiation night."

"What do you mean?" asked Arianna, barely able to control her building rage. She would have challenged Grinda Risso to another duel then and there to avenge her slain friend if not for the ongoing festivals.

"You really didn't know? That's how they form their group," he said. "Only Pippa was just for a laugh. They knew she wouldn't be able to go through with it. I overheard them talking, but I didn't think she'd actually be naïve enough to try—" He looked to the sky. "Her challenge was to sneak into the Dining Hall and kill one of the pigs they keep there for the elders. She got caught red-handed, *literally*, and the regulators killed her for it. Made a right damn show of it, though. Practically tortured her for a week." He shook his head. "She didn't deserve that."

"No… she didn't," said Arianna, feeling as if a stone had been placed in her gut. She stared at the now blood-splattered snow, and the little dead boy stared back.

FOR THE BATTLES THAT WENT on longer than thirty minutes, the panel introduced new lethal creatures or obstacles. Most of the slaves who had to fight off an extra enemy or survive some horrible 'surprise' died in pairs. And twice Arianna was forced to stand idly by while people she knew were eliminated by a shower of arrows. As the sky grew darker and the snow fell harder, more and more people became absent from her group.

The winners made their way through the crowd to sit in the elders' section, receiving their congratulations. The losers were piled in the corner, outweighing the winners by half.

"Slaves Ninety-One and Fifteen take center," said a stern voice from the panel.

Arianna felt Liam's whole body go rigid beside her; he fingered the silver ninety-one embroidered on his cloak.

"Just one more battle. Then we're free," he said after a moment. He squeezed Arianna's hand and then let go.

Suddenly the bodies heaped in the corner seemed to weigh on her heart, her soul—the slaves who would never fly free.

Not Liam. They can't have Liam, too.

He stood and reluctantly drew a slender sword from the scabbard at his hip.

Arianna felt herself shrivel with the pain of possibly watching him die as Liam leaped the small wall, walking proudly toward his fate. Now she understood how he must've felt during her Warrior's Challenge… so helpless. They'd survived so much together, and she just couldn't fathom a world where he didn't exist.

Then she laid eyes on his opponent and froze, stunned with the reality of the situation; Grinda Risso was waiting for him in the center of the Square, axe in hand.

"No, no, no," she whispered.

Leaning forward, Arianna gripped the stone wall, trying to steady her crumbling world.

"I had hoped for a worthy opponent, but I suppose this will do," she heard Grinda say with that maddening self-righteous sneer plastered across her face.

Liam didn't respond—he normally couldn't be coaxed by the likes of her—but Arianna saw that this time, in this moment, she'd got under his skin a little. His lips curled over his teeth and his brow furrowed as he readied his weapon.

Grinda snickered, following suit.

The falling snow speckled her black hair white as she tossed it over her shoulder; combined with fair skin under the light of the lanterns sparking up around the Square, she appeared as if she were a living corpse. And even though blood drenched the ground they stood upon, marking the places where their peers had brutally died in the hours before, Grinda sniffed at the air, sucking it in through her nose as if she enjoyed the stench of death. She passed her weapon back and forth between her hands. But Liam didn't seem to be worried in the slightest. He just hopped up and down, cracking his neck, as he warmed up for the fight.

Arianna, on the other hand, couldn't quite say the same.

Can he beat the odds?

A hush came over the crowd, all waiting for an entertaining duel. With Liam Black as Grinda Risso's next formal opponent, it might even be as epic as Arianna's Warrior's Challenge; they were both very skilled warriors.

But Liam isn't as good a fighter as me.

Did that mean he couldn't win? Arianna's knuckles turned white as she clenched the wall tighter, the seconds ticking by slowly while she imagined the worst possible endings. In less than an hour's time, she knew very well that she may have to say goodbye to Liam again, and forever.

The bell sounded and Grinda lunged.

Liam dropped to his knees, sliding just under her axe as it sliced through the air in search of flesh. He maneuvered swiftly, jumping back to his feet and thrusting his sword forward. It slashed at her thigh, ripping the cloth of her pants but only nicking the skin as she stepped around him. Arianna could tell Grinda was acutely aware of where he'd send his sword next. They danced just like she and Solomon did during warm-ups.

Thrust, parry, step back, step forward. Thrust again.

Except this time, it wasn't for practice.

Returning Liam's attack, Grinda swung her axe with effortlessness and the blade swiped at his chest. He didn't dodge fast enough, so she drew blood, ripping a gash in his shirt. Arianna winced at the impact, and Liam cursed, jumping back.

Regaining balance, Liam threw off his cloak and darted forward. Sweat dotted his forehead, and his sandy hair looked wild in the wind as it picked up. Now he moved faster, angrier than before. He ran toward Grinda with his sword raised.

Feigning an attack with the blade, he smashed his foot into her chest, and she buckled backward from the force, coughing up blood. He tried to land a deadly blow with his weapon, but it wouldn't be that easy—the clock had only just begun its countdown; Liam would have to really tire her out before he truly caught her off guard.

For what seemed like the longest hour of Arianna's life, she watched Liam and Grinda trap themselves in a whirlwind of metal and snow. They aimed relentless strikes at each other and drew blood time and time again, but they seemed so evenly matched. Not even the elders added any surprises to throw the duel, just as enthralled at who might come out on top in a fair fight as everyone else. And as the hour wound down, the crowd stood to watch for the end. Arianna chewed on her lip, at the edge of her seat.

Grinda lunged at Liam again, this time with the dull end of her axe; the move caught him by surprise. Liam flew off his feet and landed hard on his side, losing grip on his sword. Before he could push his way back up to find his weapon, Grinda had kicked it out of reach.

Arianna knew this move intimately and suddenly felt as if she were the one staring up at the sharp end of Grinda's blade, not even a moment to wonder what death might truly be like. But Arianna *wasn't* the one at her mercy this time... it was Liam. And, true to her nature, without hesitation, Red Risso brought her axe down to open up his skull.

RESURRECTION

WAITING FOR IMMINENT DEATH, Liam kept his eyes shut tight and tried to block out the sound of the screaming, chanting, cheering. Yet the crowd only seemed to grow louder, louder, *louder*, a frenzied roar of excitement echoing around the Square.

It was so loud that he thought that not even the walls of Blancoren could lock in the noise.

Why am I still breathing?

He'd expected to be off to the next life by now.

The sound of metal scraping on metal pierced his ears, and his eyes flew open. Arianna stood over him, using her swords and body like a shield.

"Ara, what are you doing?" he gasped, gaping up at her from the ground. It was as if he'd laid eyes on her for the first time. From this angle, she looked like a goddess sent from the heavens to spare his life.

"Just get out of here," she snapped, barely glancing his way. She held off Grinda's axe long enough for him to crawl to safety. "Go!"

With shaking hands, Liam collected his sword from the snow and rolled up to his feet.

"But I *killed* you," snarled Grinda, shoving off Arianna's swords and looking her up and down with nothing less than ire in her expression. The scar on her face twitched as she glowered at her. "Guess I'll have to do it again."

"You can try," said Arianna, sweeping her swords down by her sides as she observed her opponent—*his* opponent.

She looked like a fiercer warrior than he'd ever realized her to be before, any trace of nerves or fear from earlier replaced with unyielding strength and valor.

"Are you sure you want to do this?" he asked from behind.

"It's already done," she replied, tightening her grip on her weapons.

"Okay, Ara," he said, touching her gently on the shoulder. "I'm sorry you had to…" He shook his head. "Just stay alive."

They locked eyes for a moment, and she tried to offer him a reassuring smile, her defensive stance remaining steadfast.

"Win or die," she said with a shrug, looking back to Grinda.

"Win," he said, firmly. "I know you can."

Liam bowed his head low and moved to the side, knowing himself no longer welcome in this battle. Then Arianna Belvedor stepped forward to challenge Grinda Risso one last time, and the crowd went wild.

THE ADRENALINE PUMPING through Arianna's veins gave

her more courage than she knew reasonable, but she had made her choice. In one rapid move, she lunged forward and begun manipulating her swords in intricate attacks. Grinda struggled to block with her large axe as Arianna moved fast, but she still held her own and wouldn't be easy to take down.

Arianna could hear shouts from the crowd, floating down to them from the stands, questioning who had interrupted the duel. She was still dead to them, and with her cloak wrapped around her and her hood pulled up over her head, it would be hard for them to see anything of her.

From the corner of her eye, she saw that regulators had moved in on the undeclared battle, but the general signaled to them to wait. Grinda thrashed her weapon back and forth, but Arianna dodged her in a lethal dance about the Square, never losing her grip on her swords or her focus.

Thrust, parry, step back, step forward. Thrust again.

The battle seemed to continue on forever before Grinda took the lead. She threw her leg out, and Arianna tripped, giving Grinda just long enough to smash the dull end of her axe into her side. Arianna flew backward to the snow, landing on her back and her head smacking against the ground.

In that moment, the events of her failed Warrior's Challenge flashed through her memories, so clear. She remembered it all. The battle, the blood, the pain. And Grinda standing over her with her own sword as the district cheered her on.

A roar of anger ripped out of Arianna like she had never let free before; she thought of how hard she'd fought to get to this very day. And all for *what?* She stole a glance toward General Ivo, sitting there on his pedestal with a smug look on his face, so amused at this thrilling Free Falls Festivals surprise.

For the crowd's entertainment.

It wasn't fair. Her life wasn't someone else's to control. It belonged to her. It was *hers*, and it enraged her that she had to keep fighting to live it.

But Arianna had survived that Warrior's Challenge, and she would survive this, too. Clearing her mind as she lay there, atop a bed of crimson snow, atop the blood of her fallen peers, she willingly relinquished her hold on her weapons and got to her feet, the fire in her heart surely burning in her eyes.

Grinda took a step back, weapon raised as she observed her. She was scared, and Arianna could feel it.

Locking eyes with Grinda in that instant, unhindered by fear of the unknown and of breaking the rules, Arianna knew she truly existed. And it was an existence unlike any of her peers could possibly fathom. Arianna *lived*, resurrected by magic, and she wasn't going to let Grinda Risso, or anyone else, take her life from her again before she even had a chance to live it.

She saw her own strength reflected in Grinda's wide-eyed stare—the strength of a girl who had cheated Death. The fear, the uncertainty, the mysteries of life were scribbled all over Grinda's floundering face. And it broke her. In that weak moment, she knew Grinda saw herself as dead, slave to a world where she'd never escape her demons. There would never be freedom for her, never be a place for someone who had fallen so far. And Arianna saw that too; she saw Grinda as dead as the corpses in the corner.

The air stilled all around the Square, the crowd hungry for blood, and Arianna thought not to make them wait much longer. She removed her cloak, letting it fall to her feet as her eyes swept the watchers in the stands; it was time she came back from the dead.

Everyone leaned in for a closer look.

Crouching to retrieve her swords from the snow, Arianna could've sworn she saw silver streak across her own eyes, reflecting in the worn metal of her blades. Then she straightened her back and confronted Grinda once more, giving all of the Warrior's District a clear view of her face.

Whispers grew into howls of astonishment as people began to recognize who she was. The golden emblem on the back of her shirt and the twin swords in hand screamed warrior, but Arianna was determined to finally win that title. She felt powerful with the audience cheering on her return and shouting her name. Nothing and no one could stand in her way.

Let them try if they wish.

The crowd continued to roar and applaud her resurgence, sending her name floating in and out through the sea of red in a wave of booming sound. Turning away from them, her confidence soaring to a world beyond King Devlindor and his rules, Arianna glared toward the elders' section, setting eyes on General Ivo. He rose from his throne-like chair to meet her challenge, and the Square grew silent as they waited for him to finally react.

"Arianna Belvedor," he said after a moment. "So you live? *Bravo.* I'm shocked, indeed, at your full recovery." His glance shifted momentarily to Solomon who was still seated with the other elders, but then he signaled something to the regulators; they began to move slowly until Arianna found herself surrounded on all sides. "Such a waste that your time here is short. You should've waited for your number to be called."

He lowered himself back to his seat, taking a sip of something from a goblet and smacking his lips.

"You've broken the rules," he said, sternly. "I'm very sorry, but you're hereby disqualified."

He flashed a condemning smile, the regulators unsheathing their swords, lifting their shields, and closing a tight circle around Arianna in the same second.

Win or die.

There were too many for her to take alone and survive, but she wouldn't run; she wasn't going down without a fight or without taking Grinda Risso with her. Arianna steadied her weapons, and General Ivo gave a single nod to Westing, who was now front and center of the enclosing circle.

"Goodbye," Westing mouthed as he motioned for his men to attack.

Arianna faintly wondered if this was the surprise he'd had in store for her duel all along or if she'd screwed up his prior plans to torment her today. Then she readied herself for battle.

AS FORTY-ODD REGULATORS lifted their swords to cut her open, two things happened at once that Arianna couldn't readily explain. First, the regulators dropped dead or dying at her feet within moments, groaning as they collided with the ground. Second, the elders' section of the crowd began to scream. Their shrieks mixed eerily with the howls of the wind as they herded away from the Square, followed by a stream of terrified slaves.

Before Arianna could even begin to comprehend the situation, Liam had grabbed hold of her hand. He tried to guide her across the grounds to safety, but they kept stumbling over the bodies of the regulators; Arianna noticed some without any wounds to speak of, looking as if they'd choked to death the way their faces appeared so blue. Others had multiple arrows protruding from their backs.

"Liam, what's going on?" she yelled over the commotion. "What about Grinda?"

She glanced back and didn't see her anywhere now.

"Damn, she's gone!" Then the reality of what she'd just done set in. "I can't believe I'm still alive," she muttered to herself.

"Yeah, well, let's try to stay that way," said Liam, breathing hard as he pulled her along.

When they made their way outside of the circle of dead regulators, Arianna looked up to the stands and noticed that others had also met their ending, lying for dead across the stone benches of the amphitheater, sprawling over each other as the crowd pushed and shoved to take leave.

"Watch out!" Liam shouted suddenly, whipping out his sword and pushing Arianna back. She collided with the ground so hard that she could taste mud on her tongue.

Glancing up, she found Westing's and Liam's swords locked together; somehow the general's right hand had managed to dodge the freak attack upon the other regulators in the field. He lunged at Liam without a second thought, and the two begun to battle around the bodies and the blood like it was a regular training day in the Dueling Arena—a master versus apprentice.

Except this was the Free Falls, and in keeping with its rules, Arianna knew that one or both of them would die.

"By gods, Ara, are you all right?" Lessa was running toward her with Sano on her shoulders and her bow across her back.

"I'm fine," said Arianna, letting her help her to her feet. "But what in the King's name is going on?"

"You can thank me later," she said, gesturing to her bow. "It's a good thing your district doesn't turn heads at people walking around with weapons. I felt like a misfit without it."

"This was all you?" asked Arianna, gawking at her.

"Of course not!" replied Lessa with the wave of her hand. "Talis and Solomon took out one or two." She smiled and then leaned in to whisper, "Magic can be *really* dangerous." Her tone was so serious, frightened almost, as all traces of joking wiped from her face.

Arianna nodded as clarity struck her—the regulators had been no match for seasoned sorcerers. She glanced up to see Talis and Solomon racing across the grounds to join them.

Solomon looked exhausted, flashing a scowl at Arianna before running over to Liam; he was still exchanging blows with Westing and clearly struggling under the man's expertise. Scooping up a discarded shield, Solomon threw his body in front of Liam, blocking Westing's next swing of the sword.

"Son, you've done bravely," he said as he maneuvered Liam out of the battle, taking his place. "I'll take it from here."

Sir Dean Westing morphed from arrogant to livid in the split second it took for Solomon to enter the duel. Spit started flying from his lips and his face turned a bright orange as he thrashed his sword about with more ferocity than before.

Not at all troubled, Solomon seemed almost bored as he blocked the careless attacks with ease.

"Emotions have no place on the battlefield, young man. You would've done well to remember that," he said, coolly.

In a blur of silver, the Great Wolf of the East delivered Westing one final lesson. His neck opened up at the unforgiving slice of Solomon's blade, and Arianna saw that his blood matched the color of his red locks now lying limp in the snow.

After a moment of silence to observe the slain warrior, Solomon spoke, "Now we must be off. Quickly, follow me!"

As they all turned to take leave, a cry stopped them short.

"I win," said a soft, snakelike voice.

Arianna stiffened. In all the disorder, she'd forgotten about Grinda lurking somewhere nearby; she'd recognize that voice anywhere. Turning on her heels, slowly, she was terrified at what she might find. And when she saw what Grinda had done, her heart shriveled in her chest as she witnessed new, innocent blood staining the snow—there lay Liam Black, in all his glory, wounded by the likes of Red Risso. A pool of dark red grew around his body from a deep gash at his side.

Arianna ran to kneel beside him.

He moaned, blood sputtering from his mouth as he clutched at her face.

"End her," he said through clipped breaths.

Talis came over with Lessa right behind. They pushed Arianna aside and started working together to try to mend his injury. They shouted commands for her to help, but she didn't hear the words. Arianna couldn't hear anything other than the rage pounding in her ears and calling for Grinda's head.

Liam's words took over her mind. *End her.* She heard nothing else but his voice. *End her.*

She stood, leaving her beloved friend in the hands of the healers as she marched toward where Grinda stood waiting. Storm-gray eyes smiled in conquest, and Arianna beckoned her forward with her swords to initiate their final battle.

End her.

Grinda lunged, twirling the long axe with new confidence, Liam's blood dripping from the blade.

Arianna cried out in fury—a warrior's cry—as she ran forward to meet her. She swung both of her swords in unyielding attacks; the metal sparked and screeched with each hammering blow. Grinda tried her best to defend herself, but she was faltering. Catching a break between Arianna's attacks, she held her axe high over her head and sprang toward her, a scream tearing from her throat.

This time, though, Arianna felt compelled to try something new… something dangerously different in defense. Placing her swords down by her sides, she closed her eyes, focusing. There was something strong, an energy, scratching at her mind that desperately wanted to be released.

If I can only reach it.

She'd felt it before as a dull ache thrumming in the background, but now it was loud, banging on the walls of her brain relentlessly. And she knew it wouldn't stop until it broke through. Feeling the air shift as Grinda brought her axe down hard and fast, something fierce, something transformative, took hold of her at that moment.

She grasped that energy.

Her eyes flew open, and she knew this was her time. "*Luzcora*," she said in a whisper.

She raised her swords, quick as lightning, and crossed them in front of her chest. With her feet planted firmly on the ground, she wouldn't let Grinda's axe push through her barrier, and she held strong. For a second, everything was silent, still, save for the grunts and groans of the two warriors, but then Arianna truly felt a new power pulsing through her veins, coursing beneath her skin—as the magic took hold and joined her in battle; after this, she would *never* doubt Solomon's wisdom again.

Arianna lifted her gaze to meet Grinda's just as a burst of light grew from the collision. It sizzled like fire until it eventually exploded, sending sparks in every direction. A shield of air encompassed Arianna, keeping her safe from the backfire. Grinda, on the other hand, flew backward, landing in a heap on a blanket of snow.

When Arianna went to look upon Grinda's face, she only saw death; her axe had shattered into a thousand pieces, the remnants of the metal and wood buried in her chest and face. Blood drenched her pale skin, and her gray eyes clouded over permanently.

"I suppose you *yield*," spat Arianna, feeling dazed, drained, and powerful.

As she gazed upon the body of her first kill, she felt like a real warrior. And yet, a small pang of guilt grew in her gut for adding another lost soul to the City of the Four Corners—even if it was Grinda Risso's.

Shut it out, shut it out.

A skill she'd already mastered.

Looking up, Arianna searched for any sign of General Ivo, wanting to avoid any other nasty surprises, but found him to be missing from the Square. Instead, she saw Solomon standing not too far off, regarding her with a strange expression. He looked from her to the slain girl at her feet and back, but she looked away to the stands, no strength to try to decipher his judgments right now… nor the magic she'd just summoned. The Free Falls crowd was still in chaos, scrambling in every direction. However, to Arianna's utter disbelief, several slaves were actually struggling against the regulators—they were starting to fight back, too.

Could this really be happening?

"Ara!" she heard someone call.

She snapped back to reality, back to where Liam lay dying, and found that a new but familiar face had joined them.

"Noah?" she gasped, sheathing her swords. "You shouldn't be here! It's not safe for you with us."

"I was so worried when I realized it was you down there… fighting her again," he replied. "I thought you were dead! He'll be all right, won't he?" He glanced to Liam, his face splotched with tears.

"He'll be okay," said Arianna, firmly. She trapped her emotions inside and put on a brave face for Noah, locking him in her arms. "He has to be."

They pulled apart and went over to Talis and Lessa. Arianna sought for some sign of hope that her words spoke a truth but found it to be missing from their faces. As they rubbed something around Liam's wound, she heard Talis whispering a familiar incantation, one that she'd heard Lessa recite many times during training hours.

"We need to get back to the sparring room," interjected Solomon. He turned his attention to Arianna. "Take Liam there. I'll meet you as soon as I can, but I must fetch something first. They'll be searching for you soon. We have to hurry!" He ran off without another word, leaving them alone.

The four took hold of Liam, lifting him into the air and

heading back to the Dueling Arena as fast as they could manage. Outside, the district had lost all sanity. People ran riot in the streets, and robes of red and black clashed as regulators and slaves scattered in every direction. Some fought, some ran, and some hid from the disarray. Arianna and her group stayed in the shadows, hoping not to be spotted or confronted before they made it somewhere safe.

Finally reaching Arianna's private training quarters, Lessa unlocked the door with the stolen key and they all hurried in. The air inside was warm and welcoming, the fire from earlier still burning.

"Let's take him to the well room," said Arianna.

They all shuffled through the other door and placed Liam on the bed.

"Should I stay and help?" asked Lessa as they all observed the bloodied boy on the table.

Arianna was speechless as she really took him in, so ravaged. She wondered if this horrible image was what she must have looked like after Grinda had gotten to her, too. Her fists balled at her sides. She was suddenly so contented that Red Risso would never taste freedom; she didn't deserve it.

But Liam did.

Just survive.

"No, you've done enough," answered Talis. "Leave the rest to me." He shooed them out and closed the door.

Leaving Talis to work his magic, Arianna, Lessa, and Noah all sat in silence, the screams and shouts from the streets trickling in through the walls to fill the quiet. So many thoughts fought for Arianna's attention as she waited to see if Liam would live. She wanted answers, confused about the turn of events following her return to the living, though now hardly seemed the time to ask.

"Girls, what are you doing just sitting around! Gather your things," barked Talis, popping out of the well room after what felt like years, sweat beading on his forehead. "You'll be leaving very shortly."

He disappeared back into the room, leaving the door wide open as he worked so that they all had a clear view of Liam—he looked like a ghostly version of himself.

"What does he mean?" stuttered Noah. "Where are you going, Ara?"

Arianna and Lessa locked eyes with each other for a moment, hardly able to fathom Talis' words.

"It's okay, Noah," said Arianna, patting his leg. "Everything's going to be all right. Just stay here a moment." Her own stomach was in knots that she wasn't sure could ever be untangled.

The girls flew into action, gathering their belongings and tossing the essentials into two separate rucksacks. Then suddenly, the doors of the sparring room burst open and everyone drew their weapons.

"Relax, it's just me and Cyn!" said Solomon, holding up his hands as they slipped inside and shut the door. "Put those things away before you hurt someone."

Arianna let out a sigh of relief at seeing her master and caretaker, placing her sword back in its sheath.

"Oh, my," said Cyn, a hand on her heart as she took in all of their faces. She sucked in a deep breath and then turned to Arianna with a serious expression, so unlike her. "I heard what happened out there, heard what you did, and thought you could use a hand. Take these and use them wisely. I'm sure Lessa will know how. I've also brought some food." She pushed a small bundle and a leather water canteen into her hands. "I hope to see you again, but take care of yourself, you hear? I can't be there to fix you up anymore."

"I'll try," stammered Arianna, perplexed at Cyn's parting words as she added the care package to her rucksack. "Thank you, Cyn."

She didn't know what else to say, focusing on steadying her emotions.

"Please try your very best," she replied with a soft smile. Then her gaze set on Talis in the well room. "I see the boy's pretty bad off?"

"It's not looking good," called Talis as he worked. "I can't seem to stop the bleeding."

"It never does after the festivals. That much is still normal tonight," she said. "Do what you can, and I'll be back to check on him when all this dies down. If he makes it, maybe he'll have another chance to fight." She looked again to Arianna, pulling her into her chest for a moment. "I'm proud of you, dear. You've been *so* brave." She pushed her back to arm's length, eyes glimmering as she observed her. "Yes, so very brave. Stay strong out there."

Then she flew out the door before Arianna could even think of how to respond.

"How did all this happen?" she asked Solomon, unable to hide the panic in her voice. "What are we going to do?"

Solomon lowered his voice to a whisper, pulling Arianna away from where Noah still sat in tears near the well room.

"After you jumped the wall to save Liam, Talis and I had already resolved to do something," he said. "But before we could, *someone* started firing arrows from the elders' section."

His eyes flicked to Lessa, who still ran around the room adding to their rucksacks, though there was no anger there.

"There were archers on duty all throughout the Square," he continued, "so I stopped them with magic before they could send an arrow toward you or pinpoint Lessa. The crowd ran scared when people started falling dead around them in the stands." For a moment he looked thoughtful. "It was the perfect cover, really. Then Talis took out the rest of the regulators on the ground with a spell."

Arianna's mind buzzed with his explanation; all of a sudden, magic was a part of her life, uprooting it in the most incomprehensible of ways.

"But what about the general? Where is he?" she replied. "How could we go anywhere with him—"

"General Ivo won't be able to get orders to any of the regulators right now," said Solomon. "Especially with Westing dead and a good chunk of his warriors in the same predicament." He glanced out of the window. "It's calming down out there, though. Once they regroup, they'll be coming for you next. We need to get you out of here, and fast."

"But *how*, Master Bell? No one's ever escaped the Four Corners before!" said Arianna, pulling at her hair. Was he really suggesting this? It all felt so surreal.

"Think," he said with a smirk, tapping his temple.

"I don't know. We can't just start walking through the Vanishing Tunnels—" she choked on her own words as a wild thought flew into her mind. She laid eyes on Lessa. "Wait, you don't mean to say… the caves? *Our* cave?" She swallowed the lump in her throat. "Are you serious?"

Quite literally, Arianna had escaped her district before, though not intentionally. And Lessa had escaped hers, too, in the very same way. But what Solomon was suggesting, the idea that their utopia could be a genuine underground escape, a way to *actually* break out of the Jar, terrified her beyond words.

"You know," said Solomon, "when I said surprise them, I really didn't have all this in mind." He pursed his lips, crossing his arms at his chest as he narrowed his eyes at her.

"Master, I—"

"Yes, your way was much more effective, wasn't it? Definitely moved things along." He walked over and gave her a strong, unexpected hug. "Now grab your things. I have to get you and Lessa out of here before it's too late."

Arianna stumbled out of his embrace and then strapped on her rucksack and made sure her swords were fastened securely in the sheath at her back. Lessa did the same, fixing Sano and her bow and arrows safely around her shoulders.

"Ready?" said Lessa, her face scrunched up with worry.

"As I'll ever be," said Arianna with a shrug. "But what about Liam? Will he be all right?" She looked to Talis from across the room.

"I'm sorry, but there's nothing more I can do," he called back, leaning against the doorframe of the well room, a haggard expression on his face. "He's lost so much blood." He wiped his hands on his pants, staining the fabric red. "I'll have to wait and see, but I don't think he'll pull—"

"*What?* No!" Arianna ran to Liam's side before Solomon could protest. She had thought Talis had everything under control, but everything was so clearly the opposite.

Her soul ached for justice as she watched Liam die; it wasn't enough that she'd killed Grinda. Arianna massaged his cold hand in hers, and even so near death he looked handsome.

"Use your magic," she blurted out to Talis, pleading with watering eyes. "You healed me, so you can heal him too!"

Noah came into the room behind her, sobbing silently. Arianna could tell that he didn't understand half of what was going on.

"I've tried," replied Talis, glancing uneasily at Noah, "but I've told you before that such power can only be summoned. Either he's rejecting my... *treatment*, or it's rejecting him. Whatever the reason, it's not working." He whispered now so that only she could hear. "And the spell I used to bring you back is not something I would do again lightly. It can have dangerous consequences and only rarely works for the better. You're a lucky one, Arianna. I really am sorry, but that's just not something I'm willing to do for your friend. It's too big a risk." He pushed the silver hair from his face, so nonchalantly, as if her friend's life were inconsequential.

Arianna wanted to scream for Talis to take back his words. What made Liam's life any different from hers?

He deserves the same chance!

Just as she thought she might lose all control over her emotions, Arianna felt a consoling hand on her shoulder. Lessa was by her side.

"Can really nothing be done?" she asked Talis.

He dabbed a wet cloth on Liam's skin. "All we can do is wait now and make him comfortable for what comes next," he said, evenly.

"And what comes next?" asked Arianna, regarding her friend with new sorrow like she'd never felt before. "What is there after this life? If he dies, all of this was for nothing!"

You must live, Liam. You must!

Sano jumped down from Lessa's shoulders and onto Liam's stomach.

"*Sano,*" gasped Lessa. "Come back here. I'm sorry, Ara."

"Get off!" shrieked Arianna, appalled as the little monkey paced back and forth across her dying friend. "Get him off."

Before Lessa could snatch Sano back into her arms, he pressed his silver paws against Liam's bloodied and bruised skin, a soft, silver light glowing from beneath them. The fatal wound at Liam's side started to shrink as the light rolled all across his body—the room went silent as they all watched a miracle happen.

When all was through and the light was gone, a silver, iridescent scar had replaced the gash at Liam's side, glittering where before there had been nothing but blood. His eyes were still shut tight, but his breathing had stabilized and the color was returning to his cheeks.

Arianna gently placed a hand across his chest and felt a strong heartbeat there, thumping beneath her palm. "He's... I think he's been healed." She gazed at Sano with new eyes.

"Mercy be the gods!" said Talis, glancing to Solomon who stood in the doorway. "We were right. He *is* an avatar." Were those tears Arianna saw? Talis wiped them away quickly.

Solomon remained speechless, staring wide-eyed at Sano and Liam from across the room. Noah had his eyes clamped shut, muttering calming words to himself—Arianna was sure he'd missed it all.

"What just happened?" asked Lessa, warily, as Sano sauntered back to his perch at her shoulder. "What's an *avatar?*" She scrutinized her furry friend who only gazed back at her with large, mocking eyes.

Arianna recalled the word from one of Talis' scrolls, but it was part of a world yet to be properly defined for her; she had no idea what it actually meant, how a monkey could have possibly saved Liam's life. Clearly this had something to do with magic, but that was even more bizarre to comprehend than her own enchanted revival story.

"Never mind that now!" snapped Talis. "There isn't the time. We can't risk you two staying here a moment longer. You just take good care of Sano. There's more to him than meets the eye."

"But, Master Churry—" started Arianna.

"You must go! I promise Liam will be fine now," he said.

"Aren't you coming with us?" asked Lessa.

Talis gave her a gentle smile and shook his head. "It looks like I'm needed here, but don't worry. We'll meet again," he said, giving her a quick squeeze around the shoulders. "Just don't forget your lessons and all will be okay. You'll always find the answers if only you remember to keep faith, even during the darkest of hours. Isn't that right, Solomon?"

Solomon nodded, a solemn expression across his face. "That's right," he said.

Then Talis pulled away. "Remember that, child."

Silent tears streaked Lessa's cheeks, no more words left to

say; Sano nudged her affectionately, trying to wipe them away.

"Here, put these on," said Solomon, walking over to Arianna. He shrugged out of his cloak. "They'll stop you for sure if you wear your own."

"Really? You're okay to part with them… for me?"

He nodded. "Oh, I have plenty of the same. And whatever the general said of the Free Falls, the number one rule is to survive. You earned these tonight."

Arianna didn't shed her district robes lightly, the number twenty-two permanently imprinted on the old cloth. But when Solomon laid his own cloak over her shoulders, white velvet trimmed with fur and lined with crimson silk on the inside, the cloth slid across her skin deliciously.

My name is Arianna Belvedor, and I'm a—

Suddenly, she didn't feel like such a slave anymore.

"It's time to say goodbye, Ara," said Solomon.

The thought of leaving anyone behind made her sick, but Arianna saw no other choice. She tried to think positively now.

For whatever reason, Liam lives. And Talis will make sure he stays that way.

Arianna reached for his hand, and suddenly his eyes flew open. "He's awake!" she cried. "Liam, oh, I'm so happy you're awake."

"He's really alive?" sniffled Noah from across the room.

"He really is," she laughed, wiping the tears from her eyes.

"What… what happened?" said Liam, trying to sit up.

Arianna pushed him back down, still holding his hand.

"You were trying to save me," she replied. "I told you not to do that." She forced a smile on her lips.

"Ara, we *have* to go," called Lessa near the doorway with Solomon now. Arianna ignored them.

"Liam, listen, there isn't much time," she said. "My friend and I have to leave now. The regulators will be looking for us soon. But now that you're awake, you can come too!" She squeezed his hand tighter. "Do you remember anything? Can you get up?"

Liam's eyes flicked around sporadically, clearly confused as he registered all the faces hovering in the well room. Then his attention landed on Noah cowering in the corner.

"Yes, I remember," he said with a clenched jaw. "But leave? Leave how? Where?" Liam scrunched his eyes closed. "No, no, I… I can't leave Noah."

Arianna looked to Noah and then to Solomon but he shook his head, confirming what she already knew; they couldn't drag Noah into this, and she wasn't sure if he even had all his wits about him right now to make it very far. He would stay here with Talis and be in good hands.

"Noah will be fine," she said, turning back to Liam and tugging his hand. "Nobody knows he has anything to do with what happened. His life will go right back to normal when things calm down, but you and I… we *have* to go."

"Arianna," he said, resisting her, "I don't know how I'm even alive right now. My whole body aches, and I can barely move. And Noah looks like he might lose his stomach." She glanced to her young friend again and saw his face to be the color of the slop they served in the Dining Hall. But she didn't have time to comfort him now. He'd have to figure things out on his own from here on out, and she had every faith Noah could survive without her and Liam watching over him—he'd have to. "I don't know where you're planning to go or how you're going to get there, but don't worry about us. We'll just slow you down."

Arianna shook her head at that thought, afraid for Liam's future. What would General Ivo do to him after losing to Grinda during the Free Falls? Surely he wouldn't let him live after such a failure. Now was their chance to leave this place, together, for better or for worse.

"Liam, I'm not leaving here without you. I… I love you!"

she said, averting her eyes. Finally, she let the words which had been locked in her heart for too long spill from her mouth, and it was such a relief. Fairytale or not, she needed Liam to know that what she felt for him ran deeper than just friendship. "I can't just leave you here to the gods know what fate. *Please*, just try and get up. I know you can. You're so strong."

For a moment, Liam just seemed surprised, but then his expression wavered into something else.

Angry? Sad? Offended?

Arianna had no idea what he was thinking or feeling, but he yanked his hand away—she froze with fear.

"Love? What place does love have in this wretched world? And how could I love you after all you've put me through, Ara, after all of *this*?" he shouted, eyes glistening and face red, contorted with… definitely anger.

His voice sent chills to Arianna's core, and the air grew cold all around her.

"I didn't even know you were alive until tonight. How could you do that to me?" he said. "Maybe if I hadn't been so distracted by you none of this would've…" He let out a long, exasperated exhale and turned away from her, looking toward the window so that she could no longer see his face. "Just go already! Get out of here. Then Noah and I can just go back to how things were. When we thought you were dead."

Of all the wounds Arianna had ever lived through, this one hurt the most—a blade stabbed straight through the center of her heart. She stumbled away from Liam's bedside, her head spinning with his words. After muttering quick goodbyes to Talis and Noah, she burst out of the well room and didn't look back. Solomon and Lessa gave her space, but they stayed close behind as they all stepped back out into the cold.

LEAVING THE DUELING ARENA—and Talis, Noah, and Liam—behind, the girls ran toward their secret caverns with Solomon as their escort. The pandemonium from the botched festivals had died down, but so far there were no regulators in sight. "Hurry," whispered Solomon, ushering Arianna and Lessa toward the barracks. "We're nearly there."

The voice of a man reached their ears from down the street. "Got 'em. That's them over there!"

By the time they'd turned around to see, his black cloak was disappearing around a corner.

"Damn," spat Solomon, growing tense. "It's a trap. They were waiting us out. Keep going!" He pressed against their backs to run faster.

Before Arianna could even comprehend the situation, the pounding of hooves on the ground reached her ears, heading toward them fast. The snowy streets had cleared of people now, so she, Lessa, and Solomon stood out like sores on the land. A group of about thirty regulators on the backs of hefty horses surrounded them moments later.

As the horses came to a halt, locking them in a circle back to back, a gust of wind blew up the snow, blurring Arianna's vision. When it settled, she saw how close they actually were to the barracks where the entrance to her utopia was hidden against the walls of Blancoren. She also spotted the occupants of the slave quarters peeking out of windows and doors as war broke out in the street, as if they'd been waiting for exactly this to happen.

Solomon had been right—they'd realized the trap much too late; the regulators had surely known they would try to head toward the Vanishing Tunnels. For all they knew, there was only one way out the Jar, and that entrance was not too far off from where they were now.

"What do we do?" cried Lessa, hugging Sano close. "It's ten to one!"

Arianna had already unsheathed her swords. She and Solomon locked eyes then, and she understood with just one look at his face that this was her real Free Falls test of the night.

"Ready your bow," said Arianna to Lessa, trying to remain calm. It wouldn't serve her to panic now. "Remember what we practiced before. It'll be fine. We just have to make it to the tunnels."

Lessa swallowed her fears and nodded, whipping her bow and arrows around to her front and preparing for battle.

"We can take them," added Solomon, pulling out his swords in one fluid movement. "The element of surprise is ours tonight." He ran forward to fight, and Arianna and Lessa followed his lead.

"Let the Free Falls Festivals begin," whispered Arianna as the familiar clashing of metal began once more.

"Kill them!" one of the regulators shouted. "General Ivo demands their heads."

The horses kicked their hooves into the air and circled them ruthlessly as their opponents swung their weapons around, trying to hack them apart. It was hard to defend from such a disadvantage, and just one true hit could mean the end.

Solomon covered Lessa at first until she eventually found a higher perch on a nearby fallen rock; she fired as many arrows as she could, taking down a few horses by accident and knocking some of the regulators onto more even ground for Arianna and Solomon to spar with.

Arianna struggled under their numbers as the regulators came at them in waves, but Solomon had taught her well and she managed to avoid any fatal attacks. If there was one thing she'd learned, it was how to defend herself, and these warriors were nothing compared to her master's skill with a sword. She used to think all regulators invincible, but now that she was actually testing them out in battle, she thought they must've grown lazy during their time being pampered in the district for how slow and sloppy they proved to be.

How naïve I've been.

If it had been thirty organized warrior-slaves against these thirty *skilled* regulators, one-to-one, she was sure their opponents wouldn't have lasted even this long.

Nevertheless, Solomon did most of the real work in the end. Once he really got going, there was hardly anything for Arianna and Lessa to do. The regulators' fancy shields, armors, and weapons meant nothing against his power—both magic and metal alike.

He worked his best moves, tearing through their opponents so quickly that Lessa and Arianna had to duck out of his path just to be safe.

Horses scattered every which way as more regulators were brought to their knees by the minute. At one point, Solomon slammed the tip of his sword into the ground, whispering spells all the while—enchanted flames burst out from the blades, searing everything in their paths at his command; it looked as if a blazing octopus stormed the night, whipping at anything that moved.

When the magical fire had dissipated, Solomon set his swords on the ground and abruptly clapped his hands together. A burst of energy exploded from his fingertips, knocking the regulators in the vicinity off their feet. Then, picking up his weapons, he began to sing incantations, swirling like a deadly wind around their attackers who still dared to draw breath. As his magic joined them in battle, the night dissolved into a spectacle of vivacious color, regulators dropping dead at their feet with each flick of Solomon's sword.

Arianna couldn't believe his display of power. These warriors hadn't stood a chance against the Wolf of the East. And soon, they all reached the peace of the grave together.

The battle was won.

Everything was silent a moment, and Solomon stood in

the center of the chaos, struggling to catch his breath. He clutched at his chest and leaned on the handles of his swords for support, the battle clearly taking a toll on him.

"There's more coming!" shouted Lessa, gathering back some of her arrows as quickly as she could.

After sheathing her swords and grabbing hold of Solomon's hand, Arianna hurried up the street with Lessa by her side, not wasting a second. She knew there were still eyes on them all over the district, her peers watching closely as they raced past the never-ending line of slave barracks plastered against the mountains.

"Under here," she said not moments later.

They ducked underneath one of the barracks and out of sight. They had to crouch low as they walked, but they traveled along the wall of the Blancoren for several minutes, trying to wipe their tracks so that no one could follow. Then finally, Arianna reached the loose stone in the wall and pushed so that it fell inward.

Thud.

The sound seemed to echo on forever.

Lessa crawled inside the tunnels first, followed by Arianna. She turned back for Solomon, but he shook his head.

Her heart sank as terror took its place. "What are you doing?" she said. "We must hurry!" Arianna reached out her hand to aid him.

"This isn't a journey we can take together," he said. "I have to stay with Talis. I can't leave him alone here after this. They know he was my guest, and they'll eat him alive if I don't protect him." His voice was thick with dread, and he held a grave expression. "And I'm not young anymore. All that magic really weakened me. You'll be better off on your own."

Arianna heard the pattering of footsteps, angry voices, and more horses as what sounded like an army edged closer, patrolling the outskirts of the barracks to try to figure out a lead.

The seconds ticked by fast.

"But, Master, you can't hold off all those regulators on your own," said Arianna, beginning to really panic. It was now or never. "Especially not if your energy is drained. You'll be dead before you reach Talis! Please, just take my hand. We can all escape." She couldn't hold back her tears any longer, her cheeks running hot as they fell.

"Then I shall die fighting for him, and for *you*," he said, sternly. "As you would've for Liam tonight."

The idea of losing both men in her life so abruptly was an excruciating thought, and she began to sob even harder.

"Arianna, stop blubbering and give me your swords!" he commanded, holding out his hand to her.

Too distraught to question this strange request, she unsheathed her bronze blades and offered them over with shaking hands. The storming of footsteps and voices grew louder; regulators were starting to search under the barracks.

"You were the perfect apprentice," said Solomon, setting them aside, so calm even as the world seemed to crumble all around him, "and I think you deserve your reward."

He slid his own magnificently molded twin swords from their sheaths and gave them to her. The hilts were jeweled in a rainbow of hues, and their combined weight felt like feathers in her hands.

"Master Bell, I… can't possibly accept these from you," she breathed as he bestowed the extraordinary gifts.

"In this, you don't have a choice, girl. Though, I'm certain you'll have many others in your future. Use them wisely," he said. "They've seen many battles, of both man and magic. If you let them, they may teach you something special."

He flashed that smile Arianna loved so much. Then he fished something out from his robes.

"And here, take this too. It's what I had to run and collect earlier." He handed her a rolled, tattered parchment tied with a ribbon. "It's a map that I hope you'll find most useful on your journey."

"But I don't—"

"Arianna, I've seen your strength. You're a true warrior now." He planted a quick kiss on her cheek and tried to wipe away her tears, though they kept falling.

"I never beat you, though," she said in barely a whisper.

Solomon began inching away, taking Arianna's old swords with him. "You've got my blades, haven't you?" he replied. "A master swordsman doesn't just relinquish his most precious of weapons without an epic fight."

The voices of the regulators were more distinct now, almost upon them.

"They must be won by determination and relentless fight," he added. "I think it's safe to say that you've proven yourself worthy, Arianna Belvedor—Warrior of the Olleb. Now you must go and protect her."

The regulators closed in now, and Arianna could clearly hear General Ivo relaying commands.

"Protect her from what?" she asked, unable to even blink as she watched him retreat.

"If and when it's your destiny to know, then you will know," he said with a little chuckle, looking at her curiously. "Girls, journey well and keep each other safe. Everything will unfold with time... *should* you make the right choices. First and foremost, find yourself new, worthy trainers. Go to the City of Luose and seek Ferlon Ragaric. He can help you there." He gave them one last look. "And do remember to never lose your faith. If nothing else, that will keep you safe. You're not free yet, so go now!"

Arianna flinched at his final command. And this time she didn't dare disobey. She sucked in the last of her tears, her voice unwavering. "Goodbye, Master Bell," she called. "I hope we meet again someday."

He gave her a respectful bow of the head. "Let's see what Destiny has in store for us."

Arianna held her head high, wanting to be strong for him—for the man who had taught her to always be strong. Then Solomon turned his back to her and ducked out from under the barracks.

When he was out of sight, reluctantly, Arianna replaced the small stone in the mountainside and she and Lessa were plunged into momentary darkness. The sound of magic on metal came thunderous to their ears as the Great Wolf of the East added more notches to his blades; Arianna only hoped no one would add a wolf's life to theirs on this dark night.

22

VANISHING TUNNELS

TAKING HER BY THE HAND, Lessa led Arianna through the familiar passage away from the Warrior's District and toward the sanctuary they had both stumbled upon years ago. The firebugs buzzed and blazed along the ceiling and walls of the tunnel as if nothing at all had changed, as if she hadn't just left her friends behind… likely to their deaths. Sounds of a battle were replaced with the roaring gush of the waterfall, and fresh memories of blood and tears were wiped clean in a reflection of glittering jade stones.

Arianna had to stop. She had to have this moment of serenity one last time.

Dropping to her knees on the shore of the springs, she tilted her head up to the crowning dome of her utopia. Its walls twinkled under a canopy of firebug light, the waterfall humming in welcome as the spray lapped at her face. She reached down, letting her hands rest in the warm waters, mesmerized as the clear blue took on some of her burden—adding the blood, mud, and sorrow to its depth.

"We need to keep moving," said Lessa, shooting nervous glances back to the tunnel they'd just left. "There's no telling if anyone saw us come this way. We could've been followed."

Arianna murmured her agreement, but her body felt weighted like stone, her mind resolute in never surrendering this small sense of freedom.

Lessa came to stand in front of her, demanding her attention. Her orange boots were cleansed of dirt as the water lapped at her feet. She held out a hand. "Ara, it's time to go."

"I know," she replied, trying to keep her thoughts straight. Closing her eyes, Arianna savored one more second of this false sense of safety before allowing Lessa to drag her to her feet. "Here, maybe this map will tell us some answers."

Gently unfurling the parchment—Solomon's last guiding gesture—atop the flat surface of one of the jade stones, she searched it, hoping it might lead them out of this mess.

Alas, studying the elaborate pictures, Arianna quickly realized that it was not an elder's map of the Vanishing Tunnels but a plot of the world above that she would soon face as an outlaw; she combed it for something familiar, something to look toward, but the scribbles and marks that outlined her future meant nothing to her—she didn't recognize anything from her studies.

"Did you bring the map you started making of the tunnels?" she asked after a moment, scratching her head. "This one seems to only chart out the land above. It's no use to us now." She rolled it back up and placed it in her pack.

"That's too bad," said Lessa. "I did bring mine, just in case, but I'm afraid it'll only get us so far." She started pacing, muttering to herself. "We'll have to navigate our way *very* carefully, or we could get trapped down here. What if we—"

"That's not an option," said Arianna, laying a hand on her shoulder to stop her from pacing. Her eyes flicked toward the Warrior's District tunnel. "We can do this. Solomon and Talis believed we could, so let's not prove them wrong. Just lead the way as far as you can, and we'll figure the rest out as we go."

"You're right. I'm just…" Lessa shook her whole body, as if she could physically shake off her nerves. "There's no going back now."

"So, where to next, then?" asked Arianna, putting on a brave face. The thought of dying, buried underneath the mountains she hated so much, terrified her to a point that sent her over an emotional edge; she was suddenly filled with a bout of irrational courage, silently reassuring herself that they could actually escape the Four Corners with no elder map. And yet, she was also painfully aware that she was lying to herself. Most realistically and *rationally*, they would die down there.

Lessa pulled her self-made map from her rucksack and unfurled it across the stone. It looked just like one of the paintings from her room, the markings vibrant with color and intricate detail behind every stroke.

"See here?" She pointed to two red 'X's on the parchment, and even Sano seemed attentive as Lessa clarified the markings. "These mean dead ends. So if we exclude them along with the passageways to the Healer's and Warrior's Districts, then that still leaves us with three other options. I've traveled each one a bit, but I always end up turning around for lack of time."

She paused to get Arianna's full attention.

"You have to understand, there's no way to know where we'd end up."

"What do you suppose we do, then?" asked Arianna, curling a strand of hair around her finger to the point of breaking as she considered the implications.

Lessa shrugged. "Take your pick," she said, waving a hand over the parchment.

"Okay…" Arianna chewed on her lip, racking her brain for the right decision. Then she threw up her hands. "Let's just try this one first and hope we can count ourselves lucky." Her finger landed on the tunnel to the far left.

"After you," said Lessa with a sigh.

With Arianna leading the way, they traveled down a narrow path—away from their old lives and in search of the new.

THEY WALKED FOR A LONG TIME in silence, the only noise coming from the firebugs as Sano caused uproar in his failed attempts to catch them between his jaws. And Arianna counted the noise inside her head, of course; they each had their own thoughts to keep them occupied.

"How far can we walk before we're blind?" she asked, steering her attention away from more painful thoughts.

"I'd say we have a little while before I had to turn back," answered Lessa, eyes glued on the parchment in her hands. "Right now, everything still looks familiar. We just keep straight ahead." Her voice echoed in the tight space, ricocheting between the crystalized pillars they weaved through as they walked.

A little while later, Arianna looked back to find Lessa had stopped, poring over the map with panic in her eyes.

"Okay, now we're blind," she said in a whimper. "This is as far as I came."

Arianna gazed ahead and just saw more of the same. "Well, it looks like we can still walk straight… for now," she said. "Let's keep going."

Lessa nodded, reluctantly rolling up her map and placing it back in her rucksack. Then she called Sano back, and he obediently came to perch at her shoulder. Arianna pulled in a deep breath through her nose and straightened her back. They would continue onward with courage. Though, they both knew 'for now' held no promises, and she wasn't sure how much courage she had left.

"Ara?" said Lessa after a while, sticking close to her side.

"Hmm?"

"I just… I have this *strange* feeling that we're headed downward. Not up and out," she said. "Know what I mean?"

Arianna had the same funny feeling, but she refused to acknowledge it. "Let's just keep going."

Deeper and deeper they walked, following the twists and turns of the passageway. And soon that funny feeling started turning sour, the bright tunnel growing darker by the minute.

"Do you hear that noise?" whispered Lessa, voice shaking.

"It's just the firebugs," replied Arianna, trying to ignore her outward bursts of anxiety.

"No." Lessa stopped. "No, something's not right."

"You really worry too much." Arianna turned to flash Lessa a reassuring smile. "Everything's fine—"

She took another step forward. Her stomach suddenly felt like it had flown into her throat, and her smile was replaced with a scream—the ground disappeared before her very eyes. But before she could fall to her death, Lessa dived forward and squeezed both hands around her own, yanking her to safety.

They toppled to the ground.

"Are you okay?" gasped Lessa as they both lay there.

"Uh huh…" Arianna could hardly catch her breath, her heart beating so fast she thought it might exit her body. "Thanks for that."

"I *told* you I heard something!" replied Lessa, jumping to her feet and glaring at her. She had one hand on her hip and used the other to angrily point down—*way* far down.

Arianna slowly stood, pressing her body against the cavern

wall for support as her eyes followed Lessa's finger, calculating the new surroundings and adjusting to the sudden light. Their passageway had come to an abrupt ending, but the archway they perched under gave way to a slim cliff which encircled a deep pit. Arianna was reminded of *the* Pit in the Warrior's District, where the bones of her peers littered the bottom.

I wonder what's at the bottom of this one?

She inched backward, this new danger threatening a much worse fate than anything the Jar had to offer. Bones would disintegrate into nothingness here. All traces of a slave's existence would be wiped away in this vast, merciless crater.

A deep bowl filled with thick, rolling lava bubbled below. Smoldering steam slapped their faces, making their eyes water as their attention fixed to the waves of fire beneath them. Arianna thought it looked as if millions of firebugs had fused together to form a lake beneath the mountains.

"It's a volcano," said Arianna, mouth agape. "I never thought Blancoren... but how? It's a tundra here."

"Maybe a dormant one?" said Lessa, just as confused. "The only volcanos I learned of are on abandoned islands along the south and west coasts of the Olleb. Nothing of life there. I definitely don't remember this being in the history books." She tucked Sano safely into her robes as he latched onto her. "I bet it's how your hot springs formed. And probably why so many firebugs collect down here. They typically only flock to warm places."

Tearing her eyes away from the fiery depths below, Arianna saw firebugs swarming the walls in this part of the tunnels—it was unlike anything she'd ever seen before. Their light trailed upward for what seemed like a mile-high ceiling.

"Well... better add an 'X' to your map, Les. We need to head back," she said, dizzied by the height and the heat. "This is clearly not a way out."

"Wait!" said Lessa. "Look there. On the other side. I think

I can make out some more tunnels. Can you see?" She grabbed a handful of Arianna's robes and pulled her back to the edge. "We should try one of those. They have to lead *somewhere* this deep down. Let me just mark this so we don't get turned around later."

Before Arianna could protest, Lessa had whipped out her map, a quill and a small jar of ink, and was adding some new trails to her map. Arianna peered over her shoulder to watch and saw a striking resemblance to the magma pit flowing beneath them in rolling strokes of black.

"You can't really mean to go around the cliffs?" she asked, her voice coming out in a much higher pitch than intended.

Lessa looked up at her, nodding. "If we go back now, we'll lose so much time, and there's no telling if we've been followed or where those other entrances in the hot springs could lead us. There's only two options if we turn back, but if we go forward… just look." It was obvious there were many more tunnels to choose from on the other side of that lava pit. "Chances are, this could be our only way out."

Arianna shook her head, wanting to protest, but no words came out.

Without waiting for an answer, Lessa tiptoed forward onto the cliff, Sano snug across her shoulders. "Just follow my lead," she said, testing the ground with her foot. "I'm used to this kind of thing."

Arianna sniggered as she hugged her body close to the cavern wall, her warrior's bravery vanishing in the face of such height. She had no choice but to follow, but her courage was a thing of the past.

Who could ever be used to something like this?

They crept toward the other side of the cliff, careful not to make any sudden movements that might upset their balance or the old rock. Lessa was very nimble, a warrior of the skies. Arianna, on the other hand, couldn't have been less nimble if she tried. Her breath was hitched in her throat the entire time, and she never once looked down for fear her body might follow her eyes. Time passed unbearably slowly, but eventually they did inch closer to their goal.

"It looks like there are about five tunnels to choose from," said Lessa. "We're nearly there. Keep going."

"Your turn to pick," said Arianna, her voice trembling as she tried to concentrate on her footing.

Lessa began to mull over the decision, but before she could make an assessment of their choices, a sound ripped through the cavern as if lightning had collided with the mountainside. Arianna looked up, expecting to find boulders tumbling toward her head; she saw nothing of the sort.

Then her eyes dared to follow Lessa's to the pit below.

It seemed a rockslide had begun after all, but the boulders that fell didn't come from the sky. They crumbled beneath their feet, and the unstable cliff gave way to the fire-filled lake below.

Arianna couldn't bring herself to move. She couldn't even blink as she watched the old ground deteriorate in a wave that was catching up with them fast.

"Move!" yelled Lessa. She snatched Arianna by the arm and set off at a wobbly run, Sano clinging tightly to her neck.

Arianna ran as fast as she could behind her. But when she glanced back, she saw the cliff was giving out quicker than they could possibly outpace.

There was an opening to one of the tunnels just ahead, just ahead. She saw no other option…

"We have to jump," she called ahead.

"What?" shouted Lessa, eyes locked forward as she ran.

Arianna grabbed hold of her outstretched hand, and Lessa looked back, eyes growing wide.

"*Jump!*"

Working as one, they both leaped from the cascading floor

without a second thought.

There was a moment when Arianna thought they would never meet solid ground again as the lava grew closer—but then they did. They landed on their stomachs in the mouth of one of the entrances, feet dangling in thin air.

The rest of the skirted cliff surged downward in a waterfall of boulders and rocks. And lava splashed and sputtered at the contact, claiming the rubble to its depths.

"That was close," said Lessa, wiping the sweat from her brow as they crawled to safety. "Sano, please, I can't breathe." The little monkey clung to her neck so tightly that she had to pull him off, trying to soothe him as he shivered in her arms. Then she took out her map and diligently recorded the next path.

Arianna was still in a daze as she watched the last of the rocks slide to their demise and the lake turn calm, as if nothing at all had happened. If they hadn't been there to witness it, no one would have ever even known there'd been a cliff at all.

"How about we steer clear of anymore rock-climbing?" said Lessa as Sano finally found his calm and settled back on her shoulders.

"I thought you were *used* to that sort of thing," said Arianna, narrowing her eyes at her as she brushed herself off.

Lessa rolled the map back up. "No more cliffs."

She scoffed. "Well, I'm glad you're thinking straight now! Let's get out of here."

The girls wasted no time and set off down the next passage. They traveled away from the lava lake and through a tunnel that matched its maker formed of black and red rocks. The walls were warm to the touch, and it glowed like smoldering coal in a fire.

No turns to take, they continued down a straight path until the tunnel opened up wide, the air growing much cooler now that the lava pit was nowhere near. Then the time came to make another choice—with a dead end ahead, they'd have to veer off to the left or right.

"I say we go right," said Lessa. "It seems like it would more likely head away from where we came. What do you say?"

"What makes you think that?" asked Arianna, taking a quick sip from the water canteen Cyn had given them and passing it to Lessa.

Lessa just shrugged as she took a swig before handing it back. "Instinct?" she said. "I'd say it's the way the tunnel seems to slope, but I honestly haven't a clue."

"Right it is, then," said Arianna with an exasperated sigh.

They set off in a new direction, Lessa hastily marking it on the parchment. This tunnel twisted and turned as the girls followed along its path. And soon the flaming, coal-like stone morphed into a brilliant orange, giving off a subtle, diamond-like sparkle with the firebugs' added light. Arianna had only seen the sun in full view a few times in her life, but this entire passage seemed to be carved from it.

"I've never seen something so… breathtaking," said Lessa, eyes alit with curiosity. "There must be so many secrets under these mountains."

Arianna laughed. "We're the secrets under the mountains!" she said. "This is quite something, though." Then a new thought came to mind. "Did Talis ever tell you why they call these the Vanishing Tunnels, by chance?" The mention of him stirred up other names she'd rather not dwell on, but she'd always wondered how they'd gotten that title.

"No, but toward the end I confessed I'd been exploring them for quite some time," she said. "That I hadn't been able to help myself when I discovered another entrance. I would say he was impressed if he hadn't turned blue from all the yelling."

"I wonder if the scrolls he gave us might mention anything about that at all," mused Arianna as she let her fingertips glide over the glittery walls of the cave.

"Possibly," said Lessa as she studied her map. "You know, something else has been gnawing at my mind, Ara."

"Oh… and what's that?" she replied, attention fixed to the shimmer of the tunnels. The rock seemed to roll through all the hues between yellow and red as they walked farther in.

"Liam was practically dead on that bed, and then Sano—"

She gestured toward the little monkey whose eyes glistened much like the walls of these caves.

"His paws," interjected Arianna, "they lit up like a silver lantern." She shook her head. "I've never seen anything like that before, but I think your friend here saved him." She patted him on the head as she tried to forget Liam's scarring words. "Thanks for that, Sano."

"But truly, how can that be possible?" said Lessa, rubbing at the scar on the back of her neck.

Arianna tilted her head, watching Lessa as her fingers played with the shiny spiral mark on her skin. Then she thought of all the unfathomable power, the *magic,* that Solomon had summoned just hours before—it was one thing to learn theories of it and another to see it in practice. She knew she hadn't even scratched the surface of understanding what their masters had to teach.

"After all that's happened tonight and all we've learned in the last few weeks, I have a hard time believing that anything isn't possible now," she whispered.

Lessa let her hair fall back around her neck, hiding away her mark.

"Solomon called him an… avatar," said Arianna. "Do you know anything about that?"

"I saw that word written in one of the scrolls," replied Lessa, fingering her rucksack.

"I remember too, but there'll be time for that later. Did you bring them all?" she asked.

"I hope so," Lessa replied.

Arianna shook her head. "We have so much more to learn. But let's get out of these tunnels first and foremost."

AFTER WHAT SEEMED an immeasurable time of walking, they realized the cave to be a glittering dead end. "Now what?" said Arianna, starting to feel as if the walls were closing in on them.

"I suppose we have to go back and take the left-hand side?" replied Lessa.

"All the way back?" They'd been walking for hours and if they didn't find a place to rest soon, she thought she might collapse. Arianna slumped against the wall of the cavern, ready to give up. As she did, a large stone slab shifted under her weight and she fell forward.

"Are you all right?" cried Lessa, running to her aid.

"I think so…" she said, shaken as she looked around at the opening she'd fallen through. "I'm fine, but why do I keep falling and you—" Suddenly, she felt as if she were a ninth year again, discovering the hidden path to her utopia. "Les, are those what I think they are? It *can't* be." A rush of excitement washed over her.

"They're stairs!" exclaimed Lessa, climbing over her before Arianna could even get to her feet. "But how?" She tapped her foot on one just to be sure they were real.

"Strange… someone had to have built these here," said Arianna, also testing one. They were carved from the same sparkling sunstone of the tunnel, leading high up through the mountain from what she could tell. "But why, how?"

Lessa just shrugged. "Suppose it'll lead us up and out?"

"I say we'd better find out," said Arianna.

The girls responded to the mystery with the same fervor, both sharing a dangerously curious mind. They started the long climb upwards, and then it really began to feel as if they traveled through the sun; warm colors swam all around them like a beacon of light, guiding them toward what they hoped to be an open sky.

Focusing on anything other than their aching legs with each steep step, the girls chattered on excitedly, feeling hopeful again. They discussed the beautiful—albeit sometimes danger-ous—surprises the Vanishing Tunnels had in store. And they mused about what the real world might be like and plans to learn more about magic once they reached it. Lost in the fan-tasy of a happy future, for a moment, they really did feel free.

But only for a moment.

After what seemed like a lifetime of climbing, they reached yet another impasse.

"It's wood," said Arianna, knocking on the door standing tall before them. "Damn, and it's locked." She kicked it with as much force as she could muster after such a strenuous climb, but it didn't budge. "Now what?"

"I may have an idea, actually," said Lessa as she rifled through the scrolls in her pack. She pulled out one Arianna didn't recognize—Lessa had spent a fair amount more time studying this subject than Arianna since she hadn't had to train for the Free Falls anymore. "From what we've read, it stands to reason that humans with magical bloodlines could cast charms if they had the right knowledge, right?"

Arianna shrugged.

"Well, according to Solomon and Talis, we're those kinds of people, *and* we've been equipped with the right knowledge. Here, have a look at this."

Lessa pointed to the text, so Arianna read the description.

"Operium Undrio," she said, pronouncing the title. "Sup-posed to undo any lock not sealed with magical protection."

Arianna looked sidelong at Lessa as she peered over her shoulder at the scroll. "So…"

"*So*, should we try it?" she said, an eager pitch in her voice. "From what this says, all you have to do is place your hand on a lock and then recite those two words."

Arianna felt her stomach churn in knots, but it was the good kind—the kind that meant she was leaning into her curiosity and out of her comfort zone. She couldn't help the sudden feeling of elation that welled up inside her as she considered this option.

Should we?

Magic had summoned her back from the dead. She'd learned stories of sorcery and enchanted lands, watched a very small monkey give her friend back his life, and seen Solomon produce fire from his blade. Even Grinda Risso's bloody reign had ended with the aid of a single, supposedly enchanted word. Arianna couldn't deny that she was quickly growing a fondness for this new fantasy world, even though only a couple of months prior she'd denied its very existence. And the thought of unlocking a door with only a phrase from her mouth set the cherry on top of her euphoria.

My name is Arianna Belvedor, and I'm a…

She signaled to Lessa to stand back and placed both hands on the door to try her luck once more. "*Operium undrio!*"

23

TRAPPED

POWER SURGED FROM SOMEWHERE DEEP in Arianna's gut and gathered at her palms. Then a burst of air blew the locked door wide open. "I… did it," she said, examining her shaking hands.

Nothing about them had changed, but she felt different. And just as it had done when she'd used the *Luzcora* spell against Grinda, the magic had made her feel lightheaded. Suddenly, she understood just why Solomon had been so weak after their last battle.

Magic comes at a price.

"You did it, Ara!" exclaimed Lessa, clasping her hands over her mouth as she peered through the mysterious doorway. "I can't believe this actually worked. It all seems so—"

"Mad," breathed Arianna. "This is absolutely mad. Seeing Solomon and Talis use magic was one thing, but actually feeling it for yourself, *controlling* it." She shook her head, sinking to the ground next to the open door. "It's all so surreal. I need to rest a moment."

Lessa came to sit beside her, unable to hide the curiosity twinkling in her eyes. "Was it not like the first time?" she asked. Arianna could sense she was hungry for information. So much had happened to them tonight that they'd hardly even begun to unravel everything together.

"No, this was different," she explained, not wanting to leave her friend in the dark. "It's hard to describe, but with Grinda, I was in the heat of the battle and it just… happened. Like the magic had a mind of its own."

Lessa tilted her head to the side. "Well, from how Talis described magic, it just might," she said. Arianna let that sink in. "Strange, though, that it just appeared to you all of the sudden like this."

"I think knowing that magic exists now and the fact that Solomon was trying to see if I had any of my own through the 'meditation' words helped me to tap into the power somehow," said Arianna. "Deep down, I think it's always been a part of me, waiting for me to find it. And as soon as I realized it was there, I couldn't have resisted it if I'd tried for how strong the urge was in the moment."

"Maybe it's tied to your emotions, then," said Lessa. "I can't imagine that you weren't feeling just as strongly as the magic you created when Grinda attacked you. It was *so* powerful, Ara. You should've seen yourself."

"Perhaps," she said, massaging the muscles around her calves to alleviate them after so much walking. "I wish I could just ask Solomon. I didn't like feeling so out of control like that. When I wield my swords, every action is so deliberate. But magic is quite the opposite." She let out a long exhale. "So unrestrained."

"One day you will be able to," said Lessa. "Until then, we'll figure this out together."

"Thanks," she replied. "I hope you're right."

Lessa chewed on her lip. "So, what was it like when you…" Arianna didn't want to think about the end of that sentence.

When I… killed Grinda Risso?

She closed her eyes a moment, focusing on how it had felt to use magic.

"To be honest, it was amazing and terrifying all at once. I was completely overwhelmed by the magic while battling Grinda. But what I did just now with this lock, it came easier, *quieter.*" She searched for the right words to explain what magic meant to her, now that she'd actually experienced it for herself. "Since I've already used it once, tapped into it with the *Luzcora* spell, it's just there now, no longer hiding in my mind. I can feel the magic inside of me, stirring."

"What's it feel like now?" asked Lessa, looking her over.

"Like a heartbeat," she replied, pressing her palm against her chest. "Alive and drumming somewhere inside my body. I don't notice it really at all unless I'm focusing on it, like now. But I know it's there, somewhere beneath my skin."

Lessa smiled, putting a hand on her shoulder. "Solomon would be beside himself if he heard you talk about magic so fondly," she said.

Arianna laughed.

"Well, don't get too comfortable," she said. "Our masters saw magic in us both, and I've never known either of them to be wrong. I'm sure you'll be experiencing it for yourself *soon* enough."

Lessa glanced again at the scroll in her hands and then placed it back in her rucksack. "I honestly don't know how I feel about that," she said with a bewildered expression.

Arianna got to her feet. "Let's not worry about all this now," she said, helping Lessa up. "Another adventure awaits. Shall we?"

They both stepped through the wide-open doorway and

into a large, cold room. Everything was dark and smelled of dust and mold, like the old barracks from their districts, and deteriorating furniture was strewn about the room; tables, chairs, desks, shelves, one on top of the other, were scattered about the space. It looked like a storage room.

"Have we escaped the mountains?" Lessa asked in a timid voice. "If this is the real world, I'd like to turn back now."

"There has to be another door here somewhere," said Arianna, remaining cautious. "Come on, let's have a look. We can't go back."

Large, distorted shadows loomed over them, subtly chased away by the glimmer of the sunstone tunnel shining through. But as they walked farther in, the light from the tunnels disappeared completely and darkness swallowed them whole.

"I can barely see anything. Can you? Where did you go?" said Arianna as she felt her way around to try to find Lessa. There was a loud thump as she knocked into the edge of a table. "In the King's name!" She sucked a breath in through her teeth, her knee throbbing.

"Are you all right?" came Lessa's voice. "Ouch—" Something toppled to the floor followed by a string of curses.

"Still alive?" Arianna felt her way toward the whimpering.

"Barely," said Lessa. "I can't see a thing! What *is* all this junk?"

"Stay where you are," called Arianna, hands outstretched as she followed her voice. She clutched at what she thought to be the hood of Lessa's cloak. "Ah, there you are!"

Sano screeched as she tightened her grip, jumping down from his perch on Lessa's shoulder.

"Sano, where'd you go? Get back here!" shrieked Lessa as the two girls clasped hands.

"Sorry! I thought that was you," said Arianna. Her sight was beginning to adjust to the dark. "This way. I think I see him." She pulled Lessa toward the uncanny orange gleam of what could only be Sano's eyes.

Clearly frightened, the little monkey was scraping at the ground in a corner. When Lessa scooped him up into her arms, Arianna noticed a dim light breaking through the cracks on the dirt-covered floor.

"Sano's found another door!" she said, running forward.

"Is it locked?" asked Lessa, pressing her hand against it.

"Let's hope not," said Arianna.

Lessa pushed, and the door creaked open.

A BLAST OF FRESH AIR engulfed them as they toppled out of the dingy room. The ground was soft, covered with clean, white snow that reached to their ankles. And when Arianna looked back to the door, she realized it *was* an old storage shed, built right into the wall of the mountainside. It must've been rotting there for ages, seemingly forgotten with time.

"We did it! We're finally free," said Lessa. She pulled Arianna into her arms, her smile touching her ears. "What is it? What's wrong?" Lessa freed her from her grasp.

Arianna was staring toward the sky, and what she saw gave her little comfort. The walls of the Blancoren Mountains seemed all too familiar as they curled inwards. She shivered at the sight—at the Jar of Stone she would recognize anywhere.

Taking Lessa by the arm, she put a finger to her lips, warning her to keep quiet as they moved into the shadows. "We're not free yet," she whispered. "Let's find out where we are first."

All the color ran from Lessa's cheeks, and her smile instantly vanished.

They walked for a few minutes in silence, unsure of what to do or where to go. But it didn't take long before their fears were confirmed. Lessa nearly screamed and Arianna stopped dead in her tracks, speechless as they soaked in the horrible view. There, looming in front of them like a nightmare overshadowing a dream, stood a large, decaying building with the words 'Dining Hall' etched on the front.

"Which district is this? Do you know?" asked Lessa, her voice coming out small as she pulled up her hood.

Arianna barely heard her, her heart pounding so loudly inside her chest that it almost outdid the thoughts screaming in her mind.

"I'm not sure," she said after a moment, "but we have to go back. We can't stay here. We'll have a better chance of survival if we risk the tunnels again." She started to head back the way they'd come.

"Wait! I hear something," hissed Lessa, tugging her in the opposite direction. "Someone's coming."

"This *can't* be happening," whispered Arianna as Lessa pulled her around the other side of the Dining Hall. But Arianna heard it too, the thick voices of men, of *regulators*, up ahead, forcing them to slink back toward the Dining Hall and toward a life they'd nearly escaped.

As they waited in silence for the voices to pass, Arianna spotted the guarded passageway to the Vanishing Tunnels, marking the official entrance and exit for whichever district they were trapped in. She really wanted to laugh at their misfortune, but she learned a crucial lesson from the idea of 'luck' right then, the way it played its hand at such unpredictable moments.

Some would say it was *lucky* that the guards took no notice of their hiding spot in the shadows of the Dining Hall, but where was luck to have guided them away from this situation in the first place? Where was good fortune when they'd stumbled upon a secret staircase carved through the mountains that would only lead them back to a life of imprisonment?

As Arianna stood there, pressed against the wall, exhausted and the most scared she'd been since the festivals, she was suddenly thrust back in time, into a looking-glass filled with her reckless decisions; they'd affected everyone else around her for the worse, while luck always showed up at the end to bail *her* out. She felt everything at once, as if a cold shock jolted her guiltiest memories from their hiding place at the worst possible moment—the final pinch of pain as Grinda landed the sword in her stomach in a Warrior's Challenge she should've never been part of, the fury of Solomon as he committed murder on her behalf, and the cries of poor Pippa suffering a fate not meant for her. Of her master, and Lessa's master, of Liam, Noah, and Cyn, all dragged into her mess and left behind to clean it up.

It was lucky for her that she was alive, but did she deserve to be? Arianna glanced to Lessa, registering the terror plain in her expression.

This is all my fault.

Her choices might have been a blessing for herself in finding such a wonderful new friend and learning the truth of magic, but Lessa hadn't asked for this; she could be free right now and on her way to a life in the Olleb as a true citizen, if not for her.

Arianna shook her head, trying to shove her thoughts back into the darkest corners of her mind to lock away and forget. Now was not the time to lose focus.

She spotted the regulators patrolling near the Dining Hall; they'd stop to chat with the guards at the tunnel entrance. Arianna watched them intently, thinking it a cruel joke that she and Lessa would likely never get past them unseen without a little more luck on their side.

"In here," she said after a quick scan of the area. There was a back door to the building just a few paces ahead. It opened easily, so she and Lessa slid inside.

After double-checking the hall was empty, Lessa spoke, "What should we do now? There's so many of them."

"I don't know yet," said Arianna with a sudden yawn. "But we can't go out there right now. We'll be caught for certain."

"We've been up all night," said Lessa, rubbing at her eyes. "It's still so dark out, but I bet the morning commendation is only a few hours away. There'll probably just be more of them if we wait too long." Just then, a loud, grumbling noise came from the pit of her stomach. She clutched her belly, looking around the Dining Hall as if she'd smelled food.

"Well, we're here now," said Arianna, halfheartedly. "Let's see what we can gather for food. I'm not sure how long Cyn's provisions will last us if we keep taking detours."

"Good idea," replied Lessa. "Let's be quick."

After tiptoeing to the kitchens, they rummaged quietly around the cabinets. Much to their distaste, they found the same slop that was typically served in their own districts.

"I can't believe we ended up right back where we started," said Arianna as she peeked into all of the cupboards, searching for something more edible than the daily special.

"Gold pot!" Lessa waved her over to a large alcove in the back of the kitchens.

As Arianna peered inside, her hopes were momentarily lifted with the prospect of real food; after a few minutes, they'd pillaged the elders' stock, packing up as much as they were able and scarfing down as much as they could quickly.

Arianna instantly felt more clear-headed with a little bit of food in her stomach. "I'm going to fill up the water canteen too," she said. "Then we better be off."

"Look at all this," screeched Lessa in delight, still in the elders' area. "I doubt we'll get this lucky again."

She'd found the wine storage.

"Are you sure that's a good idea?" said Arianna, cocking her head to the side with a smirk.

"We could use a little liquid courage right now," said Lessa, taking a swig from a leather pouch. "Ah, to *almost* freedom!" She walked over to Arianna and pushed it into her hands.

"To almost freedom," laughed Arianna, taking a drink and letting the wine lift her spirits; leave it to Lessa to stay optimistic with every wrong turn. "But I think this is becoming a terribly bad habit." She handed Lessa back the pouch.

"I think if we're heading back into those tunnels, you'll be glad I brought it," she replied with a wink as she filled it back up from a standing barrel and added it to her pack. "Ready?"

Arianna looked around. "I guess, but what do you suppose we do now?"

Lessa scrunched her eyebrows together as she thought. "I think we should—"

"Hey! What in the King's name do you think you two are doing in here so early?" The voice shattered any optimism Arianna had mustered up. "It's not even light yet."

The girls looked up to find what they expected to find—a regulator standing in the doorway. The woman's eyes narrowed. "Are you wearing *elder* robes?" Her face turned the color of the wine they'd guzzled down. "You're both coming with me now. I'm taking you to the general."

Her cloak fluttered around her from the howling wind that'd followed her in from the outside, and the moonlight flowing in through a window gave an eerie glint to the sword at her hip. Arianna moved to draw one of her own from her sheath, but the woman was ready. With the flick of her wrist, she removed something from her belt and sent two objects flying toward their heads.

Arianna had just enough time to react, pressing her body against the table in front of them and forcing Lessa down with her as two razor-sharp, silver throwing stars flew overhead. Sano jumped to the floor, upset by the sudden disturbance, and the weapons landed in the wall behind them with a thud.

Grabbing their packs and scooping up Sano, they dashed through the kitchens and out the closest door they could find. The regulator didn't follow, but Arianna heard the squeal of a whistle not far behind alerting her partners.

"They ran over there. Find them!" yelled the woman.

The girls didn't stop running, but they heard the patter of feet on their trail. Soon, they found themselves on a path lined with hundreds of barracks where the slaves of this district slept. Arianna noticed that the structures were unusually built, all different shapes and sizes, like botched handiwork.

"We need to hide," said Lessa as they ran farther up the street. "This way. Let's try in here." She made a sharp turn and stopped at a tall door. She groaned. "Never mind, it's locked."

"Let me," said Arianna, placing her palms on the handle. "*Operium undrio!*" She had to steady herself on the doorframe as a wave of dizziness rushed over her.

There was a click, and the large door swung open.

"You're really getting the hang of this," said Lessa, momentarily stunned. "Come on." She grabbed Arianna's hand and helped her through.

They both crouched low to the stone floor and pressed their ears against the wood of the door, not making a sound.

"I saw them run this way," shouted a regulator from the other side. "Hurry!"

Arianna and Lessa didn't dare move, dare *breathe* until the voices had died away.

"Another close call," said Lessa with a sigh, resting her head against the door when they were sure they hadn't been followed.

The girls both took a moment to scope out this new chamber, and Sano jumped down from his perch to explore. A vast room with high-vaulted ceilings lit by dying candles in every crevice made up their hiding place. The night was freezing, yet the air in here felt warm, hot even, as if numerous fires were burning in the space. Arianna thought that maybe there were as she saw several other corridors led away from this main area.

"Looks like some kind of massive workshop," said Lessa.

Heaps of wood were piled high to the ceiling, blocks of iron were stacked along the walls, and other materials littered the floor. Walking a little farther in and weaving between the haphazard stacks of materials, Arianna saw she'd been right about the fires; already she spotted a few flickering along the walls, and low embers still burned in the furnaces where a section of the room had been dedicated to welding. Hundreds of weapons hung from the ceiling in this part too, dangling like the limbs of some metal monster.

Arianna gathered the room's purpose almost instantly as a large painting of a golden snake strangling a mallet towered above them on the far wall—it even smelled like the Dueling Arena if she were pressed to find a comparison.

She wanted to run.

Had she worked this hard, sacrificed so much, just to become trapped in a different district? *No.*

The girls started to map out their next move, not planning to stay long. Just then, they heard the chime of weapons being disturbed and turned to see a large man slinking in the opposite direction.

"Stop!" screamed Arianna, unsheathing her swords. They couldn't let anyone else get away to sound the alarm.

Lessa already had an arrow pointed in his direction.

The man froze, his back to them. "Apologies, I didn't mean to disturb anybody," he said, his voice distinctly young. He turned slowly on his heels to face them, hands raised.

He flashed a disarming smile that was so much like Solomon's it made Arianna think she was beginning to hallucinate for lack of sleep.

"Who are you?" she said in a quivering voice. The young

man stepped closer, eyes narrowed as he studied her face intently in the low light of the fires. "Stay back!"

"Wouldn't you like to know," he replied, coolly, a smile still on his face. "So you can just turn me in to the general for being out past curfew? It's nearly morning, yet you would still have my head for this, wouldn't you?" He spat at their feet, his smile fading.

Arianna cocked her head to the side in confusion and then suddenly understood the strange interaction. She leaned in to whisper to Lessa. "He thinks we're elders because of our clothes," she said. "Go with it."

Lessa nodded, keeping her arrow pointed steady at his chest from across the room. "We'll be the ones asking the questions here, *slave*," she said, a little too theatrically.

Arianna fought the urge to roll her eyes.

"Now tell us, what's your name and why are you here at this hour?" she commanded.

"My name?" he said, arching an eyebrow at her. "My name is Jeom Kane."

He took another step forward, and Arianna took a step back. The closer he got, the taller she realized this Jeom actually was, clearing her by almost a foot. His skin was as dark as the coal smoldering in the fire pits, and he was dressed in only tan pants, his bare chest chiseled like a stone statue, echoing the rest of his muscled body. And in the low light, she noticed subtle scars all across his skin—scars she thought every district slave wore in one way or another.

"Like what you see, do you?" He was grinning again, but this time at Lessa who was gawking at him with her mouth wide open. With a snicker, he hastily pulled on a shirt and his cloak. Arianna knew he was getting ready to run.

"Hardly," scoffed Lessa, though her blushing cheeks would suggest otherwise. "Jeom, err... *slave*, I demand to know which district is this." If Arianna hadn't been holding a weapon in each hand, she would've slapped her forehead for how foolish her friend sounded.

"I see…" he said after a moment, contemplating them with suspicion in his eyes. "Welcome to the Creator's District, where slaves are turned into craftsmen and women," he said, arms outstretched. "Ladies, you've found yourselves in the Inventor's Zone of this deplorable place. This is where we're trained to earn our freedom." He put his arms down, taking another step forward. "Shouldn't you know this?"

"What year do you claim?" asked Arianna, curious of him.

"Seventeen," he replied with another step closer.

"Why are you out past curfew? Haven't your Free Falls already ended?" she added.

"I earned my freedom already, two weeks ago now," he replied. "I just needed to get away tonight, to take my mind off things and clear my head. I didn't expect to find anyone here at this hour. There never has been before."

Arianna and Lessa looked at each other then, both thinking the same thing—they had a lot in common with this Jeom Kane, and it would seem that the King's rules were broken in the districts more often than not.

At that moment, Jeom smiled; it was a sweet smile, and it hid the dagger behind his back just long enough for him to throw it. It was a sloppy attempt, and Arianna blocked it easily with her sword.

She actually laughed out loud.

Jeom might know how to create weapons, but he sure didn't have a clue how to use them.

Lessa, on the other hand, didn't see the humor in the attack and sent an arrow flying at him. It missed by a hair as he rolled behind a stack of wobbling slabs of wood, the arrow piercing the wood with a clunk.

Jeom watched it vibrating to a still with his mouth agape. Then tearing away an axe buried at the top of the stack, he steadied himself and the weapon, Lessa in sight.

"If you think you're going to give *me* up to the regulators, think again!" His words reverberated around the chamber in a deep hum. He barreled toward her, axe raised high.

Lessa tried to shoot another arrow as she backed away from him, but she tripped on something behind her and her precision failed, the arrow only grazing his arm so that he dropped his weapon. The wound did nothing to ail him, though, and he tackled her in the next breath, slamming her into the wall at her back. She fell to the ground, unconscious, blood trickling from the side of her forehead.

"Lessa!" screamed Arianna, running to her aid.

But Jeom raged onward, picking up the axe and turning the fight on her before she could help her friend.

Arianna manipulated her blade around him easily, for he swung his axe around like a fifth-year warrior practicing with a stick; it was all she could do to not kill him, but this was no trained fighter, hardly worthy of her energy. Eventually, she just knocked the axe from his hands.

But his instincts were quick, and he was very strong.

Lessa groaned, distracting Arianna for just a moment as she glanced her way. Jeom's fist collided with her gut in the same second, sending her flying backward. Arianna coughed, clutching at her stomach as she tasted the dusty floor, trying to pull air back into her lungs.

While she was down, Jeom grabbed her by the arm and began to drag her across the floor away from Lessa and her weapon. He was incredibly large for someone of her size to grapple with evenly, but Arianna had had plenty of practice with Solomon. Catching her breath, she maneuvered out of his grasp and knocked him to his knees in the same breath—and since he was so big, he fell rather hard.

Arianna stood, brushing off her cloak and pressing a finger to her stomach. She let out a hiss through her teeth. "Damn, that's sure to leave a bruise!" she said, glaring down at him.

Jeom was again reaching for the axe, apparently wanting to fight to the death tonight.

"Oh, you want more?" spat Arianna. She whipped out her other sword, marching forward.

"Enough!" Lessa was wobbling toward them from behind Jeom, with an arrow nocked, as furious as Arianna had ever seen her.

Lessa pressed the arrow into the nape of his neck, her eyes scrunched together as if to ward off a bad headache. Jeom shuddered as the steel tip pricked his skin, a drop of blood staining the linen on his shirt. And Arianna smiled triumphantly, savoring the expression on his face—she knew that look well, could even match the pace of his heartbeat as she remembered all too clearly the shock of being outwitted by Lessa Thur with her bow and arrow.

Lessa stood fierce while blood trickled down the side of her face, fear completely absent as her words quivered with a rage that had probably been waiting to explode since the moment she'd left the Healer's District behind.

"If you move even an inch, I'll bury this arrow in your neck before you have time to blink. Don't test me," she said. "Leave the axe on the ground and maybe I'll let you live." Lessa pulled back on the string, and Arianna thought she might actually release this time.

His fingers unfurled from around the staff of the weapon, and Arianna stepped on the blade, seeing her face reflected in the metal. "Why do you mean to kill us?" she asked, crouching down to his eye level.

"Because you mean to kill me," he replied, looking away. He trembled as Lessa pushed the arrow in more.

"Well, we're not going to kill you if you just let us alone," snapped Arianna. "I know you know we're not elders."

"Do you think I'm daft?" he said after a moment. "I know

you're both elders, and I've broken the law. Of course you mean to have me killed. And I only have a week left here! What other choices do I have?"

Arianna was actually shocked herself now. She'd truly given this young creator too much credit before. How had he not seen through their feeble disguise and Lessa's weak attempt at acting?

"No, we're *not* elders," said Lessa. "We're slaves of the Jar, and we're trying to escape!"

Jeom's glare turned from loathing to quizzical in under a second as her words settled in. "But you're wearing elder robes—"

"We don't have time for this," said Lessa, turning to Arianna. "We should just kill him, or he'll give us up." She almost let go of the arrow.

Arianna laid a calming hand on her arm.

"Just wait a second," she said, and took a deep breath. "We're all worked up here." She turned to Jeom. "I'm surprised you bought our disguise after Lessa opened her mouth, but we are telling the truth now. The regulators who run this district recognized us as imposters right away. Can't *you* tell that we're not from around here?"

Suddenly, Jeom's entire demeanor changed, softened, as he looked them up and down. Arianna knew he saw them now, for who they truly were.

"Can I lower my weapon now?" sighed Lessa, noticing the change too. He nodded. She swung her bow back over her shoulder and placed her hands on her hips.

"Why didn't you just make it known you were slaves from the beginning?" he asked, completely bewildered.

"Because we didn't know who you were, and we have to take precautions," said Arianna, returning his accusatory glare. "An elder is the safest person to be in the Jar."

"Seems we should've taken even more precaution with

you, considering that you body-slammed me and tried to chop my friend open," growled Lessa, still glaring at him as she rubbed her forehead.

Arianna snorted at his reaction as he slunk away from her. How could such a giant be scared of someone half their size?

"So…" Jeom said, as if afraid of his own words, "if you're trying to escape, then why are you running around another district? Where have you come from? Who *are* you?"

Arianna stepped forward.

"My name is Arianna Belvedor, and I come from the Warrior's District. This here is Lessa Thur, a healer-in-training." She took in the vast room one last time. "We ended up here… in the Creator's District by accident," she said, gesturing to Lessa to take leave. "And if you don't mind, we'll be on our way now."

Lessa called to Sano, who obediently jumped to her arms, and Arianna sheathed her swords.

"Wait!" said Jeom, throwing his body in front of the exit as the girls headed to the door. "How could you escape from your districts? And how have you come to journey with each other? No slave is allowed contact with someone from another sector of the Jar. It's… unheard of!"

"Well, we're the exceptions to the rules," said Lessa, daring him to stand in her way a moment longer as she feigned reaching for her bow.

His eyes bulged, so many questions clearly forming in his mind. Arianna felt something of pride in that moment, seeing herself and Lessa reflected in his astonished expression—they really did leave no rule unbroken, blazing a very new and dangerous trail.

Shoving Jeom aside, the girls listened for any voices behind the door. All seemed clear, so they cracked it open and peered down the lane. With nobody in sight, they stepped back out into the cold and headed toward the tunnels.

Jeom followed, the crunch of his heavy footsteps making Arianna's skin crawl. It had been several minutes now of them walking in the shadows with him lurking behind. Did he think he was being stealthy?

The next loud crunch of snow underfoot set Arianna off.

"What do you think you're doing?" she said, whipping around on him. "Why are you following us? You're going to get us caught!" She had to stand on her tiptoes to level herself with him.

Jeom was wrapped in plush, purple robes which complimented his skin, and he gripped the axe tightly in his hand. Outside of the Inventor's Zone, against the white of the snow, he seemed even taller, his shadow towering over them.

"I'm coming with you," he said, unwavering.

"You want to come with us?" asked Lessa, taken aback as Sano craned his neck to get a closer look at this new person.

"What? That's absurd… *no*," said Arianna with finality.

She looked to Lessa for backup, crossing her arms.

"Why not?" he asked, surprised. Then he narrowed his eyes. "Either I come with you, or I wake this whole street and we can all die together." He inhaled a huge breath, cheeks puffed out like a child threatening to scream.

Arianna held up her hands, faltering at the coercion. Dropping her voice to a whisper, she said, "Why do you want to come with us? You just tried to kill us!" She jabbed a finger at his chest as she talked through her teeth, trying not to make too much noise. "And you already have your free ticket out of here. We weren't so lucky." She gestured to Lessa. "Either we try to escape or we're dead anyways."

"That's it, then?" he said, nodding to himself. "You both failed your Free Falls."

Arianna took a deep breath, glancing to the sky as she tried to think of how to get rid of him without killing him. "You could say that," she said.

"Well, I'm sorry for before, but you took me off guard back there," he replied, kicking up the snow. "I said I thought you were elders." His voice was impossible to reduce to a whisper, the tenor sounding like the low hum of a drum. "You don't understand. Please, I want out of here! I *need* out."

He clutched at his cloak, desperation in his eyes.

"No, I don't understand," said Lessa, running her fingers through her hair. "Arianna's right. Haven't you already earned your freedom? Your festivals *have* ended, haven't they?"

It was common knowledge that the Warrior's District festivals always happened the last week of the month-long Free Falls. The healers went first, and the others followed. But before anyone was escorted toward their new lives and out of the mountains, those who had earned their citizenship were left waiting in the limbo between slavery and freedom for the Warrior's District festivals to end.

"I don't care. I can't take it anymore," he said. "I can't live another day of this death!" He looked to the sky, pulling up his hood as if to hide a shame from the world. "If I walk away from this place on *their* terms, my soul won't follow. I'll never be free knowing I let them control me. That's why I was out tonight. To find some reprieve for what I did. Maybe... maybe I wanted to get caught and pay the price." He shook his head. "I don't know."

"But if you stay, you'll be free of the Four Corners in just a few days," replied Arianna. "Think about what you'd be giving up if you join us."

Jeom clenched his fists so tight that Arianna thought he might pop a blood vessel.

"I had to kill my best friend in order to be standing here tonight. So you say I've *earned* my freedom?" His eyes glistened as they bore into hers. "I don't feel very free."

Arianna didn't know how to respond.

"But you had no other choice," said Lessa, trying to calm

him as her compassion started to surpass her earlier anger. "None of us do here."

"Didn't I?" He looked between the two of them, as if to suggest that they'd chosen differently—if only he really knew. "Just because you survive the Free Falls doesn't mean you're free." He pointed to the mountains. "And after what I've done, I'd rather die in those tunnels or at the hand of your blade than live a thousand years knowing I let them win without a fight."

He pointed his axe in their direction and both girls jumped out of the way as he ranted.

"Isn't that what you're doing?" he asked. "I see you both here, and I want that relief. I want to know that I control my own destiny. Isn't that why you're running?"

Arianna pondered his words for a moment, not quite sure how to answer. The meaning of 'destiny' was still on her list of puzzles to solve, courtesy of Solomon's last words to her.

Yes, she hated the King. She hated the regulators and the Jar. And she hated being labeled as a number, a slave, as less than human to the elders. These were the reasons she'd always dreamed of freedom—freedom from that slavery and freedom of the mountains. But now, after learning of magic and of the King's even wickeder actions than making her suffer such a horrific youth, her reasons had multiplied.

Nevertheless, in Arianna's eyes, Jeom Kane no longer claimed a number and had broken off a heavy chain. No matter how he'd come to be free of it and no matter if there were still more to break, he had earned his name in this world. Yet here he stood, willing to throw it all away. And for what?

Pride? Dignity? Resentment?

Arianna dispelled the riddle as she recognized the eagerness in his face; nothing would stop Jeom from chasing *his* dream, even if she didn't quite understand exactly what it was in this moment—just like no one could stop her.

Lessa nodded in approval at Arianna's defeated look, sympathy now shining in her eyes.

"Oh all right then, you can come. But *only* if you don't slow us down," said Arianna, throwing up her hands.

Jeom beamed at the invitation.

"Welcome to the team," said Lessa, grinning. "You've got a lot to learn." Arianna broke out in nervous laughter—he didn't even know the half of it.

"Okay, now that that's settled, can we please get out of here?" she said. "The dark is starting to lift, and I don't want to be caught in this district when the bell chimes."

"Regulators will be crawling all over this place soon," added Jeom, nodding in agreement. "Actually, I'm surprised there's not more by now."

"That's probably because of us," said Arianna. "A woman spotted Lessa and me in the Dining Hall, so they're likely all running around looking for a slave out of bed."

Jeom balked. "Well, even more of a reason for me to go with you, then. They might've already counted me missing."

"Let's not wait around to find out," said Lessa. "No matter what way I look at it, we only have two options. Either we go back the way we came in and try the other route, or we can cut our way past those guards and map a new one." She pointed toward the Vanishing Tunnels entrance, not much farther ahead. "You can choose this time, Ara."

Arianna chewed on her lip, not liking either of those odds.

"Why don't we let the new addition handle this one?" she said with a shrug. "It's a coin toss anyways."

Jeom seemed encouraged by the opportunity. "I wouldn't mind giving the regulators a taste of what they dish out," he said, gripping his axe firmly. "There's a lot of blood on my hands that needs cleaning up because of them."

Arianna glanced at the number sewn to his chest—twenty-three. "Your friend's death wasn't your fault," she said, earnestly. "You didn't have a choice."

Her thoughts flicked to Pippa.

Our fault.

"Well, I do now," he said, already marching in that direction; the girls followed him closely until they reached the entrance of the tunnels.

"Good, there's a lot fewer of them than before," whispered Arianna. "This should be easy."

She signaled everyone to attack.

They each targeted one of three guards who stood watch, Jeom and Arianna sneaking up behind the two closest. Swinging his axe with a vengeance, Jeom landed it in his target's neck; Arianna let her trusty dagger bury in the back of the second; and Lessa only needed one arrow to do the job from afar to take out the third—she aimed for the heart.

"Three on three was a fair fight, right?" said Lessa with a grave expression as she gazed down at her first kill, at least the first where she was close enough to see the life leave their eyes.

"We needed to use the element of surprise," said Arianna. "We don't want to give away our position by making a scene."

Arianna walked ahead, avoiding eye contact with Lessa while her thoughts gave her a straight answer.

No, that wasn't a fair fight. It was hardly a fight, and now there's more blood on our hands.

She, Lessa, and Jeom collected their weapons without so much as a word. Arianna shuddered as she yanked her dagger from the woman's flesh, from the regulator that looked so much like the ones she knew from her own corner of the Jar.

So much killing. So much death.

She wondered how the others felt about taking life away from the world, even if it was from people who undoubtedly would've killed them if given the chance. Since winning the duel over Grinda, Arianna hadn't given it too much thought… tried not to, anyway. But now, as she wiped her dagger clean of the blood, the guilt was starting to claw its way into her mind.

"Search them," Jeom said, breaking her string of thought. He knelt down, feeling around the waist of the regulator he'd taken out.

"Why?" asked Arianna as she sheathed her dagger. "What are you looking for?"

"I'm looking for anything that might be useful for an escape plan," he said, flashing pearly teeth as he rummaged about the man's clothes. "Say… a map?"

"Good idea," said Lessa as she bent down to search her own victim.

They collected a few small weapons, a flask of whiskey, a pack for Jeom, and a much-needed lantern. Unfortunately, though, they had found no maps.

"Okay, are we ready? Our time's up here," said Arianna, tensing as the sounds of a waking district reached her ears.

Everyone muttered their agreement, so the three set off into the labyrinths of the Blancoren Mountains and away from the Creator's District. No one hesitated except for Jeom. He gazed at the wide mouth of the Vanishing Tunnels with a touch of fear in his eyes. Then he strode inside.

24

SPELLBOUND

"HOW ABOUT A BREAK?" SUGGESTED JEOM. "We've been walking for hours, and it seems like we're just going about in circles."

Arianna immediately stopped, and Lessa didn't hesitate before plopping down on a large stone.

It was their second day of traversing through the tunnels, and they were exhausted. The three had wandered down different paths all yesterday and all this morning, making little progress. They'd escaped the Creator's District, snaking back and forth between dead-end passages and deeper into a rut. The perilous maze that was the Vanishing Tunnels proved unbeatable without a map or a navigator, and they were lacking both.

To make matters worse, Arianna noticed nothing miraculous about these particular tunnels, not like the ones she and Lessa had journeyed through. The russet-colored walls of the caverns were beginning to make her queasy.

"Good idea," she said. "This seems like as good a place as any for a rest." She passed around food and water.

Sano leaped off Lessa's shoulder and into Jeom's lap to pick at the bread in his hand. He fed the monkey tidbits, intrigued and bewildered by its presence just as Arianna had once been.

Suddenly, Jeom jumped up from his seat. "What was that?" he said, staring down the passageway. Sano squealed, his fur spiking up as he crawled back into Lessa's arms.

Arianna and Lessa watched him with concern as he strained to see through the darkness filling the caves. But eyesight could only stretch so far, the light of their single lantern illuminating only a close proximity.

"Thought I heard something. Maybe voices… or singing?" His listened intently to the hum of the caves.

Arianna crossed her arms, annoyed at his edginess. It was starting to rub off on her, making her uneasy.

The three sat in a part of the tunnels which was a lot more open than some of the paths before, the stalactites dripping with water high above their heads as they ate in silence. A low droning noise buzzed throughout the cavern, joining their chatter. It was the cries of lonely, wandering firebugs who had also lost their way. Arianna gave them a wistful look as they flew by, wishing for her utopia.

Banded together, the tiny creatures could brighten any darkness for as far as the eye could see; it was bizarre how far their light could stretch. Alas, she knew their light only proved sufficient when they fused together in a group—and there wasn't close to enough of them to chase away the darkness here.

After Lessa had finished her meal, she went to check out the only two paths available to them from here.

"I just don't understand," she said, looking around the

mouth of one tunnel with the aid of the lantern. "I've been mapping our paths in detail, but it appears we've already been here." She knelt down, touching the dirt. "These are our footsteps. But if my markings are correct, which I'm *sure* they are, then there should be another passage just over there."

She scratched her head, poring over her makeshift map before throwing up her hands in defeat. "It makes no sense! Unless the tunnels are changing, we definitely got turned around somewhere."

Arianna contemplated this, picking at some of the food Cyn had prepared for them. She knew Lessa prided herself on being a stickler for details, and it didn't seem likely she would make a mistake. Every time they took a new turn, Lessa diligently marked their direction with care. Yet, somehow, they'd ended up as lost as ever.

"They do call these the *Vanishing Tunnels*," said Jeom with a mouthful as he tore into his bread.

"Oh, they do? I hadn't heard," snapped Lessa, pausing just long enough to roll her eyes.

Jeom smiled and dropped his voice low as if to tell a secret.

"I've heard rumors of slaves like us who tried to escape through these tunnels. Trying to navigate the labyrinths finally drove them mad, and they never made it out the other side," he said, in a spooky voice. "It is said that they haunt these caverns in a jealous rage, ensuring that anybody who strays from the right path gets lost forever as well." He licked his fingers, continuing on, "Why do you think nobody ever tries to run? Haven't you heard this story? That's why there are navigators or *real* maps which only the elders have access to. Otherwise the tunnels could swallow you whole."

Jeom's mood seemed to dim as he thought about his own words. "*Us* whole," he corrected.

"He's actually right," said Lessa with a strange look. "That story is as old as the Four Corners itself. Talis told it to me once when I was younger, because he used to threaten to throw me in here when I misbehaved, and—"

"That must've been frequent," snickered Arianna.

Lessa narrowed her eyes.

"*And...* I've even heard regulators whispering about the details," she continued. "I remember it a little differently, though. Talis told of two lovers who ran away together, but in the darkness they were separated. They died alone but swore in death they'd be reunited, so they haunt the caverns in search of each other, forever and always." She gazed off, twisting a strand of hair around her finger with a thoughtful expression.

Arianna shook her head.

"But those are just rumors. Ghost stories," she said, matter-of-factly. "In my district we have a similar one, too, a tale of two friends who tried to escape on the one-year anniversary since the formation of the Four Corners. The darkness drove them apart, and they lost their faith in each other in the end. Thus, they haunt the caves forever in order to keep one another from moving on, seeking revenge as they both believe the other was the reason they failed to be free of the tunnels in the first place." Arianna shuddered. "It's dreadful to think... but it's also only a story."

"Hold on here," said Lessa, squeezing her eyes shut and pressing her fingers to her temples. "I actually believe Jeom might be on to something, though."

"You don't *truly* believe him, do you?" Arianna let out a deep groan. "They're just fables whipped up by the regulators to frighten slaves into not escaping. And they obviously work!"

Magic she was learning to deal with, but her friends believing in vengeance-seeking ghosts gave her a whole new list of worries she didn't feel like thinking about right now.

Jeom wriggled his fingers in front of her face and let out a howl, taunting Arianna as he registered her fear. She smacked away his hands, and he threw his head back in eerie laughter that echoed throughout the caverns.

"No, not about *that*," said Lessa.

Jeom looked at her quizzically. "Then what do you—"

"The tunnels must be changing!" she said, shaking Arianna by her shoulders. "What other explanation is there?"

She jumped up and down, ecstatic.

"What in the gods' names are you talking about?" asked Arianna, looking at her incredulously.

Lessa calmed herself, attempting to explain her thoughts.

"That's why they're called the *Vanishing Tunnels*. Because that's what they are! Jeom said it himself," she said, waving a hand toward him—he looked more than dumbfounded by this conclusion.

"Hold on now," he said, lifting his hands to pause their conversation. "I only wanted to set the tone for my story. It was just a joke." He shook his head, returning to his meal. "You girls are really in need of some fresh air."

Lessa and Arianna exchanged a cautious glance but said nothing. If Arianna really thought about it, after all that had happened and all that she'd done, vanishing tunnels didn't seem like that big of a stretch. It actually sounded possible that the tunnels somehow shifted or disappeared entirely as Lessa suggested.

She recalled Talis describing magic as a force connecting all of nature. And as much as she hated the Blancoren Mountains, she knew that everything about them—above and below—came to be by the creation of Nature herself.

"Do you believe in magic?" she blurted out, looking to Jeom. He nearly choked on his food, and Lessa froze, slowly sitting down beside them.

"You're taking this too far now," he said after a moment, eyeing her with caution. She could tell he searched for the underlying joke.

"I was frightened of the truth at first," continued Arianna

in a hushed voice as she carefully calculated her next words. She looked to Lessa who fidgeted, eyes darting between her and Jeom. "But my mind was changed."

She could see his skepticism growing as he stared at her, searching for the waver in her claim. He found nothing.

"What is it you're suggesting?" he asked, his voice shaking.

"I'm suggesting that the tunnels *are* changing... because of something called magic." She smiled widely, as if to welcome Jeom into the magical world with open arms.

"Ara... he's not ready for this," warned Lessa, though much too late.

Arianna frowned. "He was going to find out sooner or later," she replied.

Jeom's back straightened as he let her words sink in.

"You both are deranged!" he said, getting to his feet. "I was only fooling with you before. These tunnels are not changing because of *magic*. They aren't changing at all! We don't have time for this nonsense."

His voice was booming, filling the heavy silence.

"Jeom, I think it's time we came to know each other just a bit better," said Lessa in a gentle voice. "After we've said what we must, then you can choose to continue or separate from us. But you have to promise to open your mind and listen to us first. You wanted to join us, and this is part of that deal."

"Well, if I had known you were crazy from the beginning, I wouldn't have come. But fine! Let's hear it then," he replied.

"Good," said Lessa as he sat back down, begrudgingly. "I take it you've heard of magic, then?"

Jeom returned a curt nod. "Again... just part of another story, a legend," he mumbled. "And to quote the King, all legends are the same as lies."

"Are King Devlindor's words ones you respect because you want to or because you were told to?" said Arianna. "Because he also said that no one had ever tried to escape before, yet here we are… three slaves from different districts of the Jar on the run."

Jeom waved his hand, giving her the floor. "Go on," he said. "I'm listening."

For quite some time, he only feigned interest in their words as he studied the ceiling of the cave and the wild curls on Arianna's head. But as they retold the detailed events which had led them to the Creator's District and showed him the magic-filled scrolls in their collection, Jeom's eyes widened in what could only be some sort of understanding. No one could, or *would*, put so much uncanny detail into a lie—so Arianna knew he'd have to either accept or reject this truth.

After they'd finished, they gave him a moment to soak everything in, a moment to adjust.

Jeom cleared his throat. "Now, I'm not going to deny your ludicrous claims… because that was quite an entertaining story," he said. "But I'm *not* saying I believe you either."

"What are you saying, then?" replied Arianna, eager to hear his final verdict.

Jeom dropped his head into his hands. "Just think of me as impartial territory," he said in a muffled voice.

"So, you'll stay?" asked Lessa, reaching for his hand.

Hope sparkled in her voice.

"For now," he replied, looking up at her with a wary expression. "I still think you girls are absolutely mad, but it wouldn't help any of us to separate before we've even seen daylight. We all have the same goal here, so we should try and stick together for the time being."

He wouldn't surrender a smile, but Arianna was satiated enough that he hadn't run in the opposite direction.

"Wonderful!" said Lessa, giving him a hug that Jeom eventually had to relax into.

Arianna chuckled. "Yes, we'll be glad to keep you a while longer," she said.

She rather enjoyed Jeom's company and good humor, and it was a nice change to have someone else to split the burden of all the craziness in their lives with, even if he didn't quite know—or even *believe*—what exactly he'd signed up for yet.

"But on one condition," added Jeom, pushing Lessa to arm's length. He gazed at Sano snuggled into her robes. "How the heck did you two find a monkey out here?"

As soon as the question had left Jeom's mouth, he began to bellow in laughter at the absurdity of it all. The girls couldn't help but join in as Sano stared wide-eyed and confused at his caretakers.

"To make it simple," said Lessa, "I believe he knocked me out of a tree and still feels bad for it. Isn't that right, Sano?" She patted him on the head as he nuzzled into her palm. "Take it or leave it."

Jeom considered her for a long moment, his eyes softening. "Do I even have a choice?" he finally said.

Lessa twisted her lips into a smile and shook her head.

"Okay, then to the matter at hand," he said with a sigh. "Regardless if the Vanishing Tunnels are actually *vanishing* or not, what do you suppose we do? How can we possibly beat this maze if we keep stumbling off track?"

"We'll find the right path," said Arianna, reassured by the unity of the group. "We just need to stick together and keep moving."

They all packed up their things and let Lessa guide the way down the other tunnel where their footprints hadn't been spotted. Arianna said a silent prayer to the gods that this path might lead them up and out and not toward one of the many terrible endings that kept lurking in the back of her mind, for she'd come to believe there was truth in what the King deemed legends and lies.

"WE SURELY HAVEN'T BEEN HERE BEFORE," said Lessa, marking her map with the new tunnel.

"It doesn't even matter because it's just another dead end," said Arianna, angered as a large wall of stone materialized ahead and blocked their way forward.

She kicked the barrier with her boot, tiny rocks dusting them overhead. As the earth rained down, it poured through the top of their lantern, their only light.

In an instant, everything went dark.

"I lied. We're going to die in here," she murmured as they all brushed the rubble from their hair, feeling around in the darkness for each other.

Only the twinkle in their eyes vied with the thick blackness that engulfed them, and Sano's glowed like twin moons in a clear sky. Jeom proved to be the most difficult to spot, blending in perfectly to the dark.

"Oh, relax," said Lessa as Jeom latched onto her.

Arianna couldn't help but smile a little. Even in the dark, she could tell she was rolling her big blue eyes.

"We're not going to die," she added. "Does anyone know how to remake that fire?"

The two met her question with a long, awkward silence, thickening the black oblivion which smothered them.

"There's nothing here to make a fire anyway," answered Jeom. "Nice going."

"Sorry," muttered Arianna, her heart pounding as the darkness thickened. It was a good thing they couldn't see her face right now for how scared she felt. "Let's just go back to that clearing, then, and we'll figure something out. There's bound to be something that gives off light down here."

As they attempted to feel their way back down the tunnel,

the darkness did seem to lift slightly after a while.

"Is it just me, or is it getting brighter?" asked Lessa.

Arianna could actually make out a little more than just the silhouettes of her friends now. "I think our eyes are just adjusting to the dark."

"Not quite," said Jeom, craning his neck to look up at the ceiling. "It would seem we have some friends in high places."

His face split into a wide grin and his white teeth made him visible again.

"Firebugs! Of course," gasped Arianna, the promise of their light chasing her fear away. "We need to catch them." She turned to Lessa. "You love to climb, right?"

"Why—"

Arianna nodded to Jeom.

"Oh, *good* idea," said Lessa in a drawn-out voice as she considered this. "Jeom, think you could hold me on your shoulders so I can reach up there?"

"Surely, madam," he said, bending down to his knees. "Climb on up." She crossed her thin legs around his neck and held on to his shoulders as he stood back up.

Jeom swayed a little on purpose, making her screech.

"Ara, will you please spot me in case this oaf drops me?" called Lessa, grasping Jeom tight.

"I'd be nicer to me if I were you," he said, feigning to wobble back and forth again.

Arianna tried to suppress her laughter. "Don't worry, I'll catch you," she said. "Hurry though, you'll scare them away."

After a little while, the dark grew lighter as the group paraded through the tunnels, chasing the lost firebugs and forcing them into the glass cage of the lantern. By the time they'd rounded up about thirty, the lantern blazed bright and the darkness fled without any hesitation. In fact, the flaming critters helped illuminate every inch of their passageway now.

And unlike before, with just the dim light of the traditional flame, Arianna could see their backdrop for what it truly was—magical. The brown walls of the cave morphed into a luscious color, and the stalactites hung like thousands of bronze swords dangling from the ceiling of the cave. Even the ground was to be admired, formed by an infinite yet beautiful web of earth-crafted pillars, connecting the ceiling to the floor.

Arianna gaped at the transformation just a little light had given them, and she suddenly appreciated being a bit lost. "We're just going about this the wrong way," she said to herself, resting her hands at her hips.

She hoped the right way would come to her soon as she marveled at the rocky, russet ceiling, pondering nature's part in creating such a magnificent landmark. Then a burst of light illuminated the darkness of her mind's eye, just as the firebugs had done for the tunnels.

"I have an idea!" she exclaimed. "Lessa could you please hand me the scroll from earlier that helped unlock the door? I think I saw something there that could be useful. Our predicament is kind of in the same category, don't you think?"

"Fight magic with magic. *Brilliant!*" said Lessa, jumping up and down. "I'm still trying to get used to all of this."

She pulled out the scroll from before and handed it to Arianna as if it were as fragile as glass.

"So am I," scoffed Jeom, folding his arms across his chest. "What a big waste of time. I should've just stayed put."

"You said you were going to be neutral," said Lessa in the sweetest voice she could muster. "Besides, it's too late for you to turn back now. You might as well see it through to the end."

Jeom huffed, leaning against the cave wall as the girls conspired over the parchment.

"Here, look at this," said Arianna, pointing to the text right below *Operium Undrio*. "It says it's a 'revealing' spell that can expose something that's hidden by magic."

Lessa quickly read over the parchment, her expression just as uncertain as Arianna felt.

"Hmm…" She tapped her finger to her lips. "I'm not sure this will work since we're looking for a way out. An exit to the tunnels isn't necessarily a tangible thing. Also, has it been hidden by magic?" She shook her head. "The tunnels might be affected by some kind of magic, but it's a bit of a stretch."

Jeom snorted with laughter. "A *bit* of a stretch?"

Arianna threw an icy gaze his way but said nothing to antagonize him further. She knew it would take Jeom time to trust. But now she understood why Solomon had lost his temper at her when she refused to believe the truth he knew so well. It was terribly frustrating, and it'd only been a few hours since they told him their secret. Arianna had refused to believe for *months* after Talis had told her.

"Well we had better try anyways," said Arianna. "It's all we've got."

"I suppose," said Lessa, eyes glued to the script. "Magic sure comes in a lot of forms, doesn't it?"

The incantation didn't call for a foreign phrase like the one before. Instead, it instructed that one must recite a short, rhythmic verse with a specific request to reveal what had been lost. The spell could work in many ways, depending on how the verse was put together and the skill of the caster conducting it. Or, as Talis would probably remind them, there was just as good a chance that it may not even work at all.

"Think you can manage?" said Lessa, pushing the scroll into Arianna's hands.

"What would I say?" she replied, trying to combine words in her head that matched these descriptions.

"We cannot find what was never lost, so reveal to us the path to cross," sang Jeom, mockingly.

Lessa and Arianna gaped at him.

"What? I can't play your silly game just because I'm not

magic or whatever?" he barked.

"No, that sounded… good actually," said Arianna with a smirk. "Didn't know you were such a poet."

"Well, there's a lot you don't know about me," he said, lifting his eyebrows at them. "Now go on. Cast your *spell* so that we can all move forward with our lives." He tapped his foot impatiently.

Arianna looked back to Lessa and saw she was extremely fidgety. She had an inkling as to the reason.

"Les, would you want to give it a go?" she asked.

Immediately Lessa's eyes lit up. "Are you sure?"

"Why not?" said Arianna. "Talis and Solomon seemed to think it has just as much to do with you as with me. What's the harm in trying?"

"I guess you're right," said Lessa, excited and nervous all at once. "Do I just say it, then?"

"More or less," she replied, shrugging. "I'm no expert, but just make sure to concentrate. Also, I don't know how difficult this one will be, but you might feel a bit drained afterward."

Lessa took a deep breath and closed her eyes; Sano stayed on her shoulder. "Okay, here it goes," she whispered. "We cannot find what was never lost, so reveal to us the path to cross?" Her voice came out shaky.

Nothing happened, so she peeked an eye open to look at Arianna for help.

"Maybe I wasn't specific enough?"

"Possibly," said Arianna, reading the scroll again. "It says the 'skill' of the caster will make a difference. When I tried the unlock charm, I felt weaker right away. Probably because I've barely used magic before. Solomon said it takes a lot of prac-tice and energy to get the hang of. You haven't tapped into any yet, so maybe if we…"

She set down the scroll and grabbed for Lessa's hands.

"What are you doing?" asked Lessa.

"Let's try this one together," said Arianna with a smile.

"Think that'll work?" she replied.

"I don't know, but Solomon mentioned that the exercises I learned practicing swords with him could also double as training for magic. And as far as all that goes, he's always been an advocate for teamwork." Arianna closed her eyes, focusing on the magic she knew now to be inside of her. "Try completely clearing your mind and think only of the objective. That's what I do before a duel."

"Truly?" said Jeom. "You both look *completely* ridiculous."

Lessa and Arianna ignored his lack of faith and repeated the rhyme once more, wanting to try anything rather than do nothing at all. This was a time for last resorts. "We cannot find what was never lost, so reveal to us the path to cross," they chanted together.

Arianna concentrated on every word, and as soon as they'd finished, she felt a surge in the pit of her belly and a strong tug on her energy. She opened her eyes, expecting to see something spectacular. But when she did, nothing had changed.

"I guess it's not going to work," said Lessa, dropping her gaze to the floor. "It's odd, though. I thought it had because I felt what you said I would, like something drained my energy. My head is pounding."

"Same here," said Arianna, feeling a bit nauseous as she clutched her stomach.

"Okay, you can have at it now, Jeom," said Lessa, irritated. "But I swear, we're telling the truth about this stuff."

When he didn't reply, both girls looked his way.

"Jeom, are you all right?" asked Arianna.

It looked like he was in a state of shock, his eyes wide and wild as he tried to form words on his lips.

"What's happened?" said Lessa. "Are you ill?"

They waited for him to speak, but he couldn't.

"Spit it out!" said Arianna.

"It… it *worked*," he finally stuttered. "Look up."

He pointed to the high ceilings of the cavern, and Arianna and Lessa raised their eyes. What they saw struck them silent as well—a green, dusted trail of light shimmered above them, trickling back down the long tunnel like an emerald python.

Then Jeom retold the events in one breath. "After you said your strange, witchy spell, that light just spilled out of your hands and shot off down through the tunnels. And your eyes, they were *glowing* like… like stars for a moment there. It was astounding!" He hugged his axe to his chest in a daze. "Just incredible," he breathed.

A trace of a smile grew on his face, and Arianna knew Jeom's boggled mind was readjusting his opinions.

"Believe us now?" said Lessa, eyes glued to the glowing green river of magic.

"I'm finding it hard not to now," he replied. "At the same time, I can't find the imagination to believe in it at all."

"Well, come on, then!" said Arianna, elated at this new development in their journey. "Who knows how long it'll last." She started back down the tunnel at a jogging pace with Lessa and Jeom right behind, the magic shining above them all the while.

THE THREE BELIEVERS FOLLOWED the magic diligently, turning down many new paths as the emerald trail twisted and curved high above their heads, snaking in and out of the jagged cavern ceilings. And as they trekked farther through the perplexing labyrinths of the mountains, the green light only glowed brighter.

"I hope this is right," said Lessa. "This deep in, we'll never find our way out on our own."

"Don't worry," said Arianna. "I have a good feeling—"

"Did you hear that?" interrupted Jeom, bringing their journey to a halt.

"Not again…" said Lessa, stroking a sleeping Sano.

"I really think I heard voices this time. *Listen.*" Jeom put a finger to his lips, more on edge than usual.

Arianna listened too, noticing only the still air of the caverns and the whine of the firebugs in their lantern. Then Sano suddenly shot up, awake, clinging to Lessa as if something had spooked him.

"What is it, boy?" she cooed, cradling him in her arms.

"What if it's the revenge-seeking ghosts from the stories?" said Jeom. He tried to seem sarcastic, but Arianna caught the shake in his voice; Sano's reaction had frightened him, and it had frightened her as well.

"The tunnels aren't *haunted*," whispered Lessa, putting Sano back on her shoulders. "Sano is just jumpy. Aren't you?" She tickled the monkey under his chin.

"You expect me to believe in magic when you can't even appreciate a little ghost story?" Jeom whistled. "Mighty tall talk, I must say."

"*Please*," said Arianna. "There are no such things as ghosts, unless you count Lessa when she's sneaking up on you." She pulled her cloak tighter around herself. "Quit trying to scare us! I think we're almost out of here."

Please don't let there be ghosts.

Lessa was eager to continue on as well. "I don't hear anything anyways. Let's just keep mov—"

"Wait," said Arianna, turning suddenly serious. She put a hand out to stop Lessa from walking ahead. "Someone's coming." Her eyes were fixed on Sano.

Lessa and Jeom followed her gaze toward the monkey, and

their expressions fell, too, as they understood.

Always follow your instincts.

Sano's fur stood on edge now, and he'd gone rigid atop Lessa's shoulder, his attention fixed on the mouth of a dark tunnel—one where the enchanted trail did not enter.

Arianna lifted her hand to draw a single sword from her back but froze as a hooded figure stepped forth from the shadows. Something about the moment felt familiar in the worst ways as a distant memory lingered in the back of her mind.

"Arianna Belvedor," came the voice of a man.

An accustomed shudder ran down her spine as she recognized it—such a horrible one.

"General Ivo," she said, clenching her fists.

"My, what trouble you've caused," said the general with a little laugh. "I do admire your commitment to life, but I think you've outlived your time, *Twenty-Two.*"

He lifted his hood, and Arianna saw clearly the jagged scar across his face.

She then grasped the hilt of one of Solomon's swords and let it slide from its sheath. As she did, she saw a baffled expression cross the general's face. He was looking past her now, for the first time registering that she was joined by others. Then his gaze lifted to the ceiling, and he hesitated as the sight of pure magic came into view.

Arianna knew he didn't know what to make of it. How could he with such a magicless soul?

"My time here, General, has barely begun," she said, feeling strengthened by her mere insight into this enchanted side of the world.

She wasn't about to give up now, with a magical map floating above her head to probably lead her and her friends to freedom. If there was one thing she had learned from the King's wrongdoings, it was that information was power—and in this, she had the upper hand; General Ivo was completely ignorant to the magic before him.

"Oh, on the contrary, girl. You're very much done here," he replied. "And I see you've found some friends? Smart. You'll have companions in the grave."

Arianna moved a step forward to challenge him but felt someone holding her back.

She turned to find Lessa clutching at her robes. "Look around," she whispered in her ear. "There's more."

Arianna looked again and found General Ivo leering back at her in triumph. Then tearing her eyes and focus from him, she saw what Lessa had meant. In the mouth of the tunnel, more hooded figures began to emerge at his side, the light of the lanterns they held bouncing eerily in the dark like the eyes of a monster crawling out of a hole. They whispered cautiously as they too witnessed the miracle of magic twisting through the tunnels, but the general silenced them with only a gesture.

Arianna recognized some faces from her district—Regulators R.J., Mundar, Ida, and Orlene. But there were several other regulators who joined them that she didn't have names for. She inched backward, reconsidering their position. Magic or not, they were sorely outnumbered this time.

"If you run, that will only make my job easier," said General Ivo, seeming to read her mind. "The tunnels can have you then. But if you wish for a battle, I wouldn't mind taking the time to get a little blood on my hands. We've been tracking you for days, so it'll be well worth the effort." He brandished his sword, pointing it toward her, letting her make the choice.

Arianna heard the regulators snicker as they moved forward, closing in on them all. There was no way they wouldn't follow if they ran. She glanced to Jeom and Lessa—they both already had their weapons at the ready.

"Looks like we're a bit tired of running," she replied as she drew her swords.

25

TUNNEL OF TOMBS

ARIANNA WANTED TO PRESS HER HANDS to her ears to block out the sound. *So much screaming.*

The metal screamed as weapons collided with each other—swords on shields, arrows on swords—and the people screamed as they clashed with each other. Her mind wandered to an earlier conversation with Solomon as she stood cornered with her back against the cavern wall.

'Beyond these mountains is a land vaster and more dangerous than you can possibly imagine.'

As she fought for her life in the depths of Blancoren, she was starting to think she'd never find out what he'd meant. The battle was short and General Ivo won.

"Don't kill her yet!" said the general as he paced around the area, dictating orders to his regulators as he watched the battle wind down from a safe distance.

Ida struck Arianna across the face, and Orlene slammed

her to the ground, pressing her knee into her back to keep her still. "My, does she have fight in her," said Orlene. "Stop struggling, child. This will be over soon."

Unlike the regulators that she and Lessa had battled alongside Solomon, these were the general's best warriors, proving their years of experience quickly over Arianna. And as Lessa and Jeom still had much to learn in the art of battle, the three runaways hadn't lasted long being so outnumbered.

A snarl tore from Arianna's throat as she tried to resist Orlene. Then Ida pressed the tip of her sword into her cheek.

"Move again," she threatened. "I dare you."

Arianna stopped struggling, tasting the salty blood as it trickled down her face and touched her lips. Lifting her eyes to the chaos around her, she saw the bodies of a few regulators collapsed on the ground.

One had an arrow in his chest. Another suffered a fatal wound to their stomach, surely an axe's doing, and several had met their ending by the blade of Arianna's swords—weapons that were now out of reach as Ida kicked them away.

"Let him go!" she heard Lessa shout from down the tunnel.

Arianna swiveled her head toward her voice and saw she was being dragged back by R.J. Sano was in the clutches of General Ivo.

"Don't worry," said the general, patting his head. "I'll take good care of him." Sano reacted violently, biting his finger. "Ah, filthy rodent!" He threw him to the ground, cradling his hand. "I'm bleeding."

Lessa beamed as she watched her small friend scurry away to safety, still following the light. Then General Ivo turned and threw a punch to her stomach. Her smile didn't last as she heaved over from the blow, blood staining her teeth as R.J. kept her upright.

"I have the boy," called Mundar. "He tried to run."

"Bring him here," said General Ivo. "Bring them all here!"

Jeom groaned as Mundar shoved him toward Lessa with the dull side of his own axe. Then Ida and Orlene dragged Arianna over to her friends by her elbows. The three of them locked eyes, each looking to each for a way out.

Alas, there wasn't one—they were defenseless and trapped.

The regulators forced them to sit with their backs to one another and then tied their hands together; Arianna squirmed uncomfortably as her wrists chafed against the thick rope. Once they had restrained their captives, the regulators started circling them like hungry wolves, General Ivo leading the pack.

"Good. Very good," said General Ivo with his hands clasped behind his back as he observed his catch.

"What are you waiting for?" growled Jeom, straining against the ropes. "Get on with it already!"

"Be quiet," hissed Arianna, nudging him. "You're going to get us all killed." Jeom didn't know her general like she did; he would 'get on with it' soon enough, and she didn't want to speed up the process.

The general unsheathed the broadsword at his hip. In the next breath, the tip of his steel was scraping at the cloth above Jeom's heart. Arianna felt Jeom flinch away, leaning his body into her and Lessa.

The general let out a bark of laughter, the regulators joining in. "Are you quite sure, boy?" he said. "You don't seem very ready for me to... *get on with it*, but don't worry. You'll meet Death soon. Right after I get some answers."

Before Jeom could respond and surely bring them all swift deaths for being mouthy, Arianna vied for the general's attention. "How did you find us, then?" she asked.

"Oh, it wasn't very difficult," replied Mundar, smirking.

He unrolled a scroll from his belt and shook it in her face. She noticed drawings similar to Lessa's charts of the tunnels inked on the parchment, though not quite as elegant.

"An elder's map," she heard Lessa mutter under her breath.

"I see," said Arianna, feigning attention as she began picking at the rope around her hands.

If I can just get my hands free, maybe I can buy enough time to let Jeom and Lessa escape with their lives.

No matter how she looked at the situation, it seemed impossible that they would all survive now that they'd been apprehended—she wished she knew a spell to loosen the bind on her hands, but she was a novice witch and couldn't rely on magic; she'd tried calling to it during the battle, but it had failed her this time. Unlike with the fight against Grinda, she hadn't been able to concentrate on the spells Solomon had taught her with so many people attacking at once.

General Ivo paced out of her line of sight, and she felt Lessa go rigid as he came to stand in front of her instead, still brandishing his sword. "You all strayed down a very wrong path," he said. "If I were a lazier man, I would've let the tunnels do my work for me."

"Why didn't you?" said Arianna, still picking at the rope.

He rounded on her, his face red with anger.

"Because I owe you for what you did to Sir Dean Westing!" he shouted. "He was one of my best men, and to be killed because of you… a *slave*." He spat at her feet. "He earned his life, yet your greed and selfishness cost him everything." He tightened the grip on his blade and inhaled a long breath through his nose, his expression softening. "So you see, I couldn't let the tunnels have you. I won't let you die here. That'd be much too generous for what you deserve. No, I won't be killing you for a *long* time to come."

Arianna gulped, Pippa's tortured screams suddenly ringing in her ears.

"At a loss for words now?" said the general, a satisfied smirk growing on his lips. "In any case, it's my turn to ask the questions. I want to know about that little hideaway of yours. How did you find it?"

"What are you talking about?" said Arianna, trying to hide the shake in her voice. He was starting to get under her skin.

"The waterfall, the hot springs," he replied, crouching down so they were exactly eye level. "Your scent was easy enough to follow under the barracks after you escaped the district. Quite the intriguing place you found there, if I don't say so myself." He stood back up. "I'll enjoy it in the future."

Arianna glared up at him, and she felt Lessa cringe at the mention of their secret utopia. Just the thought of such an evil man setting foot in their sacred place made her want to set the world on fire—though she knew the King had beaten her to it, and that's why she was in this mess in the first place.

"You can wipe that self-righteous look off your face," barked the general. "You shouldn't even be alive right now. And if it were up to me, you'd have been lying at the bottom of the Pit months ago after your disgraceful Warrior's Challenge. Clearly, you're not fit for this world. If King Devlindor got even a whiff of what had happened here…" There were murmurs of disquiet from the other regulators, and Arianna realized their lives were all on the line, too, if their High King ever found out they'd let someone escape. General Ivo pointed his sword at her. "Not to mention that you stole Grinda Risso's chance at freedom. She was worthy of citizenship by the King's Law, and you took that from her."

"If the King's Law deemed Grinda worthy of anything, then maybe there's something wrong with it," spat Arianna.

She felt the sting of the general's hand on her face in the next breath, his rings ripping into her cheek. Her hair fell down around her eyes and her head whipped to the side, hiding the gleam of tears that welled in her eyes. But she wouldn't permit them to fall. Pulling in a breath through her teeth, she fought the pain and met his eyes again.

"I'll never understand how you beat her in the end," he said with a faraway look as he considered her. "It was like…"

He shook his head of whatever words lingered on his tongue, and Arianna knew he didn't have the capacity to understand. *He* wasn't worthy of magic.

"If you felt like that all along, then why not just have me taken from my sick bed and thrown to the Pit?" said Arianna, tearing so hard at the rope now that she thought her fingers bled. "Why not just have me killed? You had every excuse."

The general looked at her incredulously. "And challenge Solomon Bell after he swore you would make a full recovery? He would've had my head on the spike next to the one I chose for you!" he said. "Although, I suppose he wasn't wrong that you'd survive to fight again."

"He never is," said Arianna.

General Ivo chuckled. "He always was a pain in my side," he replied. "Never willing to take power but always willing to stand by and watch others lead, manipulating them from behind. Thankfully, he won't be a problem much longer."

With his words, Arianna felt as if the walls of the tunnel had begun to close in on her. She couldn't breathe. She couldn't think. And she didn't dare ask another question for fear General Ivo might actually confirm that Solomon would soon meet the terrible fate that his smile suggested.

He didn't wait for her to respond again, turning his attention to his regulators.

"General," she heard Mundar say. "I think these slaves are from different districts. I don't recognize them at all, and their cloaks—"

"Thank you, Mundar," hissed General Ivo in an icy voice. "I'm quite aware of this. But it doesn't matter." Mundar lowered his head as the general addressed them all. "No one can ever hear of this. This secret dies with us. The King would have our heads if he found out we let anyone escape this far, or by the gods, actually allowed slaves from different districts to meet. Do you understand me?"

"Yes, sir," they responded in one voice.

The general again faced Arianna, aiming his sword steady. Her hands were no freer than they were a few minutes ago, so all she could do was stare at the sharp end of the blade.

"Kill those two and we'll take this one back to her own little hiding spot by the hot springs," he said. "I want to make sure she suffers good and long before her life leaves her eyes."

A regulator came toward Arianna with a covering, tying it around her eyes and effectively blinding her. Then they pulled her to her feet and she could feel the point of a sword press into the small of her back.

"One more thing before we *get on with it*," said General Ivo, whispering in her ear. "I'm curious of this green light. Is it some kind of trick? Tell me what it is."

"It's magic!" she yelled back, the truth at least giving her a semblance of freedom.

The general laughed. "Magic doesn't exist. And soon, neither will you," he replied. "Say goodbye to your friends."

"Ara," Lessa whimpered.

"It's going to be okay," called Arianna, racking her brain for a way to help her friends. "Let me go!" She struggled some more but felt the sword dig deeper into her back.

Someone knocked into her and she fell to the ground, smacking her head. She heard more loud thuds and some groans, and then hands were on her again.

"Get off of me!" she screamed, kicking with all her might.

"Stop kicking or you'll give me a black eye," huffed Jeom.

The blindfold was ripped from her eyes and she found him staring down at her, somehow free of his restraints. When she looked around, she saw the regulators helping General Ivo to his feet and guessed he must've caught them by surprise, tackling the general and regaining hold of his axe.

"How did you get out of those ropes?" she gasped as he lifted her onto her feet and cut her hands free.

"I'm a creator," he said with a shrug. "We're scrappy like that. Show me a knot that I can't untangle."

He winked and then cut Lessa free as well.

With the regulators so taken off guard and worrying over General Ivo, the three had a window to collect their weapons and ready themselves for one last fight.

"You *idiot!*" roared the general as Mundar helped him to his feet. "All you had to do was tie a knot."

Arianna didn't even see his sword pierce Mundar's body until the tip had pushed straight through his stomach and out the other side. General Ivo then shoved him to the ground, stepping around his body.

"Get them and kill them. Kill them all!" he ordered to his remaining regulators.

His outrage gave Arianna courage, but their predicament hadn't changed.

"We can't take them all," said Lessa, voicing Arianna's thoughts.

"Then we die trying!" said Jeom, crouching down and ready to pounce.

"Wait, I have a plan," whispered Arianna as their enemies neared. "We have to run for it. Run toward the light, and don't look back. Trust me. Go!" Jeom and Lessa nodded to her in agreement.

Lessa threw her bow around her back, scooped up the discarded firebug-filled lantern and turned on her heels, running in the direction of the magic with Jeom right behind. Arianna turned with them but stood her ground to watch her friends flee to safety; they never once looked back, as she'd instructed, so they didn't notice that she wasn't following.

Moments later, she heard someone running up behind her. Looking over her shoulder, she saw Orlene with her sword raised high over her head.

Bad move.

Such a stance left her mid-section completely vulnerable. With a quick twist of her feet and a thrust of her sword, Arianna sank her blade into Orlene's stomach as they collided.

I'm no child.

She yanked her weapon back, blood dripping off the metal, and Orlene fell to the ground.

"No!" screamed Ida, going to her friend's aid.

With Ida distracted and the other regulators confused at what to do, Arianna was able to get to the other side of the cavern where the general had left Mundar's body. She snatched up the elder's map rolled at his belt, sheathed her swords, and bolted toward the mouth of a tunnel in the opposite direction to that which her friends had run in; it was the same path she'd first spotted the regulators on—the emerald trail didn't glow here.

"That way, after the others!" shouted the general, his voice still in earshot. "The girl is mine. Go! We cannot let them escape again. Don't come back without their heads!"

Arianna picked up the pace as she heard the patter of feet not far behind, but it was hard to run fast without much light to see. This tunnel was dark, save for a few scattered firebugs that created an eerie glimmer overhead. So, inevitably, she scraped her legs and arms pretty badly on the sharp rocks as she ran.

After a while, the sounds of someone chasing her died away and her legs grew numb. She slowed. The air in this part of the tunnel was thick and her lungs choked on a rancid smell seeping out of the walls—Arianna would know such a scent anywhere; it often wafted up into the air from the bottom of the Pit.

So much death.

As she took the next turn, a huge clearing opened up in

front of her and she stopped dead in her tracks.

"The Tombs of Blancoren," she whispered.

Silence engulfed Arianna. She couldn't hear anything but her own heartbeat as she looked upon the skeletons of the deceased slaves. Bones piled on top of bones in this vast chamber.

For the first time since she'd been forced to say goodbye to Solomon, Arianna felt a tear leave her control. She wanted to weep for them—for the ones who had never escaped the mountains—but she knew her tears would not bring them back. Then she grew angry, *enraged*, so maddened by the injustice amassed around her in this forsaken place that she suddenly felt that strange energy begin to boil up inside her again; it was her magic, and it felt like it might very well explode.

"Don't worry. Their souls are free now," came a soft voice.

Arianna whipped around, her anger turning to fear in a split second as her magic slipped away. She tried to scream, but her voice didn't come out. Stumbling backward, she joined the bones on the ground.

"But... you're *dead*," Arianna said in a whimper. Squeezing her eyes shut, she tried to rid her mind of the image.

"It would seem so... yes."

Arianna dared to open her eyes again. To her horror, what she thought she'd seen before was no figment of her imagination. Her knees shook as she stood to face the ghost of Pippa.

"This isn't happening," said Arianna, clutching her chest as she looked upon her deceased friend. "This can't be real."

Pinching herself, she tried to gather her wits and cling to reality. But Pippa still floated before her, inches from her face in a sheer form of the girl she once knew. Looking like the most beautiful version of herself, her wispy form glided with a grace Pippa had never attained in her human life.

"I don't understand. How can I see you?" asked Arianna, slowly backing away until she was flush against the cave wall.

Pippa shrugged her shoulders. "I don't know the answer

to that. Only the dead are allowed to see the dead."

Arianna gave her a curt nod, as if what she'd said made any sense at all. But it certainly didn't, and so many questions bombarded her thoughts. She wanted to reach out and touch her to see what it might feel like, but she refrained from the frightening temptation.

"Why… why are you here?" she asked as Pippa circled her, tilting her head back and forth as if to examine her.

"I don't know the answer to that either, but I'm assuming it's the same reason you're here," she replied. "I'm just waiting to move on, like everybody else."

Just then, Arianna heard an echo throughout the chamber, like rubble falling to the ground. The sound snapped her out of her trance. Fearing that General Ivo had caught up to her, she peered past Pippa. Nothing was there.

"Something is keeping me attached to my body," said Pippa after a moment. "I think so, anyways." Her translucent, shining eyes flicked toward the ground.

Arianna followed her gaze and immediately wished she hadn't as she found the rotting corpse of the ghost, the *friend*, who had appeared before her.

She squeezed her eyes shut again, trying to erase the picture from her mind as silent tears streamed down her cheeks. Lost for words, she opened her eyes and muttered, "Your body? But the Pit—"

Pippa just shook her head, and her brown hair shimmered.

"They always move the bodies to these tombs before the Free Falls. The start of a new year," she said with mock enthusiasm as she glided around Arianna.

Arianna opened her mouth to voice more questions, but Pippa interrupted her again. She might've laughed, thinking that the ghost version of Pippa didn't much differ from the person she'd known, in that regard, but laughter seemed impossible at the moment.

"There's someone else here," she said, concern in her eyes.

Arianna blinked, and the ghost of Pippa vanished. She searched everywhere in the dim light but couldn't find her. Her nerves came back full force then; had the conversation even happened at all?

"I see the labyrinths are already taking a toll on you," came the voice of General Ivo. "Don't you know it's best to keep quiet when you're trying to hide from someone?"

Arianna saw him now as he slunk out of the shadows on the far side of the tombs, crushing the bones of his former victims with every step. She reached for her sword but then stopped as Pippa suddenly appeared once more—she was floating directly behind the general as he came toward her.

"There's been enough death here," she said, firmly.

Arianna's eyes grew wide as she watched her, deciding that the ghost of her friend was real enough, whether or not she was hallucinating her. With shaking hands, she released her grip on the hilt of her sword.

The general laughed. "What? No more fight in you?"

Arianna was more than confused.

Can't he see Pippa?

She thought not for the way he was acting, so self-assured, like he knew exactly what might happen next. But he didn't know a fraction of things… least of all the future. Keeping her eyes fixed on Pippa, Arianna repeated the haunting words of her deceased friend, relying on her judgment more than her own in these parts.

"There's been enough death here," she said.

General Ivo narrowed his eyes at her. He probably thought she'd really gone mad from too much time underground.

"Well, there's about to be a new addition," he said.

He advanced with his weapon raised, closing the long space between them, and Arianna just waited and watched, unsure of what to do next as fear knotted her insides. Pippa vanished again momentarily, this time reappearing only inches from Arianna's face. She staggered backward.

"Don't worry about him," she said with a solemn smile.

Arianna just gazed back at her, *nothing* but worried as General Ivo neared. But something told her to trust Pippa, to trust in the girl she'd wronged.

A slight wind brushed her arm, making shivers run up her spine. Her mouth fell wide open as two more ghosts floated past her, both of them young men; their attire matched the purple robes Jeom wore, though with a dated look, and she made a mental note to apologize to him later if she survived this—ghosts did exist alongside magic.

That is, if I ever see my friends again.

Arianna watched in awe at how they moved, as if the wind blew beneath their feet. Then they stopped and waited for the general as he unknowingly headed straight toward them. As they lingered, one of the ghost boys glanced back to her over his shoulder with what would've been a reassuring smile... had he not been a ghost.

Just as General Ivo reached the point where the ghosts remained in waiting, the boy who had smiled at her stepped right in front of him and disappeared as soon as he and the general crossed paths. The general hesitated for moment, as if he'd felt a disturbance, and then continued his march toward Arianna.

The other ghost boy turned and followed alongside him.

Her instincts told her to run, to run forever from this place until she saw the sun again. But she didn't—*couldn't.*

Instead, she looked to Pippa, who smiled her 'don't worry' smile she missed so much these days, and stayed her ground as General Ivo came to meet her. They stood face-to-face now, and Arianna had never been this close to him in all her life. He smelled like sweat and death, and his eyes looked like dark pools of nothingness. He studied her intently, but said nothing and did nothing—he didn't attack her at all.

"General Ivo?" she said, cautiously.

He shook his head slowly and smiled.

No?

Arianna glanced to the mysterious ghost boy at the general's side and then to Pippa. "*Wait*, did that other boy just—"

"He possesses his body now," said Pippa, nodding. "That's why he can't speak."

Arianna didn't know how to respond or how to react anymore; she truly thought she was losing it.

"Hello," said the ghost boy at the general's side before her mind had a chance to fully spiral away. He was handsome, in a supernatural way. "My name is Jacob, and this is Damon."

Out of habit, Arianna reached for his hand but then dropped her arm to her side, feeling foolish.

Jacob just smiled.

"Jacob and Damon?" she said. "I've heard your names before. In the stories…"

Jacob laughed and a pleasant sound filled the tomb, lifting some of the gloom.

"I, too, have heard some of these tales. Each one with its own ending. None ever the whole truth," he replied.

"What's the real story, then?" asked Arianna, so intrigued by the old soul that she forgot for a moment that she was literally speaking to not only a stranger but a ghost.

Jacob observed her with what was clearly a similar curiosity and then he looked to Damon, as if to ask a question. Damon studied her through the general's eyes, and Arianna squirmed under the uncomfortable scrutiny. But after a long while, he nodded to Jacob, answering an unspoken question.

"The first part of the various stories remains true and constant," started Jacob. "Damon and I were once slaves of the Four Corners. Creators, in fact." He bowed his head. "Alas, time cannot erase history, though it tries with endless effort. When the slave city was first created, people still remembered a better life."

"The Golden Age?" said Arianna, recalling the scroll.

"Yes," he said, cocking his head to the side to consider her.

Arianna scrunched her eyes together as she thought. This didn't make any sense. "But I thought the King destroyed all the—"

"You cannot build a city in a day," he said. "Destruction follows the same limitations. Things take time and people whisper. When I was brought to the City of the Four Corners, I was nine years old. I still remembered my mother's name and my sister's laugh. I remembered my seaside town and my friends. I had been born into a loving family and a wonderful, enchanted life, but it was all stolen from me in the blink of an eye. And I remember that too." He closed his eyes a moment. "My family tried to hide me from the King, but we were found out. Then I was taken to the Jar and my family was killed for treason."

He looked again to the general, to Damon.

"Damon's story is quite similar too," he added. "As was the case for many others from long ago. People used to fight back, resist the way my family tried to, because hope was thicker with the remnants of the Golden Age still lingering in the air. Not every child was captured or enslaved because people tried to trick the King and hold on to their loved ones."

"Things have certainly changed now," said Arianna with a heavy heart.

"Yes, time is fickle like that," said Jacob. "Yet you still seem well-informed. You're living proof that our true history can prevail."

"So how did you come to be… here?" she asked, glancing around the tomb.

Damon shifted back and forth on his feet, and Jacob's expression turned solemn.

"Damon and I became close friends, together mastering the skills of creation," he explained. "But we both still had knowledge and capabilities of magic. The regulators gave it their best effort to try and suppress any traces of such power by enacting severe punishment if they caught children using it, but it didn't matter. Magic can be stifled, but it never goes away."

Arianna thought of her own magic, this new permanent piece of her she had barely begun to know.

"So you were caught using magic and fated to the Tunnel of Tombs then," she said.

Damon shook his head, General Ivo's hair swishing back and forth as he did.

"As part of our creator training," continued Jacob, "Damon and I were tasked with building a shed alongside the mountain. But inside we kept a secret."

"What kind of secret?" she asked, clinging to every word.

Jacob took a moment to remember his past.

"Our work building the shed disturbed the mountain," he said. "And in doing so, we revealed a hole which led to the better parts of these tunnels. However, the path was too steep and too dangerous to navigate. Thus, combining our proficiencies in magic and creation, we carved stairs into the stone and escaped the Creator's District."

Arianna clasped a hand over her mouth in surprise. Oh, how she wished Lessa was with her to hear this.

"The sunstone," she said in a soft voice.

Both Damon and Jacob seemed taken aback at her words.

"It seems that your past would make for a good tale as well," he replied. "I can't wait to hear the rumors the city will tell of you."

Arianna laughed. The idea that her name could be the object of any such story seemed ridiculous. But, then again, she was following in the *literal* footsteps of the legends before her.

"I'm more interested in your story at the moment," she said, feeling the color rise in her cheeks.

"There really isn't much more to tell," said Jacob with a solemn expression. "We escaped slavery through our sun-kissed tunnel, but Blancoren swallowed us whole." He glanced again to Damon, whose head hung low. "We became lost in its endless maze, driven mad from the hunger and darkness. Not even our magic could aid us. And there the story ends."

"But... how did you die?" whispered Arianna, afraid to meet their eyes as their 'fight for freedom' story came to a sad and sudden ending. "And why do you linger for so long in such a terrible place?"

Jacob sighed, and Arianna swore she saw a tear glistening on the general's face. "With no other options left to us but to starve to death in darkness, we killed ourselves," he said after a moment of silence. "We took our lives together so that we could move on together."

Arianna fell speechless, humbled by such a tragic ending. She couldn't even begin to imagine being in their position—if their food ran out, if the light were lost, and if the magic wouldn't come—what would she and her friends do? She didn't want to even think of it.

"And for why we're still here, it's certainly not by choice," he added. "In this world, when you take your own life, you forfeit your soul's future." He took a deep breath, or what sounded like a breath in his ghostly state. "We cannot move forward because our souls are forever attached to our bodies."

"What do you mean 'forfeit' your soul's future?" asked Arianna. The term 'soul' was as vague to her as the word 'magic' had been up until recently. Though it was used as a reference in daily life, she had never really known its definition. Now, in talking to this ghost of a Golden Age past, she sensed the two were linked.

Jacob gazed toward the bone-littered floor.

"When you die, your soul is supposed to move on from this world and into the next life," he explained. "But by taking our own lives, we naively made a declaration to the gods that our souls were not worthy of… of *whatever* comes next. Of course, had we known that at the time—"

Damon made a sound like a whimper out of General Ivo's mouth, and Jacob placed a hand on the general's chest where Arianna knew his heart should be.

If he even had one.

"A soul cannot be destroyed because it's already in the balance," he added. "But the gods can still deny us a future if they so choose. We are stuck here because the gods and goddesses of the sky, sea, sun, and earth are punishing us for destroying their gift of life. It may not last forever, but the gods who reign over Olleb-Yelfra are eternal, so for us, it might as well be." He shrugged. "It feels like forever, anyhow."

Arianna was having trouble fathoming all Jacob had said; she could barely get a grip on this life without considering that there could be more to come after, with the possibility of higher beings pulling the strings. She shoved all of that aside, no room to think beyond the fact she was talking to a ghost.

"I'm so sorry," she said. No other words came to mind, but she truly was. No one deserved to be punished like that. They'd only wanted to be free.

"I've had a long time to be sorry too, but it does no good," said Jacob, squaring his shoulders. "No life is perfect, and this is ours. Best to look on the bright side, *especially* in a place like this." He smiled genuinely, and Arianna returned it the best she could.

"And what about Pippa?" she asked, fearful for her friend's fate. "Why is she still stuck here? She didn't take her own life."

Arianna was too ashamed to even meet her eyes.

"Her time here is short," replied Jacob.

His tone suggested that he wouldn't be elaborating further, but even Pippa looked like she wanted to know more.

"Now I have a question for you," said Jacob.

"Sure…" said Arianna, warily. "What could you want to know from me?"

Jacob floated closer to her, peering deep into her eyes as if looking for something. "How can you see us?" he asked, his expression glowing with interest.

Arianna felt like she was in a dream world. She was in the presence of ghosts—Jacob, Damon, and Pippa all stared at her, anxiously, wanting to hear her explanation of something *they* thought was extraordinary.

"I'm sorry, but I really don't know," she said, wishing she had a better reply.

"Just think," said Pippa, joining the conversation now. "You must have some idea."

Arianna looked at her feet, searching her mind for answers. Unexpectedly, something actually did come to the surface. She raised her eyes to the ghosts surrounding her and voiced her thought. "Well… I did die once," she whispered.

They all seemed perplexed by her response at first, and she could tell Pippa reeled with questions of her own. But when she opened her mouth to speak, Damon raised a hand to silence her. Then Jacob nodded his head in understanding.

"Only the dead can see the dead," he said. "We need not know more on the subject. But tell me one last thing, Arianna." He narrowed his eyes at her. "What is your goal here?"

"My goal?" She pondered this for only a moment. "I just want my freedom," she said with confidence.

"Freedom from what?" he asked.

Arianna thought long and hard, realizing she could answer that question in a thousand different ways. But finally she landed on the only answer that seemed to make perfect sense.

"Free from destiny, I suppose," she replied. "I want to make my own path and be in charge of my own life for once. Must everything be predetermined?"

Jacob smiled, not acknowledging her query. "And what do you think might be your destiny?"

"I haven't got a clue, but if it's to be a slave all my life to the King, then I'm happy to run from it. All I want is to be free," she said with conviction. "*Truly* free, whatever that means in this world."

He gazed at her with a mixture of satisfaction and skepticism in his expression, a strange smile on his face.

"The universe is watching you carefully, Arianna Belvedor," said Jacob. "The breath of life is a sacred gift, and you were blessed with it twice. You must have an important destiny, and I sincerely hope you stop running long enough to find it."

Arianna chuckled, growing more and more bewildered. "If it's my destiny, then how could I not? They're set in stone, aren't they? Unchangeable?" she asked, wanting to prolong their conversation—she had a strong feeling that her time with this remarkable being would end all too soon.

"I believe so," he replied. "And do you have your stone, then?" Arianna returned a puzzled look. "Sometimes people never find their stones because they make many wrong turns in their search," he said. "Or the obstacles in the way are far too daunting, so they give up all together. Other times, people do dig them up, read what's been carved, and then bury them in their pockets to understand later." He shook his head. "Always a mistake. And then there are the lucky few who do find their stones, read their inscriptions, and spend the time deciphering the message." He circled her, studying her. "I'm guessing you've maybe glimpsed the path to yours but haven't given it much thought yet, from what I can tell."

"I don't understand," said Arianna, scratching her head. "What stone—"

"You will... *maybe,*" he replied, moving again to stand next to Damon. "We never found ours. We gave up too fast." Then he gestured to Damon that he was ready to leave.

"What are you going to do now?" asked Arianna, knowing her time with Jacob was up.

"We're going to fulfill one of our rumors and get this man so lost that he won't even be able to find his own feet when he gets his senses back," he said with a smirk. "I enjoyed our meeting this night. It's not very often I get to converse with such a fascinating soul." He winked at Damon and General Ivo rolled his eyes, playfully. "I wish you the best of luck with all your endeavors, Arianna Belvedor."

He began to float away, General Ivo walking behind him.

"I hope we meet again!" called Arianna, waving goodbye.

At this, Jacob took pause, turning back around to meet her eyes. "For your sake, I sincerely hope that we don't."

He gazed around the tomb with a somber expression.

"And, dear girl, if you *do* ever find your true destiny, your stone, don't forget to flip it over to see what's on the other side," he urged. "You don't want to miss a thing once you have it. You can run from it all you want, but Destiny has a habit of persevering."

Jacob vanished into the darkness of the tunnels with General Ivo close by his side.

"What will you do now?" asked Pippa once they had gone and all was silent again.

Arianna felt like she had just awoken from a dream, but Pippa still floated there in her ghostly form as confirmation of this strange new reality.

"I... I need to find my friends and make sure they're okay," she said, remembering Lessa and Jeom.

She hadn't had a moment to worry for them since she ran

into Pippa, but now the panic started to settle back in. She hoped that her plan had worked and the two of them were able to fight off the other regulators with the general out of the way, but she needed to get back to them and make sure.

"If they're anything like you, I'm sure they're fine," said Pippa, sounding a bit distant.

Arianna gave her a reluctant but grateful nod. It was still so awful to see Pippa like this, and she didn't know how to address any of the emotions she was feeling. And what was Pippa feeling? She seemed so confused… lost.

Instead, Arianna unfolded the map she'd taken from Mundar to try to make sense of her whereabouts. But as she read, something just didn't add up.

"This doesn't make sense. If I'm reading this map right, then the way out of the Blancoren Mountains follows this path," she said, pointing away from where she had first entered the tombs. "But the path my friends are following is going in the opposite direction. I'm sure of it." She crumpled the map in her hands as she grasped what this meant. "The spell didn't work! They'll be lost forever if I don't get to them."

Without an elder's map, it was clear that this deep into the Vanishing Tunnels, they were doomed. Arianna turned to Pippa, fear again poisoning her hopes. But before she could even speak another word, Pippa answered.

"It's okay," she said. "I can guide you to your friends."

"Thank you," breathed Arianna, tears in her eyes.

THEY LEFT THE TUNNEL OF TOMBS together in silence, taking a path Arianna hadn't noticed before in the darkness. It felt endless as they journeyed, and she saw no signs of that changing. But she was grateful Pippa was by her side through all this, even if she was a ghost. At least, she wasn't alone.

Pippa... Pippa was alone.

The memory of seeing Pippa's mangled body at the bottom of the Pit filled her eyes, and the echo of her dying screams before that moment filled her ears. She stopped walking, rubbing at her temples to try to quiet the sound.

"What's the matter?" asked Pippa, pausing alongside her.

Arianna absorbed this peaceful image of her ghost friend, so beautiful she looked now, and committed it to memory, replacing the last horrid image of her.

"Pippa, I... I'm so, so sorry to you," she said, finally finding the right words to say and the courage to say them. "It's my fault you died the way you did. *I'm* the reason those regulators were murdered that night, but they blamed you for it." She looked anywhere but at Pippa as she tried to explain. "It's a long story as to why I was even in such a mess in the first place and I'm sure you have a million questions, but I just... I can never tell you how sorry I am for what you went through because of me. I know an apology can't fix anything now, seeing as you're..."

She chewed on her lip, then forced herself to meet her eyes.

"I will *never* forgive myself for what happened," she continued. "And I shouldn't have snapped at you that morning of my Warrior's Challenge. You were my friend, and you deserved so much better." She bowed her head low. "If I'd only known the consequences of any of those choices—"

"Arianna, thank you," breathed Pippa, staring up toward the ceiling of the tunnel as a wide smile spread across her face. "You did fix it. You've just fixed everything! I never knew what was holding me back, but I guess it was you all along. Our destinies were intertwined, and I didn't even know it!"

She appeared overjoyed, but Arianna couldn't understand why.

"What are you talking about?" she said, watching as Pippa kept her eyes locked on the ceiling, waiting for something.

"I forgive you, Arianna. Whatever your part was in my death, I *forgive* you, and you must forgive yourself, too," said Pippa, glancing at her sidelong. "Whatever it is, I know you didn't mean for this to happen to me. You're a good person, and that's why I always clung to you in the district." She gave a little laugh. "And blame or no blame for some dead regulators, I broke the rules for being out past curfew. They would've killed me regardless."

She fixed her focus again to the ceiling.

"Besides, what are the chances I would've even survived the Free Falls?" she added. "Looks like they did a number on you, and you're a much stronger warrior than me." Was that a smirk on her face?

Arianna couldn't help but laugh in response.

"Yes, they did quite the number on me, you could say," she replied, hands on her hips. "But that's not the point. They tortured you! I…" She let out an exasperated sigh, vying for Pippa's attention. "What are you staring at? Why are you smiling?"

"Because now I can be free of this place forever," said Pippa. "I can finally move on." She closed her eyes and lifted her arms up high as if a soothing wind had washed over her. "Goodbye, Arianna, I hope you find your way. And if not, I'll see you on the other side."

Pippa's ghost began to slowly morph into a sparkling swirl of white light that lit the tunnel so brightly Arianna had to shield her eyes. And as she watched her friend disappear, mouth agape and astounded all the while, she heard the faintest echo of a familiar song linger in the air behind her—at that moment, with all her heart, Arianna knew that Pippa's soul flew free.

Relief rained down on her, and her mind instantly felt

lighter somehow. A smiling, glittering Pippa replaced the horrid memory of her body strewn across the Pit and in the tombs. And their last words replaced the memory of their fight before she'd died. For a moment, everything seemed better than before with her conscience cleared of that heavy guilt.

Alas, when the sparkling light from Pippa's departure had dissipated and the dark settled all around her again, Arianna's happiness began to dim just as suddenly as it had come; with Pippa gone, she no longer had a guide to her friends, and she no longer had her light to lean on.

Pulling up her hood, Arianna continued forward on the same path Pippa had been guiding her down, the bleakness of her situation weighing on her more and more with every footstep. But after a painfully long while, she noticed the darkness begin to lift. Praying this was no trick of the mind as she navigated nothing but shadows, Arianna squinted to see the cause and found a soft glow had emerged far ahead down the tunnel. She started running at full speed toward the emerald green light.

26

THE DOOR

COMING TO A SUDDEN HALT, Arianna lifted her eyes to the ceiling as the charmed path came back into view. And just as suddenly as she'd stopped, something landed on her back, making her jump out of her skin and scream as if General Ivo had snuck up on her. To her happy surprise, Sano was the culprit this time, scurrying around her shoulders and licking at her cheeks.

"By gods, Sano!" shrieked Arianna, cuddling him in her arms. "You gave me such a fright. I'm so happy to see you."

He snuggled against her chest for a split second before jumping back to the floor. Then he bounded off, down the illuminated tunnel.

"Wait, come back here!" she called, chasing after the ball of white fur. "Lessa will have my head if I lose you twice."

Arianna ran to catch up, but every time she came close to scooping him back into her arms, Sano would dart away. She kept her eyes glued to the ground, zigzagging all about the tunnel as she followed close on his trail.

"Won't you just stay still," she moaned, crouching low with her hands outstretched.

Sano again evaded her grasp, dodging to the side. Arianna lost her balance and fell forward onto her hands and knees, the impact jolting all the bones in her body as ringlets of tangled curls fell over her eyes.

"Oh, Sano…" she said with an exasperated sigh.

With dirtied palms, she swept the hair from her face so she could see properly again, just as a pair of black boots appeared in her line of sight.

"Arianna! There you are," said Jeom, not giving her even a moment to be scared. "I can't believe this. We thought we'd never find you." He turned to shout over his shoulder. "Lessa! Hurry, I found Sano. And you won't *believe* what he's dragged with him this time."

Arianna had barely caught her breath and gotten to her feet when Jeom lifted her up into a tight embrace, her toes skimming the ground. Before he could set her back down, Lessa had flown around the corner too, wrapping her arms around them both so that there was no chance of escape.

"Oh, Ara, we were so worried," she said through a stream of happy tears. "How could you *do* that to me?"

Arianna tried to speak, but her face was being smothered in their robes so effectively she thought she might suffocate.

"I couldn't think of any other way," she managed to say, wriggling out from the hug to get a good look at her friends. "I knew General Ivo would follow me. I was the one they were after, so I hoped separating would give you both a fighting chance." She noticed Jeom and Lessa both looked a little bloodied and beaten, more so than how she'd left them. "I'm so glad you're safe. But the other regulators, are they—"

"Don't insult me," replied Jeom, flexing his biceps and

grinning at her. "I handled them."

Lessa scoffed, elbowing him in the ribs. "*We* handled them," she said, rolling her eyes. "I can't believe you would do that, though, Ara. What were you thinking?"

Arianna gave her a guilty smile, flashing all her teeth. "I was thinking that I wanted you to survive," she said with a shrug—and that was the truth of it.

Lessa put her hands on her hips, narrowing her eyes at her.

"Well, it wasn't long before we realized you weren't behind us anymore," she replied, tersely. "We turned back right away to search for you." Her lips pressed into a thin line; she was clearly conflicted with her happiness at reuniting with Arianna and her anger over being separated in the first place.

"The regulators tailing us put up a fight," added Jeom. "But they were so distracted and on edge after splitting off from the general that they were easy to take on. Though, by the time we got back to where we'd split up, you and the general were already gone."

Lessa let an exhale go from her nose. "Here, we grabbed your things," she snapped, tossing Arianna the pack she'd left behind at the battle scene.

"We shouldn't separate again," said Jeom, setting a heavy hand on her shoulder. "I think we're stronger as a team if we ever want to see the sun again."

Arianna nodded. Then she glanced at Lessa.

"I really am sorry for tricking you both like that," she said, knowing firsthand how worried they must've been. "If I had seen any other way..."

Lessa averted her eyes, her lips twisted up in thought. "I understand," she said after a moment, resigned.

Arianna took that as forgiveness, so she looped her arm through Lessa's, overjoyed at being reunited with her friends.

"At least we found each other again, and we won't be bothered by any district regulators anymore," she said, trying to force a smile out of her friend. "*And* I've got an elder's map!" She shook the parchment at her. "If that's not lucky, I don't know what is."

Lessa cracked at that, a smile inching across her lips, though she tried to hide it. "Can we please just get out of here before anything else bad happens?" she said as Sano scuttled up onto her shoulder.

"Fine by me!" said Jeom, marching back down the tunnel in the direction he and Lessa had come from.

Thus, the three began their journey again, mustering all of the courage they could to finally reach their goal and find a way out of the mountains. They still followed the light, taking boundless twists and turns as the labyrinth grew even more complex with every step. Thankfully, they had the elder's map, if ever they might need it, but for now, they were all of the same mind—all dying to see what was at the end of this mysterious, magical trail.

"So… what happened to you back there?" asked Jeom, filling the silence as they walked. "Where's the general?"

"That's a *very* long story," replied Arianna. She could hardly begin to succinctly describe the strange events which had occurred in the short absence of her friends.

"Unfortunately, I think we have plenty of time," said Lessa, rocking Sano in her arms. "Do tell."

Arianna obliged, recounting her adventure in the Tombs of Blancoren—of the ghosts and General Ivo—and of all she had learned about the afterlife and the end of the Golden Age as best she could. Lessa and Jeom stayed speechless until she finished, and even for quite some time thereafter.

"Somebody say something, please," said Arianna.

Jeom cleared his throat. "Told you so," he replied.

IT HAD BEEN HOURS OF WALKING along the lighted path, but eventually they came to a stop as another obstacle materialized before them. The trail of magic had morphed into an enormous, emerald-colored wall which blocked their way forward. It looked as if one of the jade boulders from the hot springs had been struck by lightning and exploded into a brilliant green blanket of particles, surging with electricity and creating an impassable fence at the end of the tunnel.

Arianna couldn't even bring herself to blink as the green light absorbed her. And as she gawked at the magic, she was certain she could make out a solid cave wall directly behind it.

"What do we do now?" asked Jeom in an awed voice, equally entranced by the blinding barrier. "It looks like we've reached another dead end." His voice trembled, and he tore his eyes away. "Maybe we should go back."

"Go back to where?" asked Arianna in a hushed sound. She stepped nearer to the wall, drawn to it, feeling just as awestruck as the others looked. "What do you say, Les? Do you think we should turn back?"

"Well, we do have an elder's map now," she replied, locking eyes with Jeom. "It would surely lead us safely out." Then her gaze was pulled again to the barrier as it pulsated with pure magic. "But we've come all this way, and I can't help but wonder..." She edged closer to the electric wall with her fingers outstretched.

Arianna took hold of Lessa's other hand. "Me too."

As soon as Lessa's fingertips grazed the glittering green partition, the girls, along with Sano, were suddenly sucked through the wall and into the magic, leaving Jeom behind.

Arianna's entire body went pleasantly numb as the green light tickled her nerves in the strangest sensation. And her hair and robes floated all around her as if there were a wind blowing beneath her feet. Lessa appeared the same beside her, wild and free, and even Sano's fur was raised, his carroty eyes bulging with unease.

Then, in the blink of an eye, they found themselves outside of the magic and on normal ground, back in the dark.

"It must've transported us to the other side," gasped Arianna, her mind reeling with questions. "I can't see a thing."

On this side of the barrier, all traces of the emerald magic had vanished; she felt around until she found Lessa's hand.

"That was extraordinary," said Lessa, squeezing Arianna's hand tight.

"What do we do about Jeom?" mumbled Arianna as she pressed her other hand upon the cave wall—with the magic gone, it felt nothing but ordinary.

"He'll follow," said Lessa, confidently.

"He'll be furious," replied Arianna, hoping Lessa was right, hoping they hadn't just abandoned him and trapped themselves in the dark in the process.

"It's not like we could've *known* what was going to happen," said Lessa.

Arianna could hear the smirk in her voice. "I think that's a point he'll be sure to make."

They both shared in nervous laughter.

"Yes, he's certainly passionate with his opinions," Lessa replied. "But I'm glad he joined us, and I think he's quite fond of us too. So, he'll just have to get over this little detour."

Not a minute more passed before the cave wall began to sizzle with green electric magic again, a vortex in the stone forming. Then Jeom abruptly stumbled through, his cloak settling around him as if he'd just been in flight.

He was breathing heavily, a fire burning in his eyes as he towered over them, one fist clutching his axe and the other clutching the lantern.

"What in the King's name was that? You just leap through

a bloody magic wall without so much as a warning?" he bellowed, brandishing his axe in their faces. "We could've been vaporized!"

"We're sorry!" said Arianna and Lessa in unison, jumping back lest his blade accidentally nick them.

"We just wanted to find out what it was after such a journey," said Lessa in her sweetest voice, batting her eyelids at him. "Isn't this all so exciting?"

"Exciting is *not* the word I would use," he growled.

"Well, we're all still in one piece, aren't we?" said Arianna. "No point making such a fuss."

"What if I wouldn't have had the courage to follow? Or what if we ended up separated again?" he asked with a wounded expression. "Didn't you care?"

At this, Arianna and Lessa both had the good sense to look a little bit ashamed.

"Of course we cared, Jeom!" said Lessa, hugging him around the waist. "I'm really sorry we scared you like that."

He grunted in response as Lessa pulled away, clearly not convinced.

"Jeom, we had absolutely no intention of leaving you behind," said Arianna, forcing him to look at her. "What did you call us before… a *team?* Well, you're part of our team now, whether you like it or not." She tapped him playfully on his chest, which was puffed out in anger, and he deflated a little. "We just got a bit carried away is all. Won't happen again."

"Hmph… I don't believe that for a second," he said, easing up a bit. "You girls are seriously out of your mi—"

Jeom was suddenly speechless as his eyes traveled to something beyond. He lifted the lantern high so that the firebug light chased away the shadows in the vicinity. Arianna recognized the wonderment glowing in his eyes; it was similar to when he'd first seen them use magic and when they'd stumbled upon the emerald wall.

The girls turned to follow his gaze and were immediately struck silent and awed right along with him.

"Now *this* is exciting," breathed Arianna, soaking in the spectacular view.

"Where the heck are we?" murmured Jeom, his anger vanishing in the face of such a surprise.

Arianna tried to make sense of their new location. The air tasted thick here as a subtle smell stung her nose—the stench unnervingly familiar. But she pushed it aside to admire the view. The light of the firebugs spilled around them in a flood that washed away all signs of the darkness and revealed the true destination of the magical trail they'd followed.

A huge dome-shaped cavern encircled them by miles, spacious enough that Arianna was certain the Warrior's District and all its horrors could comfortably fit inside. And its walls must have reached to the tip of the tallest peak of Blancoren. Craning her neck, she found it impossible to even see where the hollow stopped as the dome narrowed inwards.

Scanning the area further, Arianna noticed fifty or so different tunnels dotting the walls of the massive chamber. She wondered where each one might lead but couldn't possibly fathom what new mysteries the tunnels might be hiding that could surpass where they stood now.

Through the middle of this chamber, two rows of white, crumbling stone columns rose tall to sustain the lower parts of a ceiling built of the same material; they created a wide, airy hallway which cut straight down the center from where they stood now. And aside from its vastness, the columns were the only noticeable feature of the cavern.

"Why would anyone build pillars here?" asked Jeom, scratching his chin. "It seems like a terribly difficult task just for the fun of it. It's remarkable craftsmanship though."

"Maybe we should've just used the elder's map as a guide..." said Lessa, sounding worried. "There's more tunnels than I care to count to choose from this time. Who knows where they lead?" She was already diligently calculating their next move.

"It's better than no options," said Arianna. "Besides, our magic must've led us here for a reason." She walked in a bit farther, still examining the strange structures. Then her eyes grew wide as she noticed something between the columns.

"There's a door!" she said, her voice echoing off the walls.

At first glance, it seemed to be just an ordinary door. Massive in size but ordinary nonetheless. Though, with a second and a third look, she knew it to be touched by some form of magic. It was centered precisely between the first set of columns and was crafted of wood with a bronze doorknob to twist—and if it wasn't suspended in thin air with nothing above or below to keep it in place, she would've considered it extremely unremarkable.

Arianna's burning curiosity again bested her reason as her feet began moving forward. Jeom stood back to observe from a distance, but Lessa followed at her heels without any persuasion. As the girls inspected this mysterious door, Arianna first tested its durability to see if it might topple over without anything holding it up. But when she pressed her hand against the wood, it stayed sturdy as stone.

"We've really found something here," said Lessa, letting Sano down to stretch his legs while they tried to solve this new puzzle.

"Yeah, I wonder…" Arianna ran toward it, throwing her entire body against the wood to get it to budge. Of course, it didn't.

She groaned, rubbing at her sore shoulder, and Lessa burst into laughter.

"Care to try that again?" said Jeom with a smirk on his lips, slinking over from behind. His curiosity had gotten the best of him too.

"Not particularly," said Arianna, sticking her tongue out at him.

"That's a fine door," he said, inspecting it for himself.

"How would you know?" asked Arianna.

Jeom tugged at his purple robes, signifying the creator in him. "Impeccably carved, smooth finish. Really a fine door," he said, whistling as he traced the intricate grooves carved into the wood.

Simultaneously, they all stuck their heads around to the other side of the door to see if it really did attach to nothing.

"Well, I'll be!" said Jeom as they found it to be an entrance to nowhere. "What do your magic books say about this?"

Arianna and Lessa just looked at each other and shrugged.

"Look, there's another!" said Lessa, pointing ahead.

Just as the large, wooden door propped upright between the first set of columns, the second set of columns also held a door of its own. This one was crafted of the solid gray stone Arianna was so accustomed to seeing in the Warrior's District.

And as they continued down this bizarre path, they passed many more doors, each one perfectly positioned between the parallel pillars. Yet, every door had been crafted from a diverse range of materials—each with their own untold stories.

Some stood twelve feet tall while others were so short Arianna would have to crouch down to enter. Several had been carved in a typical rectangular fashion, while others were in the shape of circles, diamonds, or squares. Many were constructed of wood or different varieties of stones. Others of metal and…

"Gold!" squealed Jeom in delight, setting down the lantern and rushing to the end of the hall.

As if in a trance, he stood in front of a giant gilded door hung in the air between the last two pillars, which completed the long walkway. Flecks of gold melted into his brown eyes as he stretched his arm out to twist the lustrous knob.

He tugged with all his might, but the door just wouldn't budge. Not wanting to give up his pot of gold without a fight, Jeom then swung his axe at the handle; the impact made a piercing sound that echoed to all corners of the cave, and Arianna lifted her hands to her ears, reminded of the bell.

Jeom tried to open it again and again, but the door stayed locked tight. Then, on what would be his last attempt, the doorknob glowed a menacing red as he placed his palm to it—he yanked his hand back with a terrible cry.

"Argh, it burned me!" He dropped his axe and squeezed at the wrist of his scorched hand. "What… what do I do?" Tears began to stream from his eyes as he looked to the girls for help.

Arianna saw the skin on his palm sizzle, bubbling up from the sudden heat. It looked as if it might melt off at any second.

"Here let me," said Lessa, calm and focused.

She swung her pack off her shoulder and rummaged inside for something; Jeom leaned his back against the door and slid to the floor in a heap as she pulled out one of the tubes Cyn had gifted them at the start of their journey. The liquid inside was a dark red, like congealed blood, and Lessa knew exactly how to use it.

"It's prillyberry juice," she said. "And it's already mixed to perfection, so you're in luck." Inspecting it further, she tested some between her fingers. "This will only sting for a moment, but try and be still."

He nodded, squirming from the pain.

Lessa took his blistered hand in hers and placed a few drops on his skin.

Arianna cringed as it dissolved into his flesh.

Jeom cried out again, breathing hard. "I thought this was supposed to help?" he whined in gasps as the medicine slowly worked its way around his hand.

"Hush, I need to concentrate." Lessa closed her eyes.

Arianna paid close attention now as their healer began to

recite a verse Talis had drilled into her head. Words they now knew to be magic.

"*Helthra saludis emencia*," Lessa said in a whisper.

When she opened her eyes, they were momentarily streaked by silver, and Arianna nearly jumped for joy. Lessa had finally tapped into her magic, too. She repeated the phrase over and over until Jeom visibly relaxed. And by the time she'd finished, his hand looked almost normal—save for a scar.

"You feel that?" asked Arianna as the silver magic left her eyes. Jeom was staring at Lessa with a bemused expression, hardly even noticing his hand anymore.

Lessa nodded. "It's exactly how you described it," she said.

Then she took a deep breath and turned to Jeom.

"Hopefully that will teach you a lesson," she said, smacking him lightly on the forehead. "What were you *thinking?* We just walked through a magical wall into a room with floating doors, so your first thought is to start throwing your axe around?" She pursed her lips and let his hand fall back to his side. "And you yell at us for reckless decisions…"

He lifted his hand to his eyes, examining his scar. "Most doors don't get so offended," he said, chuckling a little to himself. Lessa glared at him, and he faked a serious look. "I mean, thank you." He flashed her that white-toothed grin.

"You're an imbecile," she replied with a heavy sigh.

With a sudden spark of an idea, Arianna headed back in the direction of the first door, jiggling more handles and doorknobs on her way.

"Are you mad?" cried Lessa, scooping up the discarded lantern and chasing after her. "I don't want to waste all my prillyberry mixtures on failed attempts to open mysterious doors."

Arianna had already made it halfway down the hallway with no injuries to speak of.

"Can't you just try one of those spells from before to be on the safe side?" asked Jeom as he followed.

Arianna shook her head. "These are all obviously locked with magic," she called back as she walked down the hall.

"Obviously…" he muttered.

"That charm won't work here, but I think I know what to do." Arianna took it upon herself to test all of the doors they had passed before Jeom had injured himself at the gold one.

"Excuse me, miss," he called in a mocking tone, closing in on her, "my hand nearly liquefied back there. You're the only warrior in the gang, so it would be great if you kept yours intact, if only to continue wielding your swords." He grabbed her wrist and forced her to stop, midair, as she reached for yet another door.

"Well, I just tried several with no harm done, because I'm not trying to *force* my way in as you did," she replied, shaking free of his grasp. "I'm sure the old-fashioned way will work just fine." She pulled the handle in front of her.

Jeom flinched as her skin made contact with the metal, but nothing happened.

"You may think me insane, but I have a feeling we need to start from the very beginning," said Arianna.

"You're *insane*," said Lessa as she and Jeom both followed reluctantly in her footsteps.

Arianna came to an abrupt halt at the back entrance of the first door and circled around to the front.

"What's the harm in testing a theory?" she said, hardly hiding her frustration as her friends blocked her way. "If this doesn't work, we can have a look through those tunnels, but I'd really like to know what the secret is behind these doors. If it's worth hiding, then I think it's worth finding."

"Oh, all right," said Lessa, swayed by her own interest. She called to Sano to return. "The door option has my vote as well. You've tried them all. What's one more?"

Jeom threw his head back with an exasperated sigh.

"What?" said Lessa as Sano found his perch on her shoulder. "I'm just really bored of this endless-maze-of-tunnels nonsense. Besides, what's life without a little risk?"

"Idyllic," said Jeom, slapping his knee in laughter.

Arianna and Lessa couldn't have rolled their eyes harder.

"When we're free, you should look into some new material for your jokes," said Arianna.

He nudged her forward. "Go on, give it a go, then. I could use a break from the haunted tunnels too," he replied after catching his breath.

As Lessa and Jeom stepped aside, Arianna crossed her fingers and then placed her hand on the cool bronze of the doorknob, giving it a twist. She heard a click, and the door creaked open with a screech.

Instead of stepping through the threshold to the other side of the pillared hallway as she half-expected, Arianna found herself standing in a large room built of the same wood as the door; the columns and the cave had completely disappeared.

Lessa shifted the lantern around cautiously, and the space drank up the light like it had been lifeless for years. As the three moved inside, one after the other, thick dust billowed about their feet from the wood-paneled floor—then the door slammed shut behind them.

Everything was layered in an inch of filth, and Arianna felt Lessa recoil at her side from the sight of the grimy place. She chuckled as she spotted a broom in a far corner.

Benches long enough to fit twenty people stretched across the two nearest walls. And facing them, on the far side of the room, sat a large desk cluttered with what looked to be stacks of old parchments. Arianna also noticed the desk's matching high-backed chair had been placed in the opposite corner. Since the seat was turned toward the wall, she could see every detail of the carefully crafted wood.

The only thing not fashioned from oak proved to be a

stone door hinged on the very opposite wall from where they stood. Arianna recognized it to be the same locked door they had come to discover after the wooden one in the hallway of columns. She nodded to herself, understanding the mystery of the doors a little better.

"See, I knew it!" she said. "We have to start from the beginning if we want to get to the gold. You can't cheat magic."

She pointed a gloating finger at Jeom, and he smiled back at her, amused by this new finding as well. "Go easy on me," he said. "I'm new to the fold." He looked ahead to the stone door. "I wonder what we might find if we reach the end."

"Let's find out," said Arianna, eager to explore.

"Stop!" said Lessa. She placed a hand on Arianna's shoulder to keep her from going any farther into the room.

"It's just a little dirt, Les," moaned Arianna, impatient. "You should be used to this by now. We're cave people!"

"No, really. Something's wrong," she said. Her face had gone paler than usual.

Arianna's mind flew to alert then as she realized Lessa wasn't teasing, trusting the instincts of her friend just as much as her own.

"She's right. Look," said Jeom, gesturing to their feet.

Everything would've seemed in place, if not for the large footprints clearing the dusted floor, tracking farther than their own into the room.

"Somebody's been in here. And recently," said Lessa.

Jeom was inching back toward the door, pulling Lessa with him. "Do you think it's the lost souls of the slaves?" He was being completely serious.

"Ghosts can't leave footprints," mumbled Arianna as her friends moved to stay behind her. "And I have a feeling Jacob and Damon won't be coming to our aid again…"

"Then what do you suspect created those?" he asked.

"I don't know!" she hissed back. "It's probably a different

magical monster seeking vengeance." She tried to remain calm, but her friends' nerves were starting to pierce her composure and morph into her own.

"I believe I could be of some service," came a harsh voice from the far corner of the room.

Jeom, Lessa, and Arianna all screamed at the top of their lungs at the sudden interruption, their voices filling the space and bouncing between the walls. Then they spun on their heels to escape back through the door from which they had entered. Ghost or no ghost, the Vanishing Tunnels proved to have no shortage of terrible surprises and they were starting to get the better of them.

Alas, to their horror, they found the door locked tight.

"*Operium undrio!*" said Arianna in a panicked voice. No luck—this door had been sealed with magic.

Reluctantly, the three turned around, backs against the wall and weapons drawn, to face whatever joined them.

ANOTHER LOST SOUL

THEIR EYES WERE DRAWN to the grand, high-backed chair, which sat forgotten in the corner, as its legs scraped against the floor. Shuffling to the right for a better angle, Arianna saw that someone, or something, was seated in it. Whatever it was had blended in to the still and dark fixtures around them, hiding beneath deep olive robes, ones that appeared especially tattered, coated in white and black muck; the cloak bunched on the dirty floor and the sleeves hung long and loose so that neither hands nor feet appeared visible. And with the hood of the cloak pulled low over what Arianna hoped to be a head, all proof of what this being was remained to be seen.

Whoever—or *whatever*—the robes concealed sat completely still, seeming as if it had been waiting there forever in that rotting room. More unnerving still, the curved blade of a scythe leaned against the figure with generous portions of the steel covered in what appeared to be dried blood.

Could this be the fabled Death?

It seemed likely they might meet this god down here, in the bowels of Blancoren.

No one said anything as they waited for the startling presence to attack. With each passing second, Arianna's hopes diminished; she wondered what would happen next, wondered if they could survive yet another battle. Unable to bear the suspense a moment longer, she found her voice.

"Who... *what* are you?" she asked with shaking words, gripping her sword tighter as she stepped forward.

The question danced around the room on strings of dust while they all awaited a reply. Time ticked by slowly, and they stood paralyzed with fear for what seemed like ages before words trickled back toward them from the ominous figure.

"Just another lost soul... like you, it seems," said a splintered voice. The figure stood, ever so slowly.

Its hood hung so low that only a dark shadow appeared visible in the space where a face should be, and Arianna went rigid as she spotted a white, crinkled hand gripping the scythe, exposed as the loose sleeve gathered around its wrist.

She stifled a scream and tried to steady her swords as the monster began to glide toward them.

"Stop!" she bellowed, stumbling backward into Lessa.

The dark olive cloth rolled across the floor as the creature seemed to float like the ghosts she'd encountered in the Tunnel of Tombs, though with a physical body. Closer still it came, a cloud of dust stirring in the air around it.

"What do you want from us?" asked Jeom. His voice pitched much higher than normal, and he was ready to swing his axe.

"I need... a way out," it replied, a hand outstretched.

Weapons quivering in their grasps, the three tried to press themselves even flatter against the door as the figure approached. Then Lessa let out a shriek as it suddenly crumpled into a pile at their feet. Its robes now gathered on the floor in a mound of blackened-green thread, a mortal physique began to piece together—the hood of the cloak had inched back just enough so that Arianna could now make out the brown hairline of a head facedown on the floor, and black, muddied boots were made visible.

The scythe had also fallen away from the figure's hand, so Arianna didn't hesitate to kick the weapon out of reach. As she did, she realized that what she'd first assumed to be dried blood clinging to the blade of the weapon was actually just grimy clumps of the same mud covering the figure's robes.

"Is it dead?" said Lessa, staying a safe distance away.

Jeom drummed up the courage to investigate, prodding the figure with the dull end of his axe.

"I think so—" Suddenly, he let out a small gasp. Kneeling down to have a closer look, he rolled back the sleeve of the fallen figure and inspected something on its hand. "It can't be," he said. He shot upright.

"What is it?" asked Arianna, confused.

"This is no ghost," he replied, glancing at the girls with a mix of both horror and disbelief on his face. Then he sat down on the floor next to the figure, gently turning it onto its back and lifting its head into his lap. "I think... this is my brother."

Arianna and Lessa stood dumbstruck, trying to comprehend his conclusion. But with the figure's face now visible, they could plainly see that it was, in fact, not a ghost or a monster but a young man.

Although, he looked to be on his way to the afterlife.

"His name is Demetrius," he said with more conviction. "This is my brother. I *know* it."

Neither Arianna nor Lessa could think of a sensible response, so they warily came to join Jeom on the floor. When Arianna got a closer look at the boy, she realized that the skin didn't wrinkle at all like she had at first thought. Rather, his hand was coated in the same dirt and mud which covered both his weapon and clothes.

"But he looks nothing like you," whispered Lessa as she stared into the sallow face of the young man. "How do you figure he's your brother?"

Arianna examined the features of the boy before her, agreeing wholeheartedly with Lessa. He was much shorter than Jeom, and shaggy, golden-brown hair peeked out from under all of the muck with a little bit of chin stubble to match. Small patches of clean skin shone coppery and suntanned, and, as his eyelids hung half open, she spotted a glimpse of bright green—he and Jeom couldn't have been more opposite if they tried.

"Half-brother, then!" he snapped. "What does it matter what he looks like?" He turned to Lessa, eyes gleaming. "I think he's still alive. We need to help him, please."

"Okay, we'll help him, Jeom," said Lessa, squeezing his shoulder in reassurance. Then the young healer began issuing orders. "He looks dehydrated. Tilt his head back a bit and, Ara, please bring me the water canteen." Arianna rummaged in her pack and then handed the canteen to Lessa.

Forcing the boy's mouth open, Lessa tried to get him to sip the water. At first, he seemed unreceptive to the drink as it lapped at his cracked lips and dribbled down his mud-caked chin, revealing smooth skin underneath. But after a moment, the water began to disappear into his mouth, and Arianna saw him swallow.

Lessa pulled away to give him a moment to breathe, but the boy's crusted hand clasped around her wrist, holding the canteen steady at his mouth. She seemed taken aback by the strength of his grip, unable to pull away; he drank until not a drop could be found, and then he let her hand go.

With the last gulp, radiant green eyes sprang open, astonishing among all of the filth. He scanned his rescuers with a hazy expression, and then his eyes found Jeom.

"Brother…" murmured the boy. "Have I died? Can this really be you?" He stared up at Jeom with wonder.

"Yes, it's me," Jeom said with a laugh of relief. "I'm here, Demetrius. How do you feel?"

"Ravenous," he replied just as his stomach let out a hungry growl.

"Here, have this," said Arianna, pulling the leftover bread from her bag and handing it to him. "It might be a little stale—" He took it from her and devoured it without ever glancing away from Jeom.

"Slowly," said Lessa, hovering over him to observe every movement. "You'll put yourself into shock if you eat too fast."

Cyn flashed before Arianna's eyes as she watched Lessa transform into a true caretaker.

"How long have you been down here?" asked Arianna. "Better yet, *how* are you down here?"

He only shook his head in reply, closing his eyes as he savored every bite of the bread.

"Let's give him a moment," said Jeom. "Let him rest."

Arianna nodded, stepping back to give them room. "Why don't we have him lie on one of those benches for a bit?" she suggested. "I'm sure it would feel much better than the floor."

"Good idea," said Lessa. "Jeom, can you lift him?"

With ease, Jeom lifted Demetrius into the air, careful not to agitate him too much as he carried him over to one of the long pews lining the walls. Lessa wiped the dust off the seat so Jeom could set him down on a clean surface, and then Jeom shed his violet robes and bunched the cloth into a makeshift pillow behind his brother's head. Once he was situated, Demetrius' eyes immediately drooped and he fell into a clearly much-needed sleep. Then, Arianna, Jeom, Lessa, and even Sano sat down to watch over him while he dreamed, eventually all falling asleep as well.

WAKING AT THE SAME TIME some hours later, Lessa and Arianna left Jeom alone with his brother, wanting to clear their
heads from this new turn of events out of earshot. They wandered across the room to where the elegantly carved desk
stood; set in a protective stance near the stone door, it was a
commanding feature of the chamber. Scattered across the large
desktop were piles of rotting, yellowed parchments and dried
ink bottles and pens. And the many drawers, which decorated
the front of the desk, were filled with junk and more untouched supplies. For a while, the girls snooped over their
findings, lost in their own thoughts.

Arianna rummaged through all of the drawers, discovering
stacks of old parchment and scrolls in each. Studying one from
the top of the stack, she realized it to be a roster or checklist of
some sort. "What do you suppose this was for?" she asked,
breaking the silence.

Lessa took the parchment from Arianna and laid it flat on
top of the desk.

"I'm not quite sure," she replied, "but I found more of the
same."

"It looks like an old logbook like the ones the regulators
use to keep track of us," mused Arianna. "But what language
is this? I can't read a thing."

"I wondered too," said Lessa as she tried to decipher the
delicate handwriting. "It's definitely not one taught in the
Learning Centers. And see here?" She pointed to the top of the
parchment. "Each scroll I've seen thus far has what looks to be
a date on it, just like this one." She slid her finger across the
different columns. "And these could be the times that people
checked in and out with whomever sat at this desk. See how
there's an individual signature in each row?" Arianna peered

over her shoulder as she pointed to another column. "I can't say for certain, but perhaps these are names of places then. The people whose signatures those belong to may have been required to sign in and out for whatever lies beyond that door." She motioned to the stone door at their backs.

Arianna noted the date of the parchment.

"If you're right, then these are quite old," she said. "Older than our history is supposed to go."

"I know," breathed Lessa, flashing her a nervous glance. "Some are dated over four hundred years ago. That shouldn't even be possible."

Arianna laughed to herself, thinking of everything they'd encountered that shouldn't be possible—floating doors, long-lost brothers...

"There must still be a lot to discover in this place," she said, placing the parchment back in its rightful drawer.

When she nudged the drawer closed with her hip, the impact jostled the desk, a thin flap in the center falling open with a pop. A rain of heavy, silver coins sprinkled to the floor, tinkling like a parade of wind chimes. The girls bent down to examine them, pinching the coins between their fingers.

"I guess this wasn't a free service," said Arianna, arching an eyebrow as she studied the coinage piled at their feet. "I've never seen monies up close like this." The girls sat down among the silver for a closer look.

Coin was one of the many privileges denied to them until earning citizenship, but Arianna had learned about it during mandatory lessons and knew it to be a significant part of their world. She'd even seen intricate representations of the gold, silver, and bronze monies which ruled the Olleb—though none quite like this.

This silver seemed much larger than the ones portrayed in her studies, covering almost the entirety of her palm. Her fingers tickled as she slid them over the jagged edges of the coin, like those of an octagon. On one face of the warped circle, a single word had been engraved in the same strange language they'd seen on the parchments; it stretched across the middle in thick block letters. The other side of the coin depicted a double-sided axe in wispy, silver strokes that blended into the coin itself; and designed into the image of the axe was a gilded creature that Arianna didn't have a name for.

"Is that… a dragon?" asked Lessa, studying a coin as well. She was fixed on the side with the axe.

Arianna raised an eyebrow at her. "A dragon?"

"They were briefly mentioned in some of the scrolls Talis left us, remember?" said Lessa. "Scaly, fire-breathing creatures with wings and sharp teeth."

"Right, right," said Arianna, considering the depiction on the coin again. "I suppose it could be…" She looked up at Lessa. "But dragons, can you even conceive that?"

Lessa just shook her head. "Hardly," she said with a sigh. "Although, if these monies have anything to do with dragons, then maybe this place we've found has something to do with the Golden Age."

"I think that's your best guess yet," said Arianna in agreement. "Our magic must've led us here for a reason. Something more is down here for us to find, and underneath Blancoren seems like as good a place as any to hide a Golden Age secret."

"The spell was *supposed* to lead us out of the tunnels," said Lessa. "What good is uncovering a secret if we die with it?"

"Magic has a mind all its own," said Arianna in her best Master Churry voice, pulling a laugh from Lessa. Then she shoved some of the coins in her pockets. "Hopefully, they'll be worth something if we do ever find a way out of here."

"What trouble have you drummed up now?" said Jeom, resting his hands on the desk, concern etched across his face as he stared down at them.

Startled by the sudden intrusion, Arianna and Lessa both

jumped up from the floor, wiping the dust off their clothes.

"Sorry about the noise," said Arianna in a low voice. "It didn't wake Demetrius too, did it?"

"No," he said. "He's sleeping still."

Jeom scratched at the back of his neck, looking anywhere but directly at the girls.

"I just wanted to apologize if I was short with you before," he added. "And to thank you two for helping me save him… and, frankly, for everything else. I realize that we've only just met, but I already feel that I owe you my life." The words tumbled out of his mouth like a bird free of its cage.

"What do you mean?" asked Arianna. "You don't owe us anything. We're all in this mess together, remember?"

"You don't understand," he said, staring at his hands. "If I hadn't discovered you and Lessa in the Inventor's Zone, where would I be?"

Lessa tried to interject. "I think—"

"I'd be twiddling my thumbs," he said, his voice growing louder, "trying to go unnoticed and survive until the day those monsters handed me my freedom. But I *took* my freedom, and I owe you everything for that." He lifted his eyes to theirs. "This adventure is nothing less than spectacular!"

Arianna smiled. "Well, I can't argue with that."

"Since I've joined you on this journey, remarkable things have happened to me," he continued. "I gained two insatiably courageous, albeit a little bit crazy, new friends, I fought against district regulators, I discovered that magic and ghosts more than exist on this earth, and now *this?*" He gestured toward the bench where Demetrius slept, mouth agape.

Arianna felt her heart warm as Lessa beamed up at him.

"I never thought I'd see my brother again. Yet somehow, in all this madness and wonderful chaos, here he is." Jeom took hold of Arianna's and Lessa's hands, gripping them tight in his own as he demanded their gaze. "I owe you everything," he said. "You saved me from a pre-written destiny and opened my eyes to a whole new world. I'll always be indebted to you both for that, whatever happens next."

"Maybe this adventure is your destiny," said Arianna, remembering Jacob's words.

"We're just glad that we found someone like you to share all of this excitement with," added Lessa with a wink.

"Besides," said Arianna, "we could use another boy to even out our group. Think Demetrius will be adding to the ranks?"

Lessa was nodding emphatically.

"I was hoping you'd say that," he replied. "I can't imagine we wouldn't all stick together, at least until we get out of these tunnels."

"And hopefully long after," said Lessa.

Jeom returned a smile. "Really, after all that's happened, I'm still completely shocked that my brother was the surprise behind the first door." He sighed, closing his eyes as he said a quiet prayer of thanks to the gods of Olleb-Yelfra.

"It seems luck is on his side," said Arianna, glancing over to where he lay on the bench. "I thought he was on his way to join the ghosts I met in the tombs when I first looked upon him." She wrapped her arms around herself, skin prickling at the vivid memory.

"We were so afraid of him," said Lessa, giggling at the thought. "You'd think a brave trio like us would show a little more backbone after all we've been through already."

Jeom turned to Lessa, worry wrinkling his face.

"Demetrius was really bad off, though," he said. "Will he recover okay?"

"When he wakes, I'll give him something to remedy all that," replied Lessa. "He was literally starving to death, his skin so sunken when we found him, like some of the slaves when they're being punished without rations. But some food and a good rest will definitely have him up and going. He'll be perfectly fine. I'll keep my eye on him."

They all gazed over at the sleeping boy, relieved at this diagnosis.

"He's in good hands. Don't worry!" said Lessa, clapping Jeom on the back.

"I'm very curious about his backstory, though," said Arianna, eyes fixed on him. "I wonder how he found himself here in the first place. It's quite strange."

"Trust me," said Jeom, "I'm dying to know the same thing."

"But tell us, how could you possibly even know you're related to this boy?" asked Arianna, gently, so many questions on her tongue. "No citizen or slave has ever been acquainted with their kin. It's an act punishable by death to even voice a suspicion of meeting someone blood-related. So, how could you be so sure?"

Both girls waited eagerly for Jeom's explanation.

"I suppose now is as good a time as any," he replied, walking back over to the bench by Demetrius, waving them along.

Arianna and Lessa followed, taking a seat on either side of him, and Sano found his way back onto Lessa's shoulder.

Leaning back against the wavy sea of polished wood, Arianna let her fingers trace the simple carvings of blossoms embellished in the woodwork. Then Jeom began his story, speaking in a whisper so as not to disturb Demetrius.

"As you well know," he started, "the Opalls are where all newborns are grouped into their ceremonial years. We aren't saddled with numbers of identification until our fifth year before transitioning to the Jar. We came to the Opalls with our given names—"

"The only thing we're allowed to keep from our birth parents," added Lessa, listening intently.

Jeom gave a single nod. "Well, my name is Jeom Kane,"

he said, putting a hand on his chest, "and this is Demetrius Kane. We were brought to an Opall together and were paired in everything we did from then on. As we grew older, we realized we shared not only a ceremonial year and a surname but an unspoken bond, and we insisted to stay together always."

He stared into a space filled with his past.

"But our time together was short-lived," he continued. "We were forced apart on our fifth-year ceremony, as everyone is before entering the City of the Four Corners."

"They split you up into different districts then?" asked Lessa.

"Yes, inevitably," he said. He turned to Arianna. "And you're right. There are many precautions in place so that people can't fraternize with any of their blood relatives after early childhood, but my brother and I are an exception."

"But many people share the same surname," said Lessa, tilting her head to the side to look at Demetrius. "And you both look so different. So, what makes you certain you're actually related somehow?"

His eyes raised to the ceiling. "It's hard to explain. The emotions I felt are what's strongest in my memory of him. We were so young then, but still, we just… knew." Then he held out his hand, balling his left hand into a fist to emphasize his thumb. "But *this* is what makes me certain," he said, firmly.

Arianna and Lessa leaned in closer to look and saw that a jagged, white line shone on his dark skin at the base of his knuckle, ending at his wrist.

"What is it? A scar?" asked Arianna as she traced the line from one end to the other with her finger. The mark reminded her of the pointed peaks of Blancoren.

"This is a souvenir of my birthright and a reminder that I'm half of a whole," he said. "My life began somewhere else other than as a slave of the Creator's District."

"And mine too," came a weak voice.

All three glanced over to see Demetrius sitting upright and awake, attentive to the conversation. He used the fabric of his already dirtied cloak to wipe his hands and face free of all the filth and then carefully slid onto the floor at Jeom's feet.

Jeom unfurled his balled fist and held it out in front of him as if routine, and Demetrius copied his movement, taking his left hand and placing it firmly against his—Arianna and Lessa gaped as they realized the boys' uncanny connection.

Demetrius had the exact same markings as those on Jeom's hand, only his stood out in a black shimmer against his tan skin. Their hands mirrored each other, and Arianna saw the marks formed a picture when united together.

"It looks like a star!" said Lessa as she gawked at the perfect six-pointed emblem etched into their skin.

Her words seemed to shake the two boys out of their trance, and Jeom slid down on the floor next to Demetrius, pulling him into a tight embrace. They sobbed onto each other's shoulders while Arianna and Lessa tried to appear invisible in their intimate moment. A minute or so passed, and then they collected themselves.

"Ladies," said Jeom, wiping his eyes. "Allow me to properly introduce you to my brother, Demetrius."

"Pleasure to meet you," replied the girls.

"The pleasure is all mine," he said, shaking their hands.

Despite his weak state, he had quite the strong grip. And though he was in desperate need of a hot bath, Arianna found him to be quite handsome.

"I'm starting to see the resemblance," she whispered to Lessa as they both observed the Kane brothers side by side.

"Neither is too bad on the eyes," agreed Lessa.

Jeom cleared his throat. "You realize we can hear you, right?" he said.

Arianna looked away, pretending to be interested in Sano while trying to hide her laughter.

"So..." said Lessa, a wide grin on her face as she addressed Demetrius, "how do you feel now?"

"Much better," he replied with a smirk. "It's amazing what some food and good company will do to you. I believe I have you to thank for reviving me, yes?" He bowed low to Lessa who blushed at the gesture—slaves never bowed to slaves.

"I was almost about to give up hope," he added in a more serious tone, straightening his back. "Then I heard your voices. Just in time, really. I hadn't eaten or drank anything in days. You saved my life."

"It was nothing," said Lessa, pink color rising in her cheeks.

"You must still be so hungry," said Arianna. "I think we all could use some food, actually."

Time was lost down here in the tunnels, so instead of relying on a bell to dictate their appetites and sleep patterns, they trusted only in their bodies. And right now, stomachs rumbled all around as the idea of food crept to the forefront of their minds. Lessa and Arianna had saved a large amount from their hoard in the Creator's District, and they still had a little bit leftover from Cyn as well; there would be no shortage of food for all four of them... at least for now. They unpacked the rations and spread it out before them on the bench like a feast.

"Dig in!" said Arianna as she chomped down on some bread and passed around the other water canteen.

The atmosphere was uplifted tenfold as the four shared their first meal together in the dusty waiting room. Demetrius thanked them again with his mouth already stuffed with food, the color flushing back to his skin.

"Fancy a drink, Ara?" said Lessa after a few minutes with a sly smile on her face. She pulled out the large leather pouch of wine from her bag. "I wanted to save it for something special and now seems like the perfect moment."

"Definitely!" said Arianna. "I think I saw some goblets

near the desk." Demetrius hopped to get them, returning with four small goblets in his hands.

Arianna wiped them clean of dust with her cloak and then passed them around. After Lessa had poured everyone a generous portion of wine, she issued a toast.

"To the Kane brothers. May you never be divided again," she said as she raised her glass to Jeom and Demetrius.

"To my new family," answered Jeom with a grateful smile. "May we journey this new world together." He touched eyes with everyone.

"And to new beginnings," added Demetrius in a voice rejuvenated with life. He held his glass high to join the others.

"To stolen freedom!" finished Arianna with a restored passion in her heart.

They all clinked their goblets together, the thin metal chiming deliciously in their ears as the wine sloshed onto the wood floor panels. Then they drank, the sounds of satisfaction and delight following their first sips. Chattering away in happy conversation, they tried to avoid the fear and worries looming in the shadows of their minds—for they were still locked in this room and in the tunnels.

"So… Demetrius," said Lessa, pouring him some more wine, "care to tell us how you ended up down here in the first place?" Curiosity was shining in her eyes.

"Well," he said with a sigh, "that's an awfully long story."

"Please, enlighten us," said Arianna, eager to hear his recollection as well. "I think we have plenty of time."

"If you insist," he said, patting his belly. "I suppose you would've drawn it out of me at some point. But, I warn you, it's not my finest moment."

"You have nothing to be embarrassed about," promised Lessa. "Your brother tackled me and tried to kill Arianna upon our first meeting."

Jeom flashed a toothy grin before guzzling his drink, and

Demetrius shook with laughter.

Then Demetrius took a deep breath, and everyone else held theirs, leaning in to listen as he began to tell his own series of unfortunate events. "It all started the day after I won my freedom," he said. "The day after the Agrarian's District Free Falls Festivals."

ESCAPE

"NOT SO FUNNY NOW, ARE YOU?" said a woman in a sharp voice. She dressed in elegant, white robes trimmed in fur and olive silk, and her long, black hair was slicked back into a stiff ponytail at the top of her head.

She narrowed her hooded eyes at Demetrius as he worked to maintain the grounds.

"You may have survived the Free Falls, but that doesn't mean I won't hesitate to make sure you live out the rest of your miserable life in these mountains," she said. "There's still plenty of work available in the mines. Don't test me again. The next time you want to make a comment like that, I'll bury you in the dirt you love so much. *Understood*, number Twenty-One?"

He nodded.

"You still have another week under my watch before

you're escorted out of the Four Corners. The Warrior's District festivals have only just begun. Show some respect."

Her eyes were colder than the ice on the ground as she stared down at him.

"Yes, Mistress Serina," said Demetrius as he continued to scrape at the earth with his scythe.

The night was frigid, but his skin broke out in an uncomfortable sweat under his cloak as he hacked away at the weeds.

"That's what I thought," she replied. "Now this better be finished by the time the bell sounds, or the regulators can deal with you. Maybe you'll discover some discipline under all that mud after a few more hours of hard labor. You'll need it where you're going."

She turned on her heels, leaving him to his chores.

It was dark, but he could still make out his trainer's pasty skin as the light of the moon trickled down through the clouds and washed over her. For a moment, he became transfixed by the jade and gold stitching of a snake coiled around the stem of a rose on the back of her cloak before she disappeared around a corner.

Then he was alone.

All of his peers had already cleared out to the Dining Hall; his stomach grumbled at the thought of another missed meal.

Just one more week of her.

He enjoyed the peaceful quiet, at least. Only the sounds of earth shifting under his feet and the howling wind were noticeable. If he could ignore the mountains who mocked him in his loneliness, he might've felt content. But he couldn't—they continued to look down on him as he worked.

As a slave to the Agrarian's District, Demetrius was accustomed to spending most of his days in what they called the Dead Lands. The vast, empty space was filled with nothing but mud, dirt, and weeds, and it was where the agrarian-slaves spent much of their time training to work the land. In such a harsh environment, not much of substance could be drawn from the earth here, but those who could will any bit of valued nature into the Dead Lands almost always earned their freedom to practice their talents elsewhere in the Olleb.

Demetrius scooped up some dirt, letting the grains fall through his fingers as he remembered the day he summoned the rare snowflower to life.

Alas, despite his natural green-thumb, his mere personality frequently caused him difficulty—he was desperate to find joy in the face of all the horrors that came with life in the Jar, but he'd been saddled with a trainer who had absolutely no sense of humor and no patience for it. Consequently, though Demetrius had an uncanny ability to motivate things to grow (which should've secured him a notable placement in the Olleb), his talent couldn't outshine how much his mistress was determined to wipe the smile from his face.

On this night, just to spite him, she'd required that he complete a double-shift tending to the Dead Lands, clearing it of the fickle winter weeds which seemed to never stop appearing. As time ticked on, his clothes and skin became muddied, mirroring the ground. His hands grew blisters from gripping the hilt of the scythe for so long, and his back ached from hunching over for hours. Still, Demetrius thanked the gods he hadn't been sent to prep any of the animals for slaughter again; that always made him so sick to his stomach.

"Damn winter weeds," he growled after a while, fighting one that was particularly stuck. He used his tool to try to tear it from the earth, growing only more furious as it resisted.

Again and again, he let the blade of his scythe bite the ground with growing strength. All of his anger and passion went into each strike as the silent night abruptly overflowed with every unpleasant memory he'd ever experienced there. So often Demetrius kept them at bay with a jest or a smile, but tonight his past and predicament overcame him—he wondered if his mistress might make good on her promise to send him to the mines after all was said and done.

As the ground crunched and cracked with each thunderous blow, he felt the earth shift under his feet, forcing his focus back to reality and out of his daunting thoughts. But, before he could stop the next swing of his scythe to investigate, the blade hit the land with another smash. The ground gave way in a waterfall of rubble and mud, and Demetrius fell through the earth.

He groaned, blinking away the dirt from his eyes as he lay sprawled out on the rocky floor. Shaking his head of the stars dancing before him, he took a moment to recover from the shock of his tumble beneath the world. "How long have I been down here?" he muttered to himself.

Just then, he recognized the fading echoes of the district bell and knew that the last ring had jolted him awake.

Fear struck him into action.

I need to get to the barracks!

His mistress would never let him leave the Jar alive if he were caught outside after curfew.

Maybe I can sneak back in somehow.

Demetrius clawed his way out from underneath the rubble and looked up, realizing there was no way he would be able to climb out of this hole without help; he'd fallen too far down.

He began to call out for anybody, but he knew the Dead Lands to be quite far from everything else. After a few minutes of relentless screaming, his voice dried and cracked like the mud on his skin, he realized that the only ones who might hear him now were regulators—he closed his mouth.

When have the regulators ever once helped someone in my position?

They'd be all too happy to make an example of him.

Demetrius let his attention travel up toward the small hole

in the earth, finding the bright moon visible. Not knowing what else to do, he pulled his cloak tighter around his body, placing himself under the moon that seemed to shed a protective light, keeping the heavy night at bay. Then, he cleared his throat and started to sing through broken sobs, praying that the Olleb would not swallow him whole:

I see you down below,
As I'm flying in the sky,
Up above the mountains
To the other side.
The air here is sweet,
And it's warmer by the sun.
Nobody can catch me,
No one, no one.

Demetrius just kept singing, choking back his fears as his voice rang out; he clung to the last glimpse of the white moon as a gray cloud moved in slowly to shroud him in complete darkness.

"I SAT IN THE DARK FOR A LONG TIME, scared as ever," said Demetrius. "I thought I could just wait 'til morning. I knew more slaves would come down to the Dead Lands for work. But then I saw this… light."

He gazed up at the ceiling, using his hands to help form a better picture.

"What do you mean, a light?" asked Jeom, hanging on to his every word.

"Right before my eyes, a trail of green light appeared from

nowhere and whizzed throughout the cave. It lit up everything around me. I'd never seen anything like that, so what can I say? I just found myself meandering along with it." He wriggled his hand through the air like a fish in water as he recalled the events. "I was too curious not to."

All three of his listeners exchanged a furtive glance, but Demetrius kept on with his story.

"I know you probably don't believe that, but I swear it happened," he said. "It took me hours to find the end of the trail, and then I came upon this giant wall of… I don't even know what. I couldn't help but reach out and touch it." Jeom rolled his eyes at Lessa and Arianna who were both trying to stifle their giggles. "As soon as my fingers hit the barrier, my whole body became trapped in a pool of green *something*, and then—" He threw up his hands.

"And then what?" asked Jeom.

"I was standing in the dark again," he replied with a sigh.

"You found no light at all?" said Arianna, remembering how dark it had briefly been in this part of the tunnels, before Jeom had joined her and Lessa with the lantern.

He shook his head. "I just started blindly walking," he said. "That's how I found that damn door over there. I felt so lucky when it opened right away, but then I just got locked in here! I tried to maneuver my way around the room for a while, but it was fruitless with no light. I couldn't find a way out."

He ran a hand through his shaggy hair.

"Eventually, I found that chair and just sat down," he added. "When I heard you all barge in, I thought I was dreaming. I could barely lift my head, and it took all my energy just to make myself known." He rubbed his forehead. "And that's all I remember before now."

"I can't believe you survived down here for so long in the dark," said Jeom. "How long was it, do you think?"

"Not sure exactly, but I'd say it was about two days. No

food, no water," answered Demetrius. "I'm just as shocked as you are."

"Did you try the other door over there?" asked Lessa.

"No, I didn't even see it until you brought in that lantern. This is the first I'm even noticing another door," he replied. "I just know that as soon as I walked into this room, that one slammed shut behind me." He pointed to the wooden door. "When I tried it again, it was locked. Wish I had thought to say something when I heard you lot come in, but my head was so clouded and I was so weak."

"Don't worry," said Arianna. "We can figure this out. We've made it this far, haven't we?"

"I'd like to see the look on my trainer's face when she notices I escaped," said Demetrius, clenching his fist. "You know something? I did learn some respect. Self-respect! And that sure as heck isn't found slaving around. I'd much rather be trapped down here with freewill than up there with none."

Jeom beamed at his brother. "My thoughts exactly."

Arianna shook her head—so much alike.

"Where are we anyways?" Demetrius asked. "Any ideas?"

Everyone shrugged. "We're just as lost as you," said Lessa.

"You don't say?" said Demetrius as a chuckle burst from his lips. The wine had clearly gone straight to his head, making him giddy. "How did you all find your way down here, then? And what... what district are you from?"

His brow furrowed as he studied their cloaks, noticing for the first time that something was amiss with their group.

"Well, I ended up in the Creator's District after we were split up," said Jeom, indicating his axe.

"And I'm from the Healer's District," said Lessa. "Ara is of the Warrior's."

Arianna let out a shocked gasp as she realized something then. "An agrarian, a healer, a creator, and a warrior... all escaping the Four Corners," she said in a whisper. "This really is a day to be marked by history." They each considered one another with admiration gleaming in their eyes.

"May the gods be with us every step of the way," said Demetrius, lifting his glass once more.

After they all enjoyed another sip of wine, Demetrius rested his back against the bench. "Now, let's hear your story," he said, gesturing to all of them. "I'm sure it's quite the tale."

Arianna and Lessa looked to Jeom with an unspoken question—to tell or not to tell the truth to this newcomer?

He gave a single nod of approval. Then together, the three began to retell their stories, from beginning to end and leaving out nothing, until all four of their lives had intertwined and knotted together in that very room.

Lessa and Arianna even explained to Demetrius all they had learned about the enchantment of the world and the magic they themselves possessed, of ghosts and the Golden Age. And after they'd wrapped up their depiction of sorcery and all of the dangerous details that came with it, they patiently awaited his reaction.

Demetrius remained stunned into silence for quite some time thereafter, but then he shook his head, and his stupor fell away. "I'll believe in anything after this miracle today," he finally said, laying a hand on his brother's shoulder.

Arianna was so relieved, more than appreciative of the fact that Demetrius kept an open mind. It was stressful enough rewriting her future in a world where magic existed without having to persuade another to believe in it too; his calm reaction and even interest in the forbidden topic gave her a little more courage.

"I never thought I'd see you again, brother," said Jeom.

"I had every faith," replied Demetrius, matter-of-factly. "We can't exist without each other. We're half of the same whole." He grasped Jeom's hand and gave it a squeeze.

Arianna stared again in wonder at the union of the two

unlikely siblings; although Demetrius was quite tan in his own right, he looked starch white next to Jeom. Yet, despite their obvious differences, they had just as many similarities to note alongside their common birthmarks—they shared the same smile that touched their eyes, and they both indulged in a delightful sense of humor, adding a little more fun to the group. And Arianna even noticed the boys exhibited the same mannerisms while they ate and when they laughed, their exultant voices complimenting each other to perfection.

"So, what now?" asked Demetrius, petting Sano. Lessa's monkey kept a close watch on their new addition, and they both seemed quite fond of each other from the onset.

"Now we figure out how to escape again," said Arianna.

In unison, they all looked toward the stone door which hovered ominously over the dusty desk.

"Let's pack all this up while Lessa fixes the rest of your brother," she added, getting to her feet and pulling Jeom to his alongside her.

Soon Lessa and Demetrius had bonded over his checkup as they discussed the different uses of prillyberries, and Arianna and Jeom became enthralled in a conversation about the different cultures in their districts while they packed; the four fit together like the pieces of a puzzle. And as they set about their tasks, they fed off each other's optimism and dreams of a happy, humble future. After some time, they finally made their way across the room toward the desk.

"Did you girls find anything useful over here?" asked Jeom as he traced his fingers over the parchments.

"Just some strange coins and old records," said Lessa, kicking at the dirty silver on the floor.

"Know what they're for?" said Demetrius as he inspected one of the parchments on top of a stack for himself. "This one is dated more than two and a half centuries ago!"

His voice thundered in the space as he rubbed his hand

over the stubble on his chin, examining the scroll further.

"Many go even further back than that. We think they're old records of times people checked in and out of this room," said Arianna.

"Looks like some never did," he replied.

Demetrius' words lingered unpleasantly in the air as an uneasy ambiance returned to their wooden prison, chasing Arianna's brief feeling of enthusiasm away.

"What do you mean?" said Lessa.

"I mean, these people never checked out," he said, showing her where to look. "And no other pages are filled out after this date. This seems like the last record."

Lessa and Arianna peered over Demetrius' shoulder to scrutinize the parchment, understanding his reasoning. Sure enough, this sheet had one empty column where the sign out time should have been documented if their assumptions were correct—and there the recordings ended.

The four stared at each other as their eyes shouted warnings and unsaid questions. But no one voiced a thing, because no other options presented themselves.

Arianna patted the dagger against her thigh, and Sano climbed to his rightful place with Lessa. Then they replaced the ancient parchments on the desk.

"Ready?" said Arianna, heading toward the door, trying to ignore the butterflies in the pit of her stomach.

Please don't let it be locked.

"As I'll ever be," said Lessa, moving behind her.

The brothers nodded in unison, so Arianna pulled on the handle—the door opened.

29

THE CITY OF UNDOR

ONE AFTER THE OTHER, the four marched through the stone door, the firebug lantern filling another lifeless room with much-needed light. And quite like the wooden den they had left behind, this space also proved to be a match to their way of entry—a room of stone.

As soon as Jeom, who brought up the rear, stepped through the doorway, the towering door creaked closed with a resonating thud. Arianna knew it would be locked, just like the last, and she knew what they had to do next as they all stared ahead to the third door; it reminded her of coal, and the faintest shimmer of orange and red weaved into the material, as if a fire smoldered behind it.

The room they stood in now was much smaller than the one before, its rounded walls connecting the stone-set floor to a high-vaulted ceiling and making them appear to be trapped inside a cylinder of gray rock. As Arianna peered across the space, she noticed a tall pedestal made of glass—the only thing standing between them and the next door.

Arianna, carrying the lantern, walked forward to inspect the glass structure with the others following closely. She saw a message inscribed across the top, painted with iridescent, pearl-white letters. It only took her a moment to realize the words belonged to the same strange language they'd encountered earlier. She had to tilt her head back and forth to read the letters as they created a circular pattern which enclosed a familiar symbol.

After setting the lantern atop the podium, she pulled out one of the coins she'd stuffed in her robes and examined it under the light next to the pedestal; the very same double-sided axe that was etched into the coin had been portrayed in breathtaking detail atop the podium.

Drawn closer to the glass, Arianna now saw that the scaled, golden tail of a dragon, as Lessa had described it, snaked up the staff of the weapon, and its head rested in the center of the two blades as it brandished sharp, gilded teeth. The blades of the axe looked to be crafted of silver metal but seemed welded in place with the lustrous wings of the mighty beast, as if it could take flight in a fiery haste. And stamped underneath the dragon weapon depiction, she found the same word that also appeared on the other face of the coin.

"Wonder what it says?" mused Demetrius, coming to stand beside her.

"Wish I knew," said Arianna, showing him the coin.

"Hmm… it's in some foreign tongue that we found on the parchments too," said Lessa, snatching the coin to examine it alongside the large podium for herself.

"Prosperity," said Jeom, eyeing the podium over Lessa's shoulder with his hands in his pockets. "That's what it says."

"And how could you possibly know that?" asked Lessa, eyeing him with skepticism.

Everyone stared at him, waiting for an explanation.

Jeom's forehead crinkled in concentration as he leaned over to study the podium again.

"I don't know. I just do," he replied after a moment, scratching the back of his neck. "I see that it's written in another language, but I can understand it, I guess..." He frowned, standing up straight. "You all really can't?"

They shook their heads.

"This definitely isn't the approved language of the Olleb we were taught in the Jar," said Demetrius. "It makes no sense that you could read it."

"Well, I'm not lying!" said Jeom, scowling at him.

Demetrius threw up his hands, jumping to hide behind Lessa. "I'm just saying... doesn't make a lick of sense."

"No one thinks you're lying," said Lessa, calmly, handing the coin back to Arianna to pocket. "I'm sure there's a logical explanation, but right now we should focus on getting out of here. Can you read what it says on the podium as well? Maybe it will offer a clue about what else to expect in this game of doors."

Jeom grunted his agreement to try, so Arianna passed him the lantern and they all moved aside to give him space. Warily, he stepped forward and rested his hands on the podium. As soon as his skin made contact with the glass, the iridescent words which encircled the axe rolled in and out in a shimmering wave of white from the beginning to the end of the circle. Jeom jumped back with a shriek, but the others made him stay put, huddling closely around him to get a better look themselves.

"Go on, Jeom," urged Lessa. "It's all right. These words must be meant for you somehow. Can you try to read it?"

Jeom leaned his axe against the podium and cleared his throat, tilting his head to see. And as his eyes scanned the words, his mouth translated them into something comprehensible for the others to hear:

> *The great City of Undor is open to all who share the blood of our founder. Those without shall remain blind unless bidden entrance by one of high honor. Only then shall visitors be welcomed into the city.*
>
> *Built over centuries throughout the foundation of Blancoren, the City of Undor covets many precious resources. Kin who pass forth from this chamber to the next thus make a solemn vow to protect these sacred walls and the secrets within, which are privileged only to our kind. If those deemed worthy abstain from this promise or fail to protect what this city holds dear, a pardon shall never be bestowed and redemption never granted. Accept the rightful duties and responsibilities as a citizen of Undor and a dwarf of Olleb-Yelfra and we invite you to continue onward. We welcome you, brothers and sisters, home.*

Jeom reread it three times before he registered the most striking word. "Dwarf?" he said, a bewildered expression on his face. "What's that?"

"I've read about them before in the scrolls from my master!" said Lessa with a gasp, hopping up and down with glee. "They're magical creatures of the Golden Age, and they normally inhabit caves or places underground where their magic is strongest... places like *this*." She could hardly contain the excitement radiating off her. "It all makes sense now! These rooms, those columns, they must've been built down here by dwarves. In fact, there was a tale of a dwarf king who slayed a three-headed dragon and then became the hero of his people. I think his name was Undor! Ara, don't you remember?"

Arianna twirled a strand of hair around her finger as she let her mind become delightfully drenched in magic and Golden Age secrets once more.

"Of course, I do," she replied, recalling the many nights she and Lessa had pored over the wealth of scrolls from Talis' personal library and inundated him and Solomon with questions at every chance they got. And still, it was hard to fathom that some of the histories and tales could've ever been true— yet, the more they journeyed away from the Jar, the more she was able to see the truth behind the ancient ink.

"This city must've been built in his honor," Lessa added, as she and Arianna marveled at the chamber.

"City… you call *this* a city?" said Demetrius, glancing around, quite unimpressed. "I'm not convinced that a room made of stone, and a dusty wooden one, can be described as such. Unless there's more here than meets the eye." He tapped his finger to his chin as he stared ahead at the wall. "Nope! Don't see it."

"With magic, there's always more than meets the eye," said Lessa with confidence. "You'll see."

"Come on," said Arianna, smirking at Demetrius. "You have to admit this is pretty spectacular after all we described to you about the Golden Age. We've literally stumbled upon a piece of it!" She held out her arms wide. "An underground city touched by magic and surrounded by caverns of equal natural splendor." She sucked in a full, deep breath, trying to soak in all the wonder.

"Oh all right," sighed Demetrius with a grin, leaning into the excitement of his first exploration of magic with the group. "I suppose there's something to be said about all this. It's definitely a twist on what I was expecting we might find."

"Underground city?" said Jeom in a whisper. "Magical creatures?" He clutched the edges of the podium as if trying to steady himself from a dizzy spell. "It's just so... strange."

"Strange is that you can read it," said Arianna, glancing again to the foreign words, Demetrius and Lessa mumbling their agreement—the writing might as well have been scribbles to them. "You seem a bit tense, Jeom. Are you okay?" She laid a comforting hand on his back.

He gave a single nod, taking deep breaths. "We've just spent a lifetime believing in nothing. It's hard to grasp, is all."

"It is," said Arianna, gazing around again and contemplating such a discovery. "But think of all the remarkable things that have led us to this very spot, just like you said last night. With everything we've been through, the fact that dwarves and forgotten cities have been added to the mix..." She shook her head. "The impossible is beginning to seem pretty ordinary, wouldn't you say?"

In a way, Arianna was trying to also reassure herself of this new piece of boggling information; this place was evidence of not just magic but of actual enchanted, intelligent beings other than humans that once walked the same land.

Jeom let his eyes float closed, hands still grasping the podium. "I just..." He slammed his fist onto the surface of the podium, a large crack splitting through the center of the thick glass and making everyone jump as the sound bounced back and forth between the walls in the tight space.

Demetrius rested his hand over Jeom's fist as his breaths came heavier still. "Don't worry, brother. Everything will work itself out in the end," he said, so calm that it made Arianna think it must be true.

Jeom nodded, straightening his back and letting his focus find the ceiling. "Sorry," he grumbled. "I just need out of these caves. I need some fresh air."

"I think we all do," said Lessa as Sano started to become

very fidgety. "Shall we, then?"

"Lead the way!" urged Arianna, anxious to move on and see what lay beyond the fire-kissed door.

Lessa took one step past the podium and was flung backward by some invisible force. She landed on the stone floor with a crash.

"By gods, what *was* that?" cried Arianna as they all rushed to her aid.

"I'm fine," she said, taking Arianna's hand. "Is Sano okay?" Demetrius had already scooped him into his arms and was trying to calm him down.

"It felt like I ran into a wall or something," she said, standing.

"It looked like you were pushed," said Jeom, squinting at the thin air and grabbing his axe.

"I don't think so," she mused.

Then she walked forward again, slowly this time, with her hands extended in front of her. Sure enough, her palms flattened against something solid.

"You have to feel this for yourself," she said in bewilderment. "It has to be some kind of magic!"

Arianna mimicked her, flinching as she too felt something cool and concrete press against the palm of her hand, blocking her way forward. Demetrius followed suit and knocked on the invisible barrier, a deep sound resonating throughout the chamber like drums before battle.

"More than meets the eye," cooed Lessa, drawing cautious laughter out of him.

"But how can we pass?" asked Demetrius.

He was met with silence.

As the three remained with their hands pressed up against the partition, Jeom tentatively reached out to place his hand on the invisible fortress. He stumbled, unhindered, past his brother and the girls.

JEOM CLENCHED AT HIS HEART, gasping as he fell through some unseen energy force almost as if he'd just stepped through a wall of electrified water, or quite like when he'd passed through the emerald wall of magic… only stronger. When he looked back, he found Arianna, Lessa, and Demetrius all banging on the barrier that had now taken shape—it appeared like a glass divider encasing a wispy, indigo liquid.

He strained his eyes to try to make out his friends through the strange substance, but they all looked blurred and their voices were muffled. Still, he could *almost* make out his name, realizing they called out for him from the other side of the watery wall.

"I'm here. I'm okay!" he tried yelling back, but they didn't seem to hear or see him.

He screamed in fright as a loud voice filled the space around him, making chills run down his back. He moved away from the wall to search for the culprit, lifting his hands to cover his ears.

"Welcome to the City of Undor. You may proceed," said the voice belonging to an unseen woman.

Surveying the small space around him, with his axe held high, Jeom saw nothing but the enchanted wall, the ember-like door, and the small space in between. Then the panic began to set in.

You're not crazy, Jeom. Just remain calm. It's just the cave air going to your head.

Inching back toward the indigo barrier with his eyes peeled, he found that his friends were still pounding away with their fists and feet, trying to get to him, their stifled cries giving him courage.

Don't worry. I'm coming!

He extended his hand toward the wall. Jeom's fingers pressed through the magic and grazed the thick yet water-like threads which separated him and his friends. Summoning all of his bravery, he moved his feet forward to follow. And just as before, he was sucked through the barrier.

Jeom fell into the arms of the others, each showering him with questions and clinging to him as if he might disappear again.

"You just vanished!" screeched Arianna, eyes wide.

"Are you okay?" said Lessa, looking him over with concern. "Are you hurt?"

"No, I'm fine…" he stuttered, pushing them to arm's length. "But did you hear that woman?"

"Hear what?" asked Demetrius as he frantically examined his brother. "What in the King's name happened to you?"

"I passed through to the other side of the wall, but you couldn't see me," he tried to explain. "And then a woman spoke, welcoming me into the city." He rubbed at his temples and then went back to the podium, reading it over. "I don't understand. Why can't you all get through as well?"

"Ah ha!" said Demetrius, lifting his finger to the air. "I know exactly what this is about." A wry smile inched across his mouth. "I can't believe I'm saying this… but I think you may have a little dwarf in you, brother."

Jeom felt his blood rush to his cheeks.

"That's ridiculous. How do you mean? I'm over six feet tall! Wouldn't dwarves be… *dwarfish?*" he replied, holding his hand low to the ground. "I know you're new to this stuff, but we need solid theories here. Quit playing around, Demetrius."

The room went unnervingly quiet, and Jeom felt his skin burning from everyone's scrutiny.

"Stature aside, he may be onto something," said Lessa after a moment, chewing on her lip as she thought.

Jeom stood up straighter, scowling down at her.

"What are you suggesting?"

"Well," said Arianna, cocking her head to the side as she joined in. "You *do* know the language, bizarrely. And you were the only one of us to be able to get through." He started to open his mouth in protest, but his brother cut him off.

"Well, have you got any other explanations?" asked Demetrius. "It does *kind of* make sense."

Jeom just gawked at them in utter disbelief, unable to contradict anything anyone had said—but he knew in his soul that they'd lost their minds.

"Here's an idea," said Lessa before he could get a word in. "Why don't you try to invite us in yourself?"

Jeom felt as if he might explode as he slammed the butt of his axe down. "I'm not going to—"

"Just listen," she said, holding a hand up to silence him. "Something about you, something in your blood, *perhaps*, allows you through that magical barrier. When you read the message on the podium, it mentioned that visitors could only be invited in by those who share the dwarf bloodline and one of 'high honor.' So... what if those are literal instructions?"

"But I'm *not* a dwarf!" Jeom pursed his lips, matching her glare as they challenged each other.

These girls really are out of their minds. And now my brother is drinking the water too.

He shook his head, firmly sticking to his position.

"I didn't say you were a dwarf," said Lessa, her cheeks burning bright pink. "I said that *something* about you allows you through, and we want in!" She stood on her tiptoes to challenge him, poking him in the chest. "We're not going to just sit down and die in this room, so unless you have a better idea, start talking."

Jeom suddenly felt shorter in her presence. "You're quite frightening for someone so small, you know?" he muttered.

Lessa let out a long exhale, throwing her head back in exasperation.

"She has a good point, Jeom," said Demetrius. "All joking aside, what's the harm in trying? It won't hurt anything."

"Oh, all right," he growled. "If it will shut you all up about this, I'll try. But what should I even say?"

Demetrius slapped him on the back in reassurance, smiling as he tried not to laugh in his face.

"Great!" said Arianna, waving him forward. "I suppose, just invite us in and we'll see what happens."

Jeom was sure he must appear mortified to them for how his insides twisted in knots at such a silly idea. Yet still, he couldn't think of any other explanation as to why he could read that foreign language like the back of his hand or why he'd not been stopped by the magic.

He took a deep breath, trying to quell his spiraling thoughts.

How could I possibly be something and not know it?

"Okay… I invite you in," he said, resigned to their pressure. But when they each tested the barrier once more, nothing had changed.

"Try something more formal," suggested Lessa, clearly on edge as she pushed all her weight against the invisible wall.

Jeom puffed out his chest mockingly.

"I, Jeom Kane, humble creator of Olleb-Yelfra, invite you—Arianna Belvedor, Demetrius Kane, and Lessa Thur—into the great City of Undor." He raised his hands above his head in a dramatic fashion, bowing to the three.

Again, nothing happened.

"I know!" said Demetrius, clapping his hands together.

"No, you *don't* know," Jeom huffed. "I told you that I can't possibly have anything to do with—"

"Just humor me," interrupted Demetrius, batting his eyelids at him. "I haven't asked you for any favors in a *long* time."

Jeom scoffed, rolling his eyes. "Oh all right, spare me the act. What is it, then?"

"Think you could actually speak the language?" Demetrius had another sheepish grin on his face.

"You're enjoying this, aren't you?" he replied with a snort.

Demetrius nodded with a little laugh. "But in all seriousness." The shadows of desperation started to creep through his calm expression. "Can you?"

Jeom felt his heart go a flutter at the suggestion, but he wasn't sure why this all bothered him so much. Then he glanced to Arianna and saw that even her steadfast brave face was starting to falter.

And suddenly it clicked; as ludicrous as the idea was, if it *didn't* work, how would the others get out?

He looked to his hands. "I really don't know if I can, I… I've only just recited it before and—"

"Don't doubt yourself," said Arianna, softly. "Please, try."

Jeom walked over to the podium, grabbed the lantern in hand and assessed the script once more, feeling it so familiar somehow—though he was certain he'd never seen it before in his life other than in the last few hours. Gulping down his nerves, he opened his mouth to speak and, to his own shock, a string of foreign words poured out in a smooth slur. He was awed with every sentence, his voice sounding so different, so deep and authoritative as it mixed well with the foreign tongue.

When he'd finished, everyone appeared to awaken from a stupor. Simultaneously, they reached out to test the barrier together. Submerged again into the rolling waves of indigo energy, Jeom landed, unharmed, on the other side—though this time with his friends at his side. And as soon as their feet had all hit the floor, the mysterious voice rang out to greet them.

"Welcome to the City of Undor. You may proceed."

Demetrius looked all around. "I sure heard it that time."

"You did it!" cheered Arianna, seeming so relieved.

Lessa ran and gave him a hug, Sano smooshing up against his chest. "You were wonderful," she whispered.

"Yeah, yeah," he replied, trying to appear unperturbed, though his mind shouted so many unsaid questions.

Why me? What does this all mean? How could I be...

Before he could even wrap his head around what had happened, Arianna and Lessa raced ahead toward the next door.

"Come on, let's get out of here before another invisible wall appears," called Arianna.

"Right behind you!" said Demetrius, pulling Jeom along.

"Here we go again," he mumbled with a sigh. "Honestly."

Jeom's grimace broke into a smile, and then he followed the girls into the next chamber with his brother at his side.

They pushed open the door and looked around, beginning to realize that each one they unlocked displayed little excerpts of what they could expect inside; and this coal-crafted entrance—laced with sizzling reds and oranges—proved to be a very good depiction of the surprise in store for them next.

30

FIRE AND ICE

WHEN THEY ENTERED THE NEXT ROOM, an unpleasant blast of heat struck them. Arianna felt as if she had just stepped into a furnace. However, unlike the others, this particular chamber resembled a part of the tunnels that she and Lessa were already quite familiar with.

"The sunstone," mumbled Arianna, taking it all in.

"Sunstone?" asked Demetrius.

"We found tunnels of this same rock when we happened upon the Creator's District," explained Lessa.

"Well, it's hotter than the Inventor's Zone in here," said Jeom with a whistle as he fastened the lantern to his belt at his hip—they didn't need to rely on the firebug light in this room. "And maybe bigger too!"

They all stood a moment to admire the drastic change of scenery and the vast cavern before them.

Sweat was already beginning to bead on her skin beneath

her heavy cloak, but Arianna didn't mind the balmy temperature; it made her think of the hot springs, and she found it impossible not to be awed by the vermillion chamber. The blackened floor and walls sparkled with deep yellows, oranges, and reds, and it looked as if the entire room had been embroidered with the elements of a dazzling fire. Even the columns of earth, which sprouted up in many parts of the cave, appeared as if bright flames simmered within the rock.

Arianna had to tilt her head back for a glimpse of the high ceiling. And when she did, a scream caught in her throat as she registered the fiery sky above them—flowing over the entirety of the ceiling was a river of roaring magma. The lava burned bright red, swirling in all directions as it ruthlessly coated every inch of the ceiling in the sunstone cave.

Lessa followed her gaze, and a shriek escaped her lips. Then the boys quickly joined in with their own fits of panic, all eyes glued to the lava. It seemed as if their world had flipped upside down as they gaped upon an inverted version of a volcanic pool.

Lessa was the first to find her voice. "It must be another charm," she said. "Dwarves sure loved making a show of things from what I read." She fiddled with the fasteners on her cloak, ensuring Sano couldn't jump down as she trapped him within her robes. "Think it's safe to move forward?"

Arianna gave a shaky nod, focus still pinned on the ceiling.

"Doesn't appear to be dripping down," she replied. "Besides, we're supposedly welcomed guests here. It stands to reason that we should be safe from here on out… right?"

Nobody disagreed, so she took the first step forward.

"Don't be so hasty!" said Demetrius, holding her back by her elbow. "I wonder what they'd have to say."

He gestured toward a corner on the far side of the cave, and Arianna went rigid as she laid eyes on what he'd spotted there—the clean bones of several bodies lay scattered in a pile, skulls littering the floor. They stood out in stark contrast against the charred ground.

"What is this place?" asked Jeom, wiping the sweat from his palms onto his robes as his expression fell. "Do you think they're dwarves? How do you suppose they died?"

"I don't suggest we wait to find out," said Demetrius, holding tight to his scythe.

Everyone muttered their agreement.

"Let's save the questions for a room where lava isn't hovering over our heads," said Arianna in a low voice. "Follow me. Let's be quick."

As she scanned the remainder of the room, Arianna's defensive instincts kicked in, but nothing as unsettling as the pool of magma bubbling above their heads drew her attention. Leading the group forward, she never took her eyes off the ceiling for fear it might fall and melt them to puddles. With every step into the cavern, it grew hotter, the radiant reds of the magma glowing brighter, vivid and alive with dangerous color. Her eyes strained to keep pace with each change in direction the lava swirled in, too many paths to follow.

This dungeon of fire created the perfect playground for her imagination to run wild. At one point during their walk across the massive area, she even thought she detected something rolling along with one of the lava streams, though she couldn't be certain what.

"Did you see that?" gasped Jeom, pulling his violet hood up over his head as if it might protect him from a fiery drip. He was also still staring up.

Arianna swallowed, her throat running dry from the heat and her nerves.

"I thought I saw something too… but I'm sure it was probably nothing," she stuttered. "Let's just keep going."

Not really believing her own words, Arianna picked up the pace. By now, they'd made it halfway across the chamber, so she tore her focus away from the captivating ceiling to have a quick glance around the area. She grimaced as more and more skeletons came into her line of sight, piling in corners and near the large columns, as if they had been trying to hide from something just before they died.

What happened to you here?

She didn't care to guess.

"There are more bones over there too," she said to the group, pointing to her left. "And there."

"By gods," gasped Lessa, clasping a hand over her mouth. "There's so many."

"It's like they were all trapped or something," said Demetrius as he tore his gaze away from the lake of lava to witness the remnants of death around them.

"I think I know what happened," stammered Jeom. "Prepare yourselves for battle." His voice cracked—he was the only one still gazing upwards.

Arianna ducked as Jeom suddenly raised his axe toward the ceiling, swinging it back and forth in the air. "Jeom, stop—"

"Run!" he bellowed, sprinting forward.

When Arianna, Demetrius, and Lessa looked up, they didn't hesitate to follow in Jeom's lead, each brandishing their weapons as they raced after their long-legged friend.

Scaly paws with sharp claws slowly began to emerge from the fire pit above, followed by the large bodies of several creatures Arianna certainly didn't recognize as of their world. From this angle, they looked like wolves or wild dogs who had stolen the skins of lizards, and their coats shone sleek and black against the crimson lake they'd just crawled out of. Each had two very curved, very lethal-looking fangs hanging out of their mouths, and each looked very, *very* hostile.

One by one, they let out long, vociferous howls that made the cavern floor quiver. Then, they slithered fully out of the lava and dug their claws into the rock of the walls to climb down, magma dripping off them like water.

"What do we do?" shouted Lessa over the abnormally loud snarls as the lavahounds slunk to the floor and swiftly surrounded them, blocking their path to the next door. She swung her bow around and nocked an arrow.

"I don't know!" screeched Jeom. "It's ten to four, and these *dogs*, or whatever they are, don't look very obedient." He skidded to a halt, waving his weapon from side to side as the lavahounds inched closer, challenging them with large, silver eyes.

Their black coats still dripped with searing lava that singed the floor beneath their paws, and hooked nails scraped at the rock under their feet in an excruciating sound that made Arianna wince. Then, their black scales began to rise up, glowing a white-hot red like iron in a fire.

"They're going to attack," said Arianna, readying her swords and widening her stance. "Don't let your guard down!"

Startled by another howl, Lessa abruptly let an arrow loose; it whizzed forward, stabbing straight through the head of the nearest creature. The monster teetered and swayed, but it didn't drop, the arrow remaining stuck in its skull. Drool fizzed around its fangs as the lavahound charged toward her with its pack at its heels.

With a howl that challenged that of the lavahounds, Jeom leaped to Lessa's aid, slamming his axe into the neck of the armored creature. It screeched as a silvery liquid spilled out of the gash—yet still, it persevered in its fight. It clamped its teeth around the staff of Jeom's axe, the wood splintering as the saliva seemed to eat away at it.

"Be careful, Jeom!" said Demetrius, standing back as they all realized the lavahounds came complete with acidic slobber.

"I don't know if these things can be killed," Jeom answered, yanking his axe to safety before it split in half. Then he swung again, hitting the same spot on the animal's neck. Its legs buckled under the pressure, and it whimpered, this time backing away from the battle.

Soon, all four of them were forced to wield their weapons, the lavahounds attacking from all angles.

"We don't need to kill them," said Arianna, out of breath as she fought the ones nearest to her. "We just need to hold them off long enough to make it through that other door."

Arianna used her twin swords to battle four at a time. And unlike Jeom's axe, her blades remained resilient against the lavahounds' armored coats and acid-like saliva, piercing their skins like butter. Silver blood spilled all around her in pools.

Alas, they never died, only staying on the ground for mere moments before they were ready to fight again.

I wish I had such stamina.

Arianna struggled to keep her momentum after a while, tiring from the never-ending attacks.

"Keep your head on, Ara!" said Lessa just as a pair of sharp fangs came much too close to her neck—she threw her whole body backward to avoid it.

"Trying," she grunted, finding her balance and driving her sword into its belly. "How are you holding up?"

Lessa concentrated hard, shooting arrow after arrow at anything that moved close to her or her friends, each one giving her momentary success as she aimed for weak spots. "I'm going to run out of arrows soon if they don't stay down," she replied.

"I'm going to run out of energy," said Arianna.

She glanced to Demetrius who had the blade of his scythe hooked into a lavahound's mouth. Grasping the staff tightly, he flung the creature toward the wall. When he brought his weapon back to examine it, the blade was melted and deformed from the saliva.

"Nice throw!" said Lessa. "What did they teach *you* in the Agrarian's District?"

Demetrius somehow found the will to laugh. "Same thing as you, I'd wager," he replied, thrusting his warped blade into the side of another hound. "How not to die."

"I think we're all pretty well versed in that," added Jeom, still brandishing his weapon. "Damn, spoke too soon—"

The four found themselves back to back, cornered and exhausted. The lavahounds were clearly coordinating now; they encircled them, closing in for the kill.

"No!" shouted Arianna, as they all attacked at once.

Frantically trying to home in on the power she knew was within her, she slammed the tips of her swords into the ground, as she'd seen Solomon do before, and hoped it would prove effective. She felt an enormous tug on her energy, and the lavahounds were suddenly blown off their feet, flying into the air and crashing into the far walls.

Arianna didn't even have a name for the magic she'd summoned, but it had certainly weakened her more than anything she'd produced thus far. She wanted to drop to her knees from the exertion, but leaning on her weapons, she managed to stay upright.

"How did you do that?" asked Lessa, taking this moment to gather some of her fallen arrows.

Arianna just shook her head, unable to speak as she tried not to faint. Jeom went to her side, linking his arm through hers for support. Without him, she was sure she would collapse at any second. "Thanks," she muttered.

"They're getting back up," said Demetrius, worry creasing his normally composed expression. "What do we do now?"

Arianna looked toward the exit and it seemed to grow only farther and farther away—in all corners of the cavern, the lavahounds were beginning to get back to their feet, shaking off whatever magic she'd just produced. And there was no hope of her rousing enough energy in time to summon anything like that again.

She tried to stand up straighter, sheathing one of her swords to free up a hand. "We have to make a run for it," she said in clipped breaths. "Straight down the middle. Block anything that comes to us from the sides. It has to be now."

"*Can* you run?" asked Jeom, glancing at her with concern.

She nodded. "Just stay close to me, okay?"

"I've got you," he replied, squaring his shoulders. "Demetrius, you watch Lessa's back. She can't run and shoot at the same time."

"Don't underestimate me," she said, nocking another arrow. "On three."

The lavahounds were running toward them from all directions; they couldn't waste a second.

"Three!" screamed Arianna, clinging to her last scraps of energy as she launched forward.

The four let out their warrior cries and released the full force of their weapons as they ran, the lavahounds already closing in on them. Arianna led the group, slicing through anything that jumped in their path. Jeom and Demetrius followed closely, defending their sides, and Lessa brought up the rear, aiming arrows toward the beasts that closed in on them from behind.

"We're almost there," said Arianna, the sweat running hot and heavy down her back. "What in the—"

The lavahounds had suddenly ceased their attacks. Arianna couldn't help but stop just shy of the door to see what these otherworldly creatures were up to now. Demetrius, Jeom, and Lessa all turned to look too.

"Why have they stopped chasing us?" asked Demetrius, warily, as everyone took a moment to catch their breath.

The lavahounds had formed a circle among themselves in the middle of the cavern.

They began howling, their necks craned to the ceiling as if there were a moon there. The sound was eerie yet beautiful, so powerful that it even rattled the walls and the…

"Oh no," said Lessa with a frightened gasp, stumbling up against Demetrius. She flung her bow around to her back and pushed him to move. "Go! Run!"

Arianna looked up to see their worst fears play out as the ceiling of magma started to rain down in sheets. Jeom shoved her forward as it cascaded in a waterfall that thundered down behind them, racing them to the frost-covered door which lay ahead. The heat overwhelmed them as the lava met the ground, splashing every which way, and their lungs choked in the airless room. Then they reached the oval door and pushed—it opened without resistance and they tumbled through.

Blasted with a burst of freezing air, Arianna thought for a moment she'd landed back in the Warrior's District; she slammed to the ground first, followed by the Kane brothers.

Lessa was lagging behind.

Demetrius got to his knees and reached for her out-stretched hand, yanking her through the wide-open door. Lessa landed on top of them in a pile, and they all stared up from the floor of the next room to watch as the river of lava flooded the sunstone cavern, its ceiling now nothing but molten rock. The last thing they saw were the icy gray eyes of the lavahounds melting back into the fires they'd emerged from. And just as the lava seemed likely to pour over the threshold, Lessa slammed her boot against the door. It swung shut with a bang and the click of a lock.

They sat and listened in silence as the mighty force of the magma crashed into the fourth door.

"DEMETRIUS... IF IT WASN'T FOR YOU!" said Lessa, throwing her arms around him and kissing the top of his head profusely.

His cheeks reddened, and a shy smile spread across his face. "It was nothing," he said. "Really, I owed you one."

"Well, I'm sure glad you did," she replied, letting out a long exhale of relief.

"Thank the gods we're all in one piece," said Arianna, as they got to their feet and brushed themselves off.

"That was far too close for my liking," said Jeom, surveying their new environment with much more caution than the previous ones. "What's next, then?"

Arianna was already starting to feel the familiar Blancoren chills settle in, the warmth from the sunstone cavern completely absent here as shivers rolled down her spine. Pulling her cloak snug around her body and lifting her hood up over her head, she let her long curls cascade down her back to warm her ears and neck as she took in the ice-cold surroundings.

"We sure can't rest here," said Arianna, teeth chattering. "Let's keep moving."

"Maybe we should stay near the walls, just in case..." said Lessa, bundling Sano close to her chest.

Just in case there are any new monsters lurking about.

"Good idea," said Arianna. "Keep your eyes peeled."

They moved forward, side by side, each remaining vigilant as they watched for signs of a threat.

Arianna soaked in as much as she could while they hurried toward the other side of this cavernous chamber. The light of the lantern—still secured at Jeom's waist—bounded off every surface so that they could clearly see, though the subtle natural glow behind every frosty wall would have also suited their needs.

Yet, they still hadn't spotted the next door.

Impressed by the beauty of a place so cold, Arianna slipped on her leather gloves and let her fingers graze the walls; it looked like they'd stepped inside of a gigantic pearl. Every surface was covered in an opaque, white frost tinted with a deep blue sheen, creating a much more soothing setting than the last. And the walls seemed to be made of thick, impenetrable ice. What's more, almost invisible in their transparency, the ceiling was cluttered with giant icicles that appeared as if a million slender mountain peaks glittered high above their heads.

"This place is absolutely extraordinary," said Arianna as she slid forward on the frozen floor, relishing the cold air after such a heated battle and forgetting her troubles for a moment. "I never thought I'd miss the cold."

She spread her arms out wide, as if to welcome it.

Lessa tried to return her smile, but she couldn't shake her frown. "What do you think that was all about?" she asked as she checked on a sleeping Sano. "I thought we were *welcomed* guests here."

"I have a feeling that no one has been welcomed inside these walls for a very long time," answered Demetrius. "Things have obviously changed in the *great* City of Undor." He ran his fingers along the frosted wall too, gazing at the ceiling.

The old documents from the wooden room came to settle in Arianna's mind.

"I wonder what could've happened here," she mused, stretching out her sore muscles. Then she had a frightening thought. "Les, do you think it could have something to do with... with the King's cleansing of the magical world?" She tapped a finger to her chin. "I suppose one of the scrolls did mention dwarves in his long list of purges."

She recalled the history scribed in *Olleb-Yelfra the Fallen*, and another chill ran up her spine—one that she couldn't blame on the temperature.

"I would guess it has everything to do with it," said Lessa.

"What are you talking about?" asked Jeom.

"Yeah, what scroll?" pried Demetrius. The boys were

clearly interested to know more about this strange world around them.

Arianna and Lessa had given them both thorough introductions to all they'd learned of the Golden Age in their month together in the Warrior's District, but there was still a lot of ground to cover to catch them up fully. And they just hadn't found much time to spend on such conversations, having to fight for their lives with every new twist and turn of this adventure through the tunnels.

"Like we mentioned to you before, Lessa's master shared many scrolls and books with us which detailed different histories of a Golden Age filled with magic that we've hardly begun to comprehend," said Arianna. "But one in particular painted a vivid picture of how that era ended and how this magicless one began."

"To put it simply," said Lessa, "King Devlindor wiped out everything that had to do with magic, *including* entire races."

"But why?" asked Jeom, his voice echoing off the icy walls. "What did he have against magic?" He cleared his throat. "I mean, besides ceilings of magma and invincible, bloodthirsty hounds, of course."

"Oh, come off it," said Demetrius with a snort. "You know it's all incredible, the good *and* the bad. Just look around us! In all my dreams, I never would've thought falling through a hole in the Dead Lands could've landed me in someplace like this." Arianna adored his enthusiasm, his emerald eyes glittering with the possibility of it all.

"Yes, yes, brother," sighed Jeom. "It's all very wonderful."

He tried to hide his smile as he turned away from them, but they all saw the corners of his lips twitch up. Then he wrapped his arms around himself.

"And all very cold," he added. "Let's just hope the next door leads us to somewhere more temperate." He was squinting across the grounds.

"Anyways, I don't believe the King had anything *against* magic, really," explained Lessa. "What he wanted was to control it. He wanted to control everything."

"That makes more sense than anything else we've encountered so far," responded Jeom, curtly. "He still wants that."

They all fell quiet a moment, their boots crunching atop the frosted ground the only sound.

"Well, when the King supposedly started his crusade, it was about three centuries ago," added Arianna.

"Oh… that's the last date of the parchments we found back in the wooden room," said Demetrius, running a hand through his hair as he thought.

Arianna gave a little nod of acknowledgment. "Exactly," she replied. "And it *would* explain the lack of life down here."

"Guess that makes sense. I'd love to take a look at that scroll sometime, if you don't mind," said Demetrius, gazing around. "This place really is something, isn't it? Dwarves must've been excellent crafters to build such an icy fortress as this."

"Certainly," said Lessa as Sano popped his head out from her robes, awake and curious about his new surroundings. "We're happy to share the wealth."

"Dwarves…" muttered Jeom under his breath, walking faster, ahead of the group. "Sure, everything's all wonderful and magical. Until we freeze to death, or get burned alive, or run out of air, or *starve*, or go mad from… from all this madness!" He threw his hands to the air as his voice grew louder, his sudden outburst startling everyone, even Sano.

"Jeom, slow down," said Demetrius, racing after him with the girls right behind—he'd veered off from the wall and started across the grounds without caution, his steps pounding with every footfall. "You're getting yourself worked up again. Take a breath."

"No, I want to get out of this maze, now. I *can't* breathe

down here," he barked back. He pointed ahead, still marching forward. "Over there, look! *Finally.* I can see the next door—"

The room suddenly filled with a deafening crack, like the sound of shattering glass in great magnitude. The ground shook, and Jeom screamed as the floor gave way beneath his feet. Then he was gone, a gaping hole remaining in the place where he'd stood.

A split second later, Demetrius was the one screaming.

"Jeom, no!"

He lunged forward, after his brother, into the hole.

"Demetrius, wait," shouted Arianna, running to him. "You could be lost as well!" Her heart had tumbled into her stomach the moment Jeom had fallen through the earth, and she couldn't bear to watch Demetrius meet the same fate.

"Don't, Ara!" called Lessa, keeping nearer to the wall. "The floor might not hold everyone's weight. This whole place… it's all ice!"

Arianna had had the same realization as soon as the floor splintered beneath Jeom's weight—she knew ice very well, but it didn't make sense that a chamber this vast could be made of *pure* ice, from top to bottom, when the one next door was filled to the brim with lava. She'd assumed there was sturdy mountain rock behind the glossy walls and floors.

Another magic trick? Is this place melting? What's the pattern behind these doors?

Always more questions, but never any answers—she wished again for Solomon.

Just survive.

By the time Lessa had finished her sentence, Arianna was already at the edge of the hole, and Demetrius was lying on the ground, half his body hanging over the side. When she looked down, her eyes caught the last trace of the firebug-filled lantern, their only transportable light source, tumbling into the void before the blackness swallowed the poor little creatures whole. She never heard the lantern crash and she knew there was no telling how deep these mountains and tunnels— ones undoubtedly drenched in magic—truly went.

"Just hold on," shrieked Demetrius, sliding a little farther in. "Arianna, help me!"

She gasped, eyes growing wide.

He's still alive?

Sure enough, when Arianna knelt down next to Demetrius, she saw that Jeom had somehow managed to survive by plunging the blade of his axe into the icy wall. His violet robes swayed in the airy abyss, and he had only one hand grasped around the staff of his weapon, which was barely holding his weight after taking such a beating from the lavahounds.

"Les, he's still alive!" Arianna called, never taking her eyes off Jeom. "Demetrius and I are going to help him. Stay near the wall. It's not safe."

All the muscles in his arms bulged, and his eyes, bloodshot from fear, were locked in on the sea-green of his kin.

"Keep reaching for me," urged Demetrius, crawling on his belly as far into the hole as he could, hand outstretched toward his brother. Arianna squatted down behind him and clutched his legs so he wouldn't fall in, too. "Grab hold of my hand."

"It's too high," cried Jeom. "I can't reach you. My palm… it's too sweaty. I'm gonna slip."

"We're going to get you back up," said Arianna, trying to keep him calm. "You have to hold on." Then she spoke to Demetrius. "We don't have any rope with us. Can you slide any further in?" Jeom had fallen pretty far down before he'd managed to wedge the axe into the wall.

"I'm going to have to try," he replied, voice shaking. "Hold on to my ankles, and don't let go."

She took a deep breath and gave a firm nod. "I won't."

Demetrius was able to lower himself a little more with Arianna holding on to his feet, but the slippery ground prevented him from getting very far. If he went any deeper, they'd both be in danger of sliding in.

"You're almost there, brother," he said in rasped breaths. "Keep reaching."

There was another loud crack and Arianna gasped in surprise. She'd thought for a second that she and Demetrius were about to fall through the ice, just as Jeom had, and she felt her heart fly into an even worse panic. But then, peering over Demetrius and into the hole, she realized the sound hadn't been ice but wood—the staff of Jeom's axe had begun to splinter where the lavahound had bitten it.

There was a second crack, and the axe broke clean in half.

Both boys let out heart-wrenching shrieks, calling to one another in desperation. Arianna fell forward onto her stomach, still holding tight to Demetrius as he dived after Jeom, most of his body disappearing into the chasm. She dug her boots into the ice as best she could, her face scraping against the ground, but from this angle, the only leverage she had to keep him from sliding fully in was her body weight.

"I've got him! Pull us back up."

Demetrius' strained voice traveled back to her ears, and Arianna felt immediately both shocked and relieved... for a brief moment. She tried with everything she had to move even an inch back, but it proved impossible from this angle on the ice. In fact, with Jeom's added weight, she felt them all creeping forward.

"*Wrong* way," said Demetrius, trying to sound light-hearted. There was hopefulness in his voice, but Arianna wasn't as sure. "I said bring us up."

"I'm trying," she yelled back, her arms shaking from the effort. "You're not exactly light." She tried again, the panic starting to settle in. "It's... it's too slick. I don't—"

"It's okay, Arianna," she heard Jeom say, sounding both assured and defeated at the same time. "Demetrius, let go of my hand. She can't hold us both."

"No! I won't let you go," Demetrius said. "Not again."

Arianna's breath came heavier now, and she felt the heat of oncoming tears pooling in her cheeks.

"I can do this," she muttered to herself.

We can't lose anyone. We have to get free.

She took a deep breath and screamed with a final effort to try to pull them up. At that moment, she suddenly felt hands grasp around her waist.

"Hang on, Jeom! We've got you. Ara, pull!"

Lessa was behind her now, her orange boots clinging to the ice as she carefully helped Arianna into a better position. Together, they both poured every last ounce of energy possible into saving the Kane brothers. Then, the ominous sound of ice groaning underfoot pierced their ears, as if daring them to make any more sudden movements.

"Come *on!*" screamed Arianna, ignoring the warning as spit flew from her mouth. She felt like her arms might actually pop off, but it was working now. "Just a little further."

Their cries and shouts of struggle resounded across the chamber, but inch by inch, Demetrius was soon in a position where he could help too. And with the strength of all three, Jeom was quickly lifted out of the hole and into their arms.

They collapsed into a pile on the ground next to the hole, Demetrius sobbing into Jeom's chest.

"It's okay, brother," said Jeom. "I'm okay. Thank you all—"

Another crack fractured the ice in an explosive sound that made them all jump, the hole growing wider so that they had to skid backward to safety.

"We have to get out of here," said Lessa, pointing toward the jade-colored door Jeom had spotted before he'd fallen.

Everyone hurried to their feet and started sprinting across the ice in that direction, all somehow finding just a little more energy to survive.

As they ran, Arianna couldn't help but feel elated that they ran together as *four* instead of three. A myriad of colors chased them like ghosts in the walls, the colors of their cloaks reflecting on the ice from every angle, making it appear as if they ran through a frosty kaleidoscope.

Red, blue, green. And purple.

She was so overwhelmingly glad there was still purple.

Crack! The fragile floor reacted to every step they took now, the icicles on the ceiling even becoming disturbed by the sharp sound as they shook threateningly above their heads. Then one fell lose, smashing down in front of them.

"Watch out!" said Arianna, skidding to a stop with everyone at her side.

Another gaping hole formed in the ice where it had landed, and with it an unstoppable chain reaction began; more breaks in the ice formed, the intense sound disturbing other icicles and causing them to plummet toward the ground.

"Keep going, we're almost there!" said Jeom, grabbing his brother's hand. They all ran forward, the door getting closer.

Arianna found it almost impossible, though, to hurdle the many holes now forming in the ice as her eyes stayed focused on the ceiling, trying to dodge the enormous, deadly spikes that kept falling lose, shattering all around them. Left and right, back and forth, side by side, they each slid across the ice and through a maze of frosty pillars and holes.

Then Jeom and Demetrius reached the door, Arianna cheering as she followed them through, unscathed.

"What a nightmare this is," said Demetrius, throwing his head back in exasperation.

Jeom wrapped his arms around him, hugging him so tightly that he lifted off his feet. "I'm alive thanks to you," he said. "That's not a nightmare. That's a dream, brother."

"I can't… breathe," whined Demetrius. "Put me down."

"Wait," said Arianna, the smile wiping from her face. "Where's Lessa?" They glanced through the doorway, but she wasn't there.

Arianna didn't wait for an answer as she flung herself back through the open door before it could close and lock them in. The ceiling fell in masses now as she scanned the crumbling chamber for her friend. She gasped when she spotted her lying on the ground in a broken heap, her hands shielding her face from the exploding shards of ice landing all around her—a giant icicle had caught her robes, pinning her to the ground. But Arianna could also see blood pooling on the ice around her. What's worse, Sano had somehow been separated from her in the commotion; he was trying to dodge the icicles on his own a few feet away as he attempted to make his way back to Lessa.

"Les, hold on!" shouted Arianna over all the noise. "I'm coming to you."

"I'm stuck," she cried back.

Arianna ran forward, sliding to a halt just as a large icicle nearly impaled her, splintering the path before her. She felt the ground falter beneath her feet as more of the ceiling tumbled to the floor, making it quake. Maneuvering around the icicle, she had to leap a small hole just before the ground underfoot gave out. But on the way, she was able to rescue a terrified Sano into the safety of her arms just before a spike smashed down to where he had been perched.

Then she was at Lessa's side.

"My ankle," said Lessa in a thick voice as tears streamed down her cheeks. "I don't think I can stand on it."

Arianna pulled out her dagger and tore the blade right through the thick fabric of Lessa's cloak that was trapped under the icicle. With the cloth separated, Arianna now saw where the bloodstained spike had punctured her body. Instinctively, she pulled in a hiss through her teeth.

She was used to seeing blood, but not coming from Lessa.

"Here, lean on me," she said as Sano jumped onto Lessa, clinging to her neck.

Arianna draped Lessa's arm over her shoulders, carefully helping her to stand on her one good leg. Then she wrapped her arm around her waist to steady them both on top of the ice.

They took a step forward, and Lessa screamed with agony, unable to put hardly any pressure on her other foot.

"We'll be quick," said Arianna, forcing a smile on her face. "Don't worry. It'll be over soon."

"Okay," she replied through chattering teeth and blue lips.

Arianna strapped her dagger back in the sheath and took hold of Lessa's hand.

The floor shook violently now as the two navigated the obstacles before them. Voids opened up on all sides, dotting the ice in ominous shadows. If they didn't make it to the door soon, the entire chamber might fall all the way to the deepest pits of Blancoren, taking them as prisoners forever. And Lessa looked on the brink of passing out, pale from the loss of the blood now drenching her boot. "Hang on, Les, almost there," she said, seeing Demetrius and Jeom clearly now.

Another wave of enormous ice stakes dropped from the sky, forcing them to stop.

"Are you kidding me?" she shouted. "We're right there!"

When the icicles had speared the ground, they'd created an impossible path to the next doorway.

"You have to hurry!" said Demetrius as he and Jeom waved at them frantically from the safety of the next room.

Arianna assessed their only choices—either leap a small hole or tiptoe over a short but thin trail of ice.

She examined the hole before them and groaned, knowing

she wouldn't be able to exert enough power to carry them both safely across that jump, and Lessa was in no state to do so on her own. Arianna guided her toward their only option.

Deadly trail of ice it is.

Arianna had to release her grip around Lessa for lack of space on the path—a thin bridge of ice stretching across a void that she really didn't want to see the bottom of. So instead, she clutched the bow at Lessa's back and gently steered her forward.

"I'm right behind you," she whispered. Lessa whimpered with every step.

The ice held Lessa's weight just fine, but as soon as Arianna placed a foot behind her friend, a shrill snap sounded as it began to break. The floor began to fall away beneath them, so Arianna shoved Lessa forward, causing her to slide across the ice and into the safety of Jeom's extended arms.

In the same moment, Arianna lurched backward as what remained of the ground crumpled inward in a roaring avalanche and she was sucked down by the force. Her hands waved above her head and she let out a scream that was eclipsed by the final moans of the collapsing chamber. She squeezed her eyes shut as the cold shards of ice scraped at her skin, damning her to the same fate they faced.

Then, in an instant, everything was quiet.

"Have I died?" she stuttered as she tried to blink open an eye, petrified of what she might find.

"Nearly," replied a warm voice.

Only then did Arianna notice the strong grip on her hands. She looked up to find both Jeom and Demetrius staring down at her.

"Trying to outdo me?" asked Jeom with a smirk.

In all of the mayhem, Arianna hadn't even noticed that they'd caught her. Her mouth split into a wide grin and she felt her heartbeat thumping in a joyous parade as they lifted her up and out of the darkness.

"I'm *so* glad you both ran away with us," she said with a laugh of relief.

When she was on solid ground again, Arianna looked back from the shelter of the next doorway and saw the scene had entirely changed—the ice room had completely disintegrated into only smooth walls and a pearly ceiling that covered a bottomless pit. Then her eyes set on the oval, fire-touched door looming in the distance and a wave of anger rushed over her.

Slamming the new door shut, Arianna locked away the wintery chamber for good.

"What is this? The *Free* Falls?" she roared, kicking the back of the jade door as she heard the sure click of a latch.

Outraged, and terrified at what they might have to face next, she turned around to take in the fifth room. Instead, she found Lessa, Jeom, and Demetrius all staring back at her wearing solemn expressions.

Her cheeks ran hot, and she looked away. Then Lessa limped forward and drew her into a much-needed hug.

"Yes," she replied. "I'm afraid that's *exactly* what this is."

"At least we're still alive," said Demetrius.

Jeom patted him on the back, nodding his agreement.

"At least we've got each other," he added.

Arianna let out a long exhale, quieting her riled emotions. *Win or die.*

Then she gazed over Lessa's shoulder and past the Kane brothers, wondering what new horrors awaited them. Though, to her astonishment, what she saw was anything but scary.

"I thought I'd never see this place again," she whispered as she looked upon a version of her jade-riddled utopia.

MAGIC AND MYSTERIES

"THE ROOM THEY WERE LOCKED IN now was completely filled with water, a wide lake stretching out to touch every wall. The only solid surface, upon first glance, was the flat area they stood on.

And as if Jeom's earlier wish had been granted, the air was neither too hot nor too cold, the perfect temperature.

Arianna almost mistook the water as a mirror as she gawked at it—as still as glass, replicating every corner of the chamber. Brilliant jade-covered walls stacked high above them, creating cliffs in some places, and even the ceiling was decorated in smoothed cylinders of the same type of stones. Firebugs also buzzed about in swarms, their natural light adding a romantic warmth to the area.

"The only thing missing is the waterfall," said Lessa.

Arianna let out a long exhale, finally letting herself relax a little. "I wonder how Solomon and Talis are faring?" she said.

So much had happened since they'd left their masters behind, so much trouble. Now the memories came flooding back in the replica of their cavern that had started it all. Arianna dwelled for a moment on Solomon's parting words, Cyn's final gestures of kindness, and Liam's hurtful goodbye. And she knew Lessa was lost in similar thoughts as she stared to the waters, trying to hide a fresh batch of tears.

"Please don't cry anymore," said Demetrius, moving closer to Lessa to try to console her. "We're almost through it."

Lessa returned a weak smile, tossing her bow, arrows, and bag to the floor. Then she leaned her back against the door and took a deep breath.

Demetrius and Jeom didn't quite understand what they'd gone through to escape the Warrior's District yet, but they'd all get on the same page soon enough. There was nothing but time ahead of them. That is, if they could escape the tunnels…

"So how do we get from *here* to there?" said Jeom, hands on his hips.

He'd walked to the edge of the dry area, contemplating the clear water as it gently lapped at the tip of his dirtied boots.

Arianna and Demetrius went over to join him.

They could make out a smooth, triangular door on the other side of the lake. From far away, it appeared to be a blend of bright turquoise, purple, green, and black stones welded together in an intricate pattern of swirls. Arianna frowned down at her crisp reflection in the water, not detecting any way to reach it.

"Suppose we'll have to go for a swim," she said, thinking of all the supplies they'd lose—the lake was rather large.

"*Swim?*" shrieked Demetrius, his body overcome with a bout of overexaggerated shivers. "They teach you to swim in the Warrior's District?" He scoffed. "I like my feet planted on solid ground, thank you. And what if there's… you know, monsters in there?"

Arianna would've laughed at him, if not for the monsters they'd already encountered on their journey. Besides, he did have a good point… the others wouldn't know how to swim. She taught herself that skill alone in the hot springs.

"Well, do you have any other ideas?" she asked him. His lips twisted up as he thought… and thought and thought and thought. She sighed, turning to Jeom. "How about you?"

"If there was any wood around here, we could build a boat," he mused. Then he slumped. "Wish I hadn't lost my axe—"

A gasp of pain from Lessa put them each back on alert. In all the rejoicing, they'd neglected her injuries and immediately went to check on her; she was still leaning against the door, as if it were the only thing keeping her upright.

"You really should sit down and rest," said Arianna, kneeling down to examine the wound at her ankle—she cringed as she recognized bone under all the blood.

"I'm afraid if I do, I won't be able to get back up," she replied in clipped breaths.

"Tell us how we can help you," said Jeom, so much worry in his expression as he, too, witnessed the extent of her injury.

Lessa struggled to even nod as Demetrius helped her slide to the floor. Her hair was drenched in a cold sweat, and her skin appeared paler than normal.

She looked to the left. "In my pack—"

Her head suddenly slumped to her shoulder and her eyelids drooped closed. Sano jumped down to her lap, affronted by the abrupt disturbance to his position on her neck.

"Les… hey! You still with us?" said Demetrius, gently patting her cheeks. She wouldn't wake.

"What do we do?" stuttered Jeom, frozen where he stood.

"Pass me her bag," said Arianna, disregarding the fact that she didn't know the first thing about healing. "Demetrius, can you help me get her boots off, please?"

Jeom set Lessa's pack down beside her, so Arianna began to rummage around for the vials Cyn had left them. And Demetrius carefully took off Lessa's shoes, setting them aside—one orange and one blood red.

"Found them!" Arianna pulled out several little bottles from Lessa's rucksack. She inspected each one and then groaned in frustration. "I don't know what any of this stuff is," she said, glancing to the boys for help.

Jeom frowned. "Well that one's for burns," he said, reminding her of the faint scar at the center of his hand.

Arianna set that one aside, along with another that looked similar to something Cyn had used on her to cure a common sickness once. That left still five other vials to choose from, and she was certain that if she fed Lessa the wrong one in the wrong way, it could make matters worse—there was too much risk with guessing from so many choices.

"Do *you* know anything about healing?" said Arianna, looking to Demetrius. He shook his head.

"I'm sorry, I don't," he said. "I can see how I might be your best bet, but agrarians just help grow the plants that healers need for their remedies."

"Then… what do you suppose we do?" she said, feeling defeated as she sat back on her knees. "The only one who can fix her is *her*."

She felt a comforting hand on her shoulder.

"Sure about that?" replied Demetrius, his voice trembling.

Arianna looked up from the vials, glancing at Lessa's limp figure. Then she jumped to her feet in surprise, mouth agape as she stared down at her.

"How could I forget?" she said, smiling from ear to ear—Lessa's small yet loyal animal companion had positioned himself at her feet, his silver-lined paws gently placed atop the injury. Sano's long tail twitched behind him sporadically, and he appeared to be in deep concentration. Then, a familiar glow originated from underneath his tiny paws. And as the silver light grew brighter and brighter, Lessa's open flesh began to stitch itself back together.

After a moment, Sano dropped his paws and curled into Lessa's lap, the radiant glow vanishing. Arianna leaned over to get a better look at her ankle, and an iridescent, silver scar had replaced the large gash.

Demetrius' voice came out in a squeak "Is she—"

"Just wait," said Arianna, holding her breath.

Lessa fluttered her eyelids open a minute or so later, the color of health returned to her skin. She sucked in a deep breath as her hand came to rest on Sano.

"Thanks, buddy," she muttered before her eyes shut again.

Arianna let out a sigh of relief; they needn't worry one bit. Lessa was in good hands.

"Arianna, I know you said Sano had some kind of magic of his own but that was incredible…" Jeom's eyes were practically popping out of his head, his jaw about to hit the floor.

Demetrius squealed with excitement. "I can't believe Sano really just *healed* Lessa. The wound, it's completely gone!"

Arianna just nodded her head. "Told you."

"But explain to me *how*," said Jeom, waving his arms at Sano. "I mean, it's a monkey!"

Arianna thought Sano might've actually taken offense, his orange, bulbous eyes glaring back at Jeom.

"How to explain any of it?" she said with a little chuckle, shaking her head at him with a dazed look—if only she knew.

"Well, try," urged Jeom, mouth still agape.

Arianna let out a loud sigh, gazing at Sano; she longed for the answers just as badly as them.

"Well, Sano is an avatar," she said after a moment, repeating the words Talis had once spoken.

Then she took off her cloak and balled it into a pillow for Lessa, helping her to rest in a more comfortable position.

"What's an avatar?" asked Demetrius, again so intrigued by yet another piece of the enchanted world.

"I suppose it must be another Golden Age creature of some sort, but I really don't know," she said. "That's what we've been trying to help you understand. Lessa and I… this is all new for us too. We have a bit of a head start over you both, but we're about all caught up now."

"Madness, I tell ya," said Jeom, shaking his head, eyes still wide. Then he smiled. "But I *suppose* it can be… wonderful in a way, too." He winked at his brother who did a silent cheer to the air so as not to disturb Lessa.

"Some of it is, yes," mumbled Arianna, her thoughts drifting in a different direction. She couldn't help but linger on those last moments with Liam, wondering if he was still even alive, or if Sano's strange magic had been a waste on him.

She bowed her head.

"Everything's such a riddle now, and they're impossible to solve all at once," she said, too tired to think straight anymore. "We just need to focus on getting out of the mountains, and then we'll have all the time in the world to figure out the rest."

Jeom looked ready to go on another tangent of questions or comments about the oddities of this new side of Olleb-Yelfra they'd tapped open. But, instead, he closed his eyes and let a big puff of air escape his lips.

"You know something?" he said. "I don't even much care *what* Sano is. He clearly saved Lessa, and that's all that matters." He bent down to examine her newly earned scar, comparing it to his own—they were extraordinarily different. "Will she be all right now?"

"Should be," said Arianna, sitting back to observe her sleeping friend. "I've seen Sano's magic at work once before."

Jeom came to sit by her side, and Demetrius plopped down by Lessa's feet to lean against the door.

The mood began to lift then as the three went over everything that had happened in the last several hours, each one made a hero from one recollection to the next. Too exhausted to even eat or drink and feeling a sense of safety in this particular place, one by one, they all drifted into a deep sleep.

'*Freedom must be earned,*' Arianna thought before her mind fell into darkness.

THE UNFORGIVING, SHARP PEAKS of the mountain block out the sky from this angle as I stand staring at the face in the mirror—I've been here before. Yes, this is certainly my face... but it's also certainly not me.

The girl from the mirror laughs, a sweet yet sour sound that makes my skin prickle. Then she steps forth from the frame. I stumble backward, falling to the ground as she glides across the snow; her toes never seem to touch the earth as she moves—indeed, she's certainly not me.

Looking up into her eyes, I see my own. Though, it's hard not to note that something... something vitally important is missing. I can't put my finger on it, exactly, but it's like a light, a fire, has been snuffed out of them.

A cloak of crimson silk drapes around her shoulders, and tendrils of long hair cascade over her chest. Then my eyes travel to her right hand. It's clutching a dagger... my dagger. My master's gift to me.

I stand to face her with as much confidence as I can muster, but all I feel is an overwhelming fear take hold of my heart.

She looks so strong, stronger than I've ever felt, and I know I won't be able to defeat her if I must. And yet, as she smiles, I can't help but to relax. My smile... her smile, is so reassuring.

I open my mouth to speak, and she steps forward as if to welcome my questions, but my words become lost as I feel something burning in my stomach; I glance down, my lips still parted, and see the dagger buried there.

The girl from the mirror pulls it from my flesh, and I fall toward her outstretched arms. I think she'll catch me, but again, I'm wrong. Instead, I tumble through her.

And then into the mirror, I fall.

"Where am I?" I mutter, my voice barely audible.

I can see the sky now, but the mountains still surround me. My body is numb from the cold, the icy floor keeping me frozen in place. I can only stare up, into an endless black sky void of stars, void of moonlight. Then my head falls to the side, and I'm suddenly warm. I realize I lie in a bed of blood; it paints the white snow a muddied red.

Is it really all mine?

I want to scream, but my voice won't come now. That, or I'm too scared to let it. Everything is so dark.

Then the shadows roll and thicken as if a black cloud of smoke has emerged straight from the mountainside. And I can hear a hiss echoing through the air. My eyes catch something moving from far away, and I watch in helpless horror as I find scaly black cobras slithering through the new fallen snow toward me, as if beseeched by Blancoren itself.

I want to cry, realizing that they probably were.

The smoky shadow becomes denser now, bowling across the ground. It moves toward me, and wavy, black lines dot the white snow behind it—the snakes following with obedience to their dark master. The procession comes to a halt only a few feet away from where I lie, and then the shadow takes form. Someone is here. Something...

It's all I can muster to tilt my head up to see as black robes skim the snow in a train behind what appears to be a hooded man. Monster?

He's covered from head to toe, his face hidden in the shadows. I'm not sure he even has a face at all. Then suddenly, he steps forward and his boot collides with my chin. It's agonizing. But still, I can't move.

The man sighs as my howl fills the silence, the dark.

He likes this, I think.

The eerie song of the snakes grows louder now. All I can hear is them, their hisses morphing into wicked whispers, but no matter how hard I try, I can't block them out.

The snakes are by my ears, circling me like prey.

Then their master steps across me, and all I can see is this monster. I'd give anything to look away. Lowering his head toward my face, the man, this fiend, wants me to see his eyes clearly, soulless and dark. But he's still just a shadow, a monster of the shadows straddling me.

His voice fills my ears, his words melting in with the seductive sound of the snakes. More whispers I can't understand—I won't.

Yet, somewhere deep down, I think I might want to.

Then the snakes attack, burrowing inside of me with their fangs. The pain starts to sear as they cling to me like leeches, their venom causing my skin to melt away to join the snow.

I'm screaming now.

The mountains blur in and out, and the figure melts back into its smoky shadows, leaving me to the fate of his minions and to fade away, too. He's gone, though I can still feel him here—his laughter echoes everywhere.

ARIANNA'S EYES FLEW OPEN, and she sat up in a flurry, sweat dotting her forehead. Everyone else still slept.

The nightmare lingered in her mind but grew more muddled with each passing second as she clung to it, trying to understand it. Alas, as usual, the detail faded until it was replaced by reality. She wrapped her arms around herself, a little cold without her cloak.

"How long have we been sleeping?" she uttered to herself.

"Not long enough," replied Jeom, startling her with a noisy yawn.

Lessa and Demetrius stirred, too, from the disruption, and soon were sitting up from their makeshift beds.

"How do you feel?" Demetrius asked Lessa.

"I feel… perfectly fine, actually." She rubbed at her ankle with a perplexed expression. "What happened, dare I ask?" she said, cautiously, as she unfurled Arianna's robes and handed them back to her.

"Sano happened," said Arianna, glancing at the moon-eyed monkey in Lessa's lap.

Lessa's lips formed an 'O'.

"A little healing magic and a dose of sleep goes a long way, I guess," said Arianna, so happy to see her friend awake.

"Such a mystery," Lessa whispered as she pulled Sano into her arms, kissing him atop his head profusely.

Then she touched eyes with everyone.

"Well, since I'm fixed up, I'd better have a look at you all now before we continue any further. You should see yourselves," she said, already fishing for her vials.

Arianna instantly felt all her ailments then—she was so sore, scratches and bruises anywhere with skin exposed. And her throat burned for water and her stomach begged for food.

As Lessa made her rounds, tending to each of them, Arianna laid the rest of their provisions out on the ground and filled up the empty canteens with water from the lake. They all ate in silence, passing Sano well-earned scraps of leftovers—though he seemed to prefer hunting the firebugs. After a while of rest and recovery, they were finally ready to tackle the matter at hand, unable to avoid it any longer.

"So… any thoughts on how we're getting out of this one?" said Jeom.

Nobody responded right away.

"Can't anything be easy for once?" huffed Arianna.

Frustrated with yet another challenge, she picked up a large pebble from the few that lay scattered on the ground and skimmed it across the lake, as she used to do in the hot springs to help her think. The pebble hopped across the still waters—strangely though, on the third jump, it landed with a resounding thud.

Everyone looked up to see what could've made such a noise, and Arianna went to the edge of the water to investigate. As if it were floating, she found the pebble still visible on top of the clear waters.

"How in the world?" said Lessa, standing up to have a look too. "Guys, come here, you have to see this." She gestured for Demetrius and Jeom to join them.

"That's odd," said Demetrius, cocking his head to the side. "How's it possible for a rock to be floating like that?"

"Sounded like it hit something," said Jeom. "I don't think it's floating. Hmm…"

Then he scooped up four more rocks and tossed them far across the lake. The first three landed with a splash, sinking as expected, but the last collided with something hard and remained on top of the water.

Everyone was silent a moment, all staring at each other in confusion. Then realization sank in and they each started chucking stones all over the lake. Water splashed and sprayed in every direction as many of them sank to the bottom. But, yet again, a fair few stayed visible atop various transparent but tangible surfaces hidden across the lake.

Lessa picked up one more pebble and tossed it into the

water—as close to the edge as possible. Sure enough, it hit another solid surface with a loud clunk. Arianna knelt down to examine this one but could only see the reflection of herself and the jade ceiling encircling the seemingly floating pebble, no matter how hard she stared.

"What do you think this is?" she asked the others. "Some kind of game?"

"Feels like it," said Jeom with a snort.

"If this whole thing has been a game, then dwarves sure have sick minds!" said Demetrius with a smirk.

"I don't know," said Lessa. "I don't think any of this was ever meant to be a game, though it does *feel* like one. Everything just seems so… abandoned."

An unsettling feeling came over Arianna as she considered this. Did the lake hide another life-threatening enchantment?

"Well, whatever it is, I think it's our only way across the lake without getting wet," she said, eventually. "They're like… invisible steppingstones."

"Who's testing that theory, then?" said Jeom, bowing out.

"Looks like we have a volunteer!" said Lessa with a cheer.

Chasing a firebug, Sano fearlessly hopped off the bank and into the water near the nearest pebble. Arianna half-expected him to sink right to the bottom, but a foot out into the lake, he was still dry. What's more, Arianna noticed his reflection now showing too.

"I think they could be mirrors," said Demetrius, a look of bewilderment across his face.

Sano hopped to the next one and then the next, such an intuitive little thing, appearing as if he could walk across water.

"What has the world come to?" Jeom sighed.

They all broke out into laughter.

"Time to pack up our things, then?" said Arianna, after catching her breath—there were murmurs of agreement, and soon, they were all walking on water behind Sano.

32

AURORA

THE GROUP SPENT THE NEXT half hour meandering across the lake on the obscured path, careful not to slip and fall off the slippery walkway. Tossing pebbles from their pockets as they went in order to locate more mirrored steppingstones, they eventually landed safely back on dry land, the sixth door waiting to be opened. Jeom was the first to enter, having to duck his head so as not to bump it on the low ceiling of the new chamber, and then the rest followed. Without any troubles to speak of and fully restored, they were ready to take on whatever else the tunnels might throw at them.

For the first time in this bizarre quest, Arianna began to feel her hopes lift. Everything was dark at first when the door shut behind them, and she wished their firebug lantern hadn't been lost. But before she had even the time to worry, her vision adjusted to the new setting—then her breath escaped her.

A narrow and perfectly cylinder carved tunnel stretched

out before them in smooth, glistening black earth. Though not quite as bright as it would be with firebug light, the tunnel sparkled with a life all its own, appearing as if millions of stars had been sewn into the walls, ceiling, and floor.

With such a low-hanging ceiling, they all had to stoop a little to walk comfortably through this tunnel, Jeom having the worst time of it, but Arianna was entranced nonetheless. Tracing the strange stone with her fingers as they traveled onward, so cool and soft to the touch, she felt as if she walked not underneath the mountains but across a crisp and clear night sky. And the farther they trekked, the more dazzled she became until soon the tunnel opened up into an area where they could all stand up straight.

This part of the cavern was decorated with massive clusters of tinted quartz, each swirling with deep hues of indigo, blues, and greens. Arianna was curious to know if magic had something to do with their formation, for she'd never seen nor heard of such a marvelous gem in nature before. She slowed to study one closer, absorbed in every facet of the crystal—it felt very familiar somehow.

Then Lessa called from up ahead.

"I found something!" she said, excited. "I think it's a sign."

They all ran to meet her.

Sure enough, some way down from the last door, a sign had been carved from the same shimmering stone of the tunnel. Framed by pieces of the vibrant quartz jutting out from the walls, words had been scrawled atop the black rock in iridescent ink—quite like the style they'd found in the stone room at the beginning of their journey.

Everyone looked to Jeom, and he shifted nervously from side to side.

"Think you can read this too?" asked Demetrius, inspecting the sign for himself.

"Come on," said Lessa with an eager smile, poking him in

the side. "Don't be shy. This is so exhilarating!"

Jeom returned a nervous nod, a grimace on his face. Then he cleared his throat and read the words out loud, first in the guttural foreign language of the dwarves. It reminded Arianna of the few spells she'd learned thus far as those too required a foreign tongue; this language had the same enchanted ring to it, albeit with a little more weight to each word.

"What does it mean?" she asked, so keen to understand.

"We are Aura and Ora—the precious stones of astral journey," he replied. "It says nothing more."

"Astral journey?" mused Lessa, squinting at the sign, her lips twisted up in concentration. She turned to Arianna. "I don't recall anything about that in all we read, do you?"

She shook her head, hands on her hips.

"It might as well be in a foreign language still," Arianna replied, taking in her surroundings once more. Then, suddenly, realization dawned on her about why this place had piqued her interest so much.

"Wait, it can't be…"

She slipped her dagger from the sheath at her thigh and Arianna held it up for all to see; the resemblance of the weapon to this cavern was uncanny.

Its blade glittered as if miniscule black diamonds covered every inch of the surface, just like the starry tunnel surrounding them, and the winged handle and hilt had surely been forged from the same dense yet colorful crystals poking out from the walls.

"It's just like my dagger," she gasped as she examined it closely against their backdrop—the slither of yellow glinting in the black-jeweled center of the pommel was the only element of the weapon not present in this cavern. "It's Aura and Ora!" Arianna was awestruck by yet another link to this enchanted world.

Lessa's mouth dropped open as she too immediately recognized the likeness of the blue-green crystals and brilliant black stone. "Oh, of course!"

She clapped her hands together, the sound ricocheting around the tight space.

"I knew I recognized these rocks from somewhere. Ara, that really is an exceptional gift. I'm curious where Solomon got it. Did he ever say?"

Arianna shook her head, bemused just the same.

"And to think it was almost lost," Lessa added, biting her lip in mock fear. Arianna laughed at the memory, silently thanking the gods that indeed it wasn't.

"How do you mean your dagger *is* Aura and Ora?" said Jeom, not paying her much mind. He and Demetrius were still trying to figure out the meaning behind the sign.

"Just look!" she said, hardly able to contain her delight as she brought it over to show them. "My dagger is made from the same stones as this tunnel."

"Whoa…" said Demetrius as he and Jeom now gave her their undivided attention, eyes fixed to the weapon. "Where did you even get your hands on such a treasure in the Jar?"

It only occurred to Arianna now that this was probably the first time the Kane brothers had even really seen it. During their journey, she'd rarely taken it out of its sheath unless she'd needed to use it.

"My master trainer offered it to me on the day I started my apprenticeship under him," she explained, thoughts trailing off to simpler times when she was just a warrior-slave learning to fight her way to freedom and Solomon was her master, teaching her the proper way to hold a sword—no hint of magic or a Golden Age, no talk of a deceitful king or revengeful regulators.

As a young warrior-in-training, Arianna had often pondered the origin of this weapon, but the underbelly of some bewitching dwarf city had never even come close to her list of possibilities. And she'd never once questioned Solomon over it, for fear he might grow offended and take his gift back.

Arianna turned the dagger over in her hands, a dumbstruck smile growing on her face. "Stones of astral journey..." she murmured. "I wonder how they got that name."

"May I?" asked Jeom as everyone huddled around her to get a better look.

Arianna handed it over.

"Impressive," he said, squinting at the detail as he brought it close to his eyes. "It's fashioned *purely* from these Aura and Ora stones, apart from the jewel." He peered up at her. "It's not often you see a weapon without a trace of bronze or iron these days, you know." Then he flipped it over in his hands. "The rock in this cave must be rare, because I've certainly never learned of anything made of a material quite like this... it definitely seems more resilient than most. And the craftwork is extraordinary all on its own."

Jeom stroked the blade in admiration and then feigned slipping it beneath his robes.

"*Very* funny," said Arianna, snatching it back.

"That's quite some gift, Ara," said Demetrius, peering at it over her shoulder. "My mistress never gave me anything but commands."

Arianna snorted in laughter. "Well, Solomon gave me plenty of those too," she said.

"Still, Jeom's absolutely right. That dagger's really something," he replied, nodding to himself. "I know quality earth when I see it."

Demetrius took it from her hands to examine for himself, lifting it into the air as if in mock worship. "Aura and Ora," he started to hum, repeating the words over and over in a ditty. Then he bowed in front of Arianna in jest, presenting the dagger to her as if it were some kind of godly gift from the heavens. "And it shall hereby be named *Aurora!*"

Arianna snatched it from his upturned palms, placing it snugly back in the sheath at her thigh.

"Don't be silly," she said, trying not to laugh—though it was hard with Jeom cackling in the corner; the Kane brothers were certainly a pair when it came to bad jokes. "Why would a dagger have a name?"

Arianna began to lead the way farther down the tunnel, the mood of the group much more jovial now that they'd passed through yet another door with no sign of danger behind it. She soaked up every inch of this cavern as they walked, knowing that she held a piece of it with her always.

Aurora... She chuckled to herself.

Just one more beguiling mystery to hopefully one day solve.

"Don't all the greatest warriors name their weapons, though?" pried Demetrius, keeping pace with her as Lessa queried Jeom more about his life as a creator-in-training.

"I didn't even have time to name my axe," mumbled Jeom, eavesdropping from behind. "It was a good axe."

"I'm sure you'll get another chance one day," said Lessa, looping her arm through his as they walked.

Arianna turned to Demetrius, narrowing her eyes at him with a smirk on her face—at first she thought he was just playing around, but with one look at his eager expression, she could tell he was hungry for more details about her district life. Before the lavahounds, he'd probably never been part of a battle in his life; from what she knew, agrarians didn't have *quite* the same upbringing as warriors. Demetrius was likely more used to seeing mud on that scythe than he was to seeing blood.

She softened. "I think the only warriors who ever gave names to their weapons must've been in the legends of your district," she said after a moment. "Blades don't need names!

They just need blood."

Arianna withdrew one of her slender swords and jabbed it forward, wielding it in a flurry of fancy tricks as they walked—all to Demetrius' sincere enjoyment.

Jeom stopped, throwing his arm out to stop Lessa too. "Save it for the regulators," he whined. "Better put that thing away before one of us gets stuck on the end of it."

"Don't worry," said Arianna with a low bow, sheathing it again at her back. "I've had a little practice at this. Happy to teach you sometime."

Demetrius showered her in applause before attempting to mimic her moves. Jeom quickly stepped up to show off his own, and soon the Kane brothers were lost in their own world, each one endeavoring to beat the other.

Arianna and Lessa took the cue to give them a bit of quality time, walking ahead and laughing all the while.

Lessa let Sano down to stretch his legs as they continued forward, the end of this tunnel in sight. "I think it's kind of fitting, actually," she whispered. "The name, I mean."

"Not you too," said Arianna, staring at her with an incredulous smile. "It's a silly notion. I've never heard of such a thing in my district."

"But who really knows?" said Lessa, lifting her eyebrows at her. "What if the greatest warriors really *did* name their weapons... you know, before the way warriors do things now?" She chewed on her lip, so clearly enamored with the possibilities the Golden Age histories presented. "In any case, you might very well be a legend at this point in time, Ara." She gave her a gentle nudge in the ribs. "You broke every rule, escaped the Jar, and still have your head."

"I don't know about that now..." Arianna replied with nervous laughter. She let her hand rest on the handle of the dagger as she took in a full view of the tunnel. "Then again, who am I to argue if it's already been named?"

"*Yes!*" said Demetrius, running up to Arianna in the next second, fists pumping in the air. "Aurora it is?"

Arianna smiled, resigned to the silliness. "Aurora it is," she said with an exaggerated sigh.

The four continued chattering on happily, getting to know one another that much better for a little while longer before they realized they'd located door number seven.

COUNTLESS MORE HOURS PASSED before they reached the end goal they had originally set out for, and they thanked the gods that no more deathtraps awaited them on the way. It seemed that their bewitched maze had finally run out of tricks as they opened up door after door with no monsters to greet them.

They passed through a room where amethyst crystals swallowed them on all sides, and then a chamber filled with natural silver that sprouted up the walls like trees. At one point, a cavern lined with crimson jasper submerged them in a pool of blood-colored stones, and then they walked through a crater of ore pulsing with veins of platinum. Resting in a chamber of earth-toned marble, they ticked down the doors they'd passed through. They even climbed their way through a maze of sapphire, thrilled at another miraculous chance to walk on water—although this lake had been filled with gems.

They paraded along for miles, basking in the brilliance of these precious yet neglected natural phenomena. The four found caverns of sunny amber, which Sano adored, and Arianna was enthralled by what felt like a sitting room with rubies embedded into the walls.

Lessa deemed her favorite a tunnel of turquoise; it seemed

to twist like a vortex through a picturesque sky. Jeom drooled in the diamond mine where he tried to scoop sparkling souvenirs from the streams, and Demetrius favored the rosy green tourmaline shooting up from the ground like crystalized buds.

"This one… is my favorite," breathed Arianna as they paused at yet another threshold to take in the view.

A wide, arched area spilled out in a rainbow of color like the inside of a white marble splattered with paint. It looked as if someone had chiseled off a piece of all the other chambers and tossed them into a melting pot in order to create a place where each could be admired together.

"Can we stay here forever?" asked Lessa, similarly awed, watching as Sano released his most playful spirit, bouncing around the space, enthralled by the sporadic colors.

A warm feeling spread over Arianna, making her nearly forget they were still trapped underneath a snow-topped mountain. She stepped inside and then tilted her head back to look upon the vibrant, polished ceiling.

Something freeing came over her then, and she stretched her arms out wide and spun, her long curls and cloak spreading out around her. As she twirled, the colors on the ceiling melted into each other until a whirlpool of delicious hues replaced her normal vision. Moments later, she felt hands grasp hers, and she found Demetrius spinning along with her; happy and carefree just seemed to be his natural state.

"I don't think so," said Jeom as the two steadied themselves and quelled their crying laughter.

"Why not? What could possibly be better than this?" said Arianna, sighing in satisfaction as she leaned against Lessa for support—once upon a time, her vision had only been filled with the gray face of the Blancoren Mountains, but underneath it, within its heart, lay *so* much color; Arianna was desperate to soak it all in and rinse away those years filled with nothing but gray.

"That!" said Jeom as he pointed up ahead.

Following his gaze, Arianna saw the same gilded door that had first melted the flesh of his hand. It was floating atop a tall, twisting black and orange opal staircase. Gold railings curved around the sides, and each step looked as if a deep ginger moon had liquefied into the blackness of the universe.

"I'm not patching you up again," said Lessa, sternly, crossing her arms as Jeom flexed his scarred palm.

He clasped his hands together as if in prayer. Then he and Demetrius began to plot a prosperous future.

"I suppose we shouldn't linger here," said Arianna with a sad sigh, not wanting to leave so much beauty behind—she wasn't looking forward to navigating the dreary tunnels again, but they'd run dangerously low on food and water at this stage; staying here forever just wasn't an option. "After all, that damn door is the whole reason we came in the first place."

"Well, I'm sure glad you did," said Demetrius, giving her and Lessa a strong squeeze around their shoulders.

"You don't say?" replied Lessa with a snicker before calling Sano to return. "Let's get on with it, then."

"Finally!" cheered Jeom. "We earned this."

Letting the boys lead the way up the stairs to the gold, Lessa and Arianna linked arms and followed diligently behind. Jeom's eyes lit up with anticipation as they all reached the gilded door together. From top to bottom, it was embellished in a delicate pattern that repeated over and over, like layered outlines in the shape of a diamond. And surprisingly, it was attached to absolutely nothing—just like the first time they had laid eyes upon it.

"Last one! Ready everyone?" asked Jeom, the excitement in his voice palpable.

"Ready!" the others responded in unison.

Lessa squeezed Arianna's hand and let go, and Demetrius was nearly jumping out of his skin in excitement alongside his brother. Then Jeom twisted the knob and the door creaked open—one by one, they all stepped through the golden threshold, leaving the opal room and, hopefully, this enchanted labyrinth of doors behind.

Alas, to their great disappointment, light seemed always to be escorted by darkness in this topsy-turvy world they'd stumbled into. And the gleaming, golden chamber before them did nothing to shadow that fact. "Draw your weapons," instructed Arianna as the familiar stench of death filled her nose.

THE GOLDEN RULE

THEY ALL STOOD IN SILENCE as an acrid smell filled their lungs, the stench of death stifling. Heaps of skeletons in decaying dress were sprawled atop the floor and stairs of what looked to be a long, gold-plated gallery. And they could see everything, nothing obscured by shadows; this chamber was lit with fires that burned in torches hanging from the walls—flames that must've been charmed into existence for how bright they burned.

Arianna knew bones like the back of her hand, but with an up-close look at these skeletons, she was certain there was something different about them; the bones were thicker, the skeletons shorter, and she recognized that the flesh and blood which once covered them had likely been flowing with magic.

Dwarves of Olleb-Yelfra.

Even in death, they were armored; chainmail, steel plates, and horned helmets kept their skeletons intact. And weapons were scattered everywhere. All different types of swords, axes, and flails littered the ground, their blades rusted and dull. Sadly, they didn't even have to question the cause of death—thousands of steel-tipped arrows covered the room and the bones.

This was no fight. It was a slaughter.

Arianna stared ahead in disbelief at the sure remnants of a massacre. "There has to be several hundred of them," she said as she drew a single sword.

"Guess now we know why no one ever 'checked out'," said Demetrius, warily, gripping his scythe.

"It doesn't even look like they put up much of a fight," said Lessa as she surveyed the room, holding Sano close. "It's like they all just stood here and died." She looked to the others. "Why wouldn't they run?"

"Maybe they were defending something," said Demetrius.

"Maybe… but I don't think these people even had a chance to run *or* fight," said Arianna. "They were trapped."

Jeom's head was bowed in grief for the golden graveyard at their feet. "*Dwarves*," he stammered.

Arianna took a deep breath, nodding.

"Dwarves," she said, softly.

"This is what remains of the City of Undor," said Lessa, matter-of-factly, shaking her head as she stared on.

Arianna had been so desperate to get through the doors and back to the tunnels that she hadn't once really thought of it in this way since leaving the stone room.

"This… this can't be it," she replied, feeling the pit of her stomach squirm at so much wasted life and beautiful, magical things—then she thought of the King.

They took a moment of silence for the fallen city. After, with care, they crept around the skeletons and made their way farther into the area.

Wide steps created much of the walls of a large octagon

chamber; they led up to a balcony that appeared to encircle the entire room. Arianna tried to make out what lay at the top, but it was too high to see from where they stood. She dropped her gaze instead to the floor. The tile not covered in arrows or bones were patterned in swirls of glowing white—it was once a magnificent room.

Zigzagging between thick, white columns, quite like the ones which they'd first seen before entering door number one, they soon reached the center of the gallery. Here, the piles of skeletons grew denser, stacked up against a wide, glass cylinder that reached all the way from the floor to the topmost part of the chamber.

"I see what they were fighting to protect," said Arianna, craning her head back to fully see. She sheathed her sword, realizing the danger here was already long gone.

Demetrius gave a low whistle as they all gawked at the object behind the glass.

A double-edged axe, fit for a king, was floating inside on invisible strings. The staff was crafted of what looked to be black steel, and the blades glinted in the same dark metal with sharp silver edges. Twisting down the length of the staff, the golden tail of a dragon ended in a lethal spike that would make a solid weapon all on its own. And the blades of the axe were welded with the dragon's unfurled wings, its golden-fanged skull wedged in the center between the two, made to forever bare its teeth at anyone who dare attack its master.

"It's just like the coins and the podium," shrieked Lessa as she drew one of the jagged silver pieces from her pocket.

She held it up near the enclosure for comparison.

Jeom was quiet, so utterly captivated by the weapon as he walked up to the glass. He pressed his palm against the partition; it seemed to react to his touch, the glass pulsing beneath his fingertips so much that Arianna could see his whole body subtly vibrate with it. Then, as if his hand had been a hammer, the glass shattered, deteriorating in a rain above their heads.

"Look out, Jeom!" Arianna immediately grabbed a discarded shield on the ground, huddling close to Demetrius and Lessa as she lifted it over their heads. Jeom was not in close enough proximity for her to protect him.

But before the shards could reach the air above them, the glass evaporated with a sizzling pop—now nothing stood between them and the axe.

It glinted even more without the glass barrier concealing it… it was still radiant and still floating.

"The gods *do* have mercy," said Demetrius. "I thought we were about to be sliced into ribbons." Then he waved his hand forward, gawking at Jeom as if he'd done something wrong. "Don't just stand there. Take it! Before somebody else does." He feigned inching a step closer.

Jeom stole a glance to Arianna and Lessa, hesitant.

"It's obviously meant for you," assured Lessa.

"You said you needed an axe, didn't you?" added Arianna with a wink—there was no use arguing with magic; if it really had a mind all its own, then right now, its intentions were perfectly clear.

"This one will *definitely* need a name," said Demetrius, his finger tapping his lips as he thought. Arianna chuckled, seeing the wheels already turning in his head.

"Okay, then…" sighed Jeom, turning back to face the glorious weapon. "Here goes nothing."

He lifted the hood from his head, stepped forward another pace, and reached out a hand. As soon as his palm wrapped around the staff of the axe, a pressure of air exploded all around him, making his robes billow out.

For a moment, Lessa, Demetrius, and Arianna all stood on edge, waiting to see if they would need to run to Jeom's aid, for he looked frozen in place by whatever magic had hold of him now. But then, the invisible restraints released their grip on the weapon, and he was able to pull it down to the ground.

Jeom wore a dumbstruck expression on his face that Arianna wasn't sure he'd ever be able to get rid of as long as he had that axe to his name. He hardly blinked as he drank in his new treasure.

"Suits you, Jeom," she said, stunned herself as they all admired the axe, the black, gold, and silver metals all sparkling brilliantly up against the deep plum of his cloak.

"Now that puts Aurora to shame," said Demetrius, nodding with his hands on his hips.

Arianna gave him a playful punch in the arm. "Bigger isn't *always* better," she replied, sticking out her tongue. "But it is sure one heck of a weapon."

Lessa knelt down for a closer look at the detail on the staff, Sano still comfortably curled on her shoulders.

"But why me?" asked Jeom, his eyebrows wrinkling with worry as his smile vanished. "It's obvious that all of these dwarves died to protect this weapon. They're all here, in this room. There were hardly any other signs of former life in the other parts of the city." He waved the axe toward the space where they'd found it, many more skeletons gathered in this area than in any other part of the hall. "They all came *here* to die. So how is it that I could obtain it so easily?" He shook his head. "I don't want to take it if it's tainted in innocent blood."

"I don't know, brother," said Demetrius. "But don't worry. We'll figure it out. I do find it strange, though, that whoever conquered this city, didn't just take the weapon for the victory."

Arianna had to agree. "It's not something any warrior would walk away from. That's for certain."

"I have a theory," said Lessa, straightening back up. "I stand by what we only speculated on earlier. I think you have some blood tie or inherited connection with this forgotten race, and a strong one at that."

Jeom opened his mouth to retort, but Arianna put a hand up to stop him. "Let's just hear her out," she said.

"When you read that tablet in the stone room," Lessa continued, "it not only indicated that someone of high honor and dwarf blood would be required to invite others in. It *also* said that those with ties to the bloodline inherently vowed to protect the secrets of this city if they did, right?"

Jeom returned a cautious nod. "But where are you going with this?" he asked.

Lessa pointed to the axe he held firmly in his hand.

"Well, Jeom, I think this will be one of those secrets," she replied, cocking her head to the side as she waited for him to catch on. "If you're correct, and all these creatures died to protect that axe from whatever monster did all this… they would've taken it if they could have." She played with Sano's tail as she thought.

"She's right," said Arianna. "It's obvious, isn't it? Whoever released those arrows weren't *welcomed* guests in this city like us. I mean, it looks like these dwarves were surrounded by an army from the state of them." She respectfully set the shield she'd been holding back down to lie with its former owner. "We've seen for ourselves that this place is rich in magic. And I know we're new to the supernatural side of things, but the magic in Undor seems incredibly powerful."

Arianna repressed a shudder, recalling the lavahounds.

"So what are you both saying?" said Jeom, growing impatient. "Spit it out."

"My guess is that dwarves take their vows very seriously," replied Arianna. "Maybe they wouldn't give up the axe to whoever broke into their fortress, so they chose death instead. Without someone of their bloodline to release this… protective magic, the axe remained sealed away."

"Until you came along two hundred-odd years later!" said Demetrius, beaming up at his brother.

Lessa was nodding along to Arianna's conclusion. "I would wager the glass case had a powerful enchantment done to it so that it wouldn't fall into the wrong hands." She laid a hand on Jeom's arm then, glancing again at the axe. "Regardless of the 'how,' you're not *taking* anything from anyone. It was a gift."

"Okay… so basically you're saying that this magic *trusts* me because of the inexplicable connection I have to this place," he responded, dryly, raising an eyebrow. "Did I get that right?"

"Got anything better?" Lessa countered as Sano swapped his perch on her shoulders for his.

Demetrius chimed in. "Makes more sense than whatever I could've come up with," he said to Jeom. "I'd just go with it."

"I see," replied Jeom, lost in his own contemplations as they all pondered the truth of the history around them.

"You know what *my* biggest question is, though?" added Demetrius, sizing up Jeom. "I'd like to know how a giant like yourself could be labeled a dwarf."

Lessa giggled but quickly covered her mouth with her hands to suppress it. So much loss had happened here that it didn't seem appropriate to be joyful about anything.

Demetrius gestured, politely, to the skeletons on the floor, so small compared to Jeom who towered over everyone in the room—it was a fair question, and Arianna knew they were all thinking the same thing.

"I'm obviously not… not one of them," said Jeom, uncertainly, twisting the axe between his palms. "I don't know how I'm connected to all this, exactly, but we made it through to the end. We should probably just be on our way now and figure it out later. I don't want to get trapped down here, and we're running dangerously low on provisions."

"I agree," said Lessa, offering him a gentle smile. "Time unfolds everything. No use guessing at the answers." She pointed to the axe. "But just don't lose this one, okay?"

That drew laughter from them all, even Jeom.

"I'll try my best," he replied, giving it a strong squeeze.

Turning to leave, Arianna had to step over a hefty skeleton who lay sprawled out at what used to be the edge of the glass cylinder. "Thanks for the shield," she whispered.

Its ribcage was covered in dark blue and black metals and a skeletal hand still gripped the steel staff of a fine spear.

"What does this nameplate read?" Arianna asked Jeom, curious as she noted a gold engraving on the dwarf's armored chest.

"General Indra," he replied, glancing over her shoulder.

"Hmm... Arianna lingered near the remains of the dwarf, scrutinizing the armor as everyone walked ahead; it was far superior to anything she'd ever known the regulators to have. "General Indra," she mouthed, testing the words.

A gust of air mussed up her hair and a shiver rolled up her spine. She jumped back, looking around, but saw nothing out of the ordinary. Then she made to catch up with the others. Alas, when she turned to follow them, she cried out and fell backward, landing right on top of General Indra's skeleton—his ghost was floating in front her and blocking her path to her friends.

"What is it? What happened, Ara?" said Lessa as she, Jeom, and Demetrius immediately doubled back.

They stared down at her in concern, but Arianna could only gaze upon General Indra's lustrous form; he looked authoritative, more so than Jacob or Damon had appeared, and he was suited in the same armor and helmet of his death, though this version of him was much more *alive* than the bones she sat upon.

The dwarf was slightly shorter than her, but his muscles were so thick that Arianna thought he could probably crush her in one blow, if he weren't a ghost. And he had a long, braided beard that was tied with what looked to be thin gold rings at each knot. There was nothing gentle or soft about any of his features, except for maybe the blushing pink jewel embedded into the forearm above the hand which grasped his spear, visible on the crevices of weathered skin not covered by metal.

Arianna couldn't imagine that anyone could've killed such a warrior, let alone hundreds with strong magic in their arsenals; that's when it dawned on her that if an army of the King did ambush them here, they evidently had very strong magic as well to have broken down the defenses and pierced their armor.

General Indra glanced from Arianna and then to the others. The smallest hint of a smile crossed his face when he laid eyes on Jeom as he offered a hand to help her up.

"Wait," she stuttered, not taking it. "I need a moment."

"Okay…" said Jeom, stepping back, through General Indra, to stand with the others. As he did, Sano screeched and hopped back to Lessa's shoulder. No one thought anything of the little monkey's reaction, but Arianna knew he'd felt it.

That's when she realized her friends couldn't see ghosts at all—Jeom would probably faint if she told him he'd actually passed *through* one, unknowingly, and she couldn't wait to see the look on his face when he found out.

But right now, she kept her attention on General Indra, never blinking for fear the dwarf ghost would vanish before she had a chance to hear what he might have to say.

General Indra turned his gaze to the bones at Arianna's feet now, and his smile grew cold as he pointed a long finger toward his own remnants. Following his line of sight, she saw the corner of a parchment peeking out from the skeletal hand not holding the spear.

"Take this script in your heart and *not* in your pocket, sorceress," he said as she pried the parchment from his grip.

He spoke their language in a thick accent that was a bit difficult to understand.

"The City of Undor has fallen, though not in vain," he continued. "Uphold the vow, and do not ever forget the Golden Rule. This is your legacy now."

He motioned to all of them.

Arianna opened her mouth to reply, but General Indra lifted his hand for silence. And much like her own master warrior, he was not to be disobeyed.

She watched him in awe, so many questions on the tip of her tongue as he gazed toward the gilded ceiling, one ringed with small yet dazzling glass balls that glinted between the light of the torches. Then the dwarf general disappeared in a sudden burst of glittering light that mixed in with the splendor of the crystal and gold decorations.

"Goodbye," Arianna whispered, eyes still glued to the ceiling as she carefully pushed herself off his bones and got to her feet.

"What's going on?" asked Demetrius. Her friends were all staring at her as if she'd lost her mind. "Who are you talking to?"

"There was… a ghost," said Arianna. She pointed to the bones of General Indra. "*His* ghost."

Lessa, Demetrius, and Jeom all huddled closer to each other then, searching the room with wary expressions.

"He wanted us to read this," she said.

Arianna unfurled the parchment, handing it to Jeom with trembling hands. The contents had clearly been scribbled in a hurry, its script written in the language of the dwarves. Jeom read aloud, and Arianna clung to every word:

> *Light is light and dark is dark, but never shall they live apart. When one eclipses over the other, life shall end for he and his brother—this is the Golden Rule.*

Jeom finished, brow furrowed. "Wonder what it means." Then he folded the paper and began to stuff it into his robes.

"I don't know, but we should leave it here," said Arianna, seizing the parchment back from him—she heeded General Indra's words. "Take the words in your heart. Not your pocket." Then she gently placed the letter back in the hand of the fallen general.

"He's not still here, is he?" asked Jeom, pulling the axe into his chest.

"I don't think he'll be coming back, no," said Arianna.

A sigh of relief blew noisily from his lips, and Arianna hid her smile, deciding to spare him the agony of knowing he'd actually been one with General Indra's ghost for a split second.

"Damn, I think I've already forgotten the words now," said Jeom, scratching his head. "What's this Golden Rule again?"

"Light is light and dark is dark… don't worry. I won't forget it," said Arianna, patting her heart.

"Neither will I," said Lessa, before sucking in a deep breath.

"I don't think General Indra wanted that parchment falling into the wrong hands," added Arianna, starting to lead the group farther down the hall. They walked to the outer edge of the chamber where the walls formed into steps.

"I understand," replied Jeom. "If a whole city gave their lives to protect it along with that axe, we should honor their sacrifice."

Lessa and Arianna murmured their agreements.

"This can't be the whole city," said Demetrius, suddenly, his face scrunched in concentration.

"What do you mean?" asked Lessa.

Demetrius stopped at the foot of the stairs, looking back down the hall. "I mean, just look. This *can't* be all there is to the 'great' City of Undor. Where is everybody else?"

Arianna looked around again and understood his reasoning—this maze of doors could hardly be called a 'city' by their standards, even if it was doused in magic.

"Let's just hope there's a way out at the top of this climb," she said, refusing to dwell on the anxious thoughts filling her mind. "Ready?"

"More than ready," replied Lessa in a shaky voice. "Let's get out of here, finally."

Alas, when they reached the top of the stairs, the balcony orbiting the gallery held another odd, and very unwelcome, surprise. A plethora of doors—those crafted from wood, stone, jade, amber, amethyst, opal, sunstone, and every other entry they had passed through previously—surrounded them on all sides. And just as they had first appeared between the columns in the tunnels, these familiar doors were now attached to nothing but thin air, hovering over the floor.

"How are we supposed to get out of here?" yelled Jeom, starting to pace back and forth. "Which one do we open?"

The four spun in circles as they considered all of the options before them, doorways that had each led them a part of the way to this very chamber of gilded death.

What if...

Arianna began walking around to the other side of the balcony, following the nag of her instincts despite so many doubts trying to overwhelm her mind—just as Solomon would have advised her.

"Hey!" called Lessa as they ran to catch up to her. They saw where she was headed. "We should think this through. If it's locked... if it just leads us back through the maze again, we will be lost in here forever."

They each stopped to look upon the wooden door which had started it all, the beginning to their perilous adventures through the City of Undor.

"I don't know how to explain it, but something tells me

this is the one," said Arianna, sticking to her guts.

"I agree with Ara," said Demetrius, stepping up to her side.

"But why?" demanded Lessa as she and Jeom remained skeptical.

Demetrius just shrugged his shoulders. "Because we still have to check out," he replied, matter-of-factly.

Arianna smiled, trying to learn from this refreshing perspective; Demetrius wasn't impulsive, like herself. No, somehow he was just able to see things in a way that the others hadn't yet mastered, able to make snap decisions based on what he *knew* to be true in his heart. As with magic, he didn't need to see it to believe it—he trusted in himself.

And in this moment, Arianna trusted in herself, too.

She felt that something had pulled her toward that door, and with Demetrius' validation, she was even more confident in the choice. Whether intuition or a hunch, she hadn't come this far to be hindered by too many options. Arianna turned the knob and the door opened with a whoosh, the unforgettable musty odor of the wooden room spilling out into the air around them.

"Any last reservations?" she asked.

Nobody opposed, so they all stepped over the wooden threshold, leaving the golden chamber behind—the door shut and then they were engulfed in complete darkness.

The smell of death was immediately replaced with stifling dust as the doorway they'd just used vanished behind them. And with no lantern or light to their names, not even the whites of their eyes nor the glint of their weapons was visible. Demetrius grew quiet, trembling by Arianna's side, and she knew he must be feeling the most scared out of them all right now after his traumatic experience alone in this room.

She grabbed his hand, squeezing it tight.

"Everyone, take someone's hand. We stick together," said Arianna.

She felt as her friends shifted, forming an unbreakable bond. Then Arianna led the group forward.

With her free arm extended out in front of her, she walked past what she was sure was the desk until she felt the wall on the other side of the room press up against her palm. As she traced her hand along the wood panels at her front, she didn't stop until she found the door she was looking for.

"Here we go," she said with a deep breath as the cool bronze of the doorknob finally met her fingers—she said a silent prayer to the gods, begging that it wasn't still locked and that they'd beaten this bewitching game. Then she twisted it, and the door flung open.

34

THE VANISHING CITY

THEY ALL CHEERED AS THEY TUMBLED through the door-way, free at last, back where their adventure through the dwarf city had first begun. Alas, while they didn't need a lantern nor flame to see, there was still only darkness surrounding them, for now they'd found the *true* City of Undor.

Arianna was struck silent as the joy of leaving the doors behind was replaced by a myriad of feelings.

Fear, disgust, sadness, anger… and wonder. *So* much wonder filled her heart.

"Who would do this?" she said in barely a whisper after the shock had worn off. She couldn't keep from shaking as they regarded the same cavernous tunnel they'd first entered after passing through the electric, emerald wall of magic—yet it had wholly changed.

The area was lit with the subtle light of firebugs astray, so Arianna still had to squint to see everything, but what she found was a massive, complex underground fortress built within the deepest depths of Blancoren. The high, crumbling columns cutting through the middle of the area that they had gawked at before were now encased in a sturdy, cream marble worth real admiration. And the ceiling it held up was that much more magnificent with twinkling gems adding to their detail—and atop that ceiling was another, grander hall. And atop that, another…

From there, the city crawled up and up and up with the aid of wide, stone staircases that crisscrossed high above their heads, connecting too many floors to count and reaching far beyond the point that Arianna could even perceive as she craned her neck back. It was a skyward labyrinth of halls and terraces, pillars and passageways that made for the grandest architecture she'd ever laid eyes on.

Giving up trying to guess at how many floors could've been built within the height of this mountain, Arianna brought her gaze to eye level, taking in the area before her; she noted the various tunnels peppering the outskirts of the city, ones that had before appeared as nothing special. Now, they were pebbled with welcoming walkways that begged to be traveled, each entrance bordered in a metallic frame with a sign at the top.

More extraordinary still, the inner walls of the mountains this city had been built between were reinforced with a medley of light-colored stones trimmed in gold embellishments and motifs that stretched on for miles. She also found that statues of dwarves had been carved from the precious stones and metals they'd come to know from their journey through the doors.

Even the floor was to be regarded as something special, a dark stone inlaid with the faintest shimmer of metal that looked as if the ground gently rolled beneath their feet—if not for the piles of skeletons and dried blood staining the patterns, Arianna would have already been rushing to explore.

Carts of rotted food mixed with the reek of decomposed flesh that stung her nose, the smell of death surely cemented in the walls forevermore. And barrels of wine and water had long since run dry. The bones of women and children lay atop one another in their daily garb, and the skeletons of workers had collapsed over the counters of their stations. Arianna and her friends stood in the epicenter of a mass graveyard that should've been a bustling city.

As they took everything in, the splendor and the horrors alike, General Indra's words rang in Arianna's head, as sharp as the point of the spear he'd been holding.

'The City of Undor has fallen, though not in vain.'

From the looks of it, it hadn't just fallen, it had come crashing down; the death revealed to them in the room of gold was nothing when compared to the carnage that spread out before them now—the great City of Undor had been bathed in blood and then forgotten with time.

Arianna's heart ached over such loss of life, and she hoped with all her heart these beings would one day see justice.

She closed her eyes, wishing for this reality to be undone. The grandeur of Undor made it easy to imagine what life used to be like… and so she did.

Arianna's mind scurried from reality, and she transported herself to the true, thriving City of Undor. She saw children with helms too big for their heads, brandishing toy hammers and shields. And she imagined welders pounding away at some rare stone to craft another masterpiece weapon while General Indra supervised with a hard-won smile. She pictured dwarves sipping whiskey in the taverns or bartering for vegetables with the large coins they had found, the odd yet beautiful language hanging in the air, mixing with the constant flow of magic.

But Arianna pictured only the ghost of the city, and the reality came in the form of bones at her feet. Sadly, her imagination wouldn't be enough for such a revival.

Demetrius had been right—the bloodstained, gilded chamber had only been a glimpse of this collapsed dwarf city. Thousands had died here on a day erased from history long ago, and Arianna knew exactly who to blame.

"This was our King," she said, bitterly. "I know it. King Devlindor did this, and then left them here to rot. Everything we've learned is incontestably true." Arianna felt the magic inside her react to her boiling emotions, her heart thrashing within her chest as she considered what this meant.

"The tyrant," stammered Lessa, trying to stave off tears.

Jeom lowered his hood. "They just seem so... innocent. Why would he do this?"

Arianna's eyes flicked to Jeom's axe. "Power," she said, clenching her fists as she remembered the tell-all scroll about the fall of the Golden Age. "It all comes down to power."

"This is sick," agreed Demetrius. "I just can't believe such a place and such a tragedy has been buried beneath the Jar for all these years, right under our noses."

"I... I really don't want to stay here," said Jeom, twitching nervously. He seemed the most troubled of them all by this.

"Which way do you suppose we should go?" said Demetrius, turning in circles to consider the options.

Lessa glanced toward the column of doors. "I think if we go through the wooden door again, we'll just 'exit' the city and end up back in the Vanishing Tunnels," she explained. "And they obviously *are* bewitched by the same magic that built this city, probably to keep away unwanted guests."

"So much that did," mumbled Demetrius.

"You were right all along, Jeom," said Arianna with a soft smile. He hardly acknowledged her, fixated on his axe and lost in his own thoughts.

"Can't we just use the elder's map to navigate the tunnels properly?" suggested Demetrius. "You mentioned you got your hands on one."

Lessa shook her head. "I thought about that, but I believe the tunnels started changing the further off track we got," she replied. "That map certainly doesn't go this far in."

"It'd basically be up to luck, then," said Arianna. "And we don't even have a lantern anymore." She thought of Jacob and Damon's sad ending. "No, it's too risky. There has to be another way out of this place. It's absolutely massive, so I can't imagine that door is the only option."

"Shall we explore, then?" said Demetrius. Everyone except for Jeom answered, so Demetrius waved his hand in his face. "Hey, snap out of it! We're leaving."

Jeom jumped, shaking out of his daze.

"Sorry," he said, rubbing the back of his neck. "I really don't get it, though." His voice was thick with grief. "How is it possible that we didn't see any of this before when we first found the door? We just… walked right through this—"

"I don't think we had really *entered* yet," answered Demetrius. "Magic obscured our vision."

"What makes you say that?" asked Jeom.

"You really aren't very good at remembering what you read, are you?" said Lessa, giving him a supportive hug around the waist. "The podium in the stone room said that all would remain 'blind' unless 'bidden' into the city. That door—" she pointed to where they had just exited "—it's the entrance *and* exit to Undor. I think when you invited us in as guests, the magic was lifted and we were allowed to see it truly."

"We just had to make it through to the end of the doors," added Demetrius.

"So, if we go back the way we came in," continued Lessa, "we'll leave this place behind for good but probably be lost in the tunnels forever. I don't know if *that* maze is beatable."

She let go of Jeom and pulled Sano into her arms as he vied for attention, quite squirmy since his encounter with the ghost of General Indra—though Lessa remained unaware.

"Hmm…" said Jeom, letting all that sink in. "Wow, all we went through and we've only just arrived."

Both Lessa and Demetrius nodded.

"I can't imagine those obstacles have always been there, though," mused Demetrius, scratching at the stubble on his chin. "This place seems like it used to be pretty peaceful."

Arianna knew exactly why they had had to face such dangers in order to even enter the city. And again, King Devlindor was to blame. "With no one left to contain the magic or secure the fortress, I think it must've gone wild after so many years unchecked," she said, knowing by just the itch of her own magic that it had the power to take over if she let it.

Jeom returned a sorrowful nod.

"All we can do now is keep walking," she said, gently. "There's nothing left for us here."

THE FOUR TREKKED ACROSS THE CITY in silence, heading toward the farthest wall, where there were several tunnels to choose from, and looking for any signs of a different way out.

"Dwarves were quite the artisans," said Jeom in awe. "This architecture… it's incredible."

"I know," said Arianna. "I can't believe this place had never been discovered before—"

"Look! It's the axe," shouted Demetrius, startling everyone. He grabbed Jeom's hand, leading him ahead in a hurry with Arianna and Lessa in tow.

Soon, they came upon a statue plated in gold. It stood about thirty feet tall and was fenced in by a grand fountain. When they reached the edge of it, as if triggered by a physical presence, water shot up from the bed of the fountain and danced in strings all around the sculpture.

For a moment, the devastation around them was erased in light of this spectacular charm.

"It seems like this city's magic might live on forever," said Arianna, enthralled by the enchanted demonstration.

When the water had settled, they took a moment to admire the statue itself; Arianna was astounded at the level of detail in which it had been carved. And sure enough, as Demetrius had exclaimed, Jeom's axe was also part of the display. A very regal-looking dwarf boasting a full suit of armor and a scowl on his face gripped the weapon in his hand—a near perfect resemblance of the real thing, though on a much grander scale. What's more, this dwarf was seated upon an ornate throne, sure royalty of his kind.

"There's a plaque over here," called Lessa, circling the fountain. "It must be some sort of tribute."

There was a moment of quiet.

"*Jeom?*" Arianna could hear the smile in Lessa's voice.

He chuckled, walking over to meet her, starting to seem more comfortable with this strange skill he'd acquired. He bent over to read the inscription:

King Undoriamus—founder of the City of Undor.

The mighty king slayed the three-headed dragon of Crissy who once dwelled in the tunnels of Blancoren. He crafted the golden axe from the bowels of the Vanishing Tunnels, the first of its kind. The Axe of Crissy, fused with the teeth of the slain dragon, is said to possess peculiar powers as the essence of the creature flows within the weapon. The beholder must have unbendable loyalty and strength in order to retain true control over the axe, for our king was a believer in both, as are all dragons of Olleb-Yelfra.

One by one, they all turned to gawk at the axe in Jeom's hand.

"What's a dragon?" said Jeom, holding the axe out to arm's length as he observed it with new eyes.

"That…" said Demetrius, pointing to the open mouth and teeth of the creature crafted into the axe.

"Do I have to repeat *everything?*" said Lessa, tossing her head back in annoyance—the girls had gone over their Golden Age findings with the boys in great detail by now, but unlike his brother, Jeom didn't appear to be the best listener.

"Special powers, huh?" said Arianna, tilting her head back and forth to see if she could figure out what it might do. "Why am I unsurprised?"

"That's no ordinary weapon," said Demetrius with a whistle. "Does it say anything else?"

Jeom nodded. "The text just goes on to tell of how the king died in a later battle, defending the city." He glanced to Lessa. "You were right earlier. That's how this place came to be called Undor long ago."

"So you were listening," she said with a smirk.

Jeom winked and finished summing up the plaque.

"King Undoriamus left the Axe of Crissy in the protection of his people," he said, "and it's been passed down for centuries to his descendants ever since." He lifted his gaze to the statue, entranced by it just as he had been the axe. "I wonder what it could mean… powers?"

"Somehow I'm certain we'll find out," said Lessa.

A chill ran over Arianna's body, and she looked up, half-expecting to encounter another ghost. To her relief, she saw nothing lurking nearby.

"I think we ought to keep moving," she whispered, wondering if it really had been nothing *or* if her instincts had been right; if so, they were not alone down here.

"Well, we've come pretty far across the city now and haven't seen anything for directions yet," said Lessa. "I guess it's time to pick a tunnel."

They all turned in circles, taking in the countless options.

"Or we could just follow the birds," said Demetrius, casually. He began walking away without explanation.

"What are you talking about? What birds?" asked Lessa as they all chased after him.

"We're in an underground fortress," said Arianna with a sigh. "Birds might be a bit hard to come by at the moment…"

She'd assumed everyone was bound to lose their wits at some point with no fresh air and only scraps of food and water left to share between them, but she wouldn't have thought Demetrius would be the first to go.

"Those look like birds to me," he replied, his focus pinned to the nearest wall.

When Arianna followed his gaze, to her surprise, she did find a flock of birds—although not real by any means.

These were painted in wispy, shimmering hues barely discernible in the dark against the light-colored stone of the main walls. And still, they were dazzling, part of a vast mural which created the façade of a peaceful outside world inside of the mountains. The birds joined portrayals of forests, rivers, and an open sky, the high walls mimicking the best of nature, she was sure. And as Arianna's sight adjusted in the dim lighting, she thought the images actually glowed slightly in the dark.

She found it impossible to see where the mural stopped as the dome-like ceiling tapered inward with the mountain peaks; if time had permitted, she would've insisted on climbing the stairs to the top to see the complete picture, but she would have to carry on with her imagination.

"It's incredible," breathed Lessa, her voice lost with the wind painted in thin strokes above her head. "I wonder why dwarves would have such decoration across their city if they chose to live underground?"

"Maybe so they could have some fresh air down here in the dungeons of the mountains. Just like your paintings," mused Arianna. "A break from reality."

"It's really something," said Jeom. "But what do you mean 'follow the birds,' exactly?" he asked his brother.

"Look," started Demetrius, "I spent all my life learning about nature and how things work. See how the birds are all flocking in one direction?" He pointed up ahead. "Even the trees and the grass are swaying in the same breeze, because that's the way it works." His enthusiasm for the subject was on par with Arianna's enthusiasm for a swordfight. "If we follow the nature, maybe it'll lead us to the real thing! We can only hope, but that's my best guess."

"Okay…" said Jeom, glancing sidelong to the girls.

Lessa just shrugged in response, and Arianna wasn't sure what to think. But it was clear that no one else had an idea as to where to go.

"What do we have to lose by trying?" said Arianna after a moment of deliberation.

"You can have my rations if I'm wrong," said Demetrius, patting his stomach. "But my gut tells me those birds are going to lead us somewhere worth going."

His zest for adventure was certainly contagious, and Arianna wanted to be as hopeful as him. In any case, she knew better than to argue with instinct, so instead of trusting in her own this time, she would trust in Demetrius'.

"After you, then," she said with a grin. Jeom and Lessa were also willing to let him test out his theory—they began to walk.

The birds flocked over flimsy white clouds and through green swaying trees, guiding the group farther through the city. Bizarre orange, pink, and lilac flora sprouted from the bottom of the walls, and wild creatures lurked through tall grasses. Even a sun with swirling, golden rays melted into a vermillion sky some way down—it was such a beautiful depiction of the outside world that Arianna had trouble believing any of this could be found within the Olleb.

So beautiful. Too beautiful.

She doubted the mural had even come to life by brush; this art was touched by magic, the colors almost standing free from the walls if she stared long enough.

Steered further by this unknown dwarf artist, they found shining tigers watering by a lake and antelope galloping through the pastures. Even a myriad of butterflies suckled at the painted flowers on the ground. Arianna thought the images so lifelike that it felt as if they already walked free of the mountains. Then, abruptly, the mural was wiped away in the face of an enormous mirror.

Arianna stood frozen as she was suddenly looking upon her nightmare.

That isn't me.

She took a step forward—drawn to her reflection.

This figure was just as alluring as the ghosts she'd seen thus far, a vision of beauty Arianna certainly couldn't have achieved in her current filthy state, or maybe ever. And she donned the same crimson robes of her district, yet Arianna knew she herself was wearing Solomon's white elder cloak.

Then the reflection smiled, a flash of silver flickering across her eyes.

I am not her.

The reflection reached out her hand, and Arianna took another step forward; she wanted to grasp it.

"It's a door!" yelled Lessa, snapping Arianna out of her trance as she pushed past her to lay her hands on the mirror.

The girl of her nightmares vanished.

Arianna faced the mirror with Lessa by her side, only now she saw her true self—white robes covered her skin, tangled curls fell down around her face, her cheeks smeared with dirt and dried blood, and brown eyes stared back in fright.

"A door?" she stuttered, putting her mind back on the present. "By gods, it is." Her eyes grew wide with realization. "It's a door!"

Sure enough, the dusty mirrors created tall double doors that reached from the ground all the way to the lowest ceiling above them. Arianna also noticed that many dwarves had died very close by, though the doors remained closed.

Could some of them have escaped?

It seemed unlikely that any of these Golden Age creatures could've survived, given the state of their world today. Yet, still, she wondered.

"Yay…" said Jeom with a face full of skepticism. "Another door."

Demetrius slapped him on the back. "Have a little optimism, brother!"

Jeom feigned a smile.

Moving around the bones, the four placed themselves directly in front of the mirrored gateway, all reflected side by side, all considering the others. Their faces appeared tired and long from the trying journey, and their eyes burned with a lust for fresh air.

"This *has* to be it," said Demetrius.

"What if it's locked?" asked Jeom.

"It won't be," replied Lessa, closing her eyes as she mouthed a silent prayer.

Everyone shared one last eager, hungry glance—one that longed for freedom. Then Arianna grabbed the coiled, golden handles with both hands and pushed.

The doors slid open with a loud groan, and a cool breeze splashed her face. They cautiously peeked inside; a long, twisting hallway stretched out before them.

"It looks clear," said Arianna, testing the durability of the seemingly fragile floor. It didn't budge in the slightest, so she started through the golden-glass portal before her, beckoning her friends along. "Let's see where this goes."

The hall was absolutely breathtaking, maybe even more so than the city itself as everything here was clear of any indication of death or despair—only images of an ideal, golden world filled their future as they all ambled inside.

Glancing back for one last look at the City of Undor, Arianna swore she saw several sets of eyes, ghostly ones, watching as they went. Then the mirrored doors swung shut behind them, sealing off the city tomb and replacing her immediate thoughts with visions of hope.

Every inch of this tunnel of mirrors was clad in glass and gold, and the architecture also mimicked the City of Undor with a kaleidoscopic fresco decorating the mirrored walls, floor, and ceiling. Soft, enchanted strokes of gold created a sunny meadow filled with wild flowers whose seeds whisked off into the breeze. And golden-leafed trees with swaying limbs sprouted up the glass walls, trying to touch the gilded clouds that floated across the ceiling.

Arianna even witnessed her first full depiction of dragons, ones with golden scales and eyes, swimming in the rays of a beaming sun. And the more she looked, the more she was certain the pictures actually moved, the dragons slowly soaring across the sky. "What magnificent magic this is," she stuttered, head tilted back as she studied their every detail.

"Can you imagine such creatures ever existed?" said Lessa.

"Not at all," answered Jeom.

Demetrius ran ahead of them, frantic with excitement. "I see a light!"

Tearing her gaze from the Golden Age mirage etched into the glass, Arianna saw it too, a soft glow filtering through to the hall. And as they traveled farther down the corridor, the light grew brighter, and the space grew colder. Lessa bundled

Sano into her robes, and everyone began to button up their cloaks and pull on their hoods as even their breath became visible in the unexpectedly chilly air.

Then, finally, they all reached the end of the tunnel to confirm the source of the light and cause behind the drastic temperature change.

"We made it," said Arianna, tears in her eyes.

35

STOLEN FREEDOM

GATHERING AT THE END OF THE TUNNEL, the four sucked at the fresh air. Mirrors of gold no longer filled their vision, and the dark engulfed them once more. But this time, it was pleasant and most definitely welcomed.

They stood on a rocky platform covered in a light frost, and when Arianna turned around to have one last look at the gold and glass tunnel, she saw nothing but stone.

"The entrance… it's gone," she said.

The others looked too, and Jeom pressed his hand upon the wall. "So long," he muttered with a thoughtful expression.

Good riddance, magical mystery maze of doors!

Arianna hoped the next door she opened was to a warm bed with nothing magical or mysterious about it. But, for now, she put her hopes aside and just enjoyed the moment. Her eyes traveled up the cliff, and her heart skipped a beat as she gazed upon the other side of the Blancoren Mountains.

It rose tall above their heads in dark gray slants—beautiful, she had to admit. Bright white peaks curved inward, away from them, and flimsy trees trickled up the sides. Shelves of rock were also covered in thick bushes with sun-colored leaves, and enormous boulders surrounded them at every angle.

Arianna tilted her head toward the midnight sky, and the moon smiled down at her, accompanied by an immeasurable number of twinkling stars. She couldn't help but smile back. Never before had she seen such a clear night sky. Nobody could move nor speak as they all reveled in the spectacular view; from the wide platform on which they stood, they could see everything, and Arianna tried to memorize every detail.

At the foot of the mountain, feathery flowers spread out in a massive, silvery sea toward the edge of a tiny town set in the midst of a boundless landscape. And in that town, many lanterns lined a single street and flickered in small windows.

Life outside the Jar.

A winding stream created a barrier between the town and the field, and Arianna could just barely make out a bridge connecting the two. Squinting, she also saw a frost-covered trail which led all the way from the town to the edge of the mountains; a stampede of white and black horses galloped across it.

Apart from the meadow and the village, there was nothing else really to note for miles, so Arianna inspected the rocky platform. At the edge of it, she found a trail of stone steps that led down the mountainside, coiling all the way to the bottom, from what she could tell.

Anxious to get on with her life, she took a step forward.

"When we reach the ground, consider your freedom earned," said Arianna, holding her breath for what might come next.

"Don't you mean, *stolen?*" replied Lessa in a whisper, closing her eyes and savoring the moment.

"I can't believe it," said Demetrius, blinking away tears.

Jeom responded with a bellow of infectious laughter, and then they all let the overwhelming bliss of their victory wash away every trouble and fear from before. Even Sano seemed to brighten as he popped his tiny head out of Lessa's robes to breathe in the fresh air for the first time.

"Stolen freedom…" said Arianna. Then she smiled to herself. "Yes, I suppose I do."

"We've got the world at our fingertips now," shouted Jeom, opening his arms out wide. He squeezed the axe between his fingers as a Solomon-like grin grew across his face.

"I've never seen so much… green!" said Demetrius, looking ready to fly off his feet and explore the forest around him. "So, where to next?"

"Why don't we start with getting away from this forsaken heap of rock?" Lessa started down the steps.

"Hold on!" said Arianna, tugging at her robes for her to come back. "We *almost* forgot something—"

Lessa gave her a perplexed look, but before she could form a question on her lips, Arianna threw her arms out wide and tilted her head back to see the stars in full view, taking a cue from Jeom.

"I'm free!" she cried out in pure joy. Her voice bounced around the walls of Blancoren, echoing with a limitless range into the open skyline, never to be caged again.

Lessa, Jeom, and Demetrius didn't hesitate to join her, each letting their voices be heard, carried off into the welcoming wind.

Then one by one, with Arianna in the lead, they climbed down the stairs.

THE FARTHER DOWN THE MOUNTAIN they went, the denser the undergrowth of the forest became. In the shade of the giant trees, the path grew very dark, and everyone kept their eyes on the ground, careful not to lose their footing on the steep trail.

"Ara," said Lessa a little while later. "What's that there in your pack?"

Arianna stopped, glancing over her shoulder to try to see. "What is it?" she asked, swinging the sack off her shoulder.

"Here, let me," said Lessa, taking the pack from her to inspect it. "Looks like there's a hole, but I thought I saw…"

She dug around for a second, and then pulled out one of the parchments Talis had given them—Arianna and Lessa had split them up between themselves before fleeing the Warrior's District.

"This was poking through," said Lessa, unfurling it. "And I swear there was—"

"Hey, what's the hold up?" called Jeom, bringing up the rear of the group.

"There's a hole in my bag," said Arianna, peering around Lessa. "Things were falling out."

With the stairs being so narrow, the boys had to stop directly behind Lessa. "Can we patch it up?" asked Demetrius.

Arianna shrugged and looked back to Lessa who was deeply enthralled with the scroll now; with a closer glance, she realized it was *Olleb-Yelfra the Fallen.*

"Well get on with it," whined Jeom. "I'm freezing my butt off back here."

Lessa still didn't respond, never taking her eyes off the parchment, reading furiously.

"How can you even read right now?" asked Arianna, wrapping her arms around herself to keep warm. "It's too dark, and I'm sure you know that story like the back of your hand by now. Is this really the time?" She was anxious to plant her feet on solid ground. "What's got your attention there?"

Demetrius and Jeom huddled closer to Lessa too, reading the parchment over her shoulder from behind and seeming to be just as captivated by the story.

"Ara, you *have* to see this," said Lessa, finally looking up.

Her voice quivered and her hands shook as she held the scroll open.

"Okay…" she replied, hesitant. Arianna scooched as close as she could to the others on the trail, careful of the steep edges. "Oh, now I see what all the fuss is about!"

She didn't have to squint to read the parchment, for the words were now glowing bright—red letters blazed between the lines of the calligraphy which detailed the downfall of the Olleb. It was as if the dark had triggered some reaction from the ink… a magical one. What had stayed invisible by day burned a luminous red by night.

Arianna felt compelled to read the words out loud:

> *Light is light and dark is dark, but never shall*
> *they live apart. One shall seek what the other*
> *denies. If it is found, thus follows the demise.*
> *When one eclipses over the other, life shall end*
> *for he and his brother.*

For a moment, they all remained quiet, each contemplating the words for themselves, though Arianna immediately recognized the verse.

"Strange we didn't see this script in the ink before," she said in a hushed voice, leaning in closer. "It's definitely another charm of some sort."

Lessa's mouth fell into a frown. "I wonder if Solomon and Talis knew it was there all along?"

"Wouldn't they have told us if they did?" replied Arianna. Lessa's expression told her she wasn't so sure—the more they learned about this new world their masters had introduced them to, the more it was clear that they hadn't really known them that well at all.

"It's the Golden Rule!" said Demetrius, snapping his fingers at his own quick wit. "From the parchment you found on that dwarf's remains back there. Right, Ara?"

"I believe so," she replied, chewing on her lip as she thought of General Indra's note. "Or a version of it, at least."

"Absolutely it is," said Lessa. "But I also think it could be… the prophecy." Her expression was twisted with confusion, and she brought the parchment closer to her face to re-read the ink that wasn't glowing.

Arianna's jaw dropped, recalling the first time she and Lessa had read that scroll and learned about a prophecy which had changed the world for the worst.

"Could it be?" she gasped.

"What… could it be *what?*" asked Jeom, growing impatient.

"This is *Olleb-Yelfra the Fallen*," replied Arianna. "It's the scroll we told you of that details the end of the Golden Age. The last part of it mentioned something about a seer who gave the King the idea of creating the Four Corners, incited by a prophecy she foresaw—"

"But we could never find any other information about what this prophecy actually said," added Lessa.

The girls were growing increasingly excited as a new piece of the Golden Age unfurled before them.

"What's a seer?" asked Jeom, leaning in.

"What's a… prophecy?" added Demetrius.

"I'm not *exactly* sure," said Lessa, "but I think a seer could be another type of magical creature from that era, or maybe a sorceress of some kind?" Her forehead scrunched together as she tried to form her ideas into words. "The text here says King Devlindor 'spared' her from the crusades against magic."

"And from what I could gather, a prophecy must be a vision of the future," mused Arianna. "A dream, maybe? Or a nightmare..." A memory of the girl in the mirror flashed within her thoughts, and suddenly she was very aware of how dark it was; she moved closer to her friends.

"I think so, too," said Lessa. "And *this* one supposedly alludes to a future without the King... if he hadn't created the slave city."

Tracing the letters on the parchment with her finger, she read an excerpt:

> *She foresaw a future that could—although very unlikely—result in the High King's death, and consequently the end of peace in Olleb-Yelfra, if her advice were not taken into consideration. Thus, for the world's continued wellbeing, the prophecy was written with the seer's binding blood and locked away in the darkest labyrinths of the palace to be seen only by the eyes of those it avowed.*

Lessa finished reading. "It's all such a lie," she growled. "There is *nothing* peaceful about the Jar."

Suddenly, Arianna understood just exactly what the charm was behind this magical ink, and she froze with realization.

"It's the seer's... it's her binding blood," she stammered, pointing to the glowing script. Her eyes grew wide. "It is a lie, Lessa. King Devlindor wrote this! Why else would it paint him as the hero when he so clearly wasn't? This is *his* side of the story."

Arianna's mouth hung open at her own words.

"By gods, you're right," Lessa breathed, looking at the parchment with new eyes. "How did I not see this before?"

"Put it away now," said Arianna, sickened at the thought

of being so near to him, even if just through ink.

Lessa rolled the scroll up, carefully placing it in her own bag for safekeeping.

"King Devlindor actually wrote that?" said Jeom. "Wonder what the real story is, then."

Arianna tried to swallow the lump growing in her throat, wondering the exact same thing.

"Wow," said Demetrius, shaking his head and using the butt of his scythe to steady himself on the path as they lined back up. "Just wow... can you imagine if the seer hadn't warned the King about his possible death day?"

A world without King Devlindor?

Arianna's imagination didn't stretch that far.

"Let's keep going," urged Jeom. "We can discuss it more as we run *away* from the Jar, but I want to put this behind us forever."

No one had any disagreement with that sentiment, so the four continued the long journey down the mountain, deliberating the possible meanings of the hidden message they'd found within the scroll.

"I don't see how this gibberish alludes to anything about the King," said Jeom after a while. "The Golden Rule could be referring to anyone... anything. It's so vague."

"It is quite cryptic," agreed Arianna. "I wouldn't be surprised if Talis Churry wrote it."

Lessa made a noise that was a mix between a laugh and a sigh.

Arianna's mind flooded with more depressing memories along the same line, but she tried to ignore them, thinking of all the good to be celebrated this day—she hoped Solomon and Talis would be proud.

"Any ideas, Les?" she said, wanting to shift the focus away from contemplations over their masters' uncertain fates.

"Too many," she replied with a sigh.

"Well, I don't think this Golden Rule... or prophecy, whatever we're calling it, is all there is to the truth," added Demetrius. "If the vision the seer told to the King scared him enough to create the City of the Four Corners, shouldn't there be more to it?"

"I'm not sure," said Lessa, "but the words seem to be centered around an idea of balance. Light and dark, life and death. They cancel each other out."

"So, then, what's left?" asked Jeom.

"I suppose nothing..." she replied.

"Or everything," said Arianna.

"Do you think it could have something to do with us?" mused Demetrius.

Arianna couldn't help but snicker at the suggestion—how could something so significant and preconceived centuries ago have anything to do with them?

"I suppose, like Jeom said, it *could* be about anybody," replied Lessa. "Though if we believe in the King's written words, then it was, I gather, meant for him."

Arianna knew enough not to believe in him at all. "If it was only meant just for him, then why did the dwarf General Indra carry the words in his pocket?"

Nobody had the answers—just more questions. So rather than continue speculating, they walked in silence the remainder of the way down. A long time passed, but they made it to the bottom. And not one of them looked back as they came toward the edge of the trail they had seen from up top; a wooden sign had been posted there with an arrow pointing back toward the mountain; it read 'Vanishing Tunnels.'

"Ah, sweet freedom!" sang Jeom, marching in the opposite direction, toward the little town.

The meadow they had seen from afar swallowed them on all sides now. The flowers crunched under their heavy boots, and the cream-colored petals reached up past their heads as they waded through the field.

"Wish we would've taken the trail," mumbled Demetrius who stepped with care, trying not to disturb the plants.

"It's too dangerous to be out in the open," said Jeom.

"I've never seen a flower like this before," said Lessa, unwilling to be troubled in this moment. She plucked one from the ground and held it to her nose to sniff the pleasant aroma.

"These are snowflowers," said Demetrius. "They only grow in the coldest places, but they still need a lot of sun. It sure was a feat to get them to sprout in the Jar, but I did have a few successes." He smiled, dimples forming on his cheeks.

"Why don't we rest here?" suggested Arianna, stopping in the middle of the meadow. She stared ahead but still couldn't see the town for how tall the snowflowers grew. "It's much farther than I thought, and we should probably rest before we start another adventure anyways."

"Fine by me," said Jeom as he plopped down, making a bed of the cottony flowers—Demetrius winced with every broken stem, but then he settled in next to his brother.

With a big yawn, Arianna sat too. And as soon as she did, she wondered if she'd ever be able to get back up for how exhausted she was. Turning her robes inside out, she laid the crimson cloth on the outside so the white wouldn't get any more muddied. Then she wrapped her cloak around her body like a cocoon.

"We can make a plan tomorrow," said Lessa, following Arianna's lead as she wrapped herself in a silky, sapphire blanket of Talis' elder robes.

Snowflowers rose high above them as they all laid their heads back—their colorful robes created a mosaic 'X' in the middle of the meadow, replicating the flag Arianna had stared upon so often in the Warrior's District. And though she had no idea of what might happen next, she hoped she'd never have to see that flag again.

The four huddled close together to stave off the cold, and then, for a little extra warmth, Jeom passed around the flask of whiskey he'd taken from one of the slain regulators in the Creator's District. They had each spent far more brutal nights in the Jar and in the tunnels, so Arianna found this makeshift bed to be quite comfortable. As they sipped the whiskey and gazed at the star-studded sky, a comet suddenly painted a trail connecting the dots.

"Is it me or is the sky getting brighter?" said Demetrius, pushing up on his elbows and squinting into the distance.

"I think you're right," said Lessa. "It does seem to be getting brighter. Ara, are you seeing this?"

Cocking her head to the side, Arianna thought that, strangely, the stars *did* seem to brighten, growing larger under the grinning moon. "That's odd," she whispered.

"See what?" said Jeom, taking the last swig from the flask.

"Wait, those aren't stars," said Arianna, tilting her head all the way back. "They're lanterns!" She reached a hand toward the sky. "I heard they mark the end of the Free Falls Festivals. They'll be letting all the new citizens go soon."

They grew silent after that, just watching the fires grow.

More and more lanterns became visible, rising high from somewhere far ahead and floating toward the heavens, orange flames flickering inside the large paper lamps. Hundreds drifted along with the guiding wind, and Arianna thought it appeared as if giant firebugs had escaped the tunnels, intending to celebrate their freedom with the stars, just like them.

The sight gave birth to a new kind of hope in her heart, and Arianna began to hum the lyrics of a song.

It is my dream. Finally, I am free...

Inevitably, sleep overcame them, and one by one, they each drifted into dreams filled with starry skies and a golden world full of endless possibilities.

THE KING

"MY LIEGE, A MESSAGE HAS ARRIVED from the City of the Four Corners," said a man as the guards escorted him into the throne room. He handed over a sealed parchment stamped with the emblem of the slave districts.

Kneeling at the foot of the stairs, he awaited the King's instruction.

King Devlindor took the parchment and opened it without the slightest glance in the man's direction. "Another successful Free Falls, no doubt." He stroked a black jaguar who sat obediently at his feet, his voice thick with authority.

But, as he scanned the hurried writing, his expression fell.

His fist clenched around the parchment, and then it burst into flames, the ashes falling to the floor.

With a long exhale through his nose, the King then stood from his throne. One hand clutching a white, wooden staff with a large ruby fixed at the top, he strode down the steps, long robes of black and gold flowing behind him like water across the red velvet.

"Come, Raja," he hissed—the jaguar, a stunning specimen for its kind, perked up at its name and shadowed the King as he walked. Her black coat gave off a sheen under the firelight spilling from the chandelier, and her eyes glowed an intense yellow, almost gold.

The messenger shrank back as King Devlindor came to stand over him; Raja sat dutifully on her haunches, a soft growl rising in her throat.

"Rise!" said the King.

"As you command," replied the messenger, trembling from head to toe as he stood to face his sovereign.

King Devlindor could see his reflection in the man's terrified stare, his jeweled crown glinting in the whites of his eyes.

"I've received some very distressing news from the Four Corners," he said, narrowing his gaze.

"How can I be of service, Your Majesty?" the messenger replied, his voice quivering.

King Devlindor let his eyes float closed, considering the words he'd just read. "Here's how," he said.

Then he snapped his fingers, and Raja responded with a roar that echoed throughout the chamber. Slamming her front paws to the ground, she bared her sharp teeth, snarling. As if reacting to her energy, the black granite tiles shook under their feet like an earthquake had hit the palace.

The messenger fell to his knees with a shriek. Then the ground stilled, and he dared to lift his eyes to the King's.

"My lord, please. I beg you," he whimpered, hand outstretched.

King Devlindor pursed his lips and tightened his grasp around the staff as he glared down at him. The gem at the center began to burn bright, as if a fire had built up inside.

The messenger started to convulse violently, and he

screamed out for the pain to stop, crawling toward the King's feet for help.

"Of course, I can take the pain away," replied the King.

He drove his staff through the messenger's back in the next breath, the sharp tip sliding with ease through his flesh. When he yanked it back out, a pool of blood spilled around the messenger's limp body.

The King kicked him away. Glancing to the mirror-clad ceiling, his own dark eyes stared back at him, judging him, reflected in the man's blood. "I am *very* displeased," he uttered, considering his reflection.

With a deep breath, he tore his gaze away from the mirrors and walked back up the steps to his throne with Raja purring at his side. He sat down and leaned back, drumming his fingers atop the wide arm of the seat, lost in thought.

"Brother, haven't I taught you to clean up after yourself?" came a soft voice.

How long has it been?

The chamber smelled like death, so the King thought likely several hours; time meant nothing to him now after so much of it had passed.

A woman walked across the room, heels clicking atop the tile. She carefully stepped around the body before stopping at the foot of the throne.

"And who told you to kill the messenger?" she added with a mock pout on her face.

King Devlindor let out an exasperated sigh, observing her with little amusement.

She wore an emerald-colored dress which clung to her curves, revealing too much of her bosom. And her skin echoed that of his own—almost as pale as the body on the floor. Her hair lay long past her chest in strings of silvery white that looked like the color of sleet as it fell, and a long leather whip draped around her neck like a shawl—though he knew it was not for decoration; he'd seen her wield it too many times to count. She was beautiful, and always had been—but made even more so with the fine, silver tiara twinkling atop her head.

To anyone else, she would have an intimidating air about her, but she served him, the High King. And brother or not, he knew she was frightened of him, as she very well should be.

"Princess Elisa," he said after a moment as he considered her. "Now is not the time for jests. What we've long since feared has finally come to pass."

It was all he could do to remain calm, taking deep, slow breaths to try to steady his nerves. As he did, the flames in the candles around the room grew with every inhale.

Princess Elisa's steely green eyes widened in shock as she comprehended his words. She tightened her painted finger-nails around the whip, and a glint of silver flashed across her pupils.

"This is quite unexpected, but it's just a small setback. Shall I call upon Sir Vladamor?" she asked, her voice coming out so even that he knew she was just trying to hold it together for his sake, always wanting to appear strong in his presence— but she wasn't *as* strong as him, and he saw straight through the act and into her weakness. "They won't get far with him unleashed. No child will be match for a necromancer."

The King returned a slight nod, so she swiveled on her heels to leave, her dress sweeping the floor, and the messenger's blood staining the fabric. But he called after her before she reached the doors.

"Let's send word to Keeper Kassime as well, shall we? His city is nearest to the Four Corners, although they shouldn't make it such a distance," he added. "And Elisa, do tell Sir Vladamor to be discreet with his tactics. Escaped slaves will cause enough uproar without him adding his tricks to the mix. We will take care of this, *quietly*. Understood?"

The Princess pursed her lips at the command, and a twinge

of a smile crossed the King's face—he loved how much it still bothered her to take orders from him. And yet, he loved her, as she did him.

"Of course, brother… my king," she replied, bitterly.

"Very well," he said with the wave of his hand. "You may go. I'll join you soon to hear the proposed plan."

She curtsied low and then left.

Soon after, King Devlindor dismissed his normal entourage of guards and departed the throne room with Raja alone, headed to the castle cellars. And while he couldn't even remember his last venture down there, he recalled the halls as if it were yesterday.

The air tasted stale and dust billowed all around, but he didn't plan to linger long. Taking a torch from the wall as he descended the stairs, he called upon his magic.

Solza ven immito.

A pink flame grew atop the torch, washing the darkness in pockets of light as he walked. And the end of his staff made a deep echo against the stone floor with every step he took.

Stacks of parchments littered his path, and countless books lined dust-covered shelves against the walls. Cobwebs clung to everything, and it was frighteningly cold compared to the warm climate above ground.

He had to step through a maze of large crates labeled 'Seized' until he eventually came to what he was looking for— a door, one he hadn't opened in a very long time.

"*Operium undrio,*" he breathed.

There was the familiar click of a lock, and then the door swung open.

Darkness stitched to every corner of the room, chased sporadically away by the firelight of his torch as he stepped inside, Raja still at his heels. There was only one furnishing in this chamber, a simple wooden table and chair situated in the corner. And on top of the table was a crate, the lid set aside.

The King moved with caution, his heart drumming inside his chest… afraid of what he might find.

You have nothing to fear. You are the High King. Do not lose control.

After leaning his staff against the wall and setting the lantern on the table, he sat down in the chair and moved the lid off the crate. Rummaging through its contents, he found a few knick-knacks and portraits from childhood that he didn't care to linger on, as well as several torn pages from a diary he'd written long ago when he was barely a man. He thumbed through the parchments, searching in vain.

"Aha!" The King pulled one from the clutter and tried to read the title; it was scuffed with old age, though the signature remained intact.

Examining the parchment further, he frowned, ultimately tossing it aside. His heartbeat quickened even more.

This isn't the one…

Skimming through more and more pages, he began to grow hot with anger. "It's not here—" he said, clenching his fist around the last scroll at the bottom of the box.

In a fit of rage, he leaped up from the chair and swept the box off the table, slamming his fist down on the wood.

The parchments from the crate littered the ground, each signed in a verse:

Inscribed by way of:
A Once Noble Man
Born of Noble Blood
To a Once Enchanted Land
And Noble Kingdom

As his past came back to haunt him, King Devlindor's voice exploded out in a thundering howl of fury and fear, disturbing the silence of the forgotten cellar and even frightening

Raja who shrank back at his feet—though no one else was around to hear.

Moments later, the ruby of his staff glowed a bright red, and a dark cloud of magic began to engulf the entire chamber, twisting in a vortex all around him.

Then he was gone.

Dear Warrior

Congratulations on escaping the Four Corners! I hope you enjoyed the beginning of your daring quest.

The peers you left behind in the districts are still in the dark—they know nothing of magic. Take a moment to show them the enchanted path to freedom.

If you could say one thing about your adventure through the Vanishing Tunnels, to help someone else follow in your footsteps, what would it be?

Share the magic on

Good luck on the rest of your journey. You are now a fugitive of Olleb-Yelfra.

Sincerely,
Ashleigh B.

ACKNOWLEDGMENTS

Thank you to the people in my corner: those who read this story when it was at its roughest and who ensured Arianna could thrive. First published on December 17, 2014, *Belvedor and the Four Corners* has come a long, long way from its origins. I've revised and republished the story countless times. I don't think I'll ever feel 'finished' with it (as is the case for many writers), but I'm so proud to see what has become of my very first novel! This book truly marks the beginning of an epic journey—for both Arianna and me.

Mom and Dad (Terri & Tony), my biggest cheerleaders— you encouraged me each step of the way, in your own ways, through every edit, update, and new edition. Without your love and support, I may have never been brave enough to share this story, let alone to continue writing it. I'm so lucky to have parents that put up with my endless imagination and support my wildest dreams, even well into adulthood.

Christina Marie, my big sister—your story alone is an inspiration to fight for what you believe in. You've always been willing to listen to me ramble about this fantasy world (a major part of the writing process), and I can always count on you to read a book faster than anyone for an honest critique.

Lisa Diane, my partner in crime—ours is truly a friendship for the books! After all our crazy adventures, I'm not surprised you also stood by my side in a world filled with swords, arrows, and magic. Your belief in me and in the *Belvedor Saga* has been invaluable.

***Hannah McCall*, my editor and storytelling guru**—you've helped me take this book to a level I have always dreamed of achieving and taught me so much in the process. I couldn't have asked for a better editor and can't thank you enough for your thoughtful treatment to my story, down to the very last comma. So glad I found you!

***Mirella Santana*, my genius cover designer**—you're a star! I'm still stunned every time I look at this cover and want to follow Arianna right through that cave. Your design skills are masterful. Thank you.

***Jessica Khoury*, my magical mapmaker and illustrator**—now I can truly picture Olleb-Yelfra for the strange and beautiful place that it is. Thank you for bringing my fantasy world to such fantastic life.

Many people, places, and experiences have inspired different aspects of my writing, and my gratitude is endless to those who have helped shape this story in any way, and to those who have supported my journey as a writer—it's been a wild ride.

Thank you!

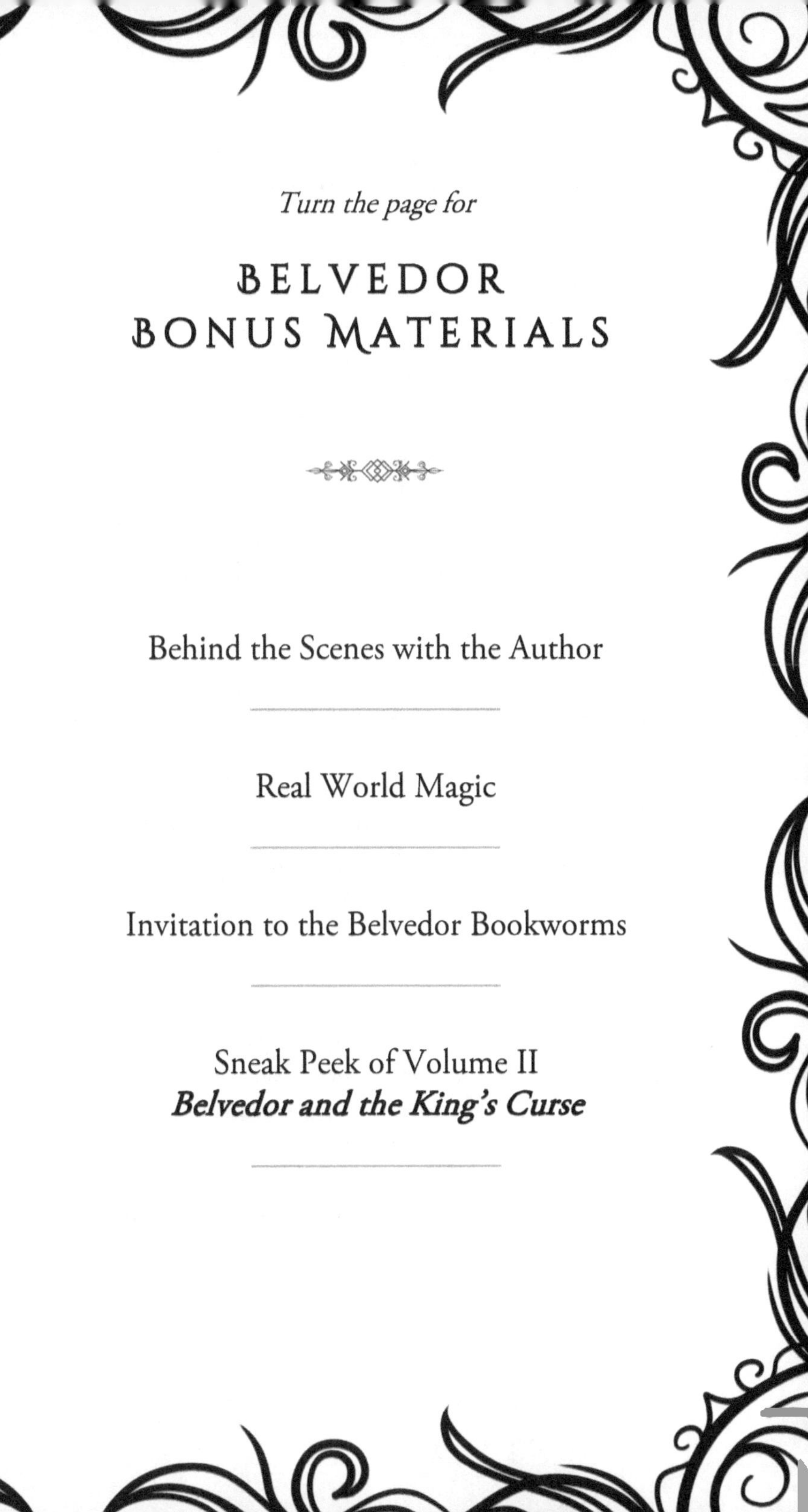

Turn the page for

BELVEDOR BONUS MATERIALS

Behind the Scenes with the Author

Real World Magic

Invitation to the Belvedor Bookworms

Sneak Peek of Volume II
Belvedor and the King's Curse

BEHIND THE SCENES

Ashleigh Bello answers questions from the Belvedor Bookworms!

What inspired you to write the *Belvedor Saga?*

It all began with *Belvedor and the Four Corners*, one word at a time—when I first started writing, I had no idea that there was an entire series of books ahead of me to create. It wasn't until I wrote the ending of Book 1 that I realized Arianna's adventures were just getting started. So you can say that *she* inspired me to complete her quest.

But this is a coming-of-age story with a lot of my heart in it, so I also think growing up in Missouri played a big part in how the beginning of her quest unfolds. Like Arianna, I craved adventure and to prove myself outside the bounds of the small society that raised me when I was young; eventually, I took the leap to start exploring the world on my own and never looked back.

It was scary and thrilling to leave my roots behind and launch myself overseas, but I learned so much. And every step led me to want even more adventure. I spent years living and working all over the world, and I found magic in each place I explored. Thus, my fantasy world was born.

But no matter what, I'll always remember where I came from.

Warrior, Healer, Creator, or Agrarian? Choose.

Warrior! I would love to be able to kick butt like Arianna and all her warrior peers. I totally live vicariously through her bravery. Alas, children don't get to choose their crafts in Olleb-Yelfra. Realistically, I think I would've been placed as a creator—I did build an entire fantasy world, after all.

What's your advice to someone starting their first book?

Just start writing and let it be messy. Refine after the story is out of your mind and on paper. And if you don't know where to begin, *literally*, just start at the beginning—this was the best piece of advice I stumbled upon in my own early research of novel-writing; it's always stuck with me.

I remember being so frustrated with how to get Arianna into action, then it was like a lightbulb went off in my head—"Just start at the beginning". In my case, that meant walking Arianna through a typical day in Warrior's District and creating the building blocks of her story with each step.

What was one of your favorite fantasy TV shows as a kid?

I wasn't an avid anime fan or anything, but I can't even really begin to explain how many times I've seen *Avatar: The Last Airbender*… whatever the staggering number, it includes re-watching the series twice during quarantine. Go, Aang!

When you're not writing, what keeps you busy?

Oh, so many things! I have a full-time career in marketing that I've been growing for just about as long as I've been writing these books. I also teach hot power yoga at a studio in Brooklyn a few times a week (I earned my 200-hour RYT certificate through *Yoga Alliance*, virtually, in the winter of 2020).

In normal, non-pandemic times, I spend a lot of hours on planes, visiting friends, family, and whichever new countries got added to my bucket list on a whim; I actually wrote a good chunk of the *Belvedor Saga* in airports or in the air over the years—I find those moments such a good time to focus.

When my feet are on the ground, a solid group of friends keeps me very busy in New York City. We find something to celebrate or explore on the regular. They definitely make this crazy city life feel like home.

REAL WORLD MAGIC

The adventure of your dreams could be just outside your door.
Take the leap and go explore!

I first started writing *Belvedor and the Four Corners* in South Korea in 2012, so it's no wonder that some of the natural beauty from this country shines through my series.

At the time of writing book one, I was living in a small city called Jeonju. During the week, I would take a bus 45 minutes from the city and through the mountains of Jeongeup-si, to the elementary school where I taught as an ESL teacher—from summer to winter, it was always such a picturesque bus ride.

I'm not entirely sure, but *maybe* that's how the idea of a mountainous Four Corners came to be. Before my time in South Korea, I had never spent much time around mountains (though, the ones I did witness in real-life were much more inviting than Blancoren turned out to be).

Photo of sweeping fields in Gunsan, South Korea (2012).
Can you spot me?

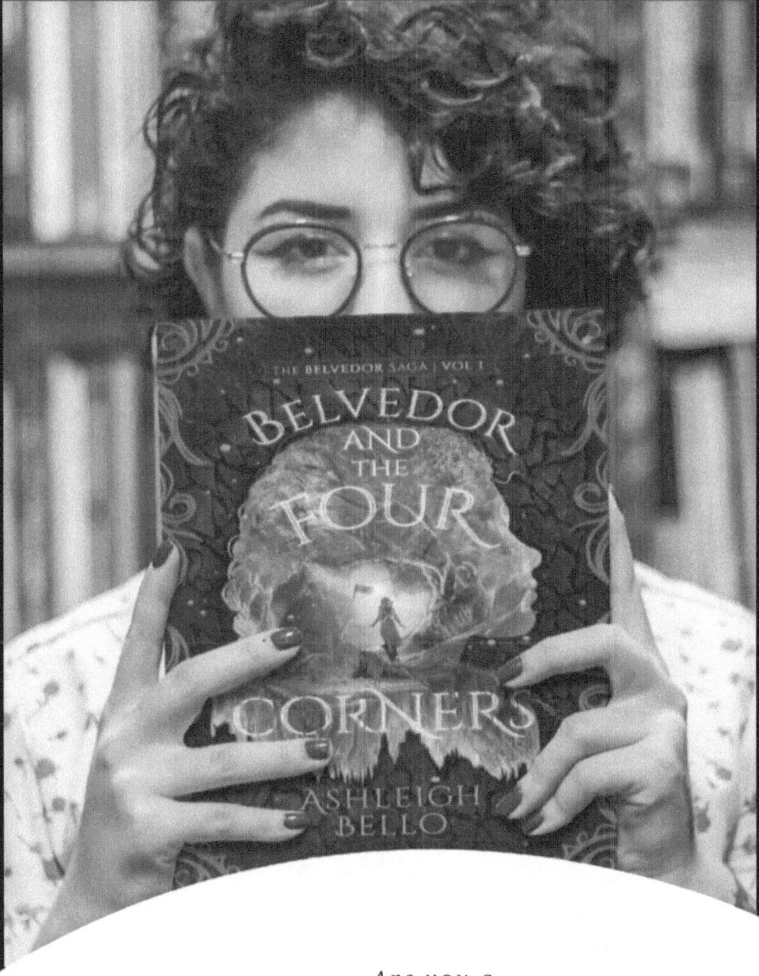

THERE'S NOWHERE TO RUN.

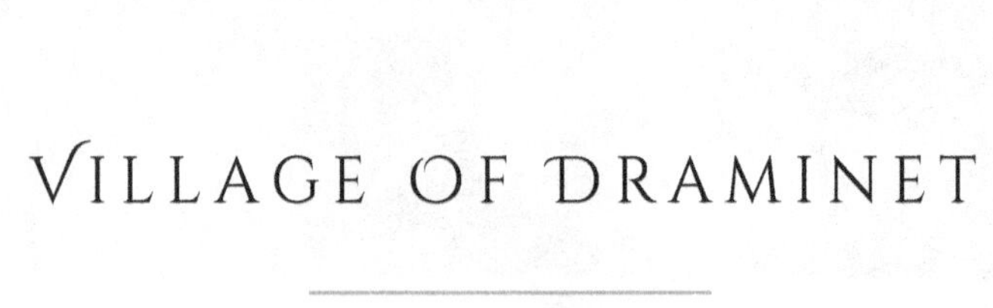

VILLAGE OF DRAMINET

AN EXCERPT

"THERE'S A FOREST UP AHEAD," said Demetrius as a seemingly endless field stretched out before them. The blade of his scythe clipped every piece of grass it touched as he headed up the group.

"Where?" said Jeom, squinting into the distance to see the cover that Demetrius claimed was so near.

Arianna could barely see a thing through the haze of fog touching the ground. She glanced at Lessa, who squeezed Sano so tightly to her chest, she thought he might combust in an explosion of fur.

"Are we almost there?" Lessa called through clipped breaths, her pack, longbow, and arrows knocking together with every step. They were all weighted down by their belongings, and this muddy field was doing them no favors.

A howling wind carried the voices of the villagers off into the distance, chasing them even this far. The town would drink themselves into a stupor this night, entertaining the new citizens of Olleb-Yelfra. But tomorrow was a new day—a day of opportunity for those who lived shadowed by the Four Corners their entire lives. Arianna knew the town would surely rally for the hunt. The luxuries of a palace post made that promise quite clear.

She halted, gasping to catch her breath as the forest suddenly became visible, piercing the fog.

Gigantic trees reached taller than the low clouds, their leaves a deep reddish-black that blended well with the night, and wide trunks shone like silver; they created a thick border against the field. And with the moonlight reflecting off the tree bark in such a way, the forest appeared like a vast, metal fence, blocking their means of escape.

Demetrius and Lessa stared ahead in astonishment, their necks craned back so they could look up high. This was familiar to them, probably a dream come true, and Lessa was the first to try to find a way through. The others followed at her heels as she searched for a clearing into the woodland, but wild bushes of all shapes and sizes barred their entry.

Jeom let out a loud groan after a few minutes of unsuccessful attempts. "Just move out of my way," he said, gripping his axe with both hands.

Everyone stepped back, and he hacked at the forest until it bent to his will and he led the way in. Branches and leaves rained to his feet with every step forward.

"You can stop now," said Demetrius after a while, placing his hand on Jeom's arm before he could take another swing—they had finally made it onto a path.

Jeom paused a moment but then swung his axe again anyway, letting out a loud yell as his blade sliced straight through a low-hanging branch.

Demetrius jumped back. "What'd you go and do that for?" he said, balking. "They have feelings, you know… spirits, I think."

"What do you mean *spirits?*" spat Jeom.

"The forest. It's alive, and it can sense everything you do."

Demetrius wagged his finger at his brother. "You should be more respectful."

"Respectful?" said Jeom, his breath suddenly heavy. "What I respect is the value of my life and the little time I have left with it." His grip tightened around his axe. "Not some stupid shrubberies!"

He hacked senselessly at another tree, his inner anger rising to the occasion and the mighty Axe of Crissy aiding it.

Demetrius opened his mouth to protest, but Lessa interrupted what was sure to be an untimely fight.

"He just needs time," she whispered. "Come on, let's keep walking." She started down the trail with the others in tow.

"Where do you suppose this leads?" said Arianna as they walked along, dwarves among the trees.

"I don't know, but I'm sure this is one of the paths the new citizens will use to journey to their placements," said Demetrius, using the butt of his weapon to help him trek. "Look, there's more up ahead."

The wide trail they traveled twisted out in all different directions from this point onward, each path leading deep into the trees—rays of moonlight shot down sporadically throughout the canopy of the forest, spotlighting their options.

"What do we do now?" said Lessa, snuggling Sano close.

"I guess we just pick one…" Arianna looked back behind her, the trail they'd just taken disappearing to the darkness. "We shouldn't linger. They'll be looking for us soon."

They kept straight until the shadows of the woodland fully consumed them. But the way the trees loomed overhead made Arianna feel as if she were back in the Jar of Stone.

"I haven't heard any voices for a long time," said Lessa, breaking the heavy silence. "Maybe we should rest soon."

"They'll figure it out," said Jeom, his voice loud—it was the first time he'd spoken in what seemed like hours. "Sooner or later, they'll realize who we were."

He pointed at Demetrius and Lessa.

"They may or may not identify you both, but I suspect someone should be smart enough to realize that Arianna and I were in the company of others. Stories *will* spread that more than one slave has escaped the Four Corners, and those portraits of us will reach much farther than just that forsaken village."

"I pray for better luck than that," said Demetrius, lowering his eyes to the ground. "Less than a week ago, everything seemed so… ordinary. And now—"

"And for now, we are alive and well," said Lessa, firmly.

"*Nothing* is ordinary about this life we were handed." Arianna stared ahead, contemplating their fates.

"Let's just try to remain positive." Lessa lifted her chin high and forced a lighter tone into her voice. "We're together, and that's what matters now. We have a chance at an extremely unordinary yet exciting existence. I'm sure everything will work itself out."

"Sure, *you* can say that," said Jeom, stopping in his tracks. His voice pitched. "At least you and Demetrius have a chance." He glowered at Arianna as they all faced him, but she refused to shrink under his scrutiny—she'd had enough of his attitude tonight.

"Jeom, you begged me to let you join us," she said. "I warned you not to come. You could be free right this very second and on your way to a normal life, so don't put that blame on me!"

She felt the itch for a fight creep under her skin, so many emotions tangling inside her in need of release.

"I still don't really understand why you even left with your freedom in hand." Her fists clenched at her sides, and she couldn't help it as her lip curled up over her teeth, her skin growing hot.

"Why I *left?*" screamed Jeom, towering over her. His knuckles turned white around the staff of his weapon.

Arianna didn't miss the intent behind his reaction; she reached for the hilt of one of the swords at her back.

"I left because I wanted to take my life into my own hands, but here we are again. On the run." He took a step forward.

"And what would you have us do?" she retorted, meeting his challenge. "Would you have us march south to Saindora and wave our swords in the air? Challenge King Devlindor so you can sleep at night… so you can have your revenge? The entire *world* wants us dead, and we know nothing of it yet!" Her voice pierced the hovering silence of the late night. "Running is our only option right now. Or haven't you noticed?"

"Wants *you* dead," said Jeom, peering down at her as she stood on her tiptoes—they were eye to eye. "We're just the tokens that come with the grand prize. What a great leader you turned out to be, hmm?"

All Arianna could see now was red; her control slipped away to make room for the warrior's rage inside her. She couldn't help the word that fell into her mind—a magical, dangerous, and unbidden word. *Luzcora!*

She hunched over, dropping to her knees as her insides burst with an overwhelming energy.

No… wait. I didn't mean it.

Digging her fingers into the cold ground, she tried to contain it, to hold this dangerous, defensive magic in the confines of her head. But it was only a matter of moments before it would explode out of her control.

"Arianna?" she heard someone say.

She strained to focus, the voice sounding so far away.

"Ara, are you all right?"

She felt the faint touch of a hand on her shoulder and looked up to find Lessa. And reflected in her friend's frightened stare, she recognized the silver, enchanted glow of her own eyes.

"Get back!" Jeom shouted, jumping in front of Lessa.

Arianna cried out, the energy releasing all around her in an exhilarating sensation; it was the same power that had ended Grinda Risso's life without remorse—the scene looked so familiar as Jeom moved behind his axe to block the attack, just as Grinda had foolishly done before she died.

THE BELVEDOR SAGA

By Ashleigh Bello

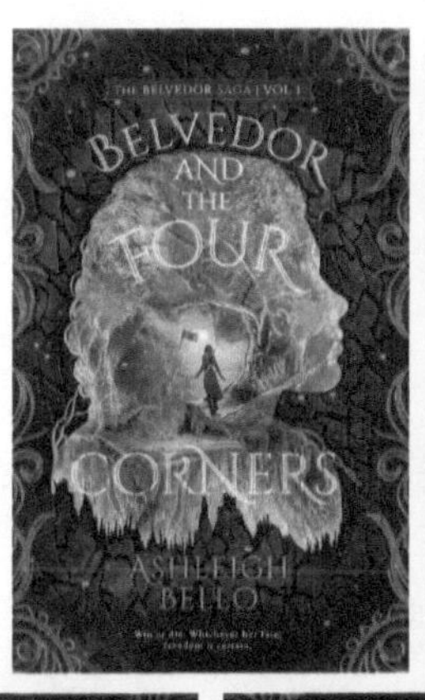

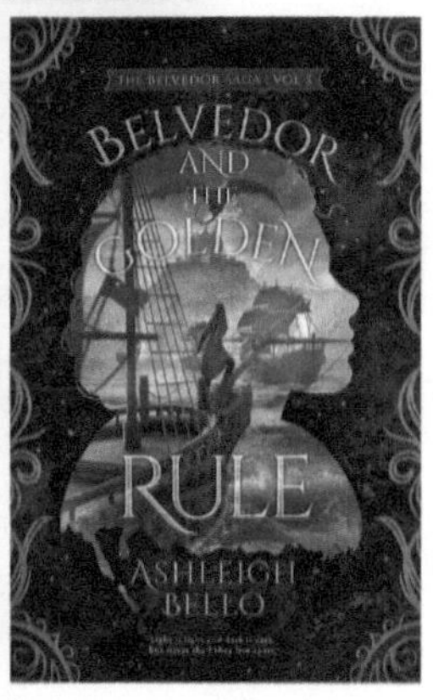

Find the completed series on Amazon.
Follow the Magic!

A S H L E I G H   B E L L O is the author of *A Myrmaid's Kiss* and the *Belvedor Saga*. She graduated from the University of Missouri-Columbia and currently lives in Brooklyn, New York. She also teaches and practices vinyasa yoga in her community and is the co-founder of Yoga Block Party, a female-owned yoga events and retreats business. She enjoys spending time with friends and family every chance she gets and is always daydreaming about her next novel. Her endless passion for travel and spontaneous adventure continues to be her inspiration for future works in the enchanting world of Olleb-Yelfra and beyond.

Connect with the Author
www.ashleighbello.com
www.goodreads.com/ashleighbello

Follow her on TikTok
Her main bookish social account

#belvedorbooks